PRAISE FOR CHARLOTTE HUBBARD AND *A PATCHWORK FAMILY*!

"Hubbard delights with the first in a five-book series that is sure to keep readers salivating for the next installment."

—*RT BOOKclub*

"*A Patchwork Family* is a wonderful adventure! Each time you think the story has finally leveled out, there is another surprise waiting at the turn of the page and around the bend... *A Patchwork Family* is a Perfect 10 and sure to become a cherished keeper!"

—*Romance Reviews Today*

"A great family story to share, [*A Patchwork Family*] will appeal to nearly every age and anyone who enjoys historical literature."

—*Fresh Fiction*

A LESSON IN LOVE

"You have no idea," Christine told Tucker, "what it's like to be betrayed by everyone you loved or trusted."

Tucker held her quaking body against his, seared by her pain once again. How could he help her see things from a different point of view?

"Do you recall Saint Thomas, the apostle—Doubting Thomas?" he asked softly. "He had to see for himself—put his hands on the Lord's wounds from those nails—before he could believe that Jesus had risen from the dead."

Her fallen expression tugged at him. Christine wanted romance, and he'd given her a Sunday school lesson.

"I hope someday you will believe in this family—in their best wishes for you, Christine," he finished earnestly. "Sometimes you must believe first, and then you will see the love in their faces, and in their hearts, for you."

Christine buried her face against his warm, solid chest. He meant well—she heard the love in his melodious voice. But sermons were the last thing she wanted from this man.

Other *Leisure* books by Charlotte Hubbard:

A PATCHWORK FAMILY

Journey to Love

Charlotte Hubbard

LEISURE BOOKS NEW YORK CITY

For my niece, Christina.
Love you, Sweetie.

A LEISURE BOOK®

July 2006

Published by

Dorchester Publishing Co., Inc.
200 Madison Avenue
New York, NY 10016

ISBN 0-8439-5566-X

Visit us on the web at www.dorchesterpub.com.

"A mother is not a person to lean upon,
but a person to make leaning unnecessary."
—Dorothy Canfield

"When you're a kid, you love your
mother no matter what she does. And you miss
her somethin' fierce when she's gone."
—Billy Bristol from *A Patchwork Family*

AUTHOR'S NOTE

The characters in my Angels of Mercy series discuss Negroes and colored men and Indians, because in the 1800s such terminology wasn't derogatory or demeaning. It simply was. The Malloys pray and discuss their faith in public, too, because a strong belief in God was the foundation these homesteaders built their lives upon.

So, at the risk of writing a politically incorrect story, I have told a more authentic, historically accurate one. I applaud my editor, Alicia Condon, for supporting me in this.

If I speak in the tongues of men and of angels,
        but have not love,
I am a noisy gong or a clanging cymbal.
And if I have prophetic powers,
        and understand all mysteries and all knowledge,
        and if I have all faith, so as to remove mountains,
        but have not love,
I am nothing.

Love is patient and kind; love is not jealous or boastful;
        it is not arrogant or rude.
Love does not insist on its own way;
        it is not irritable or resentful;
it does not rejoice at wrong, but rejoices in the right.
Love bears all things, believes all things, hopes all things,
        endures all things.
Love never ends.

When I was a child, I spoke like a child,
        I thought like a child, I reasoned like a child;
When I became a man, I gave up childish ways.
For now we see in a mirror dimly, but then face to face.
Now I know in part; then I shall understand fully,
        even as I have been fully understood.

So faith, hope, love abide, these three;
But the greatest of these is love.

—I Corinthians:13

Chapter One

October 1869

"Preacher's a-comin'!"

Christine Bristol looked out the window of her upstairs room, shaking her head at the scene below.

Asa, the old hired man, hailed the approaching preacher, while her younger brother Billy made a valiant attempt to keep three-year-old Joel out of the muddy corrals.

"Christine's gonna tan your hide if you get these new weddin' clothes dirty, boy!" Billy warned.

The feisty child ducked and ran the other way.

"Can't catch me! Can't catch *me!*" Joel taunted over his shoulder. And if the two border collies hadn't dashed over to knock him down, he'd have shot out in front of the reverend's wagon.

As it was, the preacher's horse spooked, and Reverend Larsen, a slender, bookish fellow, struggled to rein it in so the pump organ wouldn't roll off the back of his buckboard.

All the commotion provoked an adorable blond toddler to tears, which in turn set off the baby she'd been playing with.

"My Lord, it's a three-ring circus out there," Christine remarked. "I'd better go down and—"

"Let the men handle things for a few minutes more, while we put on my veil. Please?"

The willowy sixteen-year-old turned to behold Mercedes Monroe—soon to be Mercy Malloy—arrayed in an ivory gown Christine had designed. While the silk dress, made with a lace overlay and trimmed in satin ribbon, was the most elegant piece she'd ever created, it was the woman wearing it who made the whole room glow. *Radiant* didn't do justice to this homesteading widow about to take her wedding vows again.

"How do you do it?" Christine asked. "First, you took in Billy and me. You lost Judd last year, and nearly lost your mind before Solace was born. Then you had little Lily and Joel dropped in your lap. I would have gone mad, and yet you look like you're the happiest woman in the world."

"I am." Mercy took Christine's hand and approached the window. "You see that man out there? The dashingly handsome one in the new suit, who just snatched his son up from the dust?"

Christine nodded. Her temper and Mike Malloy's stubbornness had caused some strained moments, but she had to admit he was a fine catch.

"Well, when Michael smiles at me, I'm seventeen again," Mercy continued. "And when he kisses me, I'm thankful to be twenty-nine. Woman enough to appreciate him."

As though he'd heard her, Malloy looked up at them. Holding a squirming, kicking Joel against one hip, the sandy-haired man blew them a kiss.

"Lovely day for a wedding, ladies!" he called. He

looked a little rakish with his mustachioed grin. "I love you, Mercy!"

"I love you, too!" she called, returning his kiss.

Christine yanked her away from the window. "It's bad luck for the groom to see the bride—"

"Only if you believe such superstitions." Mercy smiled serenely at her, still holding her hand. "The fact that I've survived to see this happy day is proof that I'm a very blessed woman. Watched over by the angels all around me," she continued quietly. "There's a man downstairs— and a Man Upstairs—who thinks I'm really *somebody*. So I don't argue with that. I hope you'll find this same happiness someday, Christine."

"Nicely said, Mercedes. And aren't you just the loveliest bride on the face of this earth?" said a voice from the doorway.

Agatha Vanderbilt also wore a new gown Christine had created, this one from shimmering fuchsia faille. With its beaded neckline adding sparkle to her cheeks and a nosegay of ribbon roses tucked into her upswept hair, she could have passed as royalty.

"And you, Miss Bristol," the petite headmistress went on, "have come such a long way—have developed your extraordinary talent for design to such a level—that I stand in awe of you as well, my dear. It's a proud day for us all."

Christine basked in this woman's praise. It was no small favor that Mercy's Aunt Agatha had accepted her at the Academy for Young Ladies, and introduced her to the upper crust of St. Louis, and then to the esteemed seamstress she would work with after Christmas. Much as she missed her own mother, she realized such opportunities would never have come her way had she still lived in Missouri.

Mercy's voice brought her out of her daydreaming.

"Christine, I can't thank you enough for making this

gorgeous dress. And thank you, Aunt Agatha, for providing the beautiful fabrics."

As the bride turned in front of the mirror to admire her wedding gown, Christine scrutinized it a final time. More than a gift of gratitude to the woman who'd taken her in, this confection of silk, satin, and lace had won her an apprenticeship with Madame Devereaux, the most exclusive couturiere in St. Louis.

"Since this is Michael's first marriage—and since you so graciously agreed to let Christine keep the dress—nothing but the finest ivory silk and Brussels lace would do," Miss Vanderbilt replied proudly. "Its fitted bodice becomes you, Mercedes. You look even lovelier than the day you married Judd."

The three of them fell silent, recalling the handsome, loving man Mercy had lost in an Indian attack.

"Well!" Christine remarked cheerfully. "I'll need a few hairpins to secure your veil. The guests will be arriving any minute now."

"Check in my vanity, dear. They should be in the top drawer."

Christine descended the stairs with a smile of triumph. She'd designed her own gown of mint green taffeta, too, delighting in the high style that set her above their neighbors dressed in calico. No one was happier than she that the family would be leaving these dark log walls behind to move into the white frame house Michael had built. High time Mercy had something besides a calico curtain separating her bedroom from the parlor!

She yanked open the center drawer of the vanity, rummaged for the hairpins, then checked the drawers down the sides. Mercy had worn her chestnut hair tied back for so long, she'd had little use for the hairpins most women considered a necessary—

Christine gaped. Over the years, Mercy had stashed

her keepsakes in this bottom drawer, but these letters were addressed to Miss Christine Bristol! At the academy! The bold, looping penmanship made her heart skip into triple-time: Only Tucker Trudeau wrote this way.

"Of all the lying, two-faced—"

She ripped the ribbon from the bundle. Why, there must have been half a dozen letters there. And the top one had been opened! For the past three years, she'd assumed the handsome photographer from Atchison had lost track of Mama—or lost interest in her.

Ma chère Christine, she read with ravenous eyes, *A pleasure it is, to hear from you again. And you are enrolled in a fine school! A bright, pretty girl like yourself should make the most of her talents.*

She ran to the back door, scanning the yard for her brother. "Billy! Billy, you come upstairs *now!*" she hollered. Then she hurried up the steps as fast as her crinolines allowed.

Her chest felt so tight she couldn't breathe. She burst through the doorway, where Mercy and Miss Vanderbilt were attaching orange blossoms to the veil's headpiece.

"What is the meaning of—these letters are addressed to *me!* And I never got them!" she cried. "Tucker was my last contact with Mama—my only hope of finding her! But now I've discovered what a liar and a traitor you are, Mercy! And *you,* Miss Vanderbilt, saw them first!"

Mercy's face paled to the shade of her wedding dress, and the headmistress pressed her lips into a thin line. *Guilty!* One glance at the letters and the two women shrank into a strained silence. As well they should.

"You were only thirteen when those letters came," Miss Vanderbilt began. "It wasn't proper for a man of Mr. Trudeau's age to correspond with—"

"Proper?" Christine demanded, shaking the pages at them. "How *proper* was it for Richard Wyndham to sweet-talk my mother into running off with him? You all

called him a shyster, but what did you do to rescue Mama from his clutches?"

Her voice rang shrilly in the small room as she advanced toward the two women. All the humiliation and heartache of being abandoned returned in a rush, making her pulse thunder so loudly she couldn't think. If it weren't for Billy's rapid footsteps on the stairs, she'd be strangling these two conspirators.

"What's all the dang yellin' about?" he asked, breathless. "I thought the house must be afire, the way you—"

"We've got a fire, all right," Christine muttered, "and it's straight out of hell! Did you know your sweet, loving Mercy Monroe was hiding these letters? And that your buddy Miss Vanderbilt was in on it?"

Her brother's confused expression told her he'd never seen them. "They're from Mama?"

"No! But you know Tucker Trudeau gave me that photograph of her and Mr. Wyndham when I met him in Atchison," she snapped. "And now I find out he did not stop writing to me!"

"You were very upset," Mercy hastened to explain. "We were afraid you'd run off again and find more trouble than you could handle. If the Indians hadn't grabbed you, the wolves would've—"

"You could've at least opened them! You knew Tucker had seen Mama—"

Billy's low whistle silenced them. He'd opened one of the thicker envelopes, and his eyes went wet as he turned the page toward her. "Looks like you ain't the only one who has that likeness of Mama and Mr. Wyndham."

Christine gasped. The page Billy held was a WANTED poster.

"Hitch up the wagon," she breathed. "We're going to Atchison."

"But Mike and Mercy're gettin' married in—"

"How can you care about these people?" she cried.

"They've betrayed you, too, Billy! I've got to talk to the only man I can trust—and any son who loved his mother would come along. Now move!"

Her brother tugged at the collar of his new shirt, glancing nervously from Mercy to Miss Vanderbilt. "But how do you know—what if Tucker ain't—"

"Are you such a traitor you can't at least drive me to the train station?"

Billy swallowed hard. "All right, then. Let's go."

Chapter Two

"If you ladies will excuse me, I have to pack."

With her arms folded beneath her bosom and the color rushing to her cheeks, Christine Bristol cut an imposing figure. Her fury filled the room as she arched one russet eyebrow to challenge their presence.

Mercy dipped into the cooling well of emotional control that sustained her. Considering the hardships she'd endured this past year, dealing with this contrary sixteen-year-old wasn't much different from handling Lily. Why wasn't she surprised that this temperamental young woman had found those forgotten letters—and was taunting her with them—on her wedding day?

"You're making a hasty mistake,Christine. You haven't even read—"

"I don't have to!" the redhead retorted. She stalked toward her trunk and threw open the lid so hard it thumped against the wall. "Once again your meddling has kept me from reuniting my family."

"What about your apprenticeship with Madame Devereaux? And your graduation from the academy?" Aunt Agatha was shorter than her star pupil, but she'd never been one to back down from a challenge.

"Do you think dressmaking matters to me now?" Christine whirled to face them, her upswept hair vibrating with her wrath. "My mother is a fugitive from the law! The Pinkertons have probably put a price on her head! And your sense of *decency* has cost me three years of trying to find her!"

The girl yanked a dress from its peg on the wall and crammed it into her trunk. "If Mama's been hanged—or shot while outrunning a sheriff—her death'll be on your head, Miss Vanderbilt!" she cried. "Yours, too, Mercy. I thought you, of all people, would understand how badly I wanted to find—"

"What makes you think Tucker Trudeau is still in Atchison?" Mercy asked, appealing to reason. "Who says he'll still want to help you—"

"Tucker loves me!" she blurted. "Or he at least cares enough to help me search for Mama, instead of worrying about how *proper* it is! If Judd were alive, he'd have opened those letters and let me—"

"You can manipulate Billy with guilt, but don't try that trick on me."

Mercy, too, crossed her arms, restraining her rising irritation. "Judd would not have opened them because they're addressed to you, young lady. The last time you ran off, he told you we wouldn't come after you again." Mercy paused, but Christine was packing in too much of a frenzy to listen. "I'm sticking with Judd's story," she continued, turning toward the door. "You're jumping to some dangerous conclusions, Christine. But I won't waste my breath begging you to stay."

"You still don't understand!" Christine pleaded. "All I ever wanted was for my mother to be safe. No matter why she abandoned us at the depot, I just hoped she'd come back so we could be a family again. I—I just needed her to *love* us again."

The heartfelt words found their mark, for Mercy Monroe was no stranger to loss and heartache. She turned in the doorway, but the girl's theatrical nose-blowing reminded her that Miss Bristol was an accomplished actress. Maybe she was due for one of those lessons only life could teach her.

"Just leave me alone so I can pack, dammit!" Christine snapped.

"That's enough of *that*, young lady!" Aunt Agatha's index finger was pointed like a pistol. Her pumps beat a purposeful tattoo on the plank floor as she approached her student. "Maybe it was a mistake for me to intercept those letters. But I felt it was the best decision at the time, and Mercedes honored my position as your headmistress," she said. "I'm sorry if you don't believe we had your best interests at heart, Miss Bristol. I hope you won't come to regret the way you've treated us today."

Heartsick at this exchange, Mercy carefully descended the stairs—a more difficult task in this elegant, hooped gown than in her usual calico. How she'd longed to brag on Christine's rare talent today, while her friends admired her wedding dress. How she'd hoped to prove to these neighbors that she and Judd had done the right thing, sending this headstrong young lady off to school as though she were their own daughter.

"I'm sorry this came back to bite you on your wedding day, dear." Aunt Agatha's hand rested on her shoulder as they paused at the bottom of the stairs. "I didn't realize you'd kept those letters—"

"They weren't mine to throw away."

"—and I never intended for this to become another wedge between you and Miss Bristol," she said with a sigh.

"We can't control that, any more than we can control Christine."

Mercy almost got the words out without a hitch in her voice, but her aunt's apology was making her lip quiver. "Maybe those letters will help her find her mother, even now, and some good will come of all this. I can't imagine how she must feel, seeing her mother's face on a WANTED poster."

Mercy stood in the open doorway, watching neighbors arrive in their wagons and the happy way Michael greeted them . . . telling herself Christine's leaving shouldn't upset her. After all, these same friends were present the first time Miss Bristol had taken off. They'd always believed the young woman was a willful, ungrateful guest, so their opinions wouldn't change.

But still . . . it had started out to be one of the most beautiful days of her life, and now Mercy felt herself unraveling.

"She's a fool to throw away her opportunity with Madame Devereaux. If she leaves now, on the far-fetched pretext of finding her mother, the offer might not be repeated."

"She's sixteen, Aunt Ag. She doesn't see it that way."

The woman beside her let out a dignified snort. "Frankly, she's not seeing much except her romantic fantasies of that Mr. Trudeau," she said in a spinsterish whisper. "He's probably married and has a family by now."

"Which is just the sort of comeuppance she deserves," Mercy replied, more harshly than she intended. "Lord knows life isn't a bed of roses, just because we want it to be. What bothers me more is Billy's reaction."

As though on cue, a buckboard came from the barn. Billy sat relaxed in the driver's seat, because Michael had taught him the finer points of handling the reins. It was hard for Mercy to believe he'd turned fourteen last week. What a picture he made in his handsome new jacket, with a fresh white shirt and his auburn hair shining in the sun.

And what a knife he'd stuck in her heart, when he went along with his sister's plea to leave.

He pulled up alongside Michael and Asa to talk, while the arriving neighbors cast speculative glances at them. As Mrs. Reid began to play her prelude on the pump organ, everyone started toward the benches. Clyde and Nell Fergus, dressed in their stiff Sunday best, chose seats to the left of the center aisle while the Clark family sat to the right. Other homesteaders filled in behind them, still watching the conversation at the wagon with interest.

Asa glanced up, a wide grin splitting his dark face when he saw her. He came toward her at a trot, despite his age. He, too, wore new clothing made for this occasion, and his eyes shone as he approached, as though Mercy were his pride and joy.

"Reckon we'd best get you into the kitchen, Miss Mercy, so's we can have us a proper processional!" he said with a rich chuckle.

"It's time for me to take my place, too," Aunt Agatha said. She squeezed Mercy's hand, her eyes wide with love and longing. "Forget about Christine and her shenanigans. This day belongs to you, and I won't sacrifice a single moment of my happiness by worrying about her."

"Easier said than done," Mercy murmured.

As her dear aunt strolled toward the bridal arch Michael had built, Mercy noticed Billy was driving the wagon in this direction. "I never thought Billy would be drawn into this, Asa. You and that young man have been my mainstays since Judd died."

"I wouldn't worry about him, Miss Mercy," the slightly built Negro assured her as he steered her into the kitchen, out of sight. "He asked Michael's permission, nice and proper, to take that horse and wagon. Whatever his sister's up to, Mr. Billy's just lookin' out for her. Keepin' Christine from disruptin' this fine day!"

Mercy wished she could share her hired man's optimism, but she was focused on Billy's grim expression. "What if he doesn't come back, Asa? What if he goes on Christine's goose chase to find their mother—"

"That's your bride's nerves talkin'. Billy's got a good head on his shoulders—he wouldn't just up and leave," the old hand answered with a purposeful nod. "He loves you and Michael too much, after all this time."

Billy's face, still in transition from being a boy to becoming a man, looked as distressed as she'd ever seen it. He slid down from the wagon, but his actions lacked their usual energy. He couldn't look at her as he went up the stairs.

More noteworthy, however, was the set of Michael's jaw as he approached the house. With a brief word to the preacher, he strode toward them and stopped in the doorway.

"Not making any promises," he murmured, his hazel eyes alight with his mission, "but I'll speak my mind—as I know you have, honey. It's all we can do."

Nodding mutely, Mercy listened to his quick footsteps ascending the stairs.

"Let's get out of the doorway," she said. "No sense in everyone staring at us, wondering what's going on."

Malloy glanced into Billy's room, where he sat on the side of his bed, fingering the quilt Mercy had made. It had been Christine's Christmas gift, but she'd refused it—and the fact that her younger brother loved it was just another way these Bristol kids were as different as dogs from cats.

But his pitch was for Billy's sister, the young woman who'd always felt herself above Mercy's humble life. He didn't have an ice cube's chance in hell of changing Christine's mind, but Mike wanted her to know exactly where she stood if she made a shambles of their wedding ceremony. Or if she dared to belittle the woman he was about to marry—the woman who'd given these kids a home when their mother took off with a con artist after the war.

"I hear you've found some upsetting letters," he began in a low voice when he found Christine in her room. "Posters that show your ma's misadventures these past three years."

Christine looked up from cramming one last dress into her trunk. "I don't see where that's any of your business."

"It's my wedding you're disrupting. And it's my bride you're once again insulting with your thoughtless behavior." He held her gaze, struck by how womanly she looked in her fine gown. "Another day or two won't make much difference in locating your mother, honey. If you'll stay for our celebration today—look those letters over and plan your strategy—I'll do everything in my power to help you out."

"And what can *you* do to—"

"I know people all along the stage and railroad route, remember?" He wanted to slap the smirk off her face, but he leaned against the doorjamb. "A few telegrams to men with Wells Fargo and the Union Pacific Railroad could save you a lot of time and trouble. You'll be searching for a sly needle in a very vast haystack."

Christine rolled her green eyes, planting a hand on one hip. "So why are you just now offering such help, Mr. Malloy?" she demanded. "No, thank you! I'll take my chances with Tucker Trudeau."

Malloy let out the breath he'd been holding. No sense in taking her bait. Reasoning was clearly beyond her right now. "Your anger's a double-edged sword, Christine. It cuts the ones you love, and it's wounding you, too. If you'll stop and think—"

"You have no idea!" she shrieked. "No one here understands that every time I look in the mirror, I see my mother. But Mama isn't here! I may never hold her again. Because you people have kept me from finding her."

Mike eased toward her. The folks outside didn't need to hear their discussion get out of control. He'd try another angle—give her a few moments more—but then the woman downstairs deserved to reclaim her wedding day.

"More than anything in this world, I miss my mother's love," he whispered. Even now, five years after her passing, his voice shook when he spoke of it. "I was fifteen—younger than you—when I told Ma I was damn tired of being her baby boy, tied to her apron strings. I took off to fight in the war, against her wishes. When I came home, I found out she'd been dead and buried just a week, Christine."

He pushed his hair back with a hand that shook. But he didn't care if she saw his raw edges, or the way his eyes still filled with regret over a foolish mistake of his youth.

"I'll always be sorry for the thoughtless, impatient things I said as I left her," he went on. "And I was angry at God for not giving me one more day—one more conversation—to set things right with the woman who'd raised me to be better than that. Fighting in Mr. Lincoln's army wasn't dishonorable or wrong, but *how* we do things usually outlives what we tried to accomplish. I thought I was being such a man, but I was the world's biggest fool."

"I'm sorry for your loss, Mr. Malloy," Christine replied, too politely. "And I'm sorry you chased me down three years ago when I went to Atchison to find Mama. Days later I learned I was *that close*—" She held her index finger an inch from her thumb, waving it in his face. "—to finding her, before she and Richard Wyndham took off for parts unknown. I was right to track her to the Kansas border. But you hauled me back here like some stupid, senseless little girl."

"Ah, but when I see the dresses you've designed for this wedding—because Mercy sent you off to her aunt's academy," he added pointedly, "and when I feel the love you lavish on our children, I believe I was right!"

Mike gave her a final, assessing look. "The choice is yours, Christine. Stay and share our joy today—be the envy of every lady out there who sees your dresses. And then accept my best efforts at finding your mother. But if you go, you're on your own. And whatever happens to your brother will be yours to live with, too."

Her narrowed eyes and the impatient tapping of a kid-slippered toe sent him back downstairs with a sigh.

Chapter Three

"You can lead the horse to water, Miss Mercy," Asa remarked as they watched Michael stride toward the bridal arch. "But even the Lord can't make it drink. You did the best you could with Miss Christine. She's gonna be a challenge all her days!"

Mercy nodded, noting the slowing of the organ prelude poor Mrs. Reid had played at least three times.

"My family said the same thing about me as I was growing up—and especially when I left Philadelphia to homestead here with Judd," she confessed. "But I was never so bullheaded about things!"

Then she blinked. During this episode with the Bristols, she'd forgotten—

"Asa, what about the children? I asked Billy to watch them!"

"And you haven't heard a peep, have you?"

The wiry Negro stepped between her and the door, his coffee-colored eyes wide with purpose. "Miss Solace is asleep in her basket with Nell Fergus, and the Clarks have put Joel and Miss Lily between Gabe and Miss

Emma. All you have to do is be the most beautiful bride there ever was and walk toward that groom of yours. You hear me?"

He was smiling, but his tone brooked no argument. Where would she be without this faithful hired man? She simply wouldn't have survived Judd's death last September, or Solace's birth this past March.

Mercy reached out, and Asa stepped into her embrace. While she'd been born into a wealthy Philadelphia family and he had served out his slavery as a cook on an Atlanta plantation, none of that mattered now. Pioneering on these plains had made them equals, and hard times had made them fast friends.

Outside, the organist struck the opening chords of the "St. Anthony Chorale," and her pulse thrummed into a higher gear.

She was getting married! *She* was the reason their friends had come so far, on a fine October day awash in autumn's glory. In a few minutes, she'd take the name of Malloy—the name of that handsome man who'd coaxed her out of mourning and back into life again.

With a quick vision of Judd smiling down on her, Mercy nodded.

"All right," she whispered. "I'm ready."

Asa tucked her hand inside his bent arm, and they stepped into the bright sunlight. The small crowd rose to watch her approach the white bridal arch, decorated with silk ribbons and satin roses.

Mercy smiled resolutely, yet she felt a pang as they passed the wagon Billy had parked beside the house. She walked with the graceful sway Aunt Agatha taught at the academy, stepping and pausing . . . stepping and—

"Hi, Mama!" Joel called out.

"Me, too!" Lily chirped.

A sun-bronzed boy and a blond princess in pink

waved excitedly from their bench, where they stood between Emma Clark and her cousin Gabe.

Mercy grinned and waved back. She memorized this special moment, this vision of the two exuberant cherubs God had entrusted to her and Michael.

And Michael! He was gazing as though he couldn't take his eyes off her; as though the neighbors and the homestead had disappeared with the morning's mist, leaving only the two of them.

How on earth had she won such a wonderful, stunning man? What a miracle!

As Mercy stepped down the grassy aisle toward him, her heart fluttered wildly. He wore a new suit of brown serge, with a white shirt and a cravat the color of his eyes. His sandy hair glistened in the sunlight. And when his mustache lifted with that grin that always made her grin back, she remembered again what a wondrous turn her life had taken.

He came toward her, too excited to stay beside the preacher. Mercy hurried the last few feet with her hands extended, until they squeezed each other's fingers in sheer delight. A chuckle went through the crowd as they stepped into place, with Asa and Aunt Agatha flanking them. Mrs. Reid ended the bridal march with a flourish.

"Dearly beloved," Reverend Larsen intoned, "we are gathered here to celebrate a very special sacrament of holy matrimony, when—"

A loud, repetitive thumping came from the house.

"Dang it, Christine, you gotta hold up your end!" Billy called.

"I can't! I'll fall!"

Mercy swallowed, knowing the folks behind her had turned to watch the Bristols' departure. Michael's hand tightened around hers.

"It'll be all right," he murmured, willing her not to cry with his steady gaze. Then he looked at Reverend Larsen. "Please, go on."

Slightly flustered, the slender clergyman cleared his throat. "Dearly beloved, we gather here to celebrate the sacrament of holy—"

"Mama! Papa!" Joel piped up behind them. "Where's Christine and Billy goin'? Huh? Where they goin' with that big ole—"

"Shhhhh!" Emma Clark hissed.

"Kwis-teeeeeen!" Lily wailed. "Me, too! Take Lily—"

"Hush, now!" came a more dire warning from Emma's mother.

Mercy sighed, glancing from Michael to the anxious pastor. "We might as well wait. Until Christine has milked her moment of crisis, no one will be paying attention to *us*."

"Excellent point," Aunt Agatha said. "Let's turn and watch them go—if only to repay a moment of the humiliation that girl has caused you, Mercedes. As the poet Milton once wrote, 'They also serve who only stand and wait.'"

Who could argue with the headmistress of Miss Vanderbilt's Academy for Young Ladies? The guests all turned to watch a large camel-backed trunk thump down the last few stairs to land at Billy's feet. Christine, in a traveling suit of blue, scurried around to the far end, and the two of them hefted it into the buckboard.

"Wherever she's goin', she's stayin' awhile," Emma mused aloud. "Now, why didn't Billy tell me he was takin' her somewhere? I thought he'd be here for the weddin' cake—"

"If you'll notice, Billy hasn't packed anything," her cousin Gabe whispered tersely. "And he's telling the dogs to stay put. He wouldn't leave Snowy and Spot behind if he was going anywhere for long."

Mercy could've kissed Gabriel Getty for his observation: What she had overlooked in her agitation, Billy's gangly, bespectacled best friend had stated with unwavering faith.

Billy boosted his sister into the buckboard's seat, then clambered up to take the reins. He glanced back at Mercy, his expression apologetic. Then he clucked to the horse.

"Be careful," Michael called after them. "Come home when you can!"

Mercy blinked back tears. *Greater love hath no man*, she mused. *That girl has no idea what she's turned her back on.*

The two black-and-white dogs frolicked around the wagon, gazing expectantly at Billy for the invitation to hop on. But his hand signal left Snowy and Spot seated obediently at the edge of the yard, watching after them.

That's all any of us can do now: watch and pray.

With a resolute sigh, Mercy turned to face Reverend Larsen again. As Michael clasped her hand, she concentrated on the warmth and strength flowing from his grip into hers.

"All right," she murmured. "It's our turn."

Gregor Larsen, their longtime friend and pastor, spoke beneath the rustle of the crowd's sitting down. "I hope you two, as man and wife, will insist on your turn together," he admonished. "Children take their example from the parents who nurture them. If your marriage remains firm and faithful, it will be God's mirror, and they will see themselves reflected in it."

The pastor stood taller then, awaiting the guests' attention.

"It is a special day indeed," his voice rang out, "and I am honored to perform this ceremony here, at the home where we've gathered for seven years. As we witness this new beginning for Mercedes Monroe and

Michael Malloy, I ask you to invite Christ into your hearts as our most honored guest. Let us pray.

"Holy Father," he intoned, "we ask Your blessing on this couple, and upon the children You have given into their care. And we ask that You wrap Your guidance and grace around Billy and Christine Bristol as they reconcile their past and reunite their family. We pray in the name of Your Son, our Lord and Savior, Jesus Christ. Amen."

Reverend Larsen smiled at them. "Dearly beloved!" he began once again. "We are gathered here today to celebrate the sacrament of holy matrimony . . ."

Mercy let his familiar Norwegian cadence flow around her, but it was the man beside her who held her attention. With his hazel gaze fixed on her, Michael Malloy looked head-over-heels in love. His skin, tanned from hard work in the sun, glowed with vitality. His lips parted in a smile meant only for her—and when the tip of his tongue skimmed over them, she felt a secret heat pulsing inside her. What had she ever done to attract this man?

"Mr. Malloy? I believe you wanted to read the Scripture today?"

Michael blinked. "Yes, sir, I do."

He squeezed her hand, then turned to face her and their friends. "I'd like to share a passage from First Corinthians, which my mother drilled into me because I needed reminding about the proper way to treat my six sisters."

As everyone chuckled, he thumbed through the Bible's delicate pages.

"This is for you, Ma," he said, raising his face toward Heaven, "and it's a gift for my beautiful bride, Mercedes, to celebrate a love that delves far deeper than the King James translation calls up for us."

Mercy's heart raced and her eyes teared. Michael had

a way of simplifying difficult passages with his own down-to-earth interpretation. He didn't lecture on certain verses to prove his point. He simply lived his beliefs, and he lived his beliefs simply.

"If I speak in the tongues of men and of angels, but have not love, I am a noisy gong or a clanging cymbal," he began, gazing at Mercy rather than at the page before him. "And if I have prophetic powers, and understand all mysteries and all knowledge, and if I have all faith, so as to remove mountains, but have not love . . . I am nothing."

She held her breath—and those behind her were listening just as intently. By replacing the word *charity* with *love*, this man was making a statement so eloquent that even the most devout among them would feel new meaning stirring in the familiar words.

"Love is patient and kind . . . love is not jealous or boastful . . . it is not arrogant or rude," Michael continued, his eyes still fixed on her. "Love does not insist on its own way. It is not irritable or resentful. It does not rejoice at wrong, but rejoices in the right. Love bears all things, believes all things . . . hopes all things. Endures all things. Love never ends."

Tears streamed down Mercy's cheeks: Michael never once looked at the page, but spoke to her as though no one else existed. He was predicting a long and happy life for them together—giving her these words to lean upon, as they raised the children who'd come to them in different ways, from different places.

As though again aware of their guests, he spoke more quickly. "When I was a child, I spoke like a child, I thought like a child, I reasoned like a child. When I became a man, I gave up childish ways. For now we see in a mirror dimly, but then—face to face. Now I know in part; then I shall understand fully, even as I have been fully understood."

Michael handed the Bible back to Reverend Larsen, and looked over the crowd once more. "So faith, hope, and love abide—these three," he said reverently. "But the greatest of these is love.

"And today, Mercedes," he said, clasping her hands, "I set aside all that has come before, to become your husband as you become my wife. And I promise you this, sweetheart: No one can possibly love you more than I do. And I will love you even more, every day of my life."

"Me, too, Papa!" Joel piped up.

"Me, too!" chirped the little girl beside him.

Still grasping Mercy's hands, Michael smiled at the children in the first row. "Me, too, Joel. Me, too, Lily," he responded softly. Then he looked toward Nell Fergus on the other side of the aisle, as she held the sleeping baby on her shoulder. "Me, too, Solace."

"Me, too," Mercy breathed.

He tucked her hand in his arm, and they faced the pastor together.

"You've left me at a loss for words, Mr. Malloy. You have a genuine talent for—"

"Let's eat that big cake now!" Joel crowed. "Asa made it—"

"Shhhh!" Emma hissed, pressing her hand over the boy's mouth.

"Cake! Cake!" Lily cried.

Asa turned to silence them with a stern look, but he was chuckling too hard to get away with it. "Cake's for those who stay quiet while the preacher talks," he said pointedly. "Watch for when your papa kisses the bride—"

"He's gonna kiss her again? But he already—"

"Kiss me, too!"

This time Lily's shrill voice woke Solace, who began to whimper despite Nell's efforts to soothe her.

Reverend Larsen cleared his throat to begin the sacred vows they were about to exchange. Behind them, Mercy heard Rachel Clark's whispered warnings about what happened to little children who didn't behave in church. Meanwhile Solace, eight months old, was howling in a way that meant she was both wet and hungry.

When Mercy glanced up at Michael, however, she forgot about wailing babies and long-winded lessons from clergymen. Her groom's mustache was quivering with the effort it took not to laugh out loud. The sparkle in his eyes suggested that he had disrupted a wedding or two as a child, and that such heartfelt outbursts from the children would never upset him.

Mercy giggled—and then couldn't quit. Beside her, Aunt Agatha sniffed an indignant warning, but she didn't care. This was *her* day! These little interruptions foretold the life ahead, and she vowed to treasure every precious moment of this patchwork family—to enjoy all the kisses and cake life brought her way.

"Do you, Mercedes, take Michael to be your wedded husband, to live together after God's ordinance in the holy estate of matrimony? Do you promise—"

"Oh, yes, I do!"

"Oh, no, you don't!"

Billy glared at his sister, who sat beside him on the buckboard. "Wheedle and whine all you want, but dang it, Christine, I ain't takin' a train to see a man who might not be in Atchison anymore! And he might not wanna see you anymore. So you're not goin' there, either."

"You just try to stop me, Billy!"

"And how're you gonna buy your ticket?" he challenged, his voice rising right along with hers. "If you tell me you stole money outta Mercy's sideboard again—"

"I get paid for making dresses, you know." Christine leaned sideways, so her flushed face was only inches from his. "Which is more than you can say, isn't it? You're fourteen now, Billy. You do the work of two hired hands, and I bet those do-gooders haven't even offered you any money. Have they?"

He could argue until the moon turned blue, but his more worldly sister—who despised the prairie life—would never understand his gratitude to Mercy, her first husband, Judd, and now to Mike Malloy. This wasn't the time to mention the new position he'd been given when the Malloys formed the new Triple M Ranch from their two homesteads. If Christine was going to be so snooty, why, it was none of her dang business what kind of wages he'd soon be paid.

"You're changin' the subject," he replied archly. "We're talkin' about how you couldn't wait one more day to chase after Mama—how you had to storm out durin' the weddin' and be the center of attention. Even Joel has better manners than that!"

"Manners!" she cried, flapping the letters she'd found in his face. "Here we go again, talking about manners, when you and I have been kept from the truth about our mother. By my headmistress and that paragon of virtue you live with."

"Pipe down. You're spookin' Pepper."

Her fist went to her hip—which at least got those letters out of his face. "You've been lied to and betrayed for more than three years by the family who took you in to work like one of their darkies! And you're telling me to—"

Billy hauled on the reins and the buckboard lurched to a halt. He hated stooping to Christine's mean-spirited level, but he felt a twinge of satisfaction when she grabbed the wagon seat to keep from toppling off.

"I'm tellin' you to think about what you're doin', Sis," he insisted. "Those letters and WANTED posters are three years old. Who knows what Mama and Richard Wyndham have been up to since then? How many miles do you s'pose they've traveled? Assumin' he hasn't dumped her by now?"

He leaned into this argument, going toward his most important point. "Assumin' is a dangerous game, Christine. You ain't even opened all those letters."

"I don't have to!" she snapped. "Tucker kept writing to me for nearly a year—when he could surely tell by my letters that I hadn't received this information about Mama! That's all I need to know. But what would you know about such things?" she went on, rolling her eyes. "You're just a naive little idiot who—"

He grabbed her wrist until she yelped. "Get outta the wagon, then! I'm settin' your trunk and your high-and-mighty backside on the side of the road, if that's how you feel!"

Her eyes widened with fright, and she tried frantically to jerk free of his grip. Christine had used her dramatic talents against him ever since they'd been kids, but never had Billy resorted to violence.

"Sorry," he mumbled. He dropped her arm.

His sister rubbed her wrist, watching him with wet green eyes. "Why are you so dead set against me finding Mama?" she asked in a quavery voice. "Lord knows, you were so much her favorite, Wesley and I might as well not've existed!"

Billy looked away. She was toying with his feelings again, but what she said was mostly true: Mama *had* made a fuss over him, long after his larger, rowdier twin rejected such affection.

"Bad enough that I lost Mama. Watched her ride away from that depot without even lookin' back," he breathed. His chest clenched with the pain of that awful day. "You're all I have left, Sis. I don't want to lose you, too."

"Then come with me," Christine pleaded—as though her request should seem perfectly logical. "You're hanging back, just like you did last time!"

"You didn't ask me to go last time. You snuck out like a thief in the night, on the preacher's horse." It was all Billy could do not to shake some sense into her. "You had no intention of takin' your ten-year-old brother, so don't let on like you did!"

He glanced away to get control of himself. Christine seemed so grown up in that pretty blue suit, it could've been Mama sitting beside him. But his sister would never understand his side of things, much less think about all the ways this situation could go wrong.

"I'll take you into Abilene, and we'll send Tucker Trudeau a telegram," he finally said. "We'll get us a room, and we'll look at them letters real close, so's we can come up with a plan."

Billy looked her straight in the eye, so she knew exactly where he stood. "But if we don't hear back from him in a couple days, I'm goin' back to Mike and Mercy's. If you wanna get on the train then, well—that's your business. It ain't like I'm gonna change your mind."

Chapter Four

My dearest Tucker, Christine scribbled. But then, considering how many telegraph operators might read this message before it reached Atchison, she scratched that out.

From the window of their room at the Abilene House, she could see people bustling about their daily business—much as she had three years ago, when she'd walked along the sidewalk beside the photographer who spoke with a melodious French accent.

What if Billy was right? What if Tucker Trudeau had moved on, or had given up on her? His letters *had* stopped coming, after all. She must have seemed as scruffy as a homeless cat to the man who'd given her that portrait of Mama and Richard Wyndham. Maybe he'd just acted interested because he felt sorry for her.

Maybe he'd seen through her little fibs.

Memories of being abandoned—left behind while she used the privy at the stage depot—returned with a vengeance that churned her stomach. And vengeance was precisely why she'd chased after Mama right after the Monroes took her and Billy in. She needed answers. She wanted explanations for those flowery phrases in Mama's diary, about secret meetings with Mr. Wyndham before the bank foreclosed on their home in Missouri.

So much bitterness and humiliation had been heaped on her shoulders, as the oldest child . . . Mama's only daughter. Billy, at ten, had been too young to understand her devastation, her desire to set things right.

Three years at Miss Vanderbilt's Academy for Young Ladies had softened the edges of her mother's betrayal, much like an artist smudged the charcoal lines of a drawing with his fingertip. But finding Tucker's letters brought it all back: the pain, the loss of her family and her home, the bitter realization that Mama had chosen the company of a fancy man with a British accent over her own children.

Biting her lip, Christine again considered her telegram to Tucker. If he were still in Atchison, she had to give him a compelling reason to respond. Like Billy said, the primrose paths Mama followed with Mr. Wyndham had grown over, and a search was probably a waste of time.

But another glance at that photograph, where Virgilia Bristol smiled delightedly while leaning against her partner in crime, wouldn't allow Christine to leave her past—what was left of her family—behind. A WANTED poster might be the ultimate badge of shame for her genteel Southern mother, but it was the only connection she had.

And what if Billy was right? What if that weasel Wyndham had left their mother alone and defenseless? Destitute?

Christine took up her pen again.

Dear Tucker,

Just today I found those letters you sent to me at the academy—and discovered the lies that have kept me from finding my mother. May I please come and talk to you about them? Your help may be the only thing that saves Mama's life. I will await your reply at Abilene House, in Abilene.

Thank you so very much for your kindness,

Christine Bristol

She glanced at Billy, who was pacing as restlessly as one of his dogs, from one window to the other.

"Here," she said, holding out the folded note along with some money. "Take your time about getting back. Walk around town—pick out a place for dinner. My treat."

Her younger brother's auburn hair gleamed in the light from the window. Billy was taller now, lankier, yet his stiff new shirt didn't disguise the whipcord strength he got from working in the stables and corrals. For just an instant, she saw his lean features as those of a grown man. A man who might turn heads other than poor, besotted Emma's some day.

"I'll be back by six," he replied. "Got some things to look at in the Great Western mercantile, so Mike can finish out his new barn. Keep your cash."

His blue eyes locked onto hers, as though she were a book he didn't even have to open. "If you find anything in them letters—anything definite about Mama's whereabouts—you tell me, ya hear? Not just 'cause I got a right to know, but 'cause you and me oughtta be on the same side of this situation instead of fightin' about it. If there's a way to find her—or if that Trudeau fella don't answer your note," he continued, going for the door, "you and me'll be on her trail soon as we can get our things together for that long trip."

Christine stared after him, listening to his purposeful footsteps in the hall: Mama's baby boy had toughened up. But Billy would always have a cream puff for a heart, no matter how he railed at her for running after their mother. He'd tried to protect them from the emotional havoc Virgilia Bristol had wreaked when she abandoned them—and Mama's misadventures with Richard Wyndham would probably appall them both, now that this Pandora's box yawned open again.

She finally had a chance to read Tucker's letters, so she put them in order by the postmarks. The first one—which Miss Vanderbilt had opened—took her back in time, to when she'd been so eager to hear from the man with the fascinating accent. She unfolded the pages with quivering fingers. The bold, loopy penmanship brought back the memory of glossy dark hair and a close-clipped beard that accentuated his lips. Lips that had kissed her hand as he held it between his own.

She shivered. It would be hard to concentrate on Mama's plight. Christine's pulse was already racing to the catchy beat of Tucker's accented speech. She told herself to go slowly, to consider his message in light of the three years that had passed since she'd seen him . . . since the most exciting moments of her life.

Christine, ma petite princesse, he began, and she let out a gasp. His little princess, was she? Billy couldn't deny her that!

You have studied French in school, non? A bright young lady like yourself must know that Maman and I, we speak the language differently from the way you learned it. We are Cajuns, cherie, from the Bayou Atchafalaya in Louisiana. Our words, they come in a different order from yours.

It is Maman who descends from this line, and from her mother and her grandmère she got her gift

of the second sight, and her talents as a traiteur—
*a healer. By our family and friends, she is revered
as a woman touched by God. She heals to share
her gift with all who ask her help.*

*I know you find her strange, my Maman. Fright-
ening, perhaps, because she sees so much others
cannot.*

"Strange?" Christine breathed. Those beady little eyes
had been nothing short of witchy! In her flowing
clothes of mixed prints, with her hoop earrings and
necklaces, Tucker's mother had reminded her of a
Gypsy fortune-teller.

*People here in the North do not accept her vi-
sions as normal or good. Most who are not of the
Catholic faith, or who fear her mystical ways, do
not consider that Maman did not ASK for this gift of
healing—or for her ability to see spirits and into
the future. Her gifts, they have gotten her into—
how you say?—trouble sometimes. But she suffers
her persecution like the saints of old, for the cause
of God.*

Christine's eyebrows arched. *Saintly* was not a word
she'd have chosen for Veronique Trudeau—who'd
glared at her while speaking rapid-fire French to Tucker,
as though she weren't even there!

I hope you understand, ma princesse, *that she
wishes you no ill. When you came to us, Maman
had met your mother and knew,* toute suite, *that
things were being hidden by Mr. Witmer—you
called him Richard Wyndham. Like you, Christine,
we knew no good would come of him! We knew
he was luring your mama down his own crooked*

*path. He called her Veronique—Maman's own
name!—but did all the talking himself.*

*For this reason, I have kept watch. The newspa-
pers I have studied for mention of his name. The
bank account he paid me from does not exist. After
he and your mama came to fetch their photograph,
I secretly followed them around town. But I think
he knew. He stopped everywhere but at a home or
hotel. He went into shops and bought your mama
fine things to keep her happy and quiet.*

*She has your smile, Christine. Pretty and fresh as
a springtime sky.*

"Oh, Tucker," she murmured. Then she glanced out
the window to be sure Billy wasn't coming. Her brother
would never understand such poetry, or why it moved
her to tears even after all this time.

*For you see, ma petite, even though you were
dusty from traveling so far in search of her, I felt
your strength of purpose. Your honorable intent.
While Maman said you, too, were hiding the truth,
I could understand why. I admire your love for your
mother, for I cannot imagine my life without my
dear Maman.*

Did he know she'd lied about her age? Recalling the
desperate things she'd done after running away from
the Monroes, Christine grinned proudly. Not many girls
of thirteen had the grit to chase down a runaway
mother. Even Reverend Larsen, whose horse she'd
stolen, had called her resourceful. Among other things.

*I will continue to watch for your mother, cherie.
I will send you whatever I find, for as long as you
want to know. Sad to say, when I met your*

*mama—when I see her happy smile in the
photograph—I don't think she will be back to see
you. But I gave her your address with Judd Monroe, west of Abilene.*

*Like Maman, I cannot hold back what I know. I
feel it is my purpose, my duty, to help you with your
search—just as I believe it was—how you say
it?—God's providence, that you found my shop.*

She held her breath as her eyes gobbled the rest of
his letter. Unless he no longer lived in Atchison, Tucker
Trudeau would be here as soon as he read her telegram! She could feel it in his words—in the way his
handwriting took on a tighter, more intense angle.

*We must have faith that our lives will happen as
the Father wills them. If He wishes for us to meet
again, it will happen.*

I live in the hope of seeing you again someday,
ma chère *Christine. You are like the primrose that
thrives on the prairie: delicate and fresh and beautiful, yet strong enough to survive the winds and
droughts of life.*

*I will read again and again your letter of thanks.
It was my pleasure to help you—to give you the picture of your mother. You will be in my prayers as you
search for your mama, and until we meet again.*

                              Very truly yours, Tucker

Christine sprang from her chair, too excited to sit still.
How she wanted to pore over this letter again—and
again!—and then devour the rest of Tucker's writings as
well. But she didn't dare. There would be no explaining
the flush in her cheeks or her breathlessness if Billy
walked in on her.

Her brother could not see these letters!

But Billy would demand answers when he returned. He would pry and prod all during dinner if he had any inkling of the wild emotions and high hopes Tucker had stirred within her.

After watching the people thronging the street and not seeing her brother among them, Christine slipped her fingernail under each envelope's wax seal. She shook out the loose enclosures and then slipped the letters into her carpetbag. She felt like a fairy-tale princess, afloat on her true love's words of devotion but forced to keep their romance a secret.

There was no romance in these newspaper clippings, however. Neatly sliced from issues of the *Atchison Freedom's Champion*, the *Daily Capitol*, and the *Kansas City Times*, the columns of newsprint quivered in her fingers.

NEWCOMERS SUSPECTED IN LAND FRAUD SCHEME, the first headline blared. No wonder Mama's new husband had changed his alias to Dick Witmer! As Christine scanned the lines about a grandiose plan to fleece hundreds of would-be homesteaders, she sickened.

And here were half-page enticements from Atlanta, Memphis, and St. Louis newspapers as well. What respectable man would place such advertisements, promising abandoned homesteads to those who sent their money to the post office box mentioned at the bottom of the ad?

She stiffened with renewed rage. Was their ranch in Missouri one of the places Wyndham was raffling off? Had he been in cahoots with Leland Massena, the banker who'd foreclosed on them, all along?

Surely Mama would've seen through this outrageous scheme. Surely she would've known such a rogue would only bring her heartache.

And yet, as Christine compared the datelines Tucker had written on the clippings, she realized fleecing

gullible sheep from afar was Wyndham's favorite game.
And since Mama—or someone referred to as V.
Bristler—was named as this man's partner, she had to
know he was hiding behind a growing list of aliases.

By the time Christine read the final clippings, dated
nearly two years earlier, she could follow the man with
the handlebar mustache through four different names
and two additional scams involving illegal lotteries. Not
to mention notices from numerous Kansas banks about
false accounts and bank drafts.

With her heart in her throat, Christine again picked
up the WANTED poster. Hard to believe the happy couple
pictured there could be associated with charges of
thievery, fraud, and forgery, but she'd read more than
enough to know it was true.

Mama was living a life of crime. Too busy leading the
law on a merry chase to give her abandoned children a
moment's thought.

*She's having the time of her life, now that she doesn't
have us to worry about.*

Christine brushed away tears. Ten-year-old Billy's
hunches had been pretty accurate: From the day Wyndham lured her away, Virgilia Bristol had ceased to be
the mother they knew and loved.

This realization cut her so deeply, Christine doubled
over and hugged herself, struggling to hold her heart
and soul together.

In her misery, she reached for another of Tucker's
letters—anything to settle herself before Billy found her
so agitated. He'd haul her back to Mercy's if he saw the
agony Mama's misadventures were causing. The truth
hurt, but after all the time and effort she'd invested, she
couldn't just dismiss her mission to find their mother.
Could she?

Ma chère *Christine*, she read through her tears, *so
happy I am, to know you attend a fine school in St.*

Louis! Your letters make me smile and bring me hope that we will someday meet again.

There now—that was better! Sniffling into her lace handkerchief, she lost herself in Tucker's distinctive handwriting and turn of phrase. The letters she'd written him from the academy—and sneaked to the post office on her way to working at the orphanage—might prove to be the lifeline that would bring this playful Cajun back into her life.

"Oh, Tucker, if I'd only known Miss Vanderbilt was keeping your letters from me—"

An uproar on the street took her to the open window again. Christine saw a crowd gathering around an overloaded wagon, which was hitched to a mule and had two Negro women huddled together on its seat. The colored man hopping down from it had apparently sparked the interest of some drunken cowboys, and more of these mouthy men were spilling out of a nearby saloon to join the fray.

"Go on back to that plantation, slave!" someone hollered.

"Yeah, you might be free, but it'll cost ya to drive down the street!"

"Take your whores and go on home now!"

Frowning, she stuck her head outside, while other hotel guests did the same. Where was that illustrious sheriff, Wild Bill Hickok? Abilene had hired the former gunslinger to bring law and order to streets teeming with rowdy cowhands during the cattle drives, but even she could see this crowd would soon be out of control.

"Let's see how fast that sorry-ass mule can run!"

A glass bottle flew from the saloon and shattered against the animal's head. The mule brayed and shot forward, scattering the people in its path. The Negro it belonged to hollered for it to stop, but when he ran after it, cowboys grabbed him from each side. Above the pandemonium rang the frightened cries of the two women on the wagon.

Christine's hand went to her mouth in horror. The vehicle teetered from side to side with its load of household goods, behind a mule gone wild with pain and fright. Any moment now, that wagon would overturn and those women would land—

A flash of auburn hair caught the sunlight. A lithe young man sprang from the crowd to run alongside the careening wagon. He lunged high into the air, toward the crazed mule's back.

"Billy!" Christine squealed. "Billy, you'll get yourself killed!"

Chapter Five

"Whoa, now! Easy does it—whoa, now!"

Billy landed with a *whump*. He grabbed for the reins, which were flapping wildly around the wounded animal's neck, spooking it even more. The storefronts—and bystanders' startled faces—were going by at a dizzying pace, so he focused on clinging to the mule's thick gray neck.

"Easy, fella—whoa, now," he murmured.

The panicked animal's muscles bunched, his hide hot and lathered from sprinting down the street. The wails of those two scared ladies were enough to make any beast bolt—but at least the mule was slowing down.

Clenching his legs to hang on, Billy tugged steadily on the bridle, murmuring reassurances. He hadn't seen the beginning of the ruckus, but whoever had thrown that whiskey bottle deserved to be locked away! Blood was running down the side of the mule's face so fast he might bleed to death if he weren't tended soon.

"Whoooa, fella. Atta boy—we're outta trouble now," he crooned.

They were nearly to the end of the street, and close to the livery stable, thank goodness. Billy had never been so glad to see a familiar face among all the gawkers who lined the streets.

"Hank, this poor mule's bleedin'!" he called out as the animal finally came to a standstill. "Some idiot threw a bottle at him."

Hank Vance, the stable manager Billy had met when putting up their horse, hurried around to grab the bridle so Billy could climb down. As the dust settled, he saw curiosity-seekers hurrying up the street, and every window had somebody hanging out, hollering questions. Folks flocked from the stores and saloons, eager for the story behind all this excitement, which wouldn't die away any time soon.

But it was the mindless fright on those two ladies' faces that riveted Billy. They didn't look all that much older than he was, but their faded calico dresses and threadbare bonnets told a story of hardship like he'd never had to endure. The younger one hugged her belly—Lord, she looked ready to birth a baby!—and retched over the side of the wagon.

Onlookers jumped back, muttering their disgust. The other woman clutched at her, as though to keep her from falling off, and they both began to cry. It was a sorry sight, and when Billy noticed the trail of broken crates and furniture in the street behind them, he knew this family's troubles weren't over yet.

"Ladies," he said under the sound of their sobbing. He looked earnestly up at them from the side of the rickety wagon. "Ladies—please—I'm sure sorry 'bout this. If there's anything I can do to—"

"You can just back yourself away right now!" came an angry male voice. "We won't be needin' any more help like this godforsaken town's already showed us!"

The biggest Negro he'd ever seen was loping toward

him, and Billy stepped back. But it was fear in those wide, dark eyes he saw—the same terror that had sent this man's mule racing down the street with his family and possessions. He looked to be a field worker, with wide, muscled shoulders that strained the seams of his homespun shirt. His skin shone like hot coffee and he was wheezing like a locomotive from the effort of racing up the street. His overalls were patched but clean, and he wore the biggest, scruffiest boots Billy had ever seen.

"Hank here's gonna see to your mule—"

"Don't need y'all's help, I said!" the big man bellowed. "Now go on about your—"

"Reuben! Reuben Henry, you got the—"

"—business, mistah, while I sees to my women!"

"—wrong man!" the older gal scolded. "This here young fella saved our lives, praise God!"

Reuben had stepped between him and the two ladies, his nostrils flaring and his ebony gaze a definite threat—until the woman snatched off her bonnet and whacked him on the head with it.

"Are you listenin' to me?" she demanded. "You're still in a lather 'bout that man in the land office! This young fella stopped the mule. Kept the whole dern wagon from tippin' over—and us with it! So just settle yourself now, ya hear me?"

As the livery man approached, Billy realized he'd never been happier to see another white man. He grabbed one of Hank's rags and pressed it firmly against the mule's wound, while the livery man steadied the animal's head. Better to blot up blood than to get mixed up in the squabble brewing between Reuben Henry and his . . . wife?

Was the pregnant one his wife, too?

The colored man still looked dangerous, with his dark eyes bulging like an enraged bull's. He inhaled deeply as he watched the two of them tend the mule, as though trying to match the rapid-fire events of the past few minutes with what his woman was saying. Reuben didn't look the type to pay a female much heed, so Billy dipped his rag in Hank's bucket of water again. Best to give this big man all the time he needed.

"That right, what she's sayin'?" he finally asked.

Billy pressed the rag hard against the mule's skull, smiling as widely as he dared. "Yessir, I was comin' from the mercantile and dang near got hit by that flyin' bottle myself," he said in a voice low enough to keep the animal calm. "Them Texas cowpokes get all liquored up after a long drive, so Abilene ain't always a safe place even in the daylight. Sorry your mule got hit in such a bad spot. Think he's gonna be all right, though."

"What's your name?"

"Billy Bristol. What's yours?" he replied, trying to keep his voice even. The Negro was still poised to pounce. Hadn't moved a thing except his lips.

"Reuben Gates. How'd you come to be so good with animals? Matthias don't hardly let nobody touch him."

Letting out the breath he'd held, Billy grinned. "Born that way, I guess. If ya treat 'em right, most of 'em will do whatever you ask. Kinda like people."

"Well, I can't say that 'bout the people we've seen here. The cowpokes nor the land office clerk, neither," the woman behind him said.

She'd kept her arm protectively around the younger gal, who sat wide-eyed, clutching her belly. "We're just tryin' to claim a parcel of land we paid for, fair and square. That fella was makin' Reuben out to be a thief or a liar—or just a plain old fool! Never seen nothin' like it."

Billy glanced at Hank, but the livery man only shrugged. He'd wiped away most of the blood and was smearing a fingerful of thick salve on the wound.

"What parcel of land might that be? Not that it's any

of my business," Billy added quickly. " 'Cept I don't know of anythin' that's for sale hereabouts."

"We got the papers right—"

"Sedalia, don't you go botherin' Mr. Bristol with this," Reuben said sternly when she pulled papers from a carpetbag beneath the seat. "He needs to get back to whatever he was doin' before the mule got spooked."

"And who else in this lawless town is likely to help us?" she challenged. "This is our life we're talkin' about. If we don't get this land, where we gonna go, Reuben?"

Sedalia brazenly dodged the big man's hand and tossed some folded pages at Billy. One was an advertisement from a newspaper, illustrated with a sketch of a strapping, strong man behind an ox-drawn plow. He was singing the praises of land along the Kansas Pacific railroad—homesteads abandoned before the original tenants proved up. The other was a certificate printed on parchment, naming Reuben Henry Gates as the new owner of a section of land, and then listing the details of its location.

Billy blinked. "Dickinson County . . . along the Smoky Hill River?" he read aloud. "Why, that's not too far from us! But—"

He thought better of finishing his reply when he saw how intense their expressions got.

"Land agent's letter done told us the husband of that family passed on 'bout a year ago," Reuben remarked. "He said the widow, she didn't have the means to—"

"We sent 'em our money, just like it said!" Sedalia cut in, extremely agitated. "And now they's tellin' us nobody from this land office issued that certificate. That fella don't know who got our money, but it weren't him. And with winter comin' on and Libby gonna have her baby any day now, and—"

"Mr. Billy, you look like you seen a ghost," Reuben remarked.

Billy swallowed so hard his throat clicked. That pair of Kansas land agents, listed in tiny print at the bottom of the certificate, had names that did indeed resurrect faces from his past. A sick suspicion knotted his stomach. He looked again at the shabby wagon, the care-worn furniture strewn in the street, and the awkward bulge of Libby's belly—not to mention the crowd who was hanging on their every word.

It just didn't set right. But he didn't know enough de-tails to paint these desperate folks the full picture—and he didn't have the heart to disappoint them even more with half of Abilene watching. The mule whick-ered and stomped as Hank smeared salve on its wound.

"Why don't you folks come on home with me?" Billy suggested quietly. He handed the certificate back, glad to be rid of it. "We'll hitch your wagon to my horse and let your mule walk behind. Won't take us half an hour to get there. You can rest and eat a decent meal, and we'll get to the bottom of this."

All three Negroes gazed at him, dumbfounded.

The man scratched his head, raising tufts of coarse, curly hair. "Now, why you wanna go do such a thing for—"

"You lookin' for work, Reuben?" Billy asked, his heart pounding. "I'm guessin' you're no stranger to livestock and crop farmin', and I know a man needin' some good, honest help. And his new wife's taken in more lit-tle kids than she's got hands to grab 'em with," he added with a glance at the two women. "Not sayin' you're hired. Not sayin' you'll wanna stay. But it might just be the answer to a lotta prayers, you know?"

After a few moments' silence, the big man looked back at Sedalia. "I'm thinkin' we got nothin' to lose, goin' with him."

The woman replaced her bonnet at a jaunty angle, her face lighting up. "I never seen a redheaded angel before, but we sure got one watchin' over us now! Can't do no harm, can it?"

Billy grinned, suddenly ecstatic about the way this little adventure was working out. "Get your things together and I'll be right back. Gotta talk to somebody before we head out."

"And what was that all about?" Christine demanded before he was even inside the room. "My God, Billy, you could've been killed, leaping onto that crazy mule's back as though—"

"But I wasn't. And if I hadn't helped 'em out, who would have?"

He closed the door so their voices wouldn't carry out into the hallway. His sister's hair glowed with the light from the sunset coming in the window. With a few slight exceptions, Christine was so much their mother's image, it almost hurt him to look at her.

He could already guess her reaction, but her little dramas didn't bother him anymore. His sister had her mission and he had his.

"I'll be back for you tomorrow," he told her. "I'm gonna take the Gates family to Mike and Mercy's, to—"

"You're *what?*"

"—clear up a little situation they've gotten into. And probably to hire Reuben on as a field hand, while the two ladies help Mercy with the children."

Her brows arched and her eyes shone hard like green marbles, so he put his hat on before she could light into him again. "If you don't wanna stay here by yourself, you're welcome to come along. We'll drive back into town tomorrow to see if you've got a telegram."

Christine put her hands on her hips, and once again she looked for all the world like Mama. "Well, aren't you getting to be the muckety-muck, presumptuous—"

"No, I'm the livestock manager for the new Triple M

Ranch," he said, grinning broadly as surprise overtook her face. "Just doin' my job, scoutin' for the help we need to run the place. Gettin' paid top dollar for it, too. Now whadaya say to *that?*"

Chapter Six

"Say there! Might I have a few minutes of your time? If you could answer just a couple of questions—"

Billy paused on the hotel's front stairs to look at the fellow addressing him so urgently. He was tall and skinny and pink as a pig's belly, gripping a pencil and a tablet. "What kind of questions? I gotta be headin' back home."

"What possessed you to leap onto that runaway mule?" he exclaimed. "You went above and beyond the call for colored folks nobody's seen before."

"You oughtta be askin' why nobody else jumped in to help 'em," Billy replied cautiously. "Whatcha writin' this down for?"

"Sam Parsons, local man reporting on the cattle drives for *The Kansas City Times*," he said, sticking his hand out to shake Billy's. "The way Reuben and Sedalia Gates tell it, you're their guardian angel, Mr. Bristol. Certainly the man of the hour—a hero! Not only for stopping their mule, but for looking into the situation they encountered at the land office."

Glancing toward the livery stable, he saw Reuben and Sedalia loading a box back onto their wagon while Libby stared blindly at the haunches of Billy's horse, waiting. Sedalia's cheerful wave suggested she had sent this reporter his way, so he relaxed a little. Judging from what Mr. Parsons had already scrawled, he'd gotten his story and just wanted a few choice details.

Billy shrugged. "Like I said, I didn't do nothin' out of the ordinary—"

"You surely realize those Texans who taunted this family believe Negroes belong back on plantations with their masters," Parsons challenged. His Adam's apple bobbed as he watched Billy's reaction. "What possessed you to take their part when everyone else wants to drive them out of town?"

The question struck a nerve, so Billy considered his answer carefully. If he gave the wrong reply, maybe this man wouldn't print his story in the paper back home.

And maybe that wasn't such a bad thing.

"I know how it feels to be the outsider—the one who's fallen on hard times through no fault of his own," he said quietly. "If it weren't for the kindness of strangers who took me in three years ago, who knows how I mighta ended up? This family needed help and I was able to give it. Their color has nothin' to do with that."

Billy almost ended it there, but figured this fellow might as well know where he stood on the skin issue. "Matter of fact," he went on a little more boldly, "it was an old colored cook who took me under his wing when I lost most of my family to the Border Ruffians and other . . . outlaws, after the war."

Parsons had stopped scribbling to stare at him. "Pardon my saying so, Mr. Bristol, but you seem awfully young to be so—"

"I know when to tend to my own business—which is

more'n I can say for them cowboys," he replied point-edly. "So if you'll 'scuse me, Mr. Parsons, I'll be goin' now."

As he headed toward the Gates family and their wagon, Billy wondered if he should make sure Mr. Parsons didn't interview Christine. The last thing he needed was for her to run off at the mouth about those outlaws he'd mentioned—or the fact that he'd offered the Gates family jobs on the Triple M. Too many smoking coals had flared up already today without his sister fanning the flames.

"Well, Mr. Billy, you're a hero for sure!" Sedalia crowed. "That reporter's hot-footin' it down the street like he's gotta write his story *now*."

Billy smiled at her enthusiasm, and at the way her outlook had improved. Mercy Malloy needed a helper with energy and a sunny disposition—with enough patience to make Joel, Lily, and Solace behave themselves. Any woman who could keep her seat in a runaway wagon, and who dared slap her man with a bonnet after comforting her sick, upset companion, had the right qualifications for that.

"Better save your opinion till we talk to Mike and Mercy," he suggested. Vaulting up into the seat beside Reuben, he smiled at the two women, who sat squeezed into the back with their load of ramshackle furniture. "Once we straighten out that land office situation, you might not want nothin' to do with me."

"Why, there's a party goin' on! And Lord a-mercy, ain't that a pretty bride?" Sedalia piped up. "Surely this can't be the place—"

"Yep, it is."

Billy halted the wagon on the road. "I need to tell you somethin' before you meet these people. That bride is Mercedes Malloy—we call her Mercy. Her first husband Judd died in an Indian attack last year. There's a chance she's the widow you was readin' about in that land agent's letter."

He paused to let this information sink in, watching their dark faces. Meanwhile, Joel and Lily, who were chasing chickens near the corral, caught sight of them. Their squeals started the four dogs barking, and got everyone else's attention as well.

"You tellin' me our deed is for this Miz Malloy's land?" the man beside him mused aloud.

"That's what we need to find out. But let's have us some weddin' cake and get acquainted. Let the neighbors go home, 'fore we bring this up."

Billy looked first at Reuben, then back at Sedalia. "I just want you to understand that Mercy had nothin' to do with that ad or that certificate you got. She and Mike are joinin' their land into the Triple M Ranch now, and none of it's ever been for sale. Legally, leastaways."

"Are you tellin' me . . ." Sedalia's smile sagged like a pricked balloon. "Lord a-mercy, I hope that don't mean—"

"Billy! Billy!" Joel cried out as he ran toward them. His new jacket and pants were as dusty as his face, but there wasn't a happier-looking little kid on the prairie. "Who that, Billy?"

Billy hopped down from the wagon to catch the little boy who leaped at him, laughing as Joel landed with a *whump* against his chest. Snowy and Spot, the border collies, circled him in their own show of welcome as little Lily toddled along at the end of this parade.

"Joel and Lily," he said, "this is the Gates family, and they've come to see about workin' for us. The man's name is Reuben—"

"Happy to see you, Mr. Joel and Miss Lily," he responded politely. "This here's my wife, Sedalia, and my little sister, Liberty. We call 'er Libby."

"Mighty glad to meetcha," Sedalia added, her smile

wide. "And who's these fine collie-dogs? I betcha they're your best friends, ain't they?"

"Uh-huh! That one's Spot," Joel replied, pointing to the black dog with the white patch around one eye, "and that's Snowy, 'cause she gots a white face. They're Billy's dogs, really, but me 'n' Lily gets to play with 'em."

"And ain't you just the sweetest little doll-baby?"

Sedalia hopped lithely from the wagon, and—like everyone who saw Lily—crouched and held her arms open to the beautiful little girl.

Lily was all dressed up in pink, with a huge ribbon tied atop her curly blond hair. While she loved having new admirers, she wrapped one chubby arm around Billy's leg as she peered at these strangers with her fingers in her mouth.

"Lily's just a few months past her first birthday, best we can figure," Billy explained. "Her daddy dropped her off on our doorstep with a note pinned to her dress, and that's all we know about her. 'Cept that she's spoiled rotten—ain'tcha?" he teased the little girl.

She gazed up at him with huge blue eyes and giggled. "No, Joel is!"

"No, *you,* Lily Stinkerpants!" the boy teased, leaning down in Billy's arms to point repeatedly at her.

"I can see things is lively around here," Sedalia remarked, and then she looked toward the house. "And here comes Mr. Malloy—and another baby on *his* shoulder!"

"Solace was born last spring, after her daddy got killed by them Indians. And Joel here lost his mama in a gunfight last May, so Mike brought him home—just like Mercy and Judd took in me and my older sister a few years back," he went on. "We're pieced together 'bout like one of Mercy's patchwork quilts, but we get along good, mostly."

Michael's wide smile was one more reminder of why Billy would never set off across the country with his sister. Mike's face was tanned from hours of field work, and his compact body bespoke the strength of a larger man. Billy had watched in awe when this man effortlessly drove a stagecoach across the plains at full speed, but Mike Malloy looked even stronger cradling a baby. Not many men took to children, but this one was a natural daddy.

"Hey there, folks!" he called out, but his grin was for Billy. "Glad you're back, son. Didn't know when we'd see you again."

"I convinced Christine to send a telegram and wait for me in town," he explained. "But meanwhile, I met Reuben and Sedalia and Libby Gates here, and they're lookin' for work."

"And if this young fella hadn't flung himself onto our runaway mule, we'd be lookin' for St. Peter—or leastaways a good doctor," Sedalia said as she rose to her full height. "Reuben, he was testy after the fella at the land office told him the certificate we got for our life savin's was—"

"We'll settle that later," Reuben reminded his wife.

When he slid down from the wagon to approach Mike, he stood two heads taller and twice as broad across the shoulders. "I surely appreciate the way Mr. Billy brung us here to see 'bout hirin' on. He didn't say nothin' about it bein' your weddin' day—"

"And congratulations to ya," his wife said with a wide grin.

"—so we can just wait in the shade of them trees along the river—"

"You'll do no such thing." Mike gestured toward tables where food was set out. "We've got sliced ham, fried chicken, wedding cake—"

"And punkin pie, and pecan pie," Billy added with a big grin, " 'cause our cook, Asa, used to be a plantation chef in Atlanta."

"Lord a-mercy, we come up from Georgia, too!"

Sedalia's face shone as she surveyed the harvested wheat fields. "Mighty kind of ya, Mr. Malloy," she said quietly. "I can't help thinkin' the Lord's took us by the hand and led us here. We just had to come through that orneriness in town 'fore we could see the silver linin' of the clouds, was all."

She looked up at the slumped, silent girl who hadn't shifted from her spot in the back of the overloaded wagon. "Libby, girl, we gonna get you somethin' to eat and a place to rest yourself for awhile. You and that baby's gonna be just fine now. Everythin' about this place tells me so."

"Poor Libby looks miserable, even though she's sound asleep," Mercy murmured. She'd changed from her wedding gown into everyday calico and joined them at the table in the front room. The Gates girl was now asleep in Mercy's bed because the stairs to the guest rooms were too much for her.

Sedalia looked up from her plateful of Asa's ham and yams and biscuits. "Poor child ain't had a real bed for weeks. We's guessin' she's gonna birth that baby any day now."

The coffee-skinned woman let out a tired sigh. "Just so you folks understand, she ain't never told us how she come to be in the family way—who done it to her, or when or where," she said softly. "We tried ever' way we know to get her to talk, but she's been locked up inside herself since the day it happened."

"She's my little sister, and we take care of our own," Reuben insisted. "But we promise y'all, she and the baby won't be no trouble. Won't keep us from doin' our jobs, if you folks hire us on."

"I would never think that way," Mercy said as she filled her plate.

"And it ain't like she weren't raised to know better," Reuben continued. " 'Bout how she shouldn't cave in to temptation—"

"If she had a choice." Sedalia glanced sadly at Mercy from across the table. "Libby ain't but thirteen. Real smart when it comes to book learnin', but not about the way menfolk has always looked at her. Plenty of 'em coulda helped theirselves and scared her—or shamed her—into keepin' quiet." Sedalia shuddered. "That's one reason I'm so glad to leave where we was at, Miz Malloy. We heard tell of abandoned homesteads up here. Scraped together all we had, and thought the Good Lord was finally showin' us the way to the Promised Land."

She shook her head sadly, making her coarse, coiled braids shift against her scalp. "Couldn't b'lieve my ears this mornin' when that land agent shooed us out like a couple of pesky ole flies. Tellin' us he didn't know nothin' 'bout our land! It was spelled right out, on that deed we got."

Billy swallowed his last mouthful of pumpkin pie, drinking in these details. "Show 'em that certificate. They'll have a better idea 'bout the location on it."

Reuben reached into the back pocket of his denim pants and pulled out an envelope. As he handed it across the table to Michael, the paper trembled in that massive black hand—a hand that could crush the life out of any of them if Reuben's temper flared. It was something they'd have to watch, judging from how this massive man acted when he got riled.

But seeing how this family's hopes and dreams—and

all their money—rode on what Mike found inside that envelope, Billy understood why Reuben Gates was upset. He'd felt that same awful helplessness when Mr. Massena, the banker in Missouri, had foreclosed on their home a few years back, turning them out without a speck of mercy or remorse.

Mike's scowl confirmed Billy's hunch. Mercy was reading over her husband's shoulder, and her brows came together in a frown. "The land this describes can't be far from here, but I can't think of any place—"

"It's the deed for this homestead, Mercy. Somebody's pulled a fast one." He looked at Reuben over the top of the certificate. "How'd you get this, again?"

"We seen this advertisement in the newspaper," the big man replied, handing over a yellowed page that had grown limp from so much refolding. "So we sent our money to them land agents, and they sent us this here deed certificate. The land they're sellin' b'longed to homesteaders who didn't prove up, all along the railroad—"

"Look at the bottom. At the names." Billy closed his eyes, humiliation heating his cheeks.

"'Richard Bristol and Virgil Wyndham, agents and commissioners for Dickinson County, Kansas,'" Mike read aloud. "You don't suppose—?"

Mercy hurried around the table to wrap her arms around his shaking shoulders. "Oh, Billy, I'm so sorry you found this out," she said. "It's them, isn't it? That man and your mama changed their names around."

"Too close to be coincidence," Michael agreed, shaking his head with disgust. "Son, I wish it could be different. What'd your sister say about this?"

"Didn't show her," Billy mumbled. "Sis saw me stop these folks's runaway mule this afternoon, and for all she knows they're just down on their luck, lookin' for work. I didn't mention this deed, thinkin' she'd either be chasin' after that Tucker Trudeau fella or strikin' out after Mama again."

Sedalia had stopped eating to watch the conversation volley across the table. "Somebody mind tellin' me what's goin' on here?" she asked. "I'm mighty tired, and I musta missed somethin'."

The front room went silent, except for the ticking of the mantel clock. Images from his past, of his mother and a man in a handlebar mustache, collided in Billy's mind. He'd carefully tucked those memories away, for at ten, he couldn't believe Mama had abandoned them without a backward glance.

But he was fourteen now. Managing livestock for a family who treated him like a beloved son. He considered himself a man in many ways, but right now he felt like a little kid again, scared out of his mind—and swallowing back too much heartache to talk about it.

"My sister Christine and me lived on a horse ranch in Missouri till after the war. The Border Ruffians killed my daddy and kidnapped my twin brother," he explained in a thin thread of a voice. "The bank foreclosed on us, so Mama packed us up, sayin' we was headin' west to start a new life. But when Christine and me was usin' the privy, our mama rode off with an English fella we'd seen at the ranch a couple of times. Left us there with all the luggage and tickets clean to Denver—but *left* us all the same."

"Lord a-mercy, that's the saddest thing I ever—"

"Mama's name is Virgilia Bristol, and the Englishman called himself Richard Wyndham," Billy finished with a sigh. "That land agent in Abilene didn't lie to ya, Reuben. He never saw your money, and he didn't know nothin' 'bout this land bein' up for sale 'cause it *wasn't*. Richard Bristol and Virgil Wyndham are long gone by now—and your money went with 'em."

* * *

Christine patted her hair one last time and went down-stairs to sit in the hotel's front parlor. Surely someone from the telegraph office would come this morning. She planned to snatch the envelope from his hand, then read Tucker's message in the privacy of her room.

She chose a small rocking chair by the front window, where the sun would make the highlights sparkle in her auburn hair, and the watermark in her turquoise suit would set her apart from any housekeepers who might be about at this hour. The cowpokes and cattle barons might as well know she wasn't one of those "girls" who kept a room here at the Abilene House.

"Good morning, Miss Bristol. Did you sleep well?" the desk clerk inquired. The young man's hair was so heav-ily oiled, comb grooves radiated from his center part. But at least he was clean—unlike a lot of the men she'd seen here.

Christine smiled politely. "Yes, I did. Thank you for asking."

It was none of his business that she'd stayed up half the night poring over Tucker's letters. She'd also dug the red velvet diary from her carpetbag, where she always kept it. Rereading her mother's flowery accounts of meeting Richard Wyndham, and his secret visits while she and Billy were being tutored, had rekindled the re-sentment that inspired her original mission to find Mama: to get answers about why she and Billy were dumped at the depot.

Seeing new evidence in Tucker's letters—even though they were three years old—made her restless again. Christine arranged her skirts around her kid slip-pers as she perched prettily in the chair. This waiting was unbearable. Surely the fascinating man who'd penned those encouraging words would reply to her telegraph right away. Surely he would agree that they should try to find Mama together. Or just do *anything* together.

The attraction was so obvious! Tucker Trudeau had so clearly stated his affection for her, she'd heard his Cajun accent in every line.

And now that the Union Pacific Railroad stretched clear to California—why, it would be easy to trace Mama and her fancy man. According to those enclosed articles, they'd worked under many assumed names, but they seemed to settle in the more populated areas—until their chicanery caught up to them and they moved again, farther west.

"Would you care for tea, Miss Bristol? I'd be delighted to fetch it."

The desk clerk still stood before her, grinning like a lovesick puppy.

Christine blinked to clear thoughts of hale, handsome Tucker Trudeau from her mind. "How thoughtful of you. Yes, tea would be lovely."

His face flushed as he handed her a pamphlet he'd held behind his back. "I—I recall your brother being here with you yesterday, ma'am. Matter of fact, here's the piece that man from *The Kansas City Times* printed up about him! You must be very proud!"

Christine unfolded the page, which sported a two-inch-high headline across the top: BRISTOL SAVES FAMILY FROM DISASTER. Beneath that, a smaller line proclaimed: *Another Blatant Example of How Abilene Needs Real Law Enforcement.* To one side, a pen-and-ink sketch captured her younger brother's lopsided grin to perfection.

"Oh my, I—thank you for showing me this," she said. "I saw the incident from the window, but I had no idea . . . this is quite an essay."

As she skimmed the main story, she was amazed— and amused: reporter Sam Parsons had used Billy's heroism to illustrate his views that this cow town needed to clean up its streets.

So there is intelligent life in Abilene. Or one man, anyway, who sees this wicked little city for what it is.

The clerk returned with a tray of dainty cakes, a silver teapot, and a bone china cup and saucer as she finished reading.

"May I keep this?" she asked, flashing her most brilliant smile. "I'm sure Billy will want to see it."

"Oh, I—I intended for you to have it, Miss Bristol."

The clerk's grooved hair was almost making her snicker, as was his lovestruck grin. But at least he was trying to please her. "Thank you so much, sir, for—"

"Oh, please, call me Oliver! Oliver Tandy, at your service, Miss Bristol."

Make that two men who see things for what they are. Even if I don't want to encourage this one.

Christine smiled. "Thank you, Oliver. I'll enjoy my tea and cakes while I'm waiting for—"

The front door opened, and in walked Billy. His cowlick bobbed like a rooster's tail, and in his denim pants and homespun shirt he looked very much a part of the prairie. He grinned at her, his blue eyes sparkling with little-brother mischief.

"Mornin', Sis. Mornin' to ya," he said with a nod toward the clerk.

Oliver Tandy straightened to his full, lanky height, extending his hand. "What an honor to meet you, Mr. Bristol! Your sister and I have been discussing this article on yesterday's events. It seems you're a hero!"

Christine chuckled at her brother's dumbstruck expression. "Not only a hero for halting the runaway mule, but a shining example of how more men should behave—and how more lawmen should be hired. Along with an artist's rendition, suitable for framing," she added with a smirk.

He groaned. "Now what possessed Parsons to—"

"Oh, just read it and accept the notoriety you deserve."

She sipped her tea, scowling at how her script was being rewritten. She'd hoped the courier would come early—for surely Tucker had answered as soon as he received her telegram!—so she could slip upstairs to savor it. With the clerk hanging around, and now Billy, she'd look like a fool for waiting here in the parlor. Or she'd have her little brother pestering her when the telegram arrived.

How could she evade these two? A trip to her room, presumably to freshen up, would give Billy first chance to open any messages that came. Unacceptable!

"Billy, would you like the rest of my tea cakes?" she offered sweetly. "I'm sure Mr. Tandy would bring you coffee or—"

"Yes, of course. Whatever you'd like, Mr. Bristol."

Billy looked up from his reading. "Thanks, I'm fine. Sure hope this piece don't bring a parade of cowpokes to the ranch, lookin' for work—like Reuben told Mr. Parsons about."

"As many of these pamphlets as I've seen around town, you might have cowboys applying as soon as they recognize you," Oliver remarked. "The cattle drives are about over for the season. Some drovers might settle in for the winter, rather than making the long trek back to Texas."

"Not lookin' for men who'll head for the saloons every Saturday night," Billy remarked. "Don't need nobody throwin' whiskey bottles at—"

They all looked up when the little bell above the door tinkled.

"Good morning, Cal. Telegram for somebody?" Oliver asked.

As the unkempt kid squinted at the name on the envelope, Christine's teacup ticked against its saucer. This would not do! If she acted too eager to receive the message, Billy would grab it before she could.

"Christi—"

"Thank you, that's for me!" she chirped, springing up from her chair.

The sickening clatter of china announced that she'd forgotten to set down her cup and saucer—and then a swish of her skirt sent the silver tray and teapot crashing to the floor as well. As tea cakes landed in the puddle, like pretty little boats between islands of china, her face flamed.

"I am *so* sorry, Oliver, I—"

"No bother at all, Miss Bristol. I'll fetch the broom—don't you touch a thing for fear you'll cut yourself."

While the clerk hurried into the little room behind the front desk, Cal, the delivery boy, approached with her telegram. His purposeful gaze—his grip on the envelope when she tried to pluck it from his fingers—brought her out of her mortified state.

"Oh, yes, of course!" she gasped, reaching into her skirt pocket for his tip.

"Thanks a whole lot," the kid muttered at the single coin—and then he swooped down to pluck the little cakes from the puddle beside her shoe.

He wasn't out the door yet before Billy was snorting with laughter. "Wait'll I tell Miss Vanderbilt that her prize pupil—"

"You'll do no such thing!" Christine snapped, stamping her foot. "And did you see the way that ungrateful—unspeakably *crude* young man reached down and—this is beyond me! I'm going upstairs!"

Clutching the envelope, which her fingers itched to open, Christine sailed past a befuddled Oliver Tandy to take the stairs as fast as her skirts would allow. By the time she'd reached the top, she was smiling slyly.

All things work out, for those who play their parts, she thought as she entered her room.

Alone at last. Christine fell against the door to shut it, her fingers trembling so badly she could barely loosen the flap of the envelope. She held the small, folded note against her heart, closing her eyes to collect herself.

Here it was—her first message from Tucker Trudeau in nearly three years. In more ways than she dared admit to herself, Christine had awaited this sign that he still wanted to see her after his letters had so mysteriously stopped coming to the academy. Was this her ticket to the happily-ever-after she so desperately craved? The justification she longed for, after rebuffing the well-heeled suitors she'd met in the ballrooms of St. Louis society?

She unfolded the note, her heart thumping in her chest.

GO HOME, it said. TOO LATE.

Chapter Seven

"You gonna tell me what he said, Sis? I'm guessin'—"

"No! You wouldn't understand."

Christine held herself hard around the middle, trying not to cry any more . . . focusing on the withering prairie grass and the rutted, dusty road—anything, so she wouldn't have to look at Billy. His blue eyes bored into her with a curiosity—a pity—she just couldn't handle right now.

"—he told ya he couldn't help ya find Mama, or—" Billy scowled at a thought he didn't want to spend much time with. "You—you'd tell me if something had happened to Mama, wouldn't ya?"

"It wasn't that. Just leave me alone, dammit!"

He sighed, keeping his eyes on Pepper's dappled gray backside, because the sight of his sister's tear-streaked face was more than he could stand. "If that Trudeau fella said somethin' hateful and you want me to go to Atchison and set him straight—"

"I want you to shut up, all right?" she yelled. "Can't

you get it through your head that there's nothing to tell? Nothing to fish for?"

Billy smiled. While he truly hated to see Christine so upset, she wasn't going back to Mike and Mercy's with her tail between her legs by choice. Nope, his sister had disrupted that wedding with the idea that she wasn't going to face the Malloys—or Miss Vanderbilt—again any time soon. Even a blind man could see she'd been rejected. It was just a matter of whether Trudeau refused to see her, or whether Mama was too long gone to trace.

"I'm on your side, Sis," he insisted quietly. "This is my mama we're talkin' about, too. I can't help you fend off all the questions everybody'll ask unless you fill me in. What with the Gates family helpin' Mike and Mercy move into their new place today, so they can live in the log house—and Libby havin' her baby any minute now—everybody's got plenty to tend to without—"

"Did I ever ask for their help?" Christine demanded. "Can I change the way they took to you—made you the manager of their whoop-de-do livestock—"

Billy listened to that green-eyed monster, envy, in her voice as she railed about his new job and what it probably paid. But it was more than money he was hearing about between Christine's agonized words; it was disappointment. It was a betrayal as devastating as when Mama had left them at the depot ringing in his sister's tear-choked denials.

His heart ached for her as she buried her face in her handkerchief. Pulling Pepper to a halt, he awkwardly squeezed her shoulder. "I'm sorry, Sis. Maybe you oughtta just cry it all out here, before we're in sight of the new house, so—"

"All right. Here—read it for yourself, dammit!"

This wasn't the time to say he'd soap her mouth unless she quit swearing like a saloon girl. Billy unwadded the crumpled note. Then his eyes went wet.

GO HOME. TOO LATE.

"Of all the low-down—"

"Are you happy now?" Christine demanded, snatching the note back. "Do you have any inkling what it did to me, having him tell me to go home—when I don't have a home, Billy?"

Christine grabbed his arm, forcing him to look into her red-rimmed eyes. "Do you have any idea how many times my heart's been ripped out these past three years by people making polite conversation, asking me where home is?"

Billy shifted on the bench seat. He'd always figured Christine had immersed herself in her dressmaking and studies at the academy—she'd attended balls and parties in homes that would never have been open to them, even while Daddy was alive. He hadn't thought about her feeling like she'd been yanked up by the roots and never replanted. Surrounded by the love Judd, Mercy, and Mike Malloy had shown him, he simply hadn't realized that Christine still felt like an outcast even though Miss Vanderbilt had taken a special shine to her.

But it was more than that, wasn't it? Trudeau had left her to wonder *why* it was too late. Did he have a family now? Or had too much time gone by since their last letters, and too many other things taken over his life?

"I—I'm real sorry, Sis," he mumbled.

"You don't know the meaning of sorry!" she wailed. "I feel like such a fool, believing I could still—"

Billy closed his eyes. She'd arrived at the real matter now. She'd had most of yesterday to moon over those letters, convincing herself this Tucker fella felt the same about her now as he did when he wrote them. She'd let herself fall head-over-heels—in the same way Emma

Clark believed Billy was the Prince Charming in all her fairy tales.

Why did girls believe everything they saw in writing? And make up a pretty story to fill in the blanks—or read between the lines through the rose-colored glasses of their romantic notions? They were askin' for trouble, trying to outguess a man's intentions.

But a hard truth like that wasn't what Christine wanted to hear. And it wouldn't make things any easier when they showed up at the Malloys' new place, either. Agatha Vanderbilt would soon be returning to St. Louis, expecting his sister to go with her. And if she didn't, she'd have to deal with Mercy every day—the same Mercy who'd kept those letters in her drawer so long. Forgiveness didn't come easy—if ever—for Christine Bristol.

"What do you wanna do?" he asked. "Maybe we shoulda stayed in town a little—"

"If I knew that, I wouldn't be so upset! Would I?"

Billy sighed. Christine might have grown up on the outside, but down deep she was still a pigheaded, impossible little girl who didn't know how to keep her world turning unless everything went her way.

He clucked to the mare. No sense in sitting here, watching her cry. He and the good Lord both knew she'd perform as long as she had an audience—and he had chores to do.

Mercy saw the wagon—saw the slender girl beside Billy—and nipped her lip. Christine was back, but she wasn't happy about it. Even from this distance, the girl's fashionable hat couldn't disguise eyes reddened by rejection and a heart torn in two.

Was it *her* fault, for hiding those letters?

Many, many times after Aunt Agatha had slipped them to her, Tucker's notes had taunted Mercy's curiosity and conscience. Was it *her* fault the Bristols hadn't met up with their mother again? Her fault that Christine had lost a potential beau?

"Put everything where you think it looks best," she called over to Michael. He and Reuben Gates were hefting the pedestal table down from the wagon. "I'll be back in a moment. Some old fences need mending."

Her new husband, bless him, caught sight of the Bristols and flashed her an encouraging smile. "Good luck, honey. Looks like our girl got some bad news."

Mercy walked toward the barn to wait for Billy and his sister. What should she say? What could possibly make things right for a girl who'd grown to womanhood without her mother's love and guidance? Agatha Vanderbilt might have worked wonders and set Christine on the path toward a useful, lucrative career—

But that wasn't what Christine really wanted, was it?

The mare whickered as Billy pulled the buckboard to a halt. He seemed, as always, to be handling this difficult situation capably. It was his mother, too, who'd eluded them all these years. Bringing his disappointed sister back to this family—this place where she'd never felt she belonged—had been an ordeal for him. Best that Mercy state her case with all the compassion she could muster before Christine's bitterness inspired another scene they might all regret.

Lord, give me the words that will win her over with my love—and Yours, she prayed as she stepped forward. Before Billy could come around to help his sister down, Mercy reached up to clasp Christine's knee.

"I'm so sorry this didn't work out the way you wanted, honey," she said softly, "and I'm sorry for the extra anguish I've caused you by hiding those letters. It was never my intention to keep you from your mother—or from Tucker Trudeau. Please forgive me, Christine."

From beneath the brim of her lacy lavender hat, the pale-faced girl glared down at her. "That's a tall order. I'll have to think about it."

"Fair enough."

Mercy watched Christine gaze around her, at large barns, and corrals of Morgan horses, and cattle grazing beyond them. She focused then on the house, a white two-story frame creation that represented Michael Malloy's extraordinary talent for carpentry as well as his deep love for the family he'd brought together. It was leaps and bounds above the house Judd had built for her—but then, life shot up from humble roots sometimes. People were given fresh starts and second chances at love, and Mercy felt blessed to know that firsthand.

"We have a pretty yellow room upstairs just waiting for you, Christine. Stay for as long as you like. This is our home now, and you're a part of it."

The girl's backbone stiffened. "Thank you," she muttered. "I need time to decide what comes next. I'll appreciate it if you and everyone else would just leave me alone."

Mercy stepped away, nodding. The long-suffering look on Billy's face told her it was best not to challenge his sister or ask any questions yet.

"Here—let me help you with that," she said as he pushed a large trunk to the back of the buckboard. "I'll ask Michael and Reuben to carry the rest of her things upstairs before they return to the other place for more furniture."

"No need for you to help—"

"*Please,*" she insisted. "It's not like I've never toted a load."

Billy's smile spoke volumes. "Thanks for understandin'," he said in a low voice. "I don't know much about this whole thing, but it ain't pretty."

He hopped lithely to the ground and then helped his sister down. Christine gripped her carpetbag, resolutely set off toward the house—and then turned. "Where's Miss Vanderbilt?"

"Last I saw her, she and Solace were sunning on the back porch, keeping Joel and Lily out from underfoot."

"I'll go in the front door then. Like company."

Off she marched again, ramrod straight and gripping that carpetbag as though it held the last scraps of her dignity. Too preoccupied to appreciate the differences between this place and the small, dark log house she'd always detested—or to make her usual grand entrance.

Mercy had to chuckle. "I guess we shouldn't tell her how much she resembles that headmistress she's trying to avoid."

"No tellin' what she might say to that," Billy replied as they lifted the trunk between them. "'Bout as bad as when the messenger brung that telegram from Tucker this mornin'. She knocked over a teapot and a tray of little cakes in the hotel parlor, she was so excited."

Gripping the trunk's leather handle, Mercy grimaced. Christine's spirits had surely plummeted since that moment of high anticipation, before her hopes were dashed. "Was Tucker rude? Or married?" she asked quietly. "Or has something happened to your mother?"

For a few moments there was only the sound of their muffled footsteps on the hard-packed dirt driveway. "Four words—that's all he wrote her. *'Go home. Too late.'* "

"That's it?" Mercy scowled, wondering what that cryptic message *didn't* say. "Seems awfully strange, considering the long letters he wrote to her before—even when he had to realize she wasn't receiving them."

"Yeah. Begs more questions than it answers." He adjusted his grip, looking sadly toward the sway of his sister's backside, up ahead of them. "In a way, I'm sorry

she ain't takin' out after Mama. She'll never get over the
way we was abandoned if she don't work this situation
outta her system. Sis has to see things for herself before
she believes 'em."

Mercy followed Christine with her gaze, up the front
steps to pause between the two high white pillars that
gave the new house an air of true grandeur out here on
the endless prairie. At least the girl ran an appreciative
hand over the column's smoothness, letting her fingertips linger on the entwined *M*s Michael had carved into
the fretwork, so every guest could see the pride he proclaimed in his new family.

"Looky who's home!" came a voice from behind the
house. "C'mon, Lily—it's Christine!"

"Kwis-teen! Kwis-*teeeen!*"

Christine topped the steps to quickly cross the porch.
As she reached the front door, Mercy hoped the young
woman's disappointment didn't spew out to scald the
two little children who were so excited to see her.

Joel was scrambling up the steps as only a thrilled
three-year-old could. "Christine! Come see me!"

"Me, too! Me, too!" echoed Lily. Stairs were a new
challenge for her, but the little princess in pink seldom
let such things intimidate her—especially since Joel
had now latched on to one of Christine's legs.

For a moment there was only the *thump-thump*ing of
the toddler's determined feet on the stairs and the rapt
adoration in Joel's eyes as he gazed up at his idol . . . and
the exasperation of Christine, who stood with one hand
on the doorknob and the other gripping her carpetbag.

Mercy and Billy stopped walking. Both hoped two little kids didn't bear the brunt of Christine's devastation—
and then dropped the trunk to rush forward when Lily
teetered precariously on the edge of the top step.

Not daring to cry out for fear the little girl would tum-
ble backward by looking at her, Mercy breathed a des-

perate prayer. "Don't let her fall! If she hits her head on—"

Maybe it was a guardian angel whose fluttering wings kept Lily upright, or maybe that same angel gave Christine a swift kick. Her carpetbag hit the porch floor as she rushed toward the little girl with her biggest grin.

"Lily! Come here, sweetie!" she cooed as she threw her arms forward.

With a delighted cry, the little girl imitated her. Just as Lily overbalanced to fall toward the porch, Christine scooped her up to toss her into the air.

Lily laughed, wrapping her chubby arms around her rescuer's neck, blissfully unaware of the danger she'd escaped. "Kwis-teen! My angel!"

"No, *you're* the angel, Lily!" Joel crowed. "Dang! How'd you learn to fly?"

"That's enough of your cussing, Joel," came Christine's tart but relieved reply. "I'll have to wash out your mouth with—"

"But Billy says dang!"

"That's because Billy is *not* an angel."

"But we love him. And we love you, Kwis-teen!" Lily proclaimed. Her voice rang with the finality of a princess who must have her say. "Huh, Joel!"

"Double-dog right!"

Christine blinked, caught by the familiar phrase from her own childhood. She glanced at her brother, and then at Mercy, and then, still holding the little blonde to her shoulder, she sank down to sit on the top step.

"I love you, too," she whispered as she pulled Joel close.

Billy let out the breath he'd been holding. "I s'pose there'll come a time when we wish Lily and Joel didn't repeat every little thing they've heard," he whispered, "but right now, I can't argue with a thing they said."

Mercy could only nod and brush away a tear.

Chapter Eight

Unable to sleep, Christine paced between the two windows of her room. From the front of the house, she could make out the rutted road and the stubble of an endless, harvested cornfield. The Smoky Hill River wound behind the barns and corrals, its surface shining beneath a layer of mist that hovered above the moonlit water.

The silence set her on edge. Miss Vanderbilt's huge home, which housed her Academy for Young Ladies, sat on a block where, even in the wee hours, an occasional wagon clattered down the cobblestone street. Or delivery men greeted each other while leaving their ice and milk around the wealthy St. Louis neighborhood.

But here, the quiet could drive a girl insane. Or force her to face the unpleasant facts that kept her awake.

Tucker didn't want her. Didn't care that intercepted letters had kept them apart. Even though it wasn't her fault.

And Mama, well—those newspaper articles had only hinted at the sins she and Richard Wyndham had committed. When Billy told her the Gates family had come all the way from Georgia to claim Mercy's homestead because of a phony deed, she could no longer delude herself. Virgilia Bristol, by whatever name, was now a sham and a shyster like the man she'd run off with. A far cry from the mother she'd sat beside in church or shopped with in Richmond.

So what should she do? It was a sorry enough task to shove Tucker Trudeau into a dark corner of her heart after being lovestruck since the moment she'd met him. He was dashing and playful, and memories of meeting him three years ago had seen her through many a lonely weekend or boring society ball.

But how could she forget about Mama?

Reading again from that red velvet diary had called up her mother's voice, with its soft drawl . . . memories of sitting in the sun-drenched parlor, working needlepoint samplers together . . . the sweetness of Mama's magnolia perfume, dabbed behind her own ears on special occasions.

Oh, she'd been outraged and humiliated when her mother left her behind to be with that dapper Englishman. But right now just a glimpse of Mama—a single smile between mother and daughter—would wipe away her foul thoughts. She could forgive and forget her mother's misbehavior in a flash if she could have just one last glance at her.

Well, a glance and the answer to that all-important question: why?

But it looked like that was never going to happen.

She could no longer indulge in imaginative fantasies about what she'd do and say when she met her mother or Tucker Trudeau again, so graduating and then working for Madame Devereaux seemed her best option. Her friends at the academy would never know that for a few bright, shining hours, her life had taken a much more exciting turn. By comparison, she now felt like a candle with a very short wick, as though the best years of her life had already burned away.

Christine opened the window. Not a cicada sang; not a tree stirred. For miles around, the prairie appeared frozen in the moon's pale light. It could've been an enchanted land where fairies and elves held sway.

But she could no longer believe in such fanciful notions. Mama had snatched away her childish dreams, so it was time to face her future. Time to get on with life as an adult for whom a lot of people had a lot of expectations.

She turned from the window, eyeing the narrow bed, but then stopped. Had an animal made that noise?

Pressing her nose to the cold glass, Christine gazed out over the moonlit yard to where the mist hovered above the river, ethereal with mystery. There it was again, low and harmonious and—happy. It was laughter.

Gasping, she stared at one figure, and then another, darting between the trees. Christine raised the window higher, putting her ear near the opening. A lithe, long-haired woman sprang from the mist as though coaxing her companion to follow—and he did.

And they were naked!

"Oh, my Lord. . . ."

Glued to this alluring little drama, Christine put her fist to her mouth to keep from crying out. Mercy and Michael Malloy were kissing, caressing each other's bare bodies with an abandon that held her in horrified fascination.

Didn't they know children—or guests—could see them from the house? Wasn't it too cold to be outside? Surely they hadn't left the house without their clothes!

And why were her eyes glued to the clean, sleek line of Michael's backside as he held his new wife?

And why did she feel an intense tingling below her

belly? Because she might get caught spying on this wildly intimate act? Or because this was how she'd always wanted Tucker to kiss her—even though it was a sin to think such lewd, unladylike thoughts?

Yet Mercy, that paragon of prairie virtue, now stood in full moonlight, undulating in perfect rhythm with her mate. Shamelessly returning his attentions. This wasn't at all what she'd pictured when Mama had made veiled references to a woman's wifely duty. While her parents had slept in the same room, they always wore layers of nightclothes, neck to toe. And they had certainly never behaved this way!

She knew. That's what keyholes were for.

Her heart was pounding so hard she couldn't breathe. Christine sensed she should turn away from the window, but she wanted just another glimpse of the way Michael gave and Mercy took—

"You'd best get your rest, Miss Bristol. Billy's taking us to the train station tomorrow."

Christine pivoted. Thank God the room's shadows hid the flush of her face—or did her headmistress know what she'd been gawking at? Her friends often speculated that Miss Vanderbilt watched their reflections in her spectacles when her back was turned. She had a knack for knowing when any one of them wandered from the straight and narrow.

And because she was truly grateful that this woman had encouraged her design skills—and because she suspected Miss Vanderbilt didn't accept any tuition from Mercy—Christine behaved herself at school.

But now, face to face with the culprit who'd kept her from corresponding with Tucker—and perhaps even her long-lost mother—she felt something snap. It was the same release she felt when her roommate Becky unlaced her corset after a long day.

"I won't be going with you," she said, hoping her loose nightgown hid her shaking knees. "While I appreciate the many things you've done for me, Miss Vanderbilt, hiding Mr. Trudeau's letters isn't one of them. I—I feel the trust between us has been compromised. I sincerely believe I'd have caught up to Mama had I received them when they were written."

Even in her floor-length flannel nightgown, the little headmistress could fill a room with her presence. While Agatha Vanderbilt resembled a wraith, with her white braid hanging down her back and her moonlit face the shade of her nightgown, only a fool would believe she was old and helpless.

"I'm sorry you feel that way," she replied crisply. "Let us hope that you will never do what you consider best for someone and then stand accused of ruining her life. And let us hope you won't regret renouncing the opportunities you've been offered. And let us pray that if you do reunite with your mother, you won't learn things about her you don't want to know."

Christine almost lashed out at this woman, who remained totally in control even at three in the morning. But the headmistress wasn't finished with her.

"And if you find yourself with a houseful of children and guests on your wedding night," she continued in a stern whisper, "let's hope you've married a resourceful, passionate man who can't keep his hands off you—and let's hope you will respond joyfully to him. Few people follow their dreams and experience real joy, Christine. What a shame, if you were one of them who don't. Now get into bed," she said with an impatient wave. "Your pacing awakened me."

Christine searched for the perfect retort. But Miss Vanderbilt had just dismissed her. For good this time.

* * *

"Mistah Michael! Miss Mercy!" came a shrill cry from outside. "Anybody home who can help us? We got us a girl in a real bad way!"

As one they all rose from the long table in the dining room to see what the ruckus was about.

"Sounds like Sedalia Gates!"

"Bet Libby is havin' her baby!"

"We'd better put water on to boil, and fetch the rags and the laudanum," Mercy said as Michael and Billy rushed outside. "Lord only knows where those things ended up when we were moving in yesterday."

"I'll brew up some of my special tea, too," Asa remarked, already heading for the kitchen. "That little gal's gonna need all the help we can give 'er. Small as she is, it's gonna be like a dog birthin' a donkey."

"She's lucky you and Billy and Michael are here. Men of experience will have to do, since we've got no midwives close by." Mercy glanced outside and saw the young Gates girl writhing on a stretcher the men had made of sheets. The sight of so much blood made her swallow hard to keep her breakfast down.

She turned from the window to see Christine valiantly trying to keep Joel in his high chair while she balanced a whimpering Lily on one hip.

"Take the little ones outside and keep them busy—please!" she added.

Mercy's expression was a reminder of what an ordeal childbirthing could be, so Christine quickly freed Joel from his breakfast tray. She coaxed the little boy out the back door ahead of her.

"Let's chase the chickens!" Joel cried as he shot across the yard.

"Chickens! Chickens!" Lily mimicked, squirming to get down.

While the birds in the barnyard weren't what she'd had in mind for a diversion, Christine welcomed the appearance of the two barking dogs—anything to disguise the loud, keening cries coming from the house. It made her laugh, watching Snowy and Spot herd their two-legged charges away from the corrals and cattle pens. While the chickens squawked and flapped their wings, Joel was in his glory, agitating them. Lily toddled fearlessly behind him, her blond curls bouncing around a face still smeared with mush and syrup.

"It's good to be useful somewhere other than the birthing room, isn't it?"

Christine turned to see Miss Vanderbilt carrying Solace in a large, handled basket. The headmistress had been upstairs packing when the Gates family arrived, so she'd avoided the little woman's waspish looks and lectures at breakfast.

There was no escaping her now, however. And since she wasn't harping about last night's encounter, Christine was glad for the conversation. "Makes me wonder why women want to have babies at all," she murmured as another gut-wrenching cry reached their ears.

The little woman smiled wryly. "Seems childbirth is the furthest thing from anyone's mind when men and women know each other in the biblical sense. Young as that Gates girl is, she might not've realized what was happening . . . perhaps had no say about it. Some men are like that, you know," she added in a more sober tone.

Images of Mercy and Michael in the moonlight flickered through her mind, and Christine looked away, blushing. Why couldn't she stop thinking about Tucker Trudeau in that sense—or any sense at all? It was a waste of time to entertain such fantasies now! And it made her regret how many suitable young men she'd ignored—or rejected—at functions she'd attended in St. Louis.

"I—I said some things I didn't mean last night, Miss Vanderbilt. I hope you'll accept my apology for behaving so rudely."

Where had that come from? Was she so afraid of going through life alone—like this mainstay of the Academy for Young Ladies—that she was begging for a chance to return to school? Surely she could find work as a seamstress in Abilene! Surely—if she looked hard enough—there was a man in these parts who'd suit her better than Oliver Tandy or some rowdy cowpoke!

"Oh—no. No, Lily!"

Christine dashed after the little girl, who was crawling over the lowest rail of the corral. The princess in pink gingham fussed at being pried away from her pursuit of the horses, but Spot's playful licking turned her tantrum to laughter.

"Spotty!" she giggled as the dog washed the breakfast from her face. "Kiss Kwis-teen! Kiss Kwis-teen!"

Christine sent the little girl to her shoulder in a swooping motion that had them both laughing ecstatically, and without even thinking about it, she kissed Lily's damp, velvety cheek. When she turned away from the corral, she was face-to-face with Miss Vanderbilt, whose expression spoke more eloquently than any lesson she'd ever presented.

Envy. Longing. *Loneliness*. These emotions shone in the brown eyes that usually sparkled with life and purpose.

"What a gift it is, to have such a way with children," her headmistress murmured. "I meant what I said last night, when I wished you a man who would bring you joy, Christine. Your talent for design is a gift from God, but it would surely be a waste of a higher calling if you had no children. And yes, I accept your apology, dear."

Christine blinked. Had Miss Vanderbilt waxed sentimental? Or were her own jumbled thoughts about love and life—the slamming of her heart's door on seeing Mama and Tucker Trudeau again—confusing her?

"I hope you'll at least return to the academy to fetch your clothes, and to say good-bye to your friends," the headmistress continued. "You might feel your other teachers and I singled you out for discipline, or goaded you into better grades, but we'll miss you terribly, Christine. It's been a long time since I've so enjoyed watching a girl grow up."

Fetch your clothes . . . say good-bye to your friends . . . we'll miss you terribly.

Christine nuzzled Lily's wiggly, giggly softness, seeking comfort—and to blot her eyes. It hadn't occurred to her, when she'd declared she wasn't returning to school, just exactly what she was leaving behind.

And for what? To take in sewing for local women, waiting for her real life to begin? Waiting for the right man to replace Tucker Trudeau in her dreams?

"I—if it's all right with you, I *will* return to school," she blurted. "I'd be foolish not to graduate in two months— and—and it'll give me time to consider my next step, whether with Mrs. Devereaux or doing something else. I hope you understand that finding Mama's been my mission for so long, I'm at sixes and sevens now that my plans have been changed."

"I hoped you'd see it that way!" Miss Vanderbilt's face lit up like a summer sunrise as she squeezed Christine's arm. "That's a wise decision, dear. And—as Michael suggested—we can send inquiries along the railways about your mother. I'm truly sorry about the hole she's torn in your heart, Christine. Together we can—"

"Hey, mister! Whatcha got in that wagon?"

Joel's outburst made them look toward the front yard, where a large, boxlike vehicle had stopped beside the house. And who wouldn't be excited? With its bright red paint and yellow embellishments, it looked like a circus wagon. The black draft horse pulling it stood several hands higher than the Morgans that Michael raised, and his red tack glimmered with brass buckles and trim when he shook his majestic head.

Christine rushed forward, her heart in her throat. Joel was going for that animal like a shot. "Joel, no! He might bite you, or—"

"*Non, non, non!*" came a lilting reply from the side of the wagon. "Sol, he is big, but he is no bully! You would like to touch his soft nose, *oui, mon petit?*"

Christine froze. The man swinging Joel up to sit on his shoulders had lustrous black hair and a close-cropped beard. He wore a red plaid flannel shirt that hugged his flexing muscles—and his delight matched the little boy's when the huge beast nuzzled Joel's cheek.

"Pwitty hohsie!" Lily cried, flailing her arms toward it. "Me, too, Kwisteen! Me, too!"

Her heart stopped when the man holding Joel turned to smile at her. He was more solid than she recalled, and he looked a little older in the face. But those eyes shining with aquamarine mischief could only belong to one man.

"Miss Bristol?" he breathed—although he was trying not to laugh at something deliciously funny. "Why, I can no longer call you *ma princesse,* for indeed, you have grown into a queen! A fine, fiery-haired—"

Christine strode forward, clutching Lily to her hip, using her extended arm to balance herself—until she reached that exasperating man and slapped him with it!

"Tucker Trudeau!" she yelped. "Of all the low-down, despicable—! Why are *you* here, when—"

Words failed her. Her pulse was pounding so hard she couldn't breathe. So she aimed her palm at that bearded grin again—except this time he caught her mid-swing. With a glance over his shoulder at the wagon, he brought her knuckles to his lips and kissed them fervently.

"*Désolé, ma belle*—so sorry," he breathed, his gaze roving from her hair and eyes to linger on her lips. "I have some explaining to do, *oui?*"

"Wee! Wee!" Lily crowed. "Gotta go wee, Kwis-teen!"

Chapter Nine

An unearthly wail came through the open window. As Christine cringed, she wondered if things would ever *not* be in chaos at the Malloy home.

Still gripping her hand, Tucker scowled. "Someone is dying?"

"A young Negro girl is birthing a baby, and—"

"I'll take you to the potty, Lily," Miss Vanderbilt offered in a low voice.

"No! Kwis-teen!"

"—she's in such a bad way that—"

Tucker dropped her hand and sprang toward the wagon. Behind the driver's seat was a doorway, which he slid to one side.

"Maman!" he cried—and then came a syncopated volley of conversation that sped past Christine's textbook knowledge of French.

From the dark interior of the wagon emerged a birdlike woman dressed in loosely fitted prints. When those hard little eyes focused in the bright sunlight, her expression soured. Christine's hopes plummeted.

She remembered Mrs. Trudeau, all right. Was that the stench of overcooked cabbage in the swish of her Gypsy skirts as Tucker helped her to the ground?

"*Maman*, she is a *traiteur*—a healer," he explained. "And a midwife. Her angels, they have been telling her someone here needed her help! So—if we may—?"

"Of course," Miss Vanderbilt replied. She set Solace's basket down to escort the other woman inside. "We'll be thankful for any help you can provide, Mrs. Trudeau. And you—"

The headmistress pivoted to raise an eyebrow at Tucker. "You and I will have a chat when I return, young man."

"Yes, we will," Christine chimed in, "as soon as I've helped Lily. Joel—this is Tucker Trudeau. You are to see that he behaves himself."

"Me, too!" Lily said, wriggling in her embrace. "Me and Joel!"

Christine nipped back a retort. "But you said you had to go—"

"Me!" the little blonde sang out. "Not wee! Me, me, *meeeee!* Pat the pwitty hohsie!"

"Can I ride him, Mr. Tucker?" Joel pleaded. "Can I? Can I, pleeeeeze?"

"About the telegram? I am *si désolé*—so very sorry, Christine," he said beneath the children's outcries. "*Maman,* she got your message, and—"

"She still hates me."

Tucker's shrug and winsome grin made something flip-flop in her stomach. "She knows I wanted to help you—knows things about your mama. She sent that telegram before I found your note."

"But—but you're *here*."

Her heart was beating so fast and so hard she couldn't hear the toddlers' squabbling. She had eyes only for those soft, full lips . . . as they formed the words she so desperately needed to hear.

"Two reasons," he began—and then lifted Joel from his shoulders to set him firmly on the ground. "Sol, he does not give rides to children who scream and kick! You will take Lily's hand and you will *sit!* On the step of my wagon. Until I tell you to move."

Joel sucked air and Lily stuck her fingers in her mouth. While Tucker had spoken in a low voice, his size and foreign accent had made a definite impression. The three-year-old nodded, and then held out his hand to lead Lily. Still gazing at the Cajun, intimidated yet too intrigued to cry, the little girl sat demurely on the step—as though she and Joel would never dream of poking each other, or chattering nonsense in that escalating way they had.

Tucker smiled at them, nodding his approval.

And when he turned to beam at Christine, she understood perfectly why Joel and Lily had obeyed him: They were mesmerized. Tucker's smile had enchanted away any urge to challenge him.

"Now then, *ma chérie,*" he began, stepping within arm's length of her.

"Two reasons," she breathed, wondering if a proper young lady should back away from such temptation while her two young charges were watching.

"*Oui,* as I was saying—"

He reached for her hands, caressing them in his larger ones. "First, General Dodge, he has commissioned me to be—how do you say?—the official photographer for the Union Pacific Railroad! I am to take many photographs along the route. Then I travel to the next town, and the next, taking my pictures, so people, they will want to ride the train all over the West."

"That's quite an assignment! Quite an honor," Christine replied softly. "Congratulations, and—"

"And I am just starting out. I was ready to leave Atchison when I found your message," he continued. "So I said to myself, 'I wonder, is that pretty Christine living in Abilene now? To see her again—to talk about her mama—it would take only a little detour. So we stopped in town," he said as he fished a piece of paper from his shirt pocket, "and I found this article, about a Billy who must be the little brother you talked about, *oui?*"

Christine blinked at the article describing Billy's heroism. "*Oui*—I mean, yes. Except he's not so little anymore," she breathed. He was still holding her hands in one of his, and his grip felt warm and full of promise.

Tucker let out a long breath as he looked her up and down. "Nor are you, *ma belle*," he murmured cautiously. "But it seems you are, what—nineteen now? And these are your little children?"

"No! I—" Flustered by his rapt attention—caught in a fib she told him three years ago—Christine stammered, "I'm not even married—"

"And she ain't but sixteen, neither."

Billy, wiping his forehead on the sleeve of his blood-spattered shirt, scowled at the man who stood about a foot taller than he. "And what's it to ya if she's got kids, Mr. Trudeau? That telegram you sent her—"

"Was a mistake he's already explained," Christine blurted out. Of course her brother would show up now, and shoot off his mouth about her real age. "His mother received the message, and—and—"

"Tucker Trudeau," he said, extending his hand to Billy. "So pleased I am, to meet the young man all Abilene is talking about! For such a brave, kind thing he did."

Billy shook his hand, still looking doubtful. But Tucker had a way of disarming skeptics.

"How enraged you must be with me—after you read *Maman*'s reply," the ebony-haired man said apologetically. "And your sister, she was upset, *non?*"

"Upset?" Billy retorted. "Why, there weren't no talking to her for—and I couldn't blame her for bein' madder'n a wet cat about—"

Tucker's secretive grin told Christine he was better at communicating than his Frenchified accent led people to believe . . . and that he was pleased she'd been upset, when she believed she'd never see him again. Of all the sneaky—

"And it is a wise brother who protects his sister from men who are lured by her bright smile," he continued in a man-to-man tone. "Just as mothers, they protect their sons from pretty green-eyed girls who would steal their hearts with . . . stories."

Billy smirked at her. "So you lied about how old you was? To make this fella think—"

"Christine, she was trying to find her mother," the Cajun insisted quietly, "so the three of you could be together again. Because she knew how you would suffer. How could I not lo—*admire*—a young girl trying so hard to get the help she needed? For her family?"

Her brother's mouth clapped shut. Christine herself was at a loss for words. Her heart had swelled up into her throat. Tucker Trudeau had not only defended her honor, he had justified her little lies . . . had known all along that the dusty ragamuffin in his shop couldn't have been sixteen.

But hadn't he almost said he loved her?

"You have read the letters now, *oui?* The clippings about your mother and that man she is with?"

"Yeah," Billy replied, nodding toward the bedroom window, "and we're seein' firsthand how that land fraud scheme played out, 'cause that poor girl's family got bamboozled by one of their fake deeds."

The corners of Tucker's mouth dipped as he glanced toward the window from which the moans were escalating again. "How this must have stung—seeing your mama connected to such crimes! I almost didn't put those clippings in my letters to you, Christine, knowing how upset you would surely be.

"*Maman*, she is gifted with the second sight, so she knew things were not . . . as they seemed, when your mama and Mr. Wyndham came in for their portrait," he explained. "She suspects they have gone farther west—to Denver or beyond. Her spirit guides, they warned her that something was terribly wrong here, too. She believes it is her duty to help and to heal—because her powers come from God."

While she saw the cogs turning in Billy's head as he listened, Christine was hanging on Tucker's information. If Mama and Richard Wyndham had been scheming their way west, and were perhaps in Denver . . . and Tucker was working for the Union Pacific, which would take him in that direction. . . .

"Glad she come in to help." Billy glanced down, realizing how gory his blood-spattered shirt looked. "Asa and Michael and me delivered Mercy's baby durin' a blizzard—and that was bad enough. But this little gal don't seem quite . . . right. Even with your mama tryin' her best, tellin' Asa what herbs to brew up, it . . . it just don't look good."

He brushed his rust-colored hair back with fingers that quivered, glancing at Tucker's colorful wagon and the huge black horse that stood in front of it. "Fine-lookin' Percheron you got there," he said. "What's his name?"

Tucker grinned proudly. "This is Sol, and he—"

"Saul? Like the Bible guy who went around beatin' up Christians?"

"Like Solomon the king," the Cajun corrected with a laugh. "And the name, it is good, *non?* Most times, he is far wiser than I. And certainly more glorious."

Billy's grin said Tucker Trudeau had passed muster—

at least for this first round. "Tellya what—it might be awhile. We got plenty of hay and water in the barn, if you wanna let Sol—"

"But I was gonna ride him!" Joel protested, hopping off the wagon's red-enameled step. "You said if I set here real quiet—"

"Me, too!" Lily cried.

Billy was reaching up to caress the horse's glossy black neck when a frightened cry rang out from the bedroom.

"No! Don't you tell me the Lord's gonna take that girl!" Sedalia Gates wailed. "She just a child! Jesus knows some wicked man done had his way with her—"

"Out!" came a guttural command. "Ze angels, zey cannot help if you defy zem!"

Frightened, the two little children rushed toward Billy. When he scooped Lily up to silence her sobs, Joel scurried toward the folks who were coming out the front door as though the Devil himself were on their heels: Michael Malloy grabbed the little boy, while a nearly hysterical Sedalia Gates was being escorted between her wide-eyed husband and a very pale Agatha Vanderbilt. Mercy brought up the rear of this ominous parade, knuckling away tears.

Christine wavered, but her curiosity won.

To the window she went, deathly afraid yet drawn like that proverbial moth to some mysterious flame in the bedroom. Peering in, she knew better than to breathe a word when Tucker came up beside her.

"We must pray," he whispered. "*Maman*, she's going to summon God's mightiest angels. We must lend that poor girl our strength."

Petrified, Christine nodded. What was she about to witness? Who dared to call upon God's angels?

Yet she silently joined in when she heard the familiar cadence of the Lord's Prayer—even though Tucker whispered it in Latin. He was making the sign of the cross, as was the woman kneeling at the foot of the bed. A dark figure entered the unlit room.

It was Asa, setting candles on either side of the head-board and lighting them, as Veronique Trudeau instructed him. In the light of their flickering flames, Liberty Gates lay so still she might already be dead.

Seeing the poor girl distinctly for the first time, Christine pressed her fist to her lips. Libby was so wretchedly thin, her collarbone protruded above tiny buds of breasts. Her ribs were clearly visible above her distended belly.

Why had she wanted to gawk, anyway? She didn't dare move, though, for fear that oddly dressed seer might focus those evil-eye powers on *her*.

So she stood stock-still, drawing courage—and a little thrill—from the closeness of Tucker's warm body. If he felt safe standing here, Christine figured she would be all right, too.

"*Maman*, she is praying to St. Michael, the highest of the archangels, and to St. Raphael the archangel physician," he said in a reverent tone. "She will also beseech Mary, the mother of Christ, to be present."

Praying to saints and angels was totally foreign to Christine. But Liberty's situation was grave—and when the midwife pulled a large knife from her bag, Christine sucked in her breath.

With wide eyes, she watched the little midwife heat the blade in a candle's flame. Asa brought her a stack of clean rags and a pot of something with acrid-smelling steam rising from it.

"*Maman*, she is an herbalist," Tucker explained, his breath tickling her ear. "*Le bébé* is too big, perhaps, and she needs to take it out from the top."

The blood rushed from her head, and Tucker slipped an arm around her.

"She has done this many times," he reassured her. "If you don't want to watch, just keep sending prayers up for the girl. And for *Maman*, of course."

Praying for a woman who so obviously despised her didn't set well, so Christine offered another suggestion. "We should pray for poor old Asa, too. He works with herbs himself, but mostly for cooking. He probably wants to run away so fast not even Billy could catch him."

Indeed, Asa moved with a nervous energy, carrying out Mrs. Trudeau's wishes as she prepared for this surgical birthing. He stirred the pot of foul-smelling brew, then checked Libby's forehead for signs of fever.

The girl opened her eyes and caught a flicker of the knife in the candlelight. "Sweet Jesus, please don't kill me! I didn't want him to do it!" she whimpered, as weak as a half-starved kitten.

"Here, child, you drink some more of Asa's tea now," the old man coaxed.

"You go on back to sleep, and when Miz Trudeau's fixed what ails ya, why, you'll feel good as new."

Libby gulped from the cup he held to her lips, clinging to Asa's wrinkled fingers as though they might help her hold on to life itself. Her eyes rolled back in her head.

Christine gasped, afraid she would faint—or worse, vomit—on the man whose arm still supported her. Tucker was crossing himself, looking into that room as though he'd seen such trouble before and didn't like it one bit.

When his mother positioned the blade beneath the girl's navel, Christine looked away. She swallowed several times, trying not to cry while Tucker held her face to his shoulder. He surely must think her a fool for losing her nerve—and almost her breakfast—since *she* was the one who'd come to the window.

"Ah . . . that explains it," he murmured near her ear. "The cord, it was wrapped around the baby's neck.

Such an ordeal that girl has . . . oh, my. *Maman*, she is having one of her visions."

Too curious for her own good, Christine peeked through the window again. Mrs. Trudeau was handing the baby to Asa, quickly, as though it scorched her fingers. She grimaced fiercely, her body shuddering in a seizurelike convulsion. For several seconds, she was at the mercy of whatever ghastly images she saw behind her twitching eyelids. She began to babble in disjointed foreign phrases—apparently unaware of what she was doing.

Asa seemed to recognize what was going on and spoke softly to her. After a few moments, she sucked in a deep breath to compose herself again, although she still looked very upset. Then she reached inside Liberty again, raising her voice in a sing-song tone that resembled a chant.

"My God, I will never have children!" Christine rasped against the shoulder that cradled her again.

"Shhh, now. It will all be over soon, *chérie*," he crooned. "You will have fine, healthy babies, Christine, because you are a fine, healthy woman."

It will all be over soon. Just what did he mean by that?

"Keep praying," he continued, "because—oh, *mon Dieu*—"

His intake of breath made Christine peek into the room again. Libby had raised her head to cast an evil glare at Veronique, with her eyes still rolled back. The horrible image had Christine thinking the girl must be possessed by a demon, but she couldn't look away this time.

The midwife crossed herself, gazing up above the bed and to the corners of the room, beseeching the unseen powers that hovered there. As she threaded a long needle, the candle flames began to flicker wildly, as though a storm were about to break loose.

Veronique Trudeau raised her reedy voice in a prayer

that sounded desperate, even though Christine couldn't understand a word of it. Asa, too, fell to his knees beside the bed, close enough to assist with a packing of hot herbs. His eyes widened as he gazed fearfully around the room, but he kept squeezing out handfuls of the steaming greenery so the midwife could position the poultice inside Libby as she stitched. The air whirled about them—or so it seemed to Christine, as she focused on the candles rather than watching the midwife's needlework.

"It might be a while before I can stitch another sampler," she mumbled, a weak attempt at humor.

"Come away, *ma belle*," he said gently. "You've seen enough."

Christine turned—to find her brother, the Malloys, and Reuben and Sedalia Gates all wanting answers to their unspoken questions: Had it come down to life and death in that room? Which side had won?

Not ready to analyze what she'd just witnessed, Christine found herself in another awkward situation. Here she stood, in the arms of the very man who'd dumped her life upside down just yesterday. Everyone knew who he was, of course, but that didn't excuse her from making proper introductions.

"This—as you know by now—is Tucker Trudeau," she said in a halting voice. "Tucker, meet Michael and Mercy Malloy, the newlyweds who just moved into this house. This is Reuben and Sedalia Gates, who just hired on—"

"That's my little sister in there," Reuben said with a nod. "We sure glad your mama happened 'long when she did, sir."

"It weren't no accident, though—was it?" Tears trickled down Sedalia's coffee-colored face. "That woman in there, she got the power, praise Jesus! She knowed what was happenin 'fore y'all got here."

"*Oui, Maman*, she is a seer and a healer who has

birthed many babies," Tucker confirmed. "She takes the gifts that God has given her and uses them to help others. She does not charge for her help, so it is I who must see to her needs. Which is why she has come along on my new commission," he added with a glance at Christine.

Letting go of Sedalia's arm, Agatha Vanderbilt stepped forward with her hand daintily extended. "I am Agatha Vanderbilt, and I must apologize for misjudging you, Mr. Trudeau," she said quietly. "When I withheld your letters from Christine at the academy, she was only thirteen—"

"And you, too, were caring for one who depended on you," he replied with a gracious smile. "I was disappointed, *oui*, but I could not be angry. I lived hoping that someday it would be my destiny to meet Miss Bristol again."

As he raised Miss Vanderbilt's hand to his lips, Christine thought she might cry. She'd never seen such a heartfelt apology and an eloquent acceptance.

A grunt from the front of the house made them all look at Tucker's mother, whose eyes were shining like hard marbles as she glared at Christine. Veronique Trudeau obviously didn't envision the same destiny for her beloved son—which she told him in a torrent of unpleasant French.

Tucker listened, then smiled wryly at those around him. "*Maman*, she says we will stay to see that the girl awakes tomorrow. Then we must be on our way."

"Meanwhile, though," Asa said wearily, "we got us a baby to bury."

Sedalia Gates flew at him like a shot from a gun. "You ain't tellin' me you couldn't save that baby!" she cried. "Poor Libby, bearin' such a burden she durn near lost her mind over it. Possessed by a demon, she was! I thought that's why you was calling in the angels, to— you can't tell me—"

Christine held her breath. Libby's rolled-back eyes had indeed appeared demonic, and she would never forget how the girl had glared at Mrs. Trudeau with such a fiendish expression.

The wiry old cook grabbed Sedalia by the arms, pinning them to her side with more force than any of them knew he had. His white-sprigged hair shook with his wrath, and it took him a while to get the words out.

"Hear me now, woman, 'cause I ain't sayin' this but once!" he commanded. "Me and Miz Trudeau did our damnedest in there! Couldn't nothin' be done 'bout the baby's cord bein' wrapped around its neck."

An uncomfortable silence settled over them as Asa continued to rant.

"It's a wonder Libby didn't keel over long 'fore this, what with that dead baby festerin' inside her!" He dropped Sedalia's arms, but his gaze challenged them all to defy his beliefs. "I'm tellin' ya, I felt the angels' wings beatin' in that room! And they was fightin' for that little girl's life."

His voice cracked, and he stepped away with an exhausted sigh. "I see it as a sign. The good Lord's tellin' us He's savin' Libby for a special purpose," he whispered. "He's chargin' every last one of us with her care, 'cause if she lives till tomorra—it's nothin' short of a miracle. Tell that to your demon, Miz Gates!"

Chapter Ten

"This is just the saddest thing I've ever seen," Christine whispered. "We never so much as looked into that baby's face, and yet—yet—"

"It seems so unfair," Mercy agreed in a muted voice. "God surely must've known and made His plan accordingly, but I don't understand it. Makes me realize how much I have to be thankful for. How blessed I am."

They swayed together in silence then, Mercy holding a sleeping Solace to her shoulder as Christine cradled a very subdued Lily against her hip. The October morning had dawned frosty, and their breath came out in wisps of white. They stood beneath a maple tree arrayed in its red autumn glory, beside a hole that held a pitifully small box.

Michael had made the little casket with lumber and paint left from building the house. They'd lined it with the pink blanket Lily had come with in her basket last spring. He turned to them now, opening his Bible.

"As we commit this innocent child to God's care, let's also pray for Liberty. Let's ask for His tender mercies and her recovery, so she may indeed follow a higher purpose. For without our hope, our faith, and our help, these two lambs have suffered for nothing."

On the other side of the tiny grave, Tucker and his mother knelt and made the sign of the cross. The little woman looked more like a Gypsy fortune teller than ever, with a threadbare shawl around her shoulders and a lace scarf covering her head. Christine also noticed how Tucker's flannel shirt pulled across his broad back as he remained on his knees. Her gaze lingered on his lips as he murmured his prayer.

Joel tapped on Billy's thigh. "What're they doin'?" he whispered.

"Prayin' for that little dead baby and its mama," he replied quietly. "Let's listen now, while your papa reads the Scripture."

The little boy's sandy hair drifted on the breeze as he nodded, considering this. Then he, too, tapped himself on both sides of his chest and went to his knees, glancing toward Tucker to be sure he was doing it right.

"I've chosen a familiar passage from Isaiah's eleventh chapter," Michael began in a solemn voice. "To me, this has always painted a beautiful picture of how peaceful—how perfect—the Lord's dwelling will be. A place where our babies will be safe because all danger has been taken away."

He glanced at the well-thumbed page, paraphrasing for them.

"The wolf shall live with the lamb and the leopard shall lie down with the kid . . . the calf and the lion and the fattling together, and a little child shall lead them," he said softly. "The cow and the bear shall feed; their young will lie down together, and the lion . . ."

Christine let her mind drift over these images, picturing Lily walking fearlessly among the beasts he named. She hugged the little girl close. Poor Liberty would never know the joy of her child's warm weight, the soft-ness and scent of its hair.

". . . the suckling child shall play over the hole of the snake, and the weaned child shall put its hand in the snake's nest. They won't hurt or destroy in all my holy mountain, for all creatures on this earth will know the Lord."

Michael glanced at the grave, blinking. "We all recall the verses from Matthew's gospel, where Jesus opens his arms to the children, bidding them to come, for of such is the kingdom of Heaven. I find that passage a comfort, knowing this innocent baby has already been welcomed and given a home by Christ Himself.

"And now, Lord, we commit this little one to Your care and Your kingdom," Michael said as he bowed his head, "for You understand the agony of losing a child, and You grant your tender mercies to those crying out with their grief. Help us make sense of a senseless situation. Let us go forward from this day more aware of every precious moment You've given us, that we might give the best of ourselves—that we'll hear You say, 'Well done, good and faithful servant,' when our earthly time is done. Amen."

For a moment there was only the whisper of the wind in the brittle leaves, a chill reminder that winter would soon descend on the plains. It left Christine feeling bleak, knowing this funeral would weigh upon her for the rest of the day.

What if Liberty died, too? How long would it be before Tucker got back in that fancy wagon and rolled down the road?

"If it would be all right—if everyone please will stay here—I will play us a song," Tucker said, as he rose to his feet. "It is a shame, to send this little soul to God without music."

Everyone's face brightened when Tucker returned from his wagon with an accordion. He slipped his arms into its straps and placed his fingers over the buttons and keys. Then he closed his eyes and began to play.

The tone was sweet and mellow, and as the morning sun glowed over the accordion's mother-of-pearl inlay, Christine stood in awe. Lily sat straight up in her arms, watching the bellow's steady in and out as Tucker's fingers caressed the ivory keys and black buttons. When Joel went to stand closer, Tucker stooped forward so the boy could see better.

He began to sing. " 'Safe in the arms of Jesus, safe on His gentle breast—there by His love o'ershadowed, sweetly my soul shall rest.' "

Who could've guessed that this man with the mischievous eyes and dancing accent had such a wonderful voice? As his tender rendition of the song wrapped itself around them, no one could keep from swiping at tears.

" 'Hark, 'tis the voice of angels, borne in a song to me. . . .' "

Lily gazed upward then, raising her little arm in delight. "Looky, Kwis-teen," she whispered. "Angels!"

She and Mercy and Miss Vanderbilt sighed as one. When the sunlight hit the crystal-kissed leaves of crimson and gold, they did indeed sparkle and shimmer like wings.

"You're exactly right, Lily," Christine murmured, hugging the little girl hard. "Thank you for showing them to us."

When she turned back to watch Tucker sing again, it was his mother she noticed instead. Mrs. Trudeau was staring at Lily with wide eyes, as though she knew a secret about the child who'd been abandoned here last spring. The old crone actually looked happy, as she, too, raised her face to receive the blessing of the morning sun.

" 'Here let me wait with patience, wait till the night is

o'er,' " Tucker crooned, slowing down to finish. " 'Wait till I see the morning break on the golden shore.' "

A sigh hovered around them as his final note drifted off in the wind.

"What a lovely song," Mercy said in a choked voice. "I don't believe I've ever heard it. But then, out here on the prairie we miss the tunes folks out East have been singing for years."

"Fanny Crosby, she has written many hymns," Tucker replied. "That one was for mothers who've lost babies, just as she had. I'm so pleased I knew it, to end this painful service with a message of Jesus's peace."

"Amen to that," Sedalia said, glancing toward the house. "Do you s'pose Libby's feelin' any peace? Anything at all? I—I need to go look in on her."

Sedalia hurried away, as though she couldn't bear to be at the graveside a moment longer. Her hips were so slender that her threadbare calico dress swayed limply between her waist and the tops of her old shoes. Her stifled sob drifted back to them as she entered the house.

"She's takin' it real hard, 'cause she cain't seem to make no babies," Reuben remarked in a halting voice. "That's why, when we knowed Liberty was in the family way, we promised we'd take care of her—would raise the child as our own. But Libby, she been so upset, she ain't hardly said ten words," he went on, shaking his head sadly. "Why, she be so smart, the plantation owner, he done asked her back—for pay!—to teach his family's children! Only the Good Lord knows why she'd go and get herself in trouble—"

"Not ze girl's choice."

All eyes swiveled to Veronique, whose eyes were wide and shining like dark, foreign worlds.

"Who then?" Reuben demanded. "When I find out who done this to my little sister—"

"Ze overseer," the healer spat. Her voice had dropped

an octave, as though it rushed up from a Pandora's box of secrets deep within her. She looked dazed and detached, as though she had no idea what she was saying.

"He tricked her into a corner," Veronique went on with a feral grimace. "Told her she's no good—overstepped her place by teaching—"

Reuben flexed his huge hands and started toward her. "You talkin' crazy, witch! Mistah LeFourche, he's the only white man who treated us decent after we's freed! He wouldn't never—"

"Reuben, no!" Billy cried, rushing to one side of the dark giant as Michael and Tucker grabbed him, too. "You go throwin' those fists around like you did back in town, you've got no job here, mister! No place for your family to stay!"

The hired hand was wheezing like a crazed bull, his muscles bulging against the three pairs of hands that restrained him from grabbing Tucker's mother.

"How'd you know that?" he bellowed at Veronique. "You can't prove no such thing—"

"She told me that story during the birthin'," Asa chimed in, warning the larger dark man with his pointed finger. "She saw the whole thing happenin' inside her head, soon as she touched that man's child. Said the overseer wanted his own daughter to be the plantation schoolmarm—pretended he liked you folks so you wouldn't guess how he was gettin' back at poor Libby."

"*Oui*, that is how *Maman* knows things," Tucker explained urgently. "She felt the violence and hatred when the baby was conceived—saw the whole scene in her mind's eye. They come very fast, without warning, these visions. She cannot stop them. And she never makes them up."

The Cajun went over to slip an arm around his mother then, careful not to bump her with his accordion.

"Let's go inside, *Maman*," he said softly. "This darkness and shame—you have set it out in the light so it can hurt you no more. You can let it go now, on the wings of the wind."

He kept murmuring reassurances to the tiny woman, who ambled along meekly in his embrace.

Christine watched in silence, startled by this turn of events, as she hugged Lily closer. Mercy, too, seemed stunned by the sudden flare of emotions and the unearthly way Liberty's situation had been revealed. When Tucker had steered his mother inside, however, the spell of the bizarre incident was broken.

Reuben shook himself as Billy and Michael let him go. "Well, I never in my born days seen anything like— she went outta her head quicker than—"

"Stop it now," Asa commanded. "We read in our Bibles about things seen and unseen, things beyond our understandin'. Like Joseph seein' visions—nearly gettin' killed by his brothers for it 'fore he went on to be Pharaoh's own prophet."

Asa gazed at each of them in turn, trying to settle himself so he could make his point. "Tucker's mama is more aware of other worlds than most folks. My granny had the second sight, so I b'lieve it's real and true. I also know that even though it was a power God gave her, she suffered all her life from people accusin' her of makin' it all up. Sayin' she was just plain crazy."

Lily's blue eyes lit up with a need to play after so much seriousness. "Kwazy!" she mimicked, waggling her tongue. "Kwazy like *me*, Kwis-teen!"

Christine chuckled at the little girl. "You're far too smart to be *kwazy*, little girl," she teased quietly, rumpling the child's flyaway blond curls. "You're just *silly*, Lily! Silly, willy-nilly Lily!"

"Lily Stinkerpants!" Joel chimed in, coming over to join the fun.

"No, you," the girl in pink gingham replied.

"No, *you!*"

Lily pointed a queenly finger at him. "You, you, y—"

"Praise be, she's alive!" came Sedalia's cry from the house. "Libby's done opened her eyes and called me by name."

Joy tingled up Christine's spine, and Reuben loped toward the house. Leaving the children with Billy, she quickly followed Mercy and Miss Vanderbilt, excited by this wonderful news.

And yet, while she was relieved that Liberty Gates now had a new lease on life, Christine could already hear the heavy clop-clopping of huge black hooves and the clatter of a bright red wagon rolling down the road.

She had to pack and be ready. No one could keep her from leaving with Tucker Trudeau!

Chapter Eleven

"*Maman* has taken out the herbs and packing," Tucker explained quietly. He stood at the bedroom door, a sable-haired sentinel, keeping them in the hallway while his mother and Sedalia tended the girl. "Her body is clean of infection now, and healing. Liberty, she is asking for food and water. A very good sign, *oui?*"

Christine stood beside Reuben, peering between Mercy and Miss Vanderbilt's heads. Liberty was sitting up against the headboard; Sedalia had wiped her with a washcloth and was slipping one of Mercy's nightgowns over the girl's head.

Veronique Trudeau was packing her medical bag—a sure sign she and her son wouldn't be staying much longer. The healer then shooed Sedalia away so she could look more closely at her patient. She checked Liberty's eyes and pulse, talking quietly.

The girl nodded. She looked very earnest; weak, but alert.

Mrs. Trudeau took Liberty's head between her hands and began to speak in a mystical sing-song, gazing upward as though invoking those angels again. Still chanting quietly, she then followed the curves of the girl's head and body with her hands, a few inches away from her skin, like she was caressing someone a size larger than Liberty . . . or soothing her soul. Finally, crossing herself, Veronique stepped away.

Was it Christine's imagination, or was Liberty sitting taller and prouder now? When the girl turned to look at them, her eyes were large and doelike. Focused. Sparkling.

And when Liberty smiled, Christine could understand why a man would be attracted to this girl—why her fragile femininity, both a boon and a bane, acted like a magnet. It was downright humbling, to think an unsophisticated darkie from the deep South possessed the same powers of persuasion she'd been honing for most of her life.

"I want to thank you all for your help and your prayers," she said. Her voice was clear, ringing like a school bell in the little room, for she spoke in a more elevated way than the rest of her family.

"While I slept last night, I saw myself in Heaven . . . with my baby," she said in a faraway voice. "And I knew my infant was innocent—blameless—and the evil that spawned it had been cleansed from my body and soul."

Her face lit up as she continued. "St. Michael and Raphael watched over me in the night—they were in this room!—and an archangel named Ariel gave me the courage to come back. To start my life again as a new person. Free from the guilt and shame that had been my prison."

Liberty glanced up, smiling as though she still saw those heavenly beings in the corners, up by the ceiling.

"What did Asa put in that tea?" Miss Vanderbilt whispered.

"Must've been one powerful poultice, too," Mercy replied.

"Before I awoke this morning, I had a vivid dream," Liberty went on, excitement animating her face and hands. "It was like in the Bible, where Jesus was driving the money changers from the Temple in Jerusalem. While I slept, I could feel Him purging me, too! Telling me my faith had sustained me, and that I was to dedicate my new life to His service."

Liberty blinked, looking at those around her with an enviable serenity, considering the ordeal she'd been through. "Mama Trudeau has pronounced me whole—weak, but healing. A beautiful new dwelling place for the Spirit," she said in a hushed voice. "It seems fitting I should have a new name, as well. So from here on out, I wish to be called Temple. Temple Gates."

Sedalia let the washcloth drop to plant a hand on her hip. "Well, ain't you just the Queen of Sheba, tellin' us—"

"Leave her be." Reuben went to his little sister's bedside. "After what she been through, too worried sick to tell us about it, she can go by any name she wants."

In what Christine guessed was a rare display of affection, the huge man sat on the side of the bed and grasped the girl's tiny hands. Tears rolled down his rugged, dark face.

"It mighta been a phony land deed what brung us here," he said in a ragged voice, "but it just mighta been the Lord's way of gettin' this girl away from places where she ain't safe. Worth every dollar we lost to them land office leeches."

Tucker glanced at Christine. "This surely could not be the work of Richard Wyndham and—"

"I'm afraid it was, yes," she replied, her cheeks burning. "I didn't want to believe it, but the names on the deed can't be coincidence. And Wyndham had encouraged you to invest in railway land."

Tucker's aquamarine eyes shone with compassion. "*Si désolé*—I'm so sorry—you've learned these things about your mama," he murmured. "Maybe, if I hadn't sent those clippings, you would remember her as—"

"No, thank you for keeping track of her," Christine replied. And before she gave it more thought she blurted out, "Take me with you, Tucker! We know they've gone west. Probably followed the railroad—"

"You have no idea what you're asking, *chérie*."

Feeling his mother's pointed glare, Tucker quickly steered her outside. "The wagon, it is so very small. And with Maman along—"

"It will be perfectly proper," Christine finished. They were striding toward the cheerful red wagon—toward the wheels that might take her to Mama. "I can help with the cooking—or—I could be your assistant. Or—"

Tucker pivoted in front of her, as skillfully as any man she'd ever danced with. "Understand, *ma petite*, there is nothing I'd like better than to—"

"So that settles it. You're certainly old enough to decide such a thing for yourself, Tucker."

He grasped her hands, and she shivered under the intensity of his gaze. "It's not a matter of age—or what I desire," he replied earnestly. "It's—how you say?—cramped quarters already in the wagon, with my cameras and *Maman's* supplies."

She gave him her prettiest pout. "I don't take up *that* much room."

"Go inside. See for yourself," he said. He threw open the wagon's side door, pulled down the steps, and with a sweeping gesture invited her to enter what looked like a carnival on four wheels.

Christine stepped inside. Her hand went to her throat.

Wire bins holding his photographic equipment covered every inch of wall space. Around the floor were large crates of food and grain. A bunk ran across the back end of the wagon. A square trunk at its head displayed an assortment of candles and religious figurines and other trinkets.

"*Maman*'s bed and angel altar," Tucker said behind her. "She prays there and consults with her spirit guides."

"And where do you sleep?"

He pointed to the ceiling. "My hammock, it hangs from those hooks. Or, when we ride the train between photographic sessions, I'll stretch out in a passenger seat. We have passes, you see. Good for whatever train comes through when we are ready to go. We pull the wagon into a stock car, and Sol rides there, too."

"So I can buy a pass like yours," she reasoned in a rising voice, "and sleep in a Pullman berth, and—oh, Tucker, I love riding the train!"

The Cajun looked so boyishly handsome in the shadowy wagon, she almost threw her arms around his neck to kiss him. This was going to work! She wouldn't have to sleep on the floor with her carpetbag for a pillow, or share these *very* cramped quarters with Tucker's mother and her . . . spirits.

"Well, ain't this somethin'!"

Billy was coming up the wagon's stairway, peering inside with a wide grin. Of course he would have to butt in on her precious moments alone with Tucker! After he glanced at the wire bins and the wooden chests around the walls, he looked directly at Christine.

"You wouldn't last five minutes here, Sis," he announced. "No room for your trunks. No place for the chamber pot—'cept right here in the middle of the floor. And no mirror!"

Leave it to men to complicate things. Why couldn't they see the obvious?

"As I was saying when you butted in, Billy," she continued tersely, "I can get a Pullman berth—or a reclining seat to sleep in. And while Tucker's taking his photographs, I can ask around town to see if anyone knows where Mama's gone."

Tucker's face took on a patient forbearance. "And when we are off the train? Out on the prairie? In winter?" he asked gently. "*Maman*, she will tolerate such conditions rather than stay in Atchison alone.

"And what about your schooling, Christine?" he went on, grasping her hands to make his point. "You will be away from home for months if you—"

"What home is that?" she blurted. The familiar bitterness bubbled up within her. "Are we talking about the home the banker stole from us after Daddy died? The home where Mama left most of our belongings so she could run off with Richard Wyndham?"

Christine blinked rapidly and then let the tears slither down her cheeks. "Don't you see, Tucker?" she pleaded. "Yes, I could graduate. Yes, I could accept an apprenticeship with Madame Devereaux. I could've been engaged to marry, but I've turned away those boring, straitlaced men and their money. They'll never make me happy.

"So I have nowhere to go!" she cried, yanking her hands from his. "And if I can't find my mother—if I can't go with you, now that Destiny's brought us together again—well, I have no reason to go on!"

With that, she flounced down the wagon's stairs and trotted toward the house, blotting her eyes with her lace handkerchief.

Billy chuckled at Tucker's flummoxed expression.

"Better get used to it," he said. "Queen Christine needs somebody to rule and she's picked you. Not even your mama, with all her saints and angels, is gonna change that."

Chapter Twelve

"By hook or by crook, Christine'll find a way to go with you," Malloy said quietly. "And actually, that'll make things easier on both of us."

Tucker turned from putting his accordion in its bin and looked at the owner of the Triple M Ranch. Mike Malloy radiated a sense of calm control over this little kingdom, which revolved around energetic children and young women who needed immediate—and constant—attention. As he stood framed in the wagon's doorway, the sun made a halo above Michael's head.

Tucker sensed this man was by no means saintly or self-righteous, yet he seemed steeped in *goodness*. Malloy had taken in three young children—was responsible for Christine and her brother—and he'd buried Libby's baby without hesitation or judgment. He'd built a small empire for himself, too. Impressive accomplishments for a man Tucker guessed to be his own age.

"Christine, she is not one to hear the word 'no'—*non*?" he said with a shrug. "But she still wants to find her mama. I respect her for that."

"I can see that, or I wouldn't be making this suggestion." Malloy glanced toward the yard, where Joel, Lily, and the dogs frolicked around Billy as he tended the horses. "I'd like you to take some photographs—"

"*Oui*, of course! Of you and your new bride!"

"Of all of us, as a family in our new home," Malloy said with a big grin. "And of course I'll pay you for them—"

"*Non, non, non!* The pleasure, it is mine, after the way you—"

"—and give you extra, to cover expenses Christine'll run up," the rancher stated. "She has no idea about the bare-bones life you'll be living as you take your pictures. Or about the extra effort she'll cost you by coming along."

Tucker paused. *Maman* had objected strenuously to Christine's mission because of the heartache the girl was inviting—and would cause *him*—if they found her mother. But if he were paid to escort Miss Bristol . . . it wouldn't look as if he was a pretty girl's willing pawn, would it?

And what better way to see whether his dreams of her could be turned into something solid and satisfying? A home. A family. The love and devotion shared by two hearts meant to be together. *Maman* had no idea of the loneliness he endured because he'd forsaken a social life to look after her.

"You trust me with her?" he challenged. "You understand that Christine, she's become so very beautiful. And that I have ideas about—"

"You, and every other man," Malloy replied pointedly. "She took out alone when she was thirteen, and she'll do it again. I'd rest better knowing you and your ma were watching out for her. I had my doubts about you when she came back from Atchison with a headful of girlish notions about a photographer there—and secrets she'll never share with anyone.

"But I like you, Tucker," he said, focusing patient hazel eyes on him. "You'll handle the problems that'll likely arise if you find Mrs. Bristol. And I trust you to put her on a train for home if things go wrong. I have one stipulation, however."

"*Oui?* Only one?"

Tucker chuckled nervously, considering Malloy's proposition. This man had no real hold over Christine—had every reason to let her fend for herself if she walked away from the schooling he and Mercy had provided. Yet he watched over her as lovingly as St. Michael, the archangel in charge of heavenly protection and love.

"As you reach each train station, before you set out to take photographs, I'd like to know where you are. How things are going. Ideally, Christine would keep us posted, but we've learned not to rely on her letters."

"I will be sending Union Pacific's negatives and photographs back on eastbound trains," Tucker said with a nod. "It will be no trouble sending telegrams to you."

"To make it easier, I'll telegraph ahead—to men I used to work with when I drove for Ben Holladay. Fellows who went north when the transcontinental railroad was pushing through Nebraska," he proposed. "I'll tell them to watch for you. And I'll ask them to help you find Mrs. Bristol—and to keep that situation from getting nasty if you *do* run into her and Wyndham."

"Ah. So your spies will be watching us?"

Malloy's grin wasn't so boyish now. "You really think I'd let that young lady travel halfway across the country unaccounted for? My wife—and Agatha Vanderbilt—would have my hide."

Mike laughed, but then waxed serious. "If something

happens to Christine—because of her own overconfidence, or the meanness of Richard Wyndham—there'll be no consoling Billy. She's all he has left."

Tucker glanced toward the barnyard, where the boy's coppery hair caught the sunlight as he dumped water in the horse tank. "Why does he not take her himself to find their mother?"

"A good question." Malloy's expression softened. "He was only ten when he saw his ma run off. By his own account, he was her favorite—the apple of his mama's eye. Can you imagine the scar she left on that kid's soul?" he asked sadly. "I suspect he wants her back as bad as Christine does, but he's afraid of what he'll find out about her. So he started a new life here instead."

"Looking forward instead of back. A smart idea sometimes."

"Billy's smart in a lot of ways. He's watched every move you've made, Tucker, and he's as fine a judge of men as he is of horseflesh."

Malloy flashed a conspiratorial smile. "If he doesn't want you taking out of here with Christine, he'll find a way to stop it. Come time to leave, if you can't find that fine Percheron, I guarantee you Billy's behind it."

Tucker turned toward the corral. Sol stood proudly at the rail, taller and darker and stronger than the Morgans allowing him to share their pen. That ebony horse had cost him a bundle, but Sol had spirit and would see them through this adventure in fine style. He couldn't leave the Triple M with any other horse, so it was good Billy had given his blessing by saying Queen Christine wanted him as her attendant.

"Much as I'd love to see more of the West, I wouldn't trade you places for love or money," Malloy remarked. He was fishing something from his pocket—cash, which he handed up when no one was watching. "Nope. You're going to earn every cent of this, answering to both your ma and Christine these next several weeks."

"*Merci* for your kind gesture," he murmured. "And *oui,* the two women will peck at each other like jealous hens, I'm sure."

Malloy laughed, a melodious sound that carried across the yard. "I'll tell Mercy and the others to get ready while you set up your camera. But first, may I offer you one piece of advice?"

"*Mais oui.* When it comes to women, who can hear enough advice?"

Michael laughed again, shaking his hand. "If Christine gets an inkling you're sending word to us, or that I've given you money, she'll never forgive us," he said quietly. "She's proud and independent to a fault. That's why we both want to make her happy, isn't it?"

"Ah, *oui.* Yes, indeed."

Tucker glanced toward the white, two-story house, pleased by Malloy's confidence in him . . . yet aware of secrets that could come back to bite him, even if this gentlemen's agreement worked out. Even if *Maman* would be more agreeable to a paying proposition.

"I am proud and independent, too," he stated, handing Malloy's money back. "You have my word I will keep you informed. But if Christine's happiness is to be my gift to her, I'll pay for it myself."

Christine turned away from the window, fuming. If Michael and Tucker thought they could arrange everything behind her back—well! They still didn't understand her determination to go west in search of Mama. She couldn't believe that the saintly Michael was underhanded enough to bribe the photographer not to take her, and Mr. Trudeau was willing to profit from her situation. After she'd declared herself to him so openly! Well, they were both going to pay for that little transaction.

"You had the right idea, Mama," she whispered defiantly. She tucked the red velvet diary into her carpetbag
and continued to pack. "To get what we really want in
this life, we have to let men believe we're going along
with them. And then do as we damn well please."

"Smile, now! Happy faces!"

Tucker ducked beneath his camera's black cape to
squint through the lens. What a mix of calico and silk
and denim and homespun the Malloy family was, but
how loving. How happy. And how proud to be seated
on the front steps of their new home, framed between
those two impressive white pillars that showed off
Michael's carving.

"Hold very still now! I'll click on three—*un* . . .
deux . . . three!"

His gut told him it would be a portrait to prize—for
them, and in his own expanding gallery as well. While
the railroad's assignment to photograph the grandeur of
the West excited him, it was the faces he captured that
pleased him most. Michael sat with Joel in his lap, beside Mercy, who balanced Solace atop one knee. Christine and Billy sat on the step behind them, with Lily
standing in the middle. It was a likeness that would
make everyone who beheld it smile back at those faces.

Or most of them, anyway. Christine had a catlike lift
to her eyebrows as she looked toward the camera, as
though she were sending Tucker a silent message
through the lens.

But there was no time to ponder her intentions now.
He took another glass negative from his box and carefully tilted it between his fingers, coating it with wet
collodion.

He then photographed Mike and Mercy, leaning
around a column toward each other, cheek to cheek
beneath the carved *M*s. Then Mercy and her Aunt

Agatha stood with Christine between them, and then Billy and Christine held the three younger children.

At his request, Asa stood on the porch and leaned his elbows on the railing, looking down into the camera with an expression of infinite wisdom and love. The lines in that leathery face, those slender clasped hands, and the shine in those bottomless brown eyes told of a life well lived. He could call that one "God," and even the white folks who saw this old Negro would *believe*.

But the prize of the afternoon—Billy's idea—had the young man sitting with baby Solace on his shoulders, Joel and Lily on his knees, and Snowy and Spot—ears up and eyes alight—completing the pyramid's line. At the last moment, Solace laughed aloud and spread her arms wide, looking for all the world like a miniature circus rider.

"What a fine family," he cheered. Then, on impulse, he prepared one more negative and slipped it into his camera.

"Miss Christine, if you would be so kind . . . ?" he suggested playfully.

"Why would I want to—"

"Because, *mon ange*, you are the prettiest picture here," he replied in a lower voice. "Because it is a memorable occasion that we are brought together again . . . and because I have always wanted a likeness of you."

He gently leaned her back against a pillar so the afternoon sun glistened in her hair and caught the texture of the lace at her throat. Her pulse throbbed in her long, slender neck, a spot that begged to be kissed.

Tucker blinked. Christine was gazing at him with that cryptic expression again. What could it mean? Where had the unabashed happiness she'd shown for him in the wagon this morning gone?

"*Oui*, like so," he murmured, tilting her chin up slightly—mostly as an excuse to touch her exquisite skin. "Stand very still and think . . . romantic thoughts, *ma princesse.*"

He returned to the tripod, ducked beneath the cape, and grabbed the bulb that controlled the shutter. She was looking sly, and he could play that game, too—would wait until Christine relaxed slightly and glanced at him with that impetuous expression he loved.

But *non!* She lowered her eyelids and her lips parted—and Tucker squeezed the bulb out of sheer longing to taste their dewy softness.

Sacre bleu, what was he thinking? That he could escort this beautiful young girl across the West without ravishing her? Or making a *fou absolut* of himself? He took a deep breath before coming out from under the cape.

"Kwis-teen! Me, too!" Lily hollered.

The sunlight bounced in the toddler's curls as she rushed toward the young woman's arms. Tucker knew another precious moment when he saw it.

"Hold it right there, ladies!" he cried as he quickly put in his last glass negative. He let the bond between them determine their pose—let the love shine in their eyes as two strong arms wrapped beneath a pert little bottom while two pixie hands flew around that alluring neck. Nose to nose they were, laughing, when he snapped them.

He had to blink away mist before he emerged from his cape. What a beautiful mother Christine would make. Like a madonna and child of classical art, that sunlit likeness would outshine all the others. Tucker already knew he'd tuck one away in his personal album.

As the Malloys talked among themselves, *Maman* stepped onto the porch from the house. In her blend of prints and textures, with her clothes sagging on her spare frame, she seemed a world apart from these prairie homesteaders—and in a world unto herself.

"How is Miss Gates?" he asked her. "Doing well, I hope."

"*Elle va bien*," she replied in a low voice. *Allons, mon fils. Ce soir.*"

Tonight? Tucker almost challenged his mother's announcement aloud—except she wanted no gushing, grateful good-byes to prolong their leaving. It was her way of not feeling beholden to those she'd healed. And it was her way of evading a certain someone who wanted to come along. Even without eavesdropping, *Maman* picked up on such things.

Reluctantly, he gathered his gear, and Billy helped him carry it to the painted wagon. When they returned for another load, he witnessed an unusual sight: his mother—standoffish and wary by nature—was assessing the auras of the children, as though pronouncing her benediction on this family.

As she knelt before Lily, the blond doll froze in place with eyes like blue china plates. *Maman* gazed slightly above the girl's head, her hands circling the space a few inches away from those pink gingham shoulders. ". . . *claire de lune, et des étoiles filantes*," she murmured. "*Elle peut voir les anges—parce qu'elle est plus agée qu'on peut savoir.*"

Mercy, fascinated by his mother's mystical manner, was listening carefully. "Moonlight, and—?"

"Shooting stars," Tucker translated with a grin. "She will foresee momentous events, and angels—"

Lily giggled and scampered around the side of the house with the dogs.

"—because she's older than we know."

Mercy widened her eyes at Michael. "According to the note her father left, Lily would be fifteen months old now, but I've often wondered if that note was accurate," she said. "Lily is extremely precocious for that age."

"Either way, those are wonderful predictions for her to live up to," her husband replied.

Joel, however, was finding nothing wonderful about the way *Maman* scrutinized him. He doggedly turned away when she tried to engage his gaze—and ran off after Lily and the dogs when she released his hand.

"*Un esprit troublé. Prenez garde, petit fil*," she whispered after him.

As his mother moved on to gaze at Solace, sleeping in her mother's arms, Tucker worded his reply to Mrs. Malloy carefully. "A troubled spirit. And her warning to be careful—"

"Not surprising," Michael sighed, "considering how the poor kid saw his ma shot down in the street."

Nodding, Tucker nipped his lip. His mother's fingers lit like butterflies upon Solace's downy head as she dozed in her mother's arms. Would *Maman* be as delighted with Christine's aura? He glanced around, but the young woman of his dreams had apparently gone after the two children.

". . . *une fée charmante et adorable*," *Maman* breathed. "*Comme une femme, plein de grace et sagesse.*"

"I heard charming and adorable," the child's proud mother replied, sharing a tender kiss with the man beside her.

"A woman of grace and wisdom," Tucker finished. How he envied this couple, so in love it made his breath catch when he watched them together.

"Sounds just like her daddy," Michael pronounced. "No doubt in my mind Judd's going to watch over this girl as she grows up."

Mercy grew pensive then, but when *Maman's* hand gently cupped her jaw, her brown eyes widened like a doe's.

"When we see you . . . in summer," she said in careful English, "zere will be another baby girl."

* * *

From her open window, Christine rolled her eyes at Veronique Trudeau's fortune-telling act. The Cajun woman may have helped Liberty—now Temple—recover enough to walk around in the house, but Christine couldn't believe these hocus-pocus predictions about the children. And they couldn't distract her from what she'd heard earlier:

Allons. Ce soir. Let's go—tonight.

As she chose her clothing, Christine considered her options. *Maman* and Tucker slept in that bright red wagon, so they would catch her if she tried to hide it or disable it somehow.

Tucker needed that behemoth of a black horse to take him where he was going, too . . . although it wouldn't be the first time she'd ridden off on a mount that didn't belong to her. After seeing how Sol had accommodated Joel and Lily as wiggly, excited riders, Christine felt confident her riding lessons at the academy would get her onto that huge muscled back and off the homestead.

What a surprise, if she were waiting for them at the train station in Abilene! They had to go there to continue west on Tucker's assignment.

But how early would the Trudeaus pull out? And what if Michael's bribe was enough that Tucker would refuse to take her—even though he obviously wanted to be with her?

And what if Veronique let loose all those spirits on her? She'd put nothing past that witchy woman and her weird, wily ways—especially when it came to protecting her beloved son from the influence of the Bristol women.

Christine sighed, noting how many of her dresses simply wouldn't fit into the one trunk and carpetbag she was allowing herself. She should offer some clothing to Tucker's mother, considering how Veronique still wore the same gypsy-looking prints she'd seen three years ago.

But the little witch would probably pitch them out of the back of the wagon. Better to just—

She giggled, on a sudden impulse that was the answer to all her questions. She pulled back the sheets, and with great fondness—for who knew if she would ever see these pretty gowns again?—Christine arranged them in a bulky curve and covered them with the bedding. She wrote a quick note, proud of her charitable donation to a worthwhile cause, and tucked it under the upper edge of the covers.

Then she closed her trunk, listening for the sounds of supper below her.

Chapter Thirteen

"This will be a hodgepodge of a meal," Mercy fretted as she stirred batter for corn cakes. "So much of the food is still at the other house, and I haven't had a chance to—"

"Nobody's complaining, honey," Michael said. Sneaking a kiss on her neck, he added, "It's just a continuation of the wedding celebration, but with a different set of guests. Who knew we'd hire the Gates family, meet Tucker and his mother—and then deliver a baby, bury it, and have our pictures made—all in a couple of days? The Lord knows you're the best cook in the county, so He sent us new friends to appreciate you."

"Enough of your flattery, Mr. Malloy. It's your job to see that everyone has a seat around the table."

"Yes, ma'am. You're absolutely right." He dodged the wooden spoon she swatted him with.

"Don't think you said that with quite enough feelin', Mr. Michael," Asa remarked.

The old cook was slicing generous strips from a rasher of bacon, arranging them in cast-iron skillets on the new cookstove. "But you hit the nail on the head, sayin' how Miss Mercy's cookin' never falls short—and how lucky we been that these folks showed up when they did! God's a-smilin' on us, that's for sure!"

Out in the new dining room, the trestle table and benches were arranged, and Billy had placed whatever spare chairs he could find around it. Aunt Agatha was setting out plates and silverware, while Temple and Sedalia Gates sang songs with the children in the front parlor. Tucker played along on his accordion.

Michael smiled at all this. What a wonderful omen it seemed, that young Miss Gates had found a new life— maybe a new calling here with them. And while Veronique Trudeau looked lost in her own thoughts, she had agreed to eat with them before retiring to the wagon for the night.

Now that her healing had been accomplished, everything about this odd little woman said she'd be on her way come morning. This urgency meant Tucker would have to process and print their photographs on the road and send them back later.

Was he always agreeable to his mother's whims? Did he devote so much energy to pleasing her that he'd had no time to find a wife? Malloy wondered about these things as he watched the Cajun entertain Lily and Joel—a natural daddy if there ever was one.

The aroma of fried bacon and Mercy's corn cakes filled the house, as did the chatter of all the people. When Reuben stepped inside from doing the horse chores, Michael spoke above the noise.

"Shall we come to the table?" he said. "I don't know about you, but I'm plenty hungry after our busy day."

Joel came bounding out of the parlor, followed closely by his blond shadow, who looked around the gathering with bright blue eyes. "Kwis-teen?" she called in her little-girl voice. "I want Kwis-teen, sit by me!"

"Haven't seen our girl lately," Asa said as he carried

platters of bacon to the table. "Mr. Joel, you got the youngest legs, honey. Go upstairs and see about her. Please and thank you!"

Fast as a rabbit, the boy snatched a slice of bacon from a plate and then bounded up the stairway on his mission. A few moments later, with a proud clatter of his feet on the oak stairs, he bounded to the table.

"She's fa-a-a-ast asleep," he announced breathlessly.

"We'll save her a plate then," Mercy said with a little frown. "Everyone's hungry, and she'll be cranky if we wake her to eat."

"Kwanky Kwis-teen," Lily said emphatically. Then she bowed her head and pressed her hands together to say the grace. "God bwess this food. And God bwess kwanky Kwis-teen!"

Slowly, stealthily, Christine slid down the post of the widow's walk outside Mercy and Michael's bedroom, using the latticework trellis for toeholds. Having to fend for herself so often, she'd learned many skills. She hit the ground, grabbed the carpetbag she'd tossed down ahead of her, and trotted through the frosty twilight toward the corrals.

It was going just as she'd planned. With all the chatter and passing of food in the dining room and Joel falling for the "body" he'd seen in her bed, she was on her way. Tucker Trudeau and that mama of his were about to find out who they were dealing with—and the consequences of refusing her simple request to go west with them.

"Hey there, Sol!" she whispered, reaching up to stroke the velvety nose of the Percheron who'd watched her approach with interest. "Wait here, big fella! We're going places!"

Her pulse pounded in her throat as she snatched a bridle from the barn. It took three tries to get it on him, her hands were shaking so badly, but she prevailed.

Stifling a victorious cry, she led the huge horse behind the barn, back to where the trees grew along the banks of the Smoky Hill River. Stepping on a stump and hiking up her skirt—just like she had when she ran away three years ago—she swung herself high. She landed with a gasp on Sol's broad back. The horse took off before she was ready, but by clinging to his thick neck she righted herself.

She was on her way! In her dark skirt and shawl, on a mount the color of midnight, she was showing Tucker Trudeau just what she was made of. Just let him *try* to leave without her now.

Tucker felt a hand on his thigh. He looked up from the forkful of corn cake he was dragging through the sorghum on his plate. *Maman* nodded toward the window, scowling.

He almost missed it—a movement through the moonlit trees that quickly got beyond his range of vision.

"*Elle va! Avec Sol!*" his mother muttered.

"*Mon Dieu, c'est*—" Tucker tossed his napkin onto his plate and rose so fast his chair fell backward to the floor. "*Je m'excuse*—please—I must fetch my horse!"

He rushed outside, wanting to swear at her and yet laugh aloud for the sheer outrageousness of it. That feisty little—how far did she think she'd get, stealing a horse unlike any other? What was she trying to prove by—?

But he knew that answer. Christine Bristol might be older and more refined than when he'd first met her, but her mission hadn't changed, had it? And she knew exactly how to force his reaction, just as her desperate bravado three years ago had coaxed him into helping her.

He stopped at the corrals, barely hearing the diminishing hoofbeats.

Maybe he should let her go. Such a willful young

woman was more trouble than his horse was worth—and there would be no end of the sniping and pecking between her and *Maman* if he took her along. He had a schedule to keep. A reputation to maintain. Let her get into the trouble she deserved—and she could get herself out of it. Miss Bristol was due for a lesson she couldn't learn at her academy, and Sol would see that she got it.

Tucker laughed softly. At himself.

Loping toward the river, aware of the moon's beauty in the water and the trees stretching their black hands upward into the azure night, Tucker considered the best way to handle this situation. He paced himself. Fortunately, the moon was bright and the trees sparse, so he could easily keep the distant horse and rider in view. The river crooked around to the north up ahead, and if Christine were smart she'd take out across the pastureland toward the road.

And there she went, slowing Sol because she thought she'd made her escape—and probably because her thighs ached from bouncing against his broad back. How she'd remained astride the giant Percheron bareback was beyond him, but he grinned at her tenacity.

They made a wondrous sight by the light of the harvest moon, a gilded shadow gliding gracefully across the pasture. He feasted his eyes on them for a few moments more and then raised forked fingers to his lips.

He gave a shrill, warbling whistle, then three staccato blasts a few notes lower.

Sol stopped, turning his head to catch the command.

Tucker repeated the signal, almost sorry the Percheron was so well-trained. He chuckled at the frustrated curses Christine muttered when she reined the horse's head toward town again, to no avail. And then he stood at the river's edge, waiting.

*   *   *

The damn horse was backtracking toward that odd,
shrill bird cry. Ears pricked forward and nickering, his
huge body tensed with anticipation as he bounced her
with every step of his heavy yet nimble hooves.

"Sol—whoa, boy! This way!" she muttered, hauling
against his neck with the reins.

Then she saw the silhouette, backlit by the moon
shining through the trees.

How did he know? Tucker could *not* have seen her
leaving the house!

"Slow down, dammit!" Christine jerked on the bridle
again, determined not to get every bone in her body
jostled out of its socket—or worse yet, fall off this ob-
noxious horse.

It took all of Tucker's effort not to laugh out loud as
Sol came close enough that he could see Christine's
vexed expression. Her hair resembled a bird's nest
caught in the wind, and her exasperation came out as
white wisps of venom as she caught her breath.

"Of all the low-down, conniving—why didn't you tell
me Sol was—"

"Why didn't you tell me you were stealing my horse,
chérie?" He'd taken hundreds of pictures in his day, but
this image was the funniest he'd ever seen: Miss Bristol
had the pluck to be incensed when he asked such a
simple question.

"Because you weren't going to take me along! Even
after I bared my soul to you—turned down better
offers!—asked you very nicely to—" she sputtered, halting when she saw his black beard quiver with his grin.
"Don't think you can fool me, Tucker. I saw Michael give
you that money. A bribe, so you wouldn't be tempted to
let me—"

"Ah, *oui,* the money. But you didn't see me give it
back?" he asked quietly. "Michael, he wanted to cover

your expenses, *ma belle*, but I declined his offer. Because I planned to take you with me the moment I saw you yesterday."

He paused to let this sink in, and to remind himself how he, too, had once behaved as only a reckless, self-serving sixteen-year-old could. But he had never used his looks to get what he wanted. And even now, at twenty-four, he'd get into deep trouble if he let his heart do all the talking.

"You won't get far on your own, *ma belle*, jumping to untrue conclusions," Tucker reasoned. He settled Sol with the stroke of his hand, gazing into Christine's moonlit face. "What has upset you so?"

Of all the nerve, to stand there gazing up at her as though she were a witless little girl. "Why did you give me that song and dance about how crowded the wagon will be—"

"Because it will. Because I wanted you to understand, *ma princesse*, that I won't leave *Maman* and her mysterious ways behind, simply because you wish I would."

She glared, despising Tucker's too-smooth voice. This despicable man was laughing at her! He'd intended all along to take her west, and it tickled him no end to catch her in a stupid mistake—

Yes, it was stupid, thinking you could charge into the darkness again, like that girl of thirteen, and have this man fall for you—just because you wish he would.

"I am *not* your princess!" she hissed, leaning toward him to drive her point home. "You have no idea what it's like to—"

With a startled cry, she fell forward.

As Tucker caught her, he felt her body vibrating with exasperation . . . a lithe, light body rounded in all the right places, so womanly yet as full of fight as young Joel. He held her at arm's length, with her legs and skirt splayed against Sol's side. This moment would decide far too many things—set the tone for the entire trip—if he behaved rashly. He needed to be the mature one, the man both their futures depended upon.

Christine was wide-eyed, and looked mortified at getting caught. When her lips parted to rail at him again, she flailed and wiggled and kicked his horse.

Sol was the smart one; he stepped away.

She fell against Tucker, and he caught her in a kiss that stunned them both. Too many dreams and long, empty nights came rushing back at him with this first taste of her—the luck of this moonlit moment—and he couldn't let them go unanswered. He crushed her close, not letting her touch the ground as his lips delivered the message she seemed so determined not to hear.

Christine couldn't see, couldn't breathe, couldn't think—and didn't care. Wrapped in arms so strong, she only had to float and let this man lead her into the sweetness that surpassed all she'd imagined about this moment. A thousand times she'd wanted this kiss. His lips were soft and sweet like the sorghum on his corn cakes, moving restlessly against hers.

She'd always assumed lips stayed still when people kissed, yet she found her own mouth moving, too. Tucker's beard teased her cheeks, and as she wrapped her arms around his neck, she felt him groan.

But he didn't let go. He just kept tasting her, and holding the back of her head so she wouldn't pull away.

As though she could.

When he finally set her on the ground, she got a good gulp of air and then shot up at him again.

Tucker laughed, hugging her; indulging the need he now knew would never go away. She would steal kisses every chance she got, unaware of the deeper need she inspired in him with every brush of her innocent lips. Closing his eyes, he rocked her and pressed his lips to hers. When he coaxed her mouth open and slid the tip of his tongue along her inner lips, Christine gasped and stepped back.

But it wasn't fear in her eyes. It was delight.

The stomp of Sol's hoof brought him back to the reality of this October night, where those at the house awaited their return. Taking in a ragged breath, he forced himself back to their conversation. "I—I have no idea about what it's like to . . . What, *chérie?*"

Christine blinked, still riding the high tide of her pulse. They would have to go back to the house now, and everyone there would be watching them for signs of—and her hair was blowing loosely around her face, and her lips throbbed with the pressure he'd put on them. She could see the knowing expressions on their faces, and she hated being at their mercy. Miss Vanderbilt, Michael, and Mercy would no doubt lecture her about—

And then it was Mama's frown she saw, the day she'd been caught kissing Jared Mayhew at the ice cream social. It was all Jared's fault, of course, for being so careless, but *she* had caught the punishment! Yet Mama had been so brazen as to throw herself at that Englishman—

"You have no idea," she told Tucker, "what it's like to be betrayed by everyone you ever loved or trusted. First Mama running off, then Mercy and Miss Vanderbilt hiding your letters, and then—"

Tucker held her quaking body against his, seared by her pain once again. How could he help her see things from a different point of view? And then move past another false assumption?

"The Malloys—and your headmistress—" he murmured, fighting the urge to nuzzle her neck, "they love you, Christine. They have always hoped you'd find your mother without getting hurt any more.

"But you have seen them through the pieces of a little

girl's broken heart—just as you thought I was going to
ride away without you because you saw money change
hands," he added softly. "Your disbelief has blinded you,
ma petite."

He looked into her pale face, so lovely in the moonlight. But wounded, like a little bird with a broken
wing.

"Do you recall Saint Thomas, the apostle—Doubting
Thomas?" he asked softly. "He had to see for himself—
put his hands on the Lord's wounds from those nails—
before he could believe that Jesus had risen from the
dead."

Her fallen expression tugged at him. Christine
wanted romance, and he'd given her a Sunday school
lesson.

"I hope someday you will believe in this family—in
their best wishes for you, Christine," he finished
earnestly. "Sometimes you must believe first, and then
you will see the love in their faces, and in their hearts,
for you."

Christine buried her face against his warm, solid
chest. He meant well—she heard that in his low, melodious voice. But sermons were the last thing she
wanted from this man.

"Can we leave now?" she asked plaintively. "I heard
your mother say—"

"*Maman,* she hates long good-byes. And people, they
gush on and on about her healing," he explained with a
chuckle.

"She was trying to leave without *me.*"

No use in denying that. Tucker stepped back enough
to look her in the eyes again, still hoping to win the moment. "Like you, *ma princesse, Maman* cannot always
have what she wants. So we will go back for a night's
rest—and for your clothes," he added with a pointed
glance at the carpetbag on the ground. "We have a jour-

ney of several months ahead of us, and winter is closing in."

"But you said there wasn't enough room—"

"Christine," he whispered. *"Ma femme."*

She stopped midsentence, gazing at his parted lips
and shining eyes, still wondering whether this moonlit
moment was real. *His woman.*

"Do you believe there's room in my heart for you?"

It was a query he didn't sweeten with endearments, a
question she could not ignore. She nodded solemnly.

"Eh, bien. There is room for you also in my wagon."

Chapter Fourteen

Three weeks later, in late October.

I will NOT scream. I will NOT throw this pen at that despicable old Gypsy.

Gritting her teeth, Christine gripped the fountain pen poised above her letter to Billy. Bad enough to be caught in this downpour, which drowned out all rational thought and forced them to stay inside the wagon. Veronique Trudeau was performing her daily ritual, summoning her spirit guides and angels, with her back turned for more privacy while she prayed. If that chanting and muttering could be called prayer.

I will not scream! she reminded herself.

With a loud sigh she shifted on her pallet, which covered the top of Sol's grain bin. The space she could call her own was about four feet long and three feet wide—and not nearly far enough away from that angel altar, where Tucker's mother conjured up unseen beings that made her neck hairs prickle.

While spirit summonings and séances had always fascinated Christine, she put little stock in the infamous Fox sisters and their mysterious rappings. From what she'd heard, she wondered whether the world-renowned medium Daniel Dunglas Home was merely an accomplished magician and sought-after house guest of the wealthy. Their dealings with spirits from the Other Side had little connection to religion, the way she saw it. But Veronique's rituals were different.

Séances were only as genuine as the mediums who conducted them, yet Christine couldn't deny what she'd seen in Mercy's bedroom. Temple Gates had been purged by those mighty angels, and she was starting a new life. What did this say about the power Tucker's mother possessed?

The little woman was picking up the items on her altar—a rosary, small portraits and ambrotypes, a figurine of the Virgin Mary—and talking to them! As though she expected them to answer! The Latin cadence of the scriptures ran together with her Cajun French in a rush that sounded like nonsensical babbling. Did this woman speak in tongues, too?

Christine wanted to shriek. Wasn't it enough that she'd been awakened last night—again!—by Veronique's snoring?

Christine shifted impatiently, turning her back to that accented yammering. But it didn't make Mrs. Trudeau talk any more quietly. And it blocked the light from her little lamp, so she couldn't see to write.

Had she anticipated this *togetherness* back at the Malloys' ranch, she might not have come along. She'd detested the dark, claustrophobic log house Mercy had first lived in, but never again would she call it confining. *This* was confinement—this wagon with bins on the walls and storage crates covering all but the center of the floor. How had Tucker imagined he could live this way for the months he planned to travel?

Pssst! Pssst!

She glanced over her shoulder but refused to laugh. Tucker, slung in his hammock a few feet away, was waggling those black eyebrows and sticking out his tongue at her. He was making the best of a trying situation—but of course, to him, there was nothing odd about his mother's rituals. He'd designed this wagon knowing they could survive in it while he completed his commission.

And, man of his word, Tucker had made room for her in his little world. She was the one who couldn't adjust.

But of course, she couldn't report a word of this in her letter to Billy. Damn know-it-all. Why hadn't she listened to him when he'd announced she wouldn't last five minutes in here?

The incantations took on a higher pitch, and Christine clenched her jaws. *I will not scream. I will not fling my lamp across the wagon and set that altar on fire.* Although . . . burnt offerings were acceptable gifts to God in biblical times . . . .

As the thunder rumbled, Christine thought about what was probably happening at the Academy for Young Ladies. Lectures on household management, perhaps. Or sewing clothes for the orphans. How lovely it would be, to hear the steady thrum of the treadle machine as fabrics passed through her hands. Or to attend a lesson in the large, modern kitchen on how to properly carve a lamb roast.

What she wouldn't do for a taste of civilized food—even a dip of her finger in the pan drippings! While she understood the necessity of dried beans, desiccated vegetables, and the small animals Tucker shot to roast over their campfires, she might just toss the next slice of dried apple she saw into the flames. Pale and tasteless as it was, it would make better fuel than food.

And their confinement had done nothing to improve

the odor of Mrs. Trudeau's clothes. The dank aroma of the rain, coupled with the fact that none of them had bathed lately, made the witchy-woman's musky incense even more disagreeable. And she couldn't even open a window because there was none!

I will not scream! she reminded herself. The chant behind her had risen to a sing-song that sent cold shivers up her spine. It reminded her of eerie scenes from the birthing—Libby with her eyes rolled back and the candles flickering wildly beside the bed as this Gypsy summoned her saints and angels.

I asked for this. Lord love me, I insisted on coming.

Silence suddenly filled the dim wagon—a sensation nearly as unsettling as those never-ending prayers. With a wink, Tucker looked over his shoulder at the hunched figure still sitting on her bunk, gazing at her altar gewgaws—if indeed she saw them. Christine had watched Veronique Trudeau enter trancelike states that sometimes lasted several minutes and made the wagon feel like all the air had been sucked from it.

"*Tu es fini, Maman?*"

Tucker's mother gave him a blank stare. She sat so absolutely still, Christine wondered whether the woman was even breathing.

Then Veronique shuddered, focusing on *her*. Looking through her, as though she were as transparent as one of Tucker's glass negatives. It was an eerie feeling, but Christine refused to drop her gaze—refused to be intimidated by a woman who communed with unseen people. Or said she did.

Mrs. Trudeau railed at her son in rapid-fire French. He responded calmly.

Once again, Veronique was talking about her as though she wasn't even there.

Then the woman scooted off her bunk, yanked a

shawl and some flour sacks from the bin she'd been sitting on, and threw open the wagon's door. She stalked outside, muttering.

Tucker rolled over the edge of his suspended bed. "*Maman* is right. No more rain!" he said as he detached the hammock from its hooks.

Christine scowled. "That's not what she was talking about, Tucker. I might not follow every word you two say, but—"

"She insisted you need some fresh air," he said with a sly grin. He removed two of the metal bins from the wall and slipped into his coat. "*Maman*, she says you were screaming at her, inside yourself. Ready to throw your lamp and set her on fire. You will be my assistant? While I print pictures?"

Her mouth fell open. *My Lord, I can't even think without that little witch knowing*—"Yes—yes, that's a fine idea!" she blurted. "I'll get my coat and—"

He caught her by the hand as she turned. "Pack your valise, *chérie*," he murmured. "We will set up the prints, and I'll take you into town. To get us rooms. You want a nice bath—a real bed, and time for washing clothes, *non?*"

"*Non! Oui!*" Christine gasped. Her heart raced with the idea of a feather mattress, and clean sheets—a soak in hot, soapy water!

Then she narrowed her eyes. "What about you and your mother?"

"*Maman et moi*, we'll be back by nightfall. I have negatives to send back east, and then we'll eat a nice dinner," he said, brushing her knuckles with his lips. "And we'll all feel better in the morning, *oui?*"

"We must use this sunlight. In winter, the days bright enough for making prints don't come often."

Tucker watched the slender redhead place sheets of

sensitized paper along the boards he'd brought from the wagon. While she was good help, eager to learn, she would be on her guard now—afraid to speak her mind. Or to even think.

Rather than the recent landscapes of the plains he'd taken for the railroad, Tucker chose the shots of the Malloys. As he centered the glass negatives on the paper, he considered his next move.

"Oh, there's Billy and the children!" Christine studied their pale images, shifting subtly closer to him. "All you do is put these negatives on paper and it makes a photograph?"

Her green eyes gazed up into his and he melted. In the fragile autumn sunlight, her skin looked fresh and soft, while her lips parted, waiting for kisses.

But Tucker felt her wariness: *Maman* was over in the trees by the Platte River, gathering herbs. Watching them.

"The paper is specially treated," he replied, "which is why we handle it by the edges. You do well, *ma princesse*, tilting the negatives to coat them with the wet collodion, too. I'm glad you've come along."

His praise brought Christine's own special sunshine from behind her hesitant smile. "I'm quite good with my hands—"

"Ah, *oui*," he said with a chuckle. "How quickly they bridled Sol that night you rode off—"

"—and I catch on fast when . . ."

She nipped her lip at the reminder of that escapade, and he kicked himself for bringing it up. It was just as Malloy had predicted: Living with two women who competed for his loyalty was wearing on him. Best to complete this task and head into North Platte while *Maman* hunted for her herbs. She was standing now, looking right at them.

He smiled at Christine, hoping to recapture their lighter mood. "How can I ever forget you catching on to

me, *chérie?*" he quipped softly. "Out by the moonlit river.
I was good with my hands, too, *non?*"

The vein in her neck throbbed with sudden
urgency—how he longed to kiss that soft, sweet pulse
point! But Christine clutched the packet of paper, aware
of their audience. They'd stolen only a few kisses these
past two weeks—just enough to fan her innocent fantasies and set him afire, as well.

"I—can your mother really tell what I'm thinking?"
she rasped. "Have you always had to deal with that? To
live without the least little secret?"

He laughed out loud. "It is you girls who keep secrets," he teased as he positioned the last negatives.
"And I will tell you that *Maman*, sometimes she is a
lucky guesser. She was sixteen once, you know."

Her russet brow arched. She was wise in many ways
he was not, this Christine, and it tickled him that she
had such a quick wit.

"And she had me by then," he added, "so I'm sure she
had her troubled thoughts. And *oui*—she throws things
sometimes. Now—let's get you into town," he said, collecting the rest of the paper. "By the time I come back
here, these prints will be ready."

An hour later, he felt much better. Mrs. Padgett's rooming house on the edge of North Platte was clean and
reasonable, and Christine looked happier than she had
since they'd left the ranch. Perhaps it was the bathtub
down the hall from her room, or the prospect of a few
peaceful hours to herself . . . or the long, tender kiss
they'd shared before he left her upstairs.

It was the right thing to do, bringing her here. Christine was used to her little luxuries, whether or not *Maman* approved. If he had to sell extra portraits along the
way, it was worth his time to indulge her. What young
lady didn't want to be clean and presentable? She was

handling life in the wagon better than he'd expected . . . and when he looked at *Maman* from Christine's young, educated viewpoint, Tucker was well aware of how odd his mother appeared.

With that in mind, he smiled at Mrs. Padgett, a plump partridge of a woman with every hair in place. "Two dollars each room, *oui, madame*?" he asked as he reached for his money clip. "I'll pay you for two nights, and we will be three for dinner when I return with my mother."

"Let me bring you some change, Mr.—"

"I am Tucker Trudeau, and happy to leave you a little extra because—" He flashed her a conspiratorial grin. "*Maman*, she snores."

"Oh, Mr. Trudeau, that's quite all right—"

He let her chatter, guessing she was perhaps fifty; a woman without a man, if her taste for lace and pastel walls were any indication. He'd noticed not a hint of pipe tobacco, and most of the parlor chairs tended toward dainty rockers without arms.

"—and what did you say your wife's name was?"

Tucker blinked. His insides skittered at the thought of playing such a charade, but he needed no more complications than he already had with his two women.

"Miss Bristol is my—how do you say?—assistant," he announced with a grin. "I am a photographer, you see. Making pictures for the Union Pacific—but if you like, I could make your portrait, too. Or one of your rooming house, so hundreds of people who see the railroad's pamphlets will know of a good place to stay. I can print them before we leave."

Mrs. Padgett's round face radiated a matronly interest—until a frown furrowed her brow. She folded his money into her pudgy fist. "I think not," she said crisply. "A lady must be careful these days, Mr. Trudeau. You know what they say about fools' names and fools' faces."

Tucker blinked. It was a rare woman who wouldn't have her portrait made. And why didn't she want travelers to know about her boardinghouse?

"*Bien sûr.* I understand," he said, placing his hat back on his head. "*Maman et moi*, we'll be back by six for dinner. Miss Bristol, she will enjoy a hot bath and a chance to wash some clothes. *Merci, madame!*"

He paused outside the tidy house, gazing along the direction of the railroad tracks until he spotted a huge roundhouse, where he could send off his prints and plates.

Had he said something wrong to Mrs. Padgett? Misunderstood her English?

Or were some women just more complicated than others?

Chapter Fifteen

Christine let herself drift in the tub of hot, bubbly water. Smelling of lavender soap, with her hair clean at last, she felt nearly civilized again.

Since Mrs. Padgett and her sister Polly had been kind enough to heat so many pails of water, she'd brought her dirty underthings and a few dresses to wash out as well. It wasn't the modern way they'd learned at the academy, where Miss Vanderbilt stressed the use of fresh water for each new task, but it seemed the polite thing to do. While her hostess kept a proper rooming house, it was clear she couldn't afford any little extras.

A knock at the door startled her.

"Yes? I—I'm almost finished!" she yelped.

Lord, had she fallen asleep? Surely no one else wanted to bathe in the middle of the day!

"We have something to discuss, Miss Bristol—or whoever you *really* are," came a voice through the door.

Christine grabbed her towel and stood up. What on earth had Tucker told Mrs. Padgett? Perhaps it seemed unusual for a man to leave a younger woman at a rooming house while he fetched his mother, but it wasn't like they'd committed any social blunders. He'd paid for two rooms, after all!

She stopped blotting her hair. Why, it sounded like magpies were chattering in the hallway. Biddy hens gossiping about—

A key clicked in the lock and the door flew open.

"What on God's earth—? What're you—?"

Clutching the skimpy towel around herself, Christine gaped as the room filled with women old enough to be her grandmother. They surrounded the tub, glaring at her.

"Yessir, that's the one! The very woman who sold me that—"

"Shameless hussy! Showing your face in this town again, after you—"

"Polly, go get the sheriff!" Mrs. Padgett called from beside the tub. "With all of us here, she won't get away this time."

"You tell her, Matilda!" the oldest biddy clucked. The white bun at the nape of her neck began to quiver, she was so agitated.

Matilda Padgett's face contorted with rage as she planted her fists on her hips. She was standing so close, Christine could've smacked the eyeglasses from her face. But she didn't dare.

"You've got nerve," Mrs. Padgett said, and her friends hushed so they could catch every damning word. "Fool me once, shame on you. But fool me twice—well, I'm not falling for it!"

"I—I don't know what—"

"Don't play innocent with me," the landlady snapped. "You might've sashayed in here with a different man—not so polished around the edges this time—but I'd know you anywhere."

The old lady with the bun stepped forward to thrust a

large, leather-bound Bible at her. "What kind of heathen preys upon a widow in her darkest hour? Claiming that her dear, departed husband bought her this fine family Bible as a special gift, right before he died?"

"But he hadn't paid for it, you said. So you stole twenty dollars from *me!*" a lady in the back bellowed.

"Twenty?" another one cried. "This shyster cheated me out of twenty-five! And my *embossed* name is peeling off the cover like cheap paint!"

"It is cheap paint," the one in the bun said. "My name is *not* Harrie Butt."

Hairy butt! Now *there* was a story to make the girls snicker! Christine thought.

But she wasn't in school anymore, was she? She stood nearly naked in a bathtub, surrounded by angry women who expected a confession for sins she hadn't committed. Sins that baffled her.

The matron beside Matilda was holding her Bible higher now, so Christine couldn't miss the peeling personalization on the cover. The indented lettering spelled Harriet Butterfield, but through an unfortunate twist of fate only HARRIE BUTT retained its original golden luster.

The shyster these ladies were hounding her about had pressed the letters into the white leather and then filled them in with gold paint—which made the Good Book look tawdry even before the personalization began to peel. And as the others held up their Bibles in silent testimony to this cheap trick, Christine wanted to shoo them all from this airless room so she could dress—so she could think about what these outlandish accusations meant.

But they were standing fast, waiting for the sheriff. And she was shivering in a towel, completely at their mercy. And completely baffled.

There had to be some compelling reason Matilda

Padgett had rounded up her widowed friends after Tucker left her here, but her heart was pounding so hard she couldn't for the life of her think what it could be.

"I—I don't understand why—"

"Your mother would be ashamed!" Matilda hissed, her eyes narrowing behind her spectacles. "A comely young woman like yourself, helping that huckster with the handlebar mustache—"

Christine's mouth fell open. The picture Mrs. Padgett was painting became painfully clear: Mama and Richard Wyndham had suckered money from these ladies who'd lost their husbands.

And they thought she was Mama.

"I can explain everything, if you'll just—"

"Oh, don't think you'll weasel out of this!" Mrs. Butterfield said smugly. "Once we knew we'd been bamboozled, we put our heads together—"

"And then I recalled that one of my lodgers had a small press stashed under his bed," Matilda continued. "But by the time we convinced Sheriff Carson to come confiscate it, your huckster husband—or whoever he is!—with the English accent had disappeared like mist in the morning sun. And you along with him!"

Your mother would be ashamed . . . disappeared like mist . . .

The awful truth kicked her square in the chest. Her throat got so tight she couldn't speak—and what would she say? Who could admit to this roomful of spitfire widows that her own mother had done this to them?

Christine's chin dropped to her chest. Despite her efforts to think on her feet—to win them with the social skills Miss Vanderbilt had drilled into her—tears dribbled down her cheek.

"Oh, no, you don't!" Mrs. Butterfield said. "That crying over your own lost husband was just an act. A way to make us all think, when you came to call after the funerals, that you understood our grief. Get out of that tub! If the sheriff's not around, why—we'll march you over to the jail ourselves!"

"Without clothes, if we have to," another one piped up.

When they all cheered, Christine knew she was in more trouble than her academy training could help her out of. After all, when had Agatha Vanderbilt ever been caught—nearly naked—in her mother's lies?

What would Miss Vanderbilt do? What would Mercy do?

This thought made her stand taller, made her hold her head up and look at her cackling accusers and see them for the . . . plain but proper prairie women they were. Women alone, forced to get by without their husbands—just as Mercy had to run the way station after Judd was killed. They felt outraged at being taken for fools. And taken for money they couldn't afford, thinking their husbands had bought them one last gift.

Oh, Mama, what a despicable—how could you do this to them? she fretted. *How could you do this to me?*

"Ladies, please." Christine spoke above their angry chatter. "If you'll give me a moment to dress, I'll show you a photograph from my valise—"

"Oh, we won't be falling for that one," came Polly's voice from the door. "I've brought Harley Carson to settle this, once and for all!"

"High time you showed up, Sheriff!"

"How nice of you to be in town for a change."

"We told you that Englishman was a skunk!"

The short, fleshy man in the doorway wore a bemused expression. As he studied her, his crowsfeet deepened into webs . . . webs that called to mind twin spiders when she saw his dark eyes.

Christine shuddered. Spiders gave her the willies.

And when the lawman's gaze traveled up and down, as she clutched the threadbare towel around her bare body, she knew how it felt to be prey. The lamb to be sacrificed for Mama's sins—and these ladies' complaints against his lackluster performance as a lawman.

Christine blinked, refusing to cry. Tucker wasn't due back for a couple of hours—so she'd have to act fast. No hysterics, because Harley Carson was growing more disgusted with each disgruntled remark these old ladies made.

"Please! Listen to me!" she said in the strongest voice she could muster.

They turned wary eyes her way—but they stopped talking. For the first time in weeks, Christine prayed.

Lord, if You'll give me the right words, I promise You—

"So you've got a photograph? What'll that prove?" a widow in brown calico challenged. "We already know what you look like."

"But you'll see that it's my—" Christine squeezed her eyes shut against the most painful, humiliating thing she'd ever had to say. "It was my *mother* who sold you those Bibles, and—"

"Oh, for the love of God! Can you believe—?"

"What sort of girl would accuse her own mother of—"

"Quiet! All of you!"

The little room filled with the sheriff's presence, even though he remained in the doorway. The ladies pressed their lips into thin, tight lines, awaiting his judgment.

"It seems simple enough," Carson grumbled. "Not like she's pointing a pistol or can pull a knife from her stocking, for Pete's sake. Polly, you stand at the door while she gets dressed. Matilda, you go fetch the valise—and that photograph—from her room. I'll wait for you in the parlor, if you honestly think she needs to be in jail for—"

"You damn well better believe—"

"If you won't handle this, Sheriff, we'll take the law into our own—"

"Oh, shut up! All of you!" he barked. "Get back to your

own homes—or whatever it is you do all day—and I'll take care of her. Go on, now!"

Still clutching her towel, Christine caught the ladies' final dark looks as they filed out. Harriet Butterfield, waiting to be last, paused to look down her nose at Sheriff Carson as though she might whack him with her defiled Bible.

"Worthless!" she hissed at him. And then she stalked off.

Chapter Sixteen

"High time we got to the bottom of this—no thanks to you, Sheriff!"

"Now that we've corralled this crooked woman, you could at least see that justice is done."

"Amen to that!"

From behind the bars of her jail cell, Christine watched the ladies parade out the door of Harley Carson's tiny office. After the racket of their shrill voices died away, the silence was a real relief. The sheriff remained in the doorway, shaking his head.

What would he do to her? How could she make this man with eyes like spiders see her side?

When he turned around, Christine felt acutely aware that her hair was hanging in damp, uncombed clumps and that her crumpled clothes stank despite the bath she'd had. Lord, if any of her friends from school saw her this way—

But again, this wasn't the Academy for Young Ladies. She was caught in the most damning, demeaning situation of her life, and it would be hours before Tucker found her. Her fate lay in the hands of the pudgy little lawman who'd come to stand in front of her, studying her the way a circusgoer takes in the freaks at a sideshow.

He took off his hat and smoothed his thin brown hair. "I put you in here for your own protection, understand?" he said with a sigh. "Once those gals get a bee in their bonnet, there's no stopping them. And with their husbands gone, there's no one to make them behave like ladies."

Christine blinked. His voice was low, almost cordial. He'd dropped his predatory air.

"Excuse me?" she murmured. "I'm very confused by this whole—"

"I knew who you were the minute I laid eyes on you." A smile tickled the lawman's lips. "And if those ladies had really *looked* at the WANTED poster you showed them, they'd have seen that woman was, well—old enough to be your mother. But they saw what they needed to see."

An exasperated sigh escaped her. "So why didn't you just tell them—"

"Because they were on a rampage, just like the drunken-fool card sharps who shot up their men a few years back," he explained. "Couldn't see the facts, even though you were standing right in front of them telling them the truth. And I'm sorry for what that must've cost you, Miss Bristol."

Her eyes went wet at the sympathy in this man's voice. But why was he taking her part now? Yet keeping her behind bars like a criminal? "So if they don't believe me, why do you?"

He glanced toward the door, then slipped the skeleton key into the cell's lock and smiled.

"Who could forget the telegrams and stories we heard after the war about two redheaded kids abandoned by their mother at a Kansas stagecoach depot?" he replied. "When a fellow named Michael Malloy put the word out among the Union Pacific crews, trying to find Virgilia Bristol and her English escort, those ladies who just now tried to crucify you were shocked beyond belief. Real pleased to hear that a family near Abilene took you in."

Her mouth dropped open. Michael had said he sent word along the stagecoach line, but she hadn't realized how far-reaching his efforts had been. And she'd certainly never guessed these people on the Nebraska prairie would care what happened to her and Billy.

"You are the image of your mama, Miss Bristol. And when you had the grit to stand there in front of those biddies and claim her, after hearing about the stunt she'd pulled with those Bibles, I had to admire you. Had to get you out of their way, so we could . . . talk."

Harley Carson swung open the black-barred door, gesturing toward the little front room where his messy desk and chair were.

Gripping her valise, Christine stepped out of the cell. She was still confused, but a sense of hope had replaced her desperation.

"I—thank you," she said, standing taller as she remembered her manners. "I was appalled to hear—I can understand why they were so upset about paying for those vulgar Bibles—"

"It's more than the money."

He removed a pile of newspapers from the chair beside his desk, motioned for her to sit down, and then took his seat. "Matilda and her friends are looking for the villains who stripped them of their dignity—who robbed them of their confidence just days after they buried the men they'd depended on for half their lives. Today they saw their chance to make things right again. Even though they saw things wrong."

She thought about this, nodding. "That's what I'm try-ing to do, too—make things right by finding Mama. A lot of time's passed, though. I just got that WANTED poster a few weeks ago, and I don't even want to think about what she's been doing since that picture was taken."

The sheriff leaned toward her, following her story closely. "Where'd you get that poster, Miss Bristol? May I see it again?"

She smiled ruefully and fished it out of her bag.

"It's a long story. The man I'm traveling with—Tucker Trudeau, now the official photographer for the Union Pacific Railroad?" she said with a proud grin. "He sent it to me from Atchison, in Kansas. Mama and Mr. Wynd-ham were there right after she abandoned Billy and me, and I think they've been heading west ever since. Away from checks written on fake accounts and phony homestead sales, among other things."

The lawman nodded, studying the poster. At least he appreciated her predicament. He knew more than he was telling her—but he would defend her from that flock of hens that wanted to peck her to pieces.

"I remember this fellow, all right," Carson said. "Mr. Gentility, he was. Had all the ladies aflutter with that for-eign accent and his fancy clothes.

"But he was a fox in the henhouse—Matilda Padgett's house, to be exact," he added with raised eyebrows. "And because your mother stayed at the hotel, posing as a representative of the Alpha and Omega Bible Soci-ety, nobody realized they were together."

Christine sighed. She'd rather not hear about their conniving, yet knowledge was power—that was what Miss Vanderbilt always said. Best to listen and learn, so she knew how Mama and Mr. Wyndham operated.

"But how did she and Richard know who to . . . whose names to put on those Bibles?" she asked.

"Well, back when the railroad was being built, a

whole slew of gamblers, saloon owners, and soiled doves followed the construction crew. They weren't known as 'hell on wheels' for nothing, if you'll excuse my French," Carson explained. "Had a spell when tempers and guns got out of hand, and those gals' husbands stepped into the crossfire. When obituaries were posted, they gave enough details about each man's life and family that any salesman could've talked a pretty convincing piece."

The sheriff's smile was sympathetic. "Your mama had a face, and a graceful way about her, that made those widows believe their husbands bought them Bibles just before they were killed."

Christine swallowed a knot of embarrassment over Mama's dubious talents. "We lost Daddy when the Border Ruffians raided our corrals, right after the war. So Mama knew exactly what women left alone would fall for. Knew how they were . . . ripe and ready to fall."

He patted her hand, and pulled a clean bandanna from his desk drawer.

It surprised her how Judd Monroe's line about "ripe and ready to fall" could still sting—but then, who could've guessed Mama would be selling Bibles? Christine blew her nose, wishing she'd had a chance to pull up her hair before it dried looking like a rat's nest.

She glanced at Harley Carson through the slits of her eye as she dabbed at them. While it was good to have the lawman on her side, she wondered what would happen next. Most of her clothes were still at the boardinghouse, and Tucker would be coming back— with his mother!—soon.

But how could she even think of returning to Mrs. Padgett's? Matilda's flock of friends would probably spot that red wagon and then hide behind the furniture to spring at Tucker when he walked in—to grill him for sins they assumed *he* had committed, just for associating with her. They were a vindictive lot, those widows.

And when they saw Veronique Trudeau in her gypsy attire, with those ever-moving, all-seeing eyes, no telling what they'd try.

Christine shifted in the hard chair. The man studying the WANTED poster now looked every bit as tame and bland as Daddy had. When he noticed her watching him, he smiled kindly.

"Can I get you anything, dear? A sandwich from the restaurant, perhaps?"

She *was* hungry, but food seemed unimportant. "Thank you, but—"

Christine paused, thinking how very considerate he was. Nice as pie, Billy would say. Especially after she'd compared his eyes to spiders back at the boardinghouse.

"Why were those ladies so hateful with you?" she blurted. Then she realized this might be the wrong thing to ask, since Harley Carson held the key to her immediate future.

He laughed, a bitter note that sounded off-key.

"I'm their sheriff—their protector, since they have no menfolk," he said. "But the pay for lawmen in these little frontier towns won't hold body and soul together, so I sometimes take on other jobs that keep me out of the office."

"What sort of jobs?"

As the lawman leveled his gaze at her, Christine chided herself again for letting her curiosity get out of hand.

"There are things a man doesn't discuss with women—"

"Yes, of course. I didn't mean to be rude."

"—but the fact remains I haven't avenged their husbands' deaths at the hands of those fly-by-night gamblers, and—more importantly—I didn't catch that

Englishman who hid his press under the bed at
Matilda's, nor his lady confederate who sold them those
Bibles. So I'm a failure."

"That's ridiculous! Why, you're not only thoughtful,
you're—you're—"

Christine searched for the right words about this
man, who'd changed from an apparent predator to her
protector in the past hour. In his denim pants and
chambray shirt, he looked very ordinary; had the care-
worn air of an old boot about him.

Yet in a lot of ways, he reminded her of Michael Malloy. Maybe even Judd Monroe, the way he saw beneath
those women's prickly-pear exteriors to the fear and vulnerability beneath . . . just as Judd had understood
those things about her.

"You're the nicest sheriff I've ever met," she finished.
"Those women wanted to crucify you, too. Yet you're de-
fending them to me."

Harley Carson glanced away, as though wondering
whether to let her in on a secret.

"You're a bright girl, Christine. Wise beyond your
years in many ways," he remarked. "So perhaps you'll
see the twist in my situation when I tell you that Harriet
Butterfield is my mother."

Christine nearly fell from her chair. That old sourpuss
with the white bun and the—

Hairy butt.

She choked to keep from laughing. It wasn't the least
bit funny, since Mrs. Butterfield had been the loudest of
all Mr. Carson's critics. Why, as she'd left the bathroom,
she'd called this man—her son—*worthless.*

*If Mama had treated me that way, I wouldn't be chas-
ing her down!*

Again she wondered how to say the right thing.
Surely the sheriff didn't enjoy being ridiculed by those

widows. And it had to be worse because his own mother was their ringleader.

If you can't say anything nice about Harrie Butt—change the subject.

Christine smiled politely at the man across from her. "She's perhaps related to the Butterfield who ran the overland stagecoach company?"

"Married his cousin after my father died, yes. And even though the John Butterfield you speak of was ousted from his own company for going deep into debt, she can't let me forget that my career has been less than illustrious by comparison."

When he glanced out the window, a wicked grin lit his face.

"But tonight, I get to prove I was right. Here comes that black Percheron you rode in on earlier, pulling Tucker Trudeau's wagon," he said as he rose from his chair. "Tidy up in the back room if you like, while I tell him what's gone on today. Then I'll escort the two of you back to Mrs. Padgett's for dinner, so there'll be no misunderstandings about—"

"I'd rather not go back," Christine confessed as she watched the bright red wagon pass by. "And I'm such a frightful-looking—"

"It'll be all right, dear. You've done nothing wrong." He grinned at her. "And from what I observed earlier, Mr. Trudeau won't mind how you look, Miss Bristol. Love is blind, you know. But I'm not!"

As Harley Carson opened the door, Christine gathered up her courage and spoke her mind.

"Sheriff, I—thank you for taking care of me today," she said while trying to smooth her hair. "I'm sorry those ladies don't appreciate you more. And I'm sorry your mother is so—so mean."

The lawman shrugged. "She's eighty years old and

doesn't have much to hold on to except her grudges," he said softly. "I don't always like her, but I'll keep looking after her. She's my mother, after all."

Tucker hitched Sol outside the Union Pacific depot. He carefully lifted his crate of glass negatives and prints, and carried it inside to the station agent.

"The train east will be passing through soon, *oui?*" he asked loudly.

The man behind the ticket window awoke with a snort. "*Wee?* I'll thank ya not to do that *here*, sir, inside the—"

"*Non, non, non!*" Tucker eased his crate onto the countertop, chuckling. "I am Tucker Trudeau, and you have maybe heard of me? The Union Pacific photographer? This crate, it is very fragile, so I must ask you to—"

"Trudeau? Well, now, ain't *this* a fine surprise!"

The agent was all smiles then, reaching between the iron bars for such an exuberant handshake, Tucker grabbed his crate to keep it from falling off the counter.

"Why, sure I've heard all about you," the agent said. "Takin' pitchers and ridin' the rails, are ya? Sure hope you're makin' some of them stereopticon cards as you go, on account of how me 'n the wife really like to look at those on a Sunday afternoon, when all there is to—"

"Moe, you wouldn't be talking this fellow's leg off, would you?"

Tucker turned to see a rather short man in the doorway. He sported such unremarkable features and ordinary clothing he could fade into any crowd, or be forgotten moments after he turned away. Except he wore a star on his chest.

"Sheriff Carson!" the agent exclaimed. "This here's that Union Pacific photographer we got word about. I don't know about you, but I'm gonna go home and get slicked up some, just in case he wants my portrait for them boys back east. Why, I—"

"May I see you outside for a moment, Mr. Trudeau?"

While he was guilty of nothing the sheriff could arrest him for, Tucker's insides tightened. What could possibly have gone wrong since he was here this afternoon? With an apologetic glance at the station agent, he stepped out onto the platform—just as the lawman unfolded a familiar piece of paper.

"What do you know about this WANTED poster?" Carson asked.

It was a simple question, yet Tucker sensed the lawman was fishing. "You got this from Miss Christine, *oui?*" he demanded. "There is a problem, Sheriff? When I left her at the boardinghouse—"

"I see my share of these," the lawman said with a noncommittal shrug. "It's unusual for a WANTED poster to have a photograph on it, and it says nothing about the bank or agency who's after these folks. What with you being the photographer . . ."

Tucker's English wasn't perfect, but he couldn't miss the sheriff's insinuation—or the way Carson's gaze intensified. He prided himself on an artistic eye, which brought out the best in his subjects and captured them at just the right moment, but this fellow had vision of a different sort. More powerful. Potentially more dangerous.

So Tucker shrugged in that offhand Cajun way. No need for this man to know every little thing until he could find out what had happened to Christine.

"My banker in Atchison, he complained about how this man—Richard Wyndham is one of the names he goes by—wrote a check on a fake account," Tucker explained carefully. "This couple, I had just taken their wedding portrait—displayed it in my front window—where Miss Bristol first found it."

Carson nodded, remaining silent.

"After that poor little girl, she came so far to find her mama—and after my banker, he lost his money—"

Tucker dodged artfully, "I wanted to help the law find these people. You have seen them, perhaps?"

The slightest smile played on the sheriff's face.

"The two of them passed through here. Couple of years ago," he clarified. "And yes, Mr. Trudeau, I've met Miss Bristol today, as well. She's in my jail because Mrs. Padgett and her friends mistook her for Virgilia Bristol. The resemblance is amazing, don't you think?"

"My Christine? She is in jail? But why—she has surely done nothing so wrong—"

"I'm holding her for her own protection," the lawman answered, straightening to his full height. "She says you're taking her west as a favor, but if there's some sort of funny business going on—"

"*Mais non!*" Tucker insisted, scowling with his own suspicions. "My *maman*, she is with us! Michael Malloy, he has sent telegrams along the Union Pacific line, asking for word about Wyndham and Christine's mama— saying Christine is with me, *non?*"

Carson's face remained carefully composed. "It's a mighty unusual arrangement—"

"It's an unusual situation."

Tucker stuffed his hands in his pockets, fighting the urge to shake some straight answers from this presumptuous little sheriff. "And Christine, she is an unusual girl, wanting to find her mother—to bring her home. It is three years since Mrs. Bristol abandoned her, but I have to help her, *non?* I simply cannot—"

"You're in love with her."

Tucker gasped. "*Oui,*" he admitted quietly. "From the moment I met her, I have lived to see Christine again— to make her dreams come true. I cannot fail her now."

Silence shimmered between them, and then—as though some unseen hand had wiped the slate clean— Sheriff Carson smiled.

"All right, Mr. Trudeau. Since you and I want the same

thing for Miss Bristol, I'll tell you that last I heard, her mother was doing business as a medium in Denver," he said quietly. "Conducting séances, and quite successful at it. You can do what you like with that information, but I'll warn you: Christine learned some . . . unflattering things about her mother today."

Tucker's gut tightened. "What things?"

The sheriff sighed reluctantly. "Mrs. Padgett was none too happy to be reminded about how Virgilia and Richard Wyndham hoodwinked her and her friends with a Bible-selling scheme," he said. "So I advise you to move along tomorrow on your railroad business. Christine might be better off not finding that mother of hers, if you know what I'm saying."

Tucker figured he'd heard all this lawman was willing to share. But what if he'd made that remark about Denver to get rid of them? To mislead them—or give them false hopes, after so much time had gone by?

"*Merci.* Is a tricky situation, *non?*" he replied cautiously. "My negatives, I will send them. Then I'll come by the jail for Christine—"

"I'll take her back to Mrs. Padgett's. She—well, you know how girls are," Carson said with a grin. "Give her time to fix herself up while I smooth Matilda's ruffled feathers. We'll all be better off for that."

Tucker watched the sheriff start toward the boardinghouse, past the shops and churches that marked North Platte as a settled, respectable town now. Then he went to the wagon and poked his head inside.

Maman was sitting on her bed. Her arms were folded and her eyes were bright. She'd clearly heard every word between him and the sheriff.

"You knew about Mrs. Bristol being in Denver, *non?*"

She pointed her nose toward the ceiling, as though answering him was beneath her. Still peeved at him for taking that detour to Abilene, which had led him back to Miss Bristol, no doubt.

"She is still there?" he demanded. "You could find her, with your spirit guides? Or by holding something that belonged to her?"

"*C'est un mensonge*," she muttered. "*Je n'aime pas le shérif ou son village. Allons, maintenant. Sans Christine.*"

Tucker shut the door with an exasperated sigh. He would *not* leave Christine here just because his mother didn't like the sheriff or this town. Why did women have to be so damned difficult?

He stuck his head inside again. "He knows about the poster, *Maman*. I think we should tell Christine that—"

"*Fermez la bouche!*"

Her tongue-lashing stung. But he saw no point in having both women mad at him if he revealed their little secret. Just as there was no point in pressing *Maman* to eat and sleep at the boardinghouse. Her mood would only get worse.

"You knew Christine was in jail, didn't you? Because she'd been mistaken for her mama?"

His mother let out an exasperated gasp, pointing her nose in the opposite direction.

"Answer me! She has been upset enough by her own mother's trickery," he declared. "I won't have her hurt by yours as well."

Maman's obsidian gaze shot through the dimness like a bullet. Tucker felt her hostility, her alienation—her *fear*—so keenly, he stepped backward out of the wagon, quickly shutting the door. There was no reasoning with Veronique Trudeau once she summoned her spirits and the mental powers that set her apart from everyone else in his world.

So he entrusted his crate of negatives to the chatty station agent, claimed a letter awaiting Christine—and then remembered his agreement with Mike Malloy.

North Platte, Nebraska. All goes well, his message said.

"I'll send this telegram right away, sir," the station agent said when Tucker laid extra money on the counter. "And when ya have a spare minute, why—me 'n the wife, we'd like to sit for a pitcher. Got us a purty little place out in the country, where there's sunflowers tall as giraffes in the summer and—"

Tucker pasted on a patient grin. "I must rescue—how you say?—a damsel in despair now. You have a livery stable nearby, *oui?*"

The man blinked and adjusted his spectacles. "Yessir, *we* have a place right over yonder, where that big ole horse of yours can *wee* all it wants. Better'n him makin' a lake outta Mrs. Padgett's front yard, don'tcha know?"

Chapter Seventeen

". . . and deliver us from the evil in this world, oh Lord, as you deliver us from those who would deceive us," Polly prayed fervently. "Bless this food to the use of those who love You, and who make it their business to do Your will."

"Amen," her sister Matilda chimed in.

As Tucker crossed himself beside her, Christine couldn't help thinking how different this prayer sounded, compared to the way Michael Malloy offered thanks. But then, these two widows hadn't ever planned to see her again. When she'd arrived with Harley Carson, Polly had to fetch the rest of her clothes from a heap outside the back door.

Mrs. Padgett sprang up to remove the lids from the vegetable bowls. "You'll have to excuse me for having less of a dinner cooked up, Harley. I hadn't planned on you or Miss Bristol joining us," she said tartly.

"We'll make do, Matilda." He reached for the platter in front of him, smiling smugly. "Things aren't always what they seem."

"Humph!" Polly grunted, passing the bowl of boiled potatoes to Tucker. "We women have to watch out for ourselves, now that the train brings every part and parcel of humanity to our door!"

Had she not been so tired from today's misadventures, Christine would've enjoyed watching these ladies chafe at her presence while refusing to apologize for their error. She could imagine Miss Vanderbilt sitting tall, quietly triumphant. So that's what she did, too.

"It was an easy mistake since Miss Bristol looks so much like her mother," the sheriff continued. He stabbed a second pork chop, disregarding Polly's scowl. "But we can't help admiring Christine for hunting her down. We never outgrow the need for our mother's love, now do we?"

Was the lawman going to use this meal as a chance to pour salt on everyone's wounds? Christine kept her eyes on the plateful of potatoes and pork she didn't have the stomach for, avoiding another of her hostess's poisoned looks. Matilda Padgett despised being wrong. And, seeing how Harriet Butterfield had treated her son, no one could miss Mr. Carson's knife-edged sentiment about a mother's love.

"*Oui*, this is why I brought Christine west," Tucker cut in cordially. "I could not imagine worrying about my own mother—what a man like Richard Wyndham might force her to do."

"Oh, there's no doubt Mrs. Bristol enjoyed her work," their hostess snipped. "Why, she cried like a baby over my grievous loss—and then purred like a happy cat when I paid for—"

"And where is your mother, Mr. Trudeau?"

Harley Carson gazed across the table at the Cajun, as though he knew the answer but was fishing for more. "Surely she'd like to join us for this fine meal, since you've paid for it. And no doubt she'd enjoy a fresh bed, too."

Tucker made a point of swallowing and wiping his mouth—a move that had Christine watching the sharp sparkle of a challenge in his aquamarine eyes. She was greatly relieved that Mrs. Trudeau had stayed in the wagon, but she knew better than to let on.

"*Maman*, she is very shy. Very private," he replied in his most charming accent. "And, coming from the bayou of Louisiana, her English, it is not so good. I will take her a plate after we've finished—if I may?"

Matilda Padgett fluttered her lashes like a debutante as Tucker fixed her in his flirtatious gaze. "Why, certainly," she replied. "But I can't imagine any woman wanting to sleep in a wagon, in a smelly old stable, when she could—"

"She feels closer to Jesus there." Tucker lowered his voice in reverence, widening his eyes at her. "Jesus, He was born in a stable, *non?*"

"No! Er, *yes*—yes, of course He was," Matilda twittered.

The five of them ate in silence then, with the clicking of tines against china and the ticking of the mantel clock marking the moments of their discomfort. Polly seemed to be counting the spoonfuls of potatoes the sheriff took, while Matilda couldn't feed herself fast enough.

When she'd devoured her final bite, she hopped up from her chair. "I'll fetch our dessert now. I've made a raisin pie I think you'll all enjoy."

Eager for something to do, Christine began scraping their plates. Today's unexpected events had exhausted her, and the conversation was becoming strained. Had Miss Vanderbilt been here, she would've initiated some fascinating—safe—topic to elevate the room's mood.

But again, this wasn't the academy. It was the choice she'd made, and it was beginning to chafe like a cheap corset.

Polly snatched the stack of plates from her hands, then stalked toward the kitchen.

"I—I believe I'll go to my room now," Christine said. "I couldn't eat another bite, and a real bed sounds heavenly after the day I've had."

Tucker stood up, concern etching his face.

"You are all right, *oui?*" he asked, gently testing her forehead for fever. "When I take *Maman*'s plate, I will bring back my accordion. So perhaps you will stay here and sing with me?"

It touched her that Tucker wanted her to be with him, but Christine shook her head. How could she tell him the awful details about her bath without dredging up Mrs. Padgett's animosity—and her own—again?

"I'll listen from upstairs. You can play me a lullaby, all right?"

Tucker leaned closer, smiling as he did only for her. And despite the tattoo of Mrs. Padgett's returning footsteps and Polly's gasp, and Sheriff Carson watching them from across the table, he kissed her softly on the lips.

Christine sucked in her breath, desperate for more. They'd just crossed the line of polite public courtship—which meant Matilda and her sister would stay awake into the night, listening for Tucker to slip into her room.

And how she wished he would!

"A lullaby, of course I will play," he whispered. Then he pulled something from his shirt pocket. "This letter, it was waiting for you at the train station, *chérie*. You'd rather read it alone, *non?*"

A letter! Her pulse pounded like wild drums when she saw it was from Abilene. The Malloys and the children they'd taken in weren't her family, but these weeks away from school—apart from her friends and familiar routine—had taught her a new appreciation for the life Billy now lived on the Triple M Ranch.

"Thank you," she whispered, and after bidding the sisters and the sheriff good night, she hurried up to her room.

Christine closed the door with her backside while opening the letter. She saw Mercy's perfect script first, and then a folded page of Billy's irregular scrawl, and even a few paragraphs from Michael. This was a treat, indeed! She forced herself to sit in the sewing rocker beside the bed, turn up the lamp, and draw a deep breath before devouring their news. She had to make this unexpected pleasure last awhile.

Dear Sis, she deciphered, sighing over the way Billy's penmanship disgraced the page. *We're all doing fine here, but we miss you something fierce.*

She paused, a knot in her throat. This was her little brother, after all—the one who would rather romp with his dogs and rhapsodize over Asa's pie than write about his feelings.

> *I sure hope you aren't causing Tucker too much trouble with your queenly ways—*

That was more like it!

> *—and I thank you for being hardheaded enough to hunt for Mama again. After seeing what that land office scheme cost the Gates family, I hope you don't run on to any more of her and Wyndham's tricks.*

"Oh, Billy, it's best you don't know," she sighed. Blinking, she tucked his page behind the others, to finish reading when she wasn't so tired. So heartsick.

Michael's squarish printing beckoned her next. *Christine, honey, we keep you in our prayers every day, and ask God to guide your journey. While I realize you're angry at your mama, I also understand that deep down, you want her restored to her rightful place in your life, and in your heart.*

A shuddery sigh escaped her, for the words came to her in Michael Malloy's calm, reassuring voice. As always, he had seen her secret needs—and right now, his sincerity was more than she could stand. This page went behind Billy's, and Christine gazed out the window toward the street.

In the darkness, she saw her candlelit reflection: pensive and sad, she looked. Older. Not the least bit inclined to practice her smile so she could attract Tucker's affections.

"What a difference a day makes," she mused aloud.

From the parlor she heard tentative accordion chords. Tucker had returned. And while she longed to watch Tucker's eyes dance as he played, she needed this time away from the wary looks and pinched dignity that Polly and Matilda didn't wear very well.

She sat straighter, mustering the strength Agatha Vanderbilt would expect of her. The headmistress taught that even while walking through the Valley of the Shadow, a lady behaved with courage and fortitude. Christine wished she'd paid closer attention to such lessons. Who could've guessed she would ever need such reassurance?

She smoothed the final page, determined to read it. Mercy's writing flowed the way this capable, compassionate woman spoke: chatty, yet filled with news she needed to hear. Many times this woman's saintly ways had provoked her envy and anger—but truth be told, it was Mercy she looked up to. Mercy to whom she owed such an incredible debt of gratitude.

Dearest Christine, the pretty script began.

In her mind, Mercy's chestnut hair and kind brown eyes took on the glow of the lamplight she'd be writing by, probably at the new desk in the parlor.

*I hope your journey with Tucker is going well,
and that you've found a way to stay sane as you*

*share that wagon with him and his mother! I
sounded less than enthusiastic about this trip, I
know, but I'm so proud of you for taking it. It can't
be easy, finding a woman who disappeared years
ago—especially considering what we've learned
about her since then.*

*My heart goes out to you, dear. Again, I'm truly
sorry if tucking away those letters hindered your
mission. Aunt Agatha, too, realizes you always intended to find your mother, so "protecting" you
from her and Tucker was our silly mistake. I hope
you've forgiven us.*

Christine gripped the page. The anger and resent-
ment she'd hurled at Mercy—on her wedding day, no
less—had subsided after these weeks of bumping along
the rutted prairie. She suddenly longed for the soothing
sound of this woman's voice, in person rather than in
this letter. What she wouldn't give to be sitting in that
parlor now, working a sampler while Mercy quilted.

She blinked and read on.

*You'll be pleased to know that Temple Gates has
made a full recovery. She helps with the cleaning
and keeps track of Lily, Solace, and Joel while I
make this beautiful new house a home. You'll love
the lace curtains I've sewn for your room!*

*Reuben and Sedalia have settled into the log
house on my homestead, and we'll hire two more
hands to manage the stock and the planting come
spring. Asa does most of our cooking, although his
old bones are hurting him more as the cold
weather comes on.*

*And your brother—he's remarkable when it
comes to training the horses. Since that pamphlet*

appeared, we've had several cattlemen stop by (including Obadiah Jones, Mrs. Barstow's new husband). They're choosing our best three-year-olds for Billy to train over the winter, so they can claim these fine Morgans when they drive their herds here next year. He won't say so, but he's pretty "dang" proud of himself.

Christine's throat tightened. Maybe she should've held Billy to his offer to search for Mama . . . but no. He'd found a home with people he loved, and training horses had always been his special talent. She didn't expect him to give all that up for a mother who'd abandoned them.

The mellow tones from Tucker's accordion drifted upstairs, and she closed her eyes. Part of her wanted to be in the parlor, watching his face light up as he made his music . . . wrapping his arms around that fine old instrument the way she wished he'd hold *her*. He played softly, a sentimental song she recognized. It made her swallow hard and return to Mercy's letter.

Joel keeps us all busy. Thank goodness Snowy and Spot love that boy because when he takes off down the road or across the fields, only they can coax him home. Billy thinks he goes out looking for Tucker's wagon because he sometimes mentions Sol. He chatters about you in his sleep.

A tear dribbled down Christine's cheek, landing with a *splat* on the page. Mercy might as well be driving that pen through her heart, the way those words made her ache. It didn't help that downstairs Tucker was crooning, " 'Mid pleasures and palaces though we may-ay roam, be it ever so humble—' "

Christine blew loudly into her lace handkerchief. Mercy's words shimmered before her watery eyes, but it was better than following Tucker's tender song.

> *And Lily, too, asks about you every single day. You should see her now! Emma Clark's barn cat had a litter, and Lily chose a ginger kitty she calls Kwis-teen. She carries it with her everywhere—*

" '—there's no place like home,' " the Cajun continued, singing with heartfelt conviction as only he could. " 'A charm from the skies seems to hallow us there. . . .' "

Squeezing her eyes shut against a torrent of tears, Christine felt utterly, hopelessly alone. She couldn't bear to read any more about the little girl who missed her, too. Nor could she escape the sweet, sentimental music that swept her into emotions she seldom explored . . . for fear she'd be swallowed alive, like Jonah by that whale, and never find herself again.

" 'Be it ever so humble,' " Tucker concluded with a poignant pause, " 'there's no-oh place . . . like . . . hoooooome.' "

Christine crumpled, hugging her knees to hold body and soul together. How she longed to giggle with that little girl. And how she wished that kitty had any name but her own. She could hear Lily saying it so clearly, the Princess of Pink might as well be right here, climbing into her lap.

Matilda and Polly's applause drifted upstairs, with Harley Carson's compliments—for Tucker had sung the beloved song with the expression he always poured into whatever he loved.

But why did he have to pick that one? Why did he have to make her so aware, yet again, that she hadn't known *home* for such a long time?

She had been thirteen when Mama left them—which

seemed like a lifetime ago, considering all that had happened to her since—but the ache never ended. It lingered in the far corners of her heart, haunting her just when she thought she'd hardened herself and moved on.

For her, there truly was no place like home. And when she wasn't afraid to face her fears—or couldn't escape them while lying awake in the night—she wondered if *home* would ever be hers again.

Too miserable to read any more, Christine sprawled on the narrow bed to bury her face in the pillow. She cried for Lily and Joel and Solace, and for the way those border collies looked after them all—and Billy.

She cried for the comfortable routine at school, and for her friends and their gossip—and even for Miss Vanderbilt, who had warned her that chasing after Mama might not be a good idea. Would she never learn to listen?

And she cried because when they left North Platte and Mama's Bible scam behind, they might find even more horrid evidence of Virgilia Bristol's . . . heartlessness. A calculated cruelty Christine would never have believed had she not gotten caught up in its consequences.

But mostly Christine cried because she couldn't turn back. As surely as her wayward mother had fled west with Richard Wyndham to avoid detection, the angel of Fate was crooking its finger, beckoning her to follow.

Chapter Eighteen

She looked so pale, seated beside him as they drove through the morning mist, that Tucker didn't know what to say. Had her letter contained bad news?

Or was she still smarting because those ladies in North Platte had mistaken her for her cold-blooded mother? He'd cringed at every detail Sheriff Carson shared with him last night while Polly and Mrs. Padgett washed the dishes. That incident would've sent any other girl back to Kansas, yet Christine seemed to ponder these things in her heart . . . a heart filled with longing he wasn't sure he could satisfy.

He cleared his throat. "If you wish to board the train and return home—"

"No!" she said sharply.

She gathered her deep green cloak around her as though she felt cold to the core. "Please understand, Tucker, that I won't rest—I can't stop searching—until I've found Mama. If she's desperate enough to deceive widows with cheap Bibles, what else might Wyndham convince her to do?"

She paused, blinking bravely, so he slipped his arm around her.

"You're right, *chérie*," he murmured. "No matter what Mrs. Padgett said, I can't believe that your mother is cruel enough to fool—"

"She's not *smart* enough!" Christine blurted. "Mama has the charm and manners to manipulate people, but she could never have devised such a clever, conniving way to take those ladies' money."

What an awful thing to say about her own mother. But it was true, wasn't it? Mama had always gotten what she wanted—especially from Daddy—by playing the helpless, innocent victim. The rub of it was that she herself had perfected this talent. Christine gazed at the treeless prairie around them, thinking how those low-slung gray clouds signaled snow.

Perfect. They would be trapped inside the wagon again.

Tucker hated to see Christine worry. What should he suggest? Her heart was set on finding her mother . . . Denver would mean another detour that would take him away from his work—but wasn't finding Mrs. Bristol the reason her daughter was along? Should he mention Virgilia had been there? Conducting séances?

Or should he save Christine from further humiliation and pain? He wasn't sure he trusted Harley Carson's information, anyway—and by now, Wyndham and his woman had probably moved on.

"The family—everyone there is doing well, *oui?*" he asked, hoping to draw her out of her sorrow.

Everyone did a fine job of ripping my heart out, yes, she wanted to say. Good thing she'd never considered them family.

Christine inched closer to his body's warmth. "It was a very nice letter," she answered in a detached voice. "Mercy says Reuben and Sedalia Gates are living in her

little log house now, and Temple is minding the . . .
children."

Tucker felt the drop in temperature that preceded a
storm, painted in swirling, muddy grays ahead. But the
tempest brewing beside him was potentially more devastating. Christine wouldn't be avoiding his gaze with a
quivering lip simply from reading about the hired help.

Should he press for details, or leave her to her private
misery?

He smiled, with the best intentions. "They are a busy
pair, Joel and Lily! When we get back, I'm betting that
boy will want to ride Sol all by himself—even though
his little legs won't hold him on."

When we get back . . . his little legs. . . . Christine
pressed her lips together, determined not to cry again.
Surely there were no tears left.

"And Lily, her hair shines like the sun," he went on.
"She's too little to understand why you left her, *ma belle*."

Will I ever understand why Mama left me? she thought
before she could stop it. She'd never considered this
from Lily's angle—the questions and fears such a little
angel didn't even know the words for yet, about why
her daddy had dumped her off. A tear slithered down
Christine's cheek, and she was a goner.

"She—she has a ginger kitty now," she said in a wobbly
voice. "Mercy says she . . . she named it Kwis-teeeeeeen."

Christine slumped against him, and he pulled her
close. Here it was—the real reason she looked so de-
jected. He'd thought a letter from people who loved her
would cheer her up.

Tucker sighed against her soft hair, whispering endearments and wishing he knew how to soothe her
sobbing. So young to be so alone—smitten by his affection, yet still unsure where it might lead. As was he.

Was it fair to believe she could love him? To believe
that at sixteen, this beautiful but sheltered girl under-

stood the meaning of marriage? It was a commitment he longed to make—but only when Christine was ready.

More importantly, was it fair to discuss his love for her while she was so upset? After all, the one person in the world whose love she should never have doubted had abandoned her. That wound might never heal—unless he made Christine believe she was loved, and believe he would never leave her.

And a large part of that promise involved finding her mother, didn't it? If he truly loved Christine, there could be no holding back, no holding out on what he knew.

As though on cue, *Maman* began her prayers inside the wagon. Was this a reminder that she'd fight his affection for Miss Bristol every step of the way—to keep the son she depended upon?

The first fat flakes of snow swirled around them with the promise of a full-blown storm to come. Tucker clucked to Sol and they traveled faster, fueled by the Percheron's innate sense of a change in the weather.

Christine swiped at her eyes. Snowflakes stung her raw cheeks, and she knew Tucker would soon ask if she wanted to ride inside, where it was warm and dry.

She'd rather return to the jail cell in North Platte than endure the sing-song chanting within the wagon.

"Where are we going next?" she asked, trying to sound interested. "Taking photographs in this snow will be difficult if—"

"We'll stop at the next station, *chérie,* and board the train," he said, realizing now what he must do. "I have many photographs of the Nebraska plains already, so we can head on down the tracks."

And then head to Denver, he vowed silently.

Christine shifted on the upholstered seat, settling herself as the train lurched away from yet another little station. While this day coach offered considerably less luxury than the hotel express car she'd imagined riding, it was better than being exposed to the snow—or confined with Veronique—while riding Tucker's wagon.

She glanced behind her, to where his mother had stretched out in the bench built against the back wall—

As though anyone would sit beside an old Gypsy who might hex them! she mused.

Then she smiled up at Tucker. His broad shoulders took up so much of their seat, she brushed against him every time she moved—and the skirt of her green plaid traveling suit lapped over his legs even though she wasn't wearing her hoops while they were on the road.

"You are too crowded, *ma petite?*" he asked, scooting toward the aisle.

"Don't you dare move away from me," she teased. The chatter of the other passengers—and the five benches separating them from Mrs. Trudeau—were providing a chance to flirt, and she refused to miss a minute of it. "Now—what's in this mysterious box you've brought along?"

Tucker lifted the lid slowly, prolonging the suspense.

"Today, since it is snowy, we must make our own sunshine," he offered. "While I have printed many fine photographs for the Union Pacific, you might enjoy the faces of your family more."

The faces of your family. Images of Daddy and Wesley and Mama drifted through her mind. Would she ever see any of them—besides Billy—again?

But of course, Tucker wouldn't understand how he unwittingly upset her whenever he called the Malloys her family. Damn. She'd just recovered from their letters and now this.

Christine fluttered her lashes so he wouldn't realize she was crying; a little talent honed during lonely times at the academy . . . a lady's way of rising above until she could deal with her feelings in private. The car was hazy with cigar smoke, so if Tucker asked, she'd say it was making her eyes water.

She glanced at the photograph he was lifting from the box. It didn't help that the patched-together family posing between those porch pillars looked all of a piece: Michael smiled proudly over Joel's mussed hair, while Mercy held a wide-eyed Solace on her knee and Lily stood grinning between them . . . holding hands with her and Billy.

"Oh, my," she murmured, her fingertip following the length of that little dress she'd made.

Christine suddenly *felt* the grip of Lily's fingers. She swallowed hard, for Tucker had captured everyone in such perfect, sharp detail—she even looked rather fetching, seated beside her growing-up brother. The life-like clarity of his work made her insides clench with longing. How she missed these children!

"It's a fine likeness, *non?*" Tucker agreed. "I'm glad that Michael wanted these photographs to remember his wedding day. The pride in his family is written all over his face."

Christine felt a tear slip out and roll down her cheek. She realized Tucker was only trying to brighten her mood, but she was more homesick—or heartsick—than she wanted to admit.

"And how about this?" he coaxed as he slipped the print behind the others and brought out a new one. "Sometimes, the best pictures take *me* by surprise."

Christine giggled in spite of herself. There sat Billy, grinning like the imp he used to be, with Joel and Lily beaming at her from each of his knees. They looked so excited, they might just *say* something. Snowy and Spot sat alert and bright-eyed on each side of him, ready to bark out their orders.

But it was Solace who stole the show. She was stand-

ing on Billy's shoulders as he held her, with her arms
out like a circus rider's and a daredevil grin that made
Christine laugh out loud.

"Look at her!" she exclaimed, not caring if other passengers turned around to stare. "Eight months old and
fearless. Spreading her wings to fly."

Tucker chuckled fondly. "And someday she will. *Maman*, she believes this little baby will amaze us someday. Felt the spirit of her father protecting her. He was
killed before she was born, *non?*"

"Yes. Judd Monroe was a magnificent man," Christine said.

This thought nipped at her. Plenty of times she'd
railed against Judd's plainspoken sense of right and
wrong—mostly when he'd expected better of her. What
surprised her more was that Veronique Trudeau had discussed this with her son. The seer not only believed the
baby with the dark curls and bottomless brown eyes
had a special destiny, but she apparently planned to
watch Solace grow into it.

As she pondered this, Christine could feel those tiny
black eyes peering at the backs of their heads—so
pointedly she could almost hear the old witch telling
her to move away from Tucker!

"She's watching us," Christine sighed.

Tucker frowned, glancing at the passengers around
them. "Who do you say is—"

"Your mother. She hates me, Tucker. She hasn't said
one word to me in nearly three weeks." Her words came
out in a frustrated rush, despite the way people nearby
could hear her. "It's not like she can't speak English—
she just *won't.*"

"*Maman*, she does not hate you, *chérie*," he murmured. "She doesn't yet know you, so she doesn't understand you. What we don't understand, we fear."

"Oh, she understands. She knows how I feel about

you." Aware that her voice was rising, Christine sneaked a peek behind her.

Sure enough, Veronique Trudeau was sitting upright now, looking at them as though the rows of passengers between them didn't exist.

Tucker shrugged, brushing her shoulder with his as he fought a grin. "All right, so she knows you are—how do you say?—crazy for me," he teased. "*Maman*, she is afraid of losing me to you—even though I've promised I will never leave her."

Why did this man's feelings for his mother scrape her like sandpaper? Why didn't he declare his independence?

"She's afraid?" Christine blurted. "My God, she summons angels! She directs invisible forces—"

"But she cannot control her little boy." He wiggled his dark eyebrows, grinning mischievously—first at her, then over his shoulder. "I adore pretty women, and I have chosen you, *ma joie*. She will know, someday, that I chose well."

Before she could protest again, Tucker leaned down to kiss her. His hands remained on the box of photographs, but his mouth left no doubt about how he felt about her. How he wanted her.

Such soft lips, moist and warm, framed by a silky beard her fingers found themselves stroking—until she gasped and pulled away. How had she forgotten that his mother was watching them? That dozens of other people could see them kissing, right here in public!

Incorrigible, Tucker remained close enough that his eyes glimmered, mere inches above hers. "Perhaps, *ma petite*, you should fight fire with fire," he whispered suggestively. "It is Saint Michael, the head of all the archangels, who can remove our doubts and fears. If you pray to him for help with *Maman*, to help her see—"

"In my church, we don't pray to angels."

She immediately regretted saying that, since these in-

timate moments were so seldom. When a handsome, affectionate man was trying to help her, she really
shouldn't defy him.

"Then to God you should pray. You can go no higher,
after all," Tucker quipped. "The Lord, He hears the small-
est of our prayers and answers every one of them.
Sometimes not in the way we want—or in ways we can
see—but He answers. He cares."

Stifling a sigh, Christine shifted away from him. She'd
been soaring on the currents of his kiss, but now he was
waxing religious, like Michael Malloy or Judd Monroe.
It was silly to wish he'd continue along that more romantic path while they were being watched by the very
woman they discussed, so Christine focused on his next
picture.

She stood between Mercy and Miss Vanderbilt. With
their similar upswept hairstyles and figures, this might
well have been a three-generation portrait—had they
been family.

Christine squared her shoulders, as though to separate herself from the other two in the photograph. They
had the academy in common, perhaps, but beyond
that—well, she was in no mood to be like those women
who'd hidden Tucker's letters.

"If you close yourself off to *Maman*, she will not open
to you either, Christine," Tucker was saying. "When we
are young, we believe older people—our parents, our
teachers—they should be the ones to reach out with
their wisdom. And their love."

The way he was so thoughtfully gazing at their portrait, she almost rolled her eyes. Had he intentionally
put these pictures in order, to illustrate the points of this
little lecture?

"But they won't always love us, just because we believe they should," she snapped.

He smiled at her then, so profoundly handsome that she wished he'd stop preaching and kiss her again.

But no. He reached for another print. "You must offer the first olive branch, *ma belle*. A gift of your good intentions."

As though that will happen any time soon! As though Veronique Trudeau would accept anything I'd give her— especially after eavesdropping on this conversation with those powers she has.

But all doubts were forgotten when Lily appeared in the next print, utterly lovely as she threw those little arms around Christine's neck and they touched noses.

Christine held her breath, her throat tight with wanting to cry again. She could feel the wiggling solidity of Lily's warmth, could bask in the sunshine of that little girl's smile and delight in the crisp pink gingham that always smelled of a summer's day.

"Kwis-teen," she murmured in a childlike voice. "Kwazy Kwis-teen."

Tucker's tender expression told her he understood how much she missed that bright-eyed child.

"You have always needed her this way, *oui?*"

"*Oui,*" she replied without thinking. "We found her in a big basket on Mercy's porch last Easter after we'd baptized Solace. I reached for her—she reached for me—"

Christine blinked, not caring that a tear slithered down her cheek. "I loved her that fast. It was like she'd been placed there for me to find."

"It is the best way to fall in love, *non?*" he murmured. "No questions, no doubts. No looking back. If we could only feel so safe with those we don't understand . . . if only someday, you could embrace *Maman* this way— because she needs love, too, *ma joie*."

She could *not* imagine hugging Veronique Trudeau. Not only because the witchy little woman would never allow her so close, but because, well . . . she was odd. And she smelled bad.

"Your mother is a seer," she pointed out. "She'll know I'm trying to sweet-talk her."

Tucker chuckled, a low sound that danced with delight.

"I am a seer, as well—through my camera lens. Sometimes I see people as they are, sometimes as they would like to be," he continued. "I capture the yearning on their faces . . . their secret joys. The goodness inside them."

He flipped to the next print in his box. "When you look at this likeness, of Michael and Mercy, it is goodness you see, *non?* Even if you had never met them, you would trust them. These people, you want to *know* them."

How could he say that after Michael Malloy had hauled her away from Atchison three years ago and Mercy had hidden his letters? While she admired Tucker for seeing the best in people, Christine had a hard time reconciling herself to the way this pair had betrayed her. Even though their letters had made her cry last night.

But yes, it was a stunning picture of a couple so much in love, she had to look away.

"Ah, you hesitate, *ma belle*. It is clear to me how much the Malloys love you and want the best for you, but you cannot see it."

A smile crept across his face as he gazed at Mike and Mercy, who smiled beneath those entwined *M*s carved in the porch pillar.

"We should not forget, *chérie*—you might not be with me now, if you got my letters when I wrote them," he said. "You might have quit school if you'd read those clippings about your mother back then. Or—if you'd followed her trail from Atchison—your younger heart might've been broken beyond repair. Who can say?"

Should she blurt out about her hopes and dreams being shattered—or, more accurately, stuffed into a drawer—those three lonely years she hadn't heard from him? If only he didn't sound like an older, more experienced man trying to teach her something.

"It was your dusty little face that spoke to me when we met," he went on softly. "I knew—just like *Maman*—that you were not sixteen. That you had told other stories to get so far across Kansas alone. But you were doing it because you loved your mama."

Tucker brought the next portrait to the top of his box, holding her gaze. "You wanted her back, of course. You wanted her to be safe from—"

"I wanted answers!" she said harshly. "She left Billy and me behind without a backward glance."

"You wanted to go home, to know your mother's love again," he continued, ignoring her discomfort. "Love, it is what we cannot live without, Christine. We shrivel like flowers that get no rain. Which is why I knew I had to see you again someday. And here you are, ready to be my queen."

The magician beside her had timed this little show so perfectly, she wondered whether Tucker Trudeau was as potent a sorcerer as his mother. The photograph before them, where her plot to run off with this man had lowered her eyelids and given a feline lift to her lips, looked as stunning as the others. If she said so herself.

Tucker laughed softly at her transformation. Young ladies loved to study themselves, and this portrait had inspired the reaction he'd hoped for. With her green eyes alight and a flush returning to her cheeks, Christine Bristol was once again the confident young woman he'd fallen in love with—the girl who would stop at nothing to have her way.

"What do you see when you look at this likeness?" he

whispered. While he had captured her at the best possible moment, Christine herself was the work of art. He
was merely the recorder.

She chuckled, smug again. "I see a woman who has
set aside girlish games to play for keeps," she answered.
"Everyone was dead set against me leaving with you,
and when you took this, I was figuring out a way to defy
them. And you, if I had to."

Ah, it was that defiance that defined her. Tucker savored her response. She had no idea how much like her
mother she truly was.

And perhaps that was the cornerstone he had to
build a very convincing case on, if Christine was to
come through this next leg of their journey with her
emotions intact.

Tucker gazed at her with all the love in his heart—
and all the Cajun flirtation that would keep her smiling,
willing to follow his lead.

"It is that single-mindedness I have always admired,"
he began, slipping his hand around hers. "It is the will to
not only survive, but to triumph against all odds. It
shines on your pretty face again, *chérie*, and I'm happy
to see it."

Her expression softened into a demure loveliness
that teased at his better intentions. Tucker allowed himself one soft, thorough kiss . . . waiting until he felt the
breath of her surrender before he parted her lips for his
tongue, to deepen the contact . . . the commitment.

She sighed languidly when he let her go. He was gazing at her with a playfulness his black hair and beard
accented so brazenly: the look of a man who saw what
he wanted and intended to have it.

"What are you up to, Tucker?" she asked.

He feigned surprise—but only because she'd nailed
him more quickly than he anticipated. He could lead

her on no longer. While Christine was feeling strong again, he had to present his plan.

"While I don't think Sheriff Carson always told the whole story—"

"He didn't. He was nice to me because he wanted information," she stated. Then her brow puckered. "I'm not sure what I might've revealed when I told him about Mama, but I felt like a prize he'd won at the fair when he paraded me back to Mrs. Padgett's."

"Ah, *oui*. So proud of proving those ladies wrong so he could be right." Tucker shifted in the seat to face her more fully. "Christine, *ma belle*, he told me your mama . . . your mama, she has spent some time in Denver."

The rise of her eyebrows told him to go on before she got skittish.

"It was awhile back, *oui*, but—but he heard she was conducting séances there. Doing quite well at it."

The bottom dropped out of her stomach. "Mama? A *medium?*"

He shrugged, hoping she wouldn't misinterpret his idea. "We can go there, if you like. Ask around town—"

"Of course we will!"

"—to see if she is possibly still there," he finished in a rush. "We must be so very careful, you understand. The last time she learned you were looking for her—"

"In Atchison. Right after Michael Malloy hauled me back to Mercy's."

"—she disappeared."

Christine's mouth clapped shut.

"Like the mist before the morning sun," she finished sadly, knowing exactly how exasperated those ladies in North Platte had felt when Mama slipped through their fingers.

She glanced behind them, to where Veronique appeared to be sleeping again. Only the flicker of an eyelid gave her away.

"Can your mother—*will* your mother—tell us if Mama and Wyndham are still there?" she whispered. "Considering what I witnessed when she was with the Gates girl, it seems a simple enough . . . vision for her."

Tucker closed his eyes, wishing this whole thing were simpler. "She could, *oui*. And perhaps, if she realizes the advantages of *trapping* your mama once and for all—"

He smiled apologetically. "*Désolé, cherie*. I make it sound as if your mama is an animal."

"A fox. A sly cat. Obviously a chameleon, too."

Christine stared at the large hand enveloping hers in its warmth, trying to harness her racing thoughts. What if Mama were in Denver? These days, mediums were considered quite respectable, and they often catered to an elite clientele if they were accurate . . . or just very astute about duping those who sat around their table.

What if they could find out where Mama plied her current trade? How difficult would it be to—

"We're going to find her, Tucker. We're going to sit at her séance table and play her own phony game to catch her."

Tucker cleared his throat. He'd thought of this already—just as he'd considered a dozen ways Virgilia Bristol might viciously lash out and hurt her daughter again.

"Christine, *ma belle*," he murmured. "She will recognize you instantly. And we have to figure that Wyndham, he's in on this—probably pulling her strings. Certainly the purse strings."

She widened her eyes at him. "Have you never heard of disguises, dear man?"

"*Et moi?* How will we disguise *me?*" he challenged. "The moment I speak, your mama will recall the photographer from Atchison—and be suspicious because he has come to her."

Tucker leaned closer to drive home his point. This challenge—the chance that they might actually find her mother—was shining like a beacon in Christine's green eyes. In her innocence, she had no idea of the risks they'd be taking.

"It is not so simple, sitting at her table, *ma petite*," he insisted softly. "What if she really has the power? What if she truly summons spirits, like *Maman*?"

She considered this, but then shook her head. "Mama was fascinated by séances before Daddy got shot— would've gone to one had anyone she knew been a medium. But actually contacting Daddy after he was gone?"

Christine smiled with the irony of it. "She would've fainted dead away, had he—or anyone else—spoken to her from the Other Side. She would've had nightmares for weeks, and seen spirits behind every odd little thing that happened."

Her fingers drummed the arm of the seat as she gazed into space. She could do this—there had to be a way. The mysterious nature of séances, with their dim rooms and tilting tables and spectral voices from the Beyond, could play perfectly into this plan if she found out how Mama was working her hocus-pocus. She was certain her mother had parlayed her crafty imagination into becoming a medium—a socially acceptable occupation that would hide her connivery while using it to best advantage. It was only a matter of—

Turning in her seat, Christine looked at Veronique again. This time the old crone was staring back at her, as though telling her she'd be a fool to try such a charade, much less believe she'd succeed at it.

What more incentive did she need? If that witch in

the mismatched clothes thought she'd fail at this venture, then she absolutely had to do it. Even if Tucker and his mother refused to go with her, she would haunt Mama—and she would demand the answers that had driven this mission for the past three years.

"And we must consider this, *chérie*," Tucker's low voice cut into her thoughts. "Even if we cleverly disguise our looks—even if I pretend to be mute—how will your emotions not give you away? One look at your mother and you won't be able to keep quiet. You'll either shake the explanations out of her, or you'll . . . cry like a little girl who has desperately missed her mama."

Christine nearly laughed out loud, but Tucker's eyes stopped her. Luminous aquamarine they were, but their Cajun playfulness had been replaced by a sorrow so profound it took her breath away. It was as though he could see into the future—as his mother supposedly did—and had no words to express the awful consequences of meeting up with Mama.

She looked away. For several moments, there was only the steady rocking of the train and the low, repetitive song of its wheels along the track. The passengers around them disappeared, and she could think of only Tucker, herself, and Mama sitting at a séance table.

"Then what am I to do? How can I *not* go to her?"

Tucker had no answer. He held her small, damp hand between his, aware of how delicate she was . . . fragile, in ways she didn't realize. Christine Bristol had been entrusted to his care by God—regardless of how *Maman* had argued against him seeing her again.

"Think about it. Pray about it," he replied, kissing her temple. "I'm going back to talk with *Maman*."

Chapter Nineteen

When the train jerked to a stop, Christine awoke with a gasp. Had she dozed for an hour or only moments? She recalled Tucker going back to talk with his mother—and saying they'd head to Denver now, to find Mama.

Great clouds of white steam drifted up past her window, obscuring her view. Railway agents began wrestling trunks onto the platform. This station appeared larger and more impressive than most of the ones she'd seen dotting the Nebraska plains, yet it still had a rough-and-tumble frontier newness about it. Denver was not at all the impressive city she'd anticipated.

Tucker slid into the seat beside her, smiling at the sleep-glazed look on her face. "You have napped, *ma belle?* I doubt we'll get much rest on the road into Denver—"

"We're not there yet?"

"*Non, non, non!* This is Cheyenne. Now we must drive the wagon south, along the stagecoach road."

Christine scowled again, cranky from being awak-

ened so suddenly. "You can't tell me a major city like
Denver isn't on the Union Pacific's—"

"Oh, the city fathers and railroad officials, they wanted
that. But General Dodge, when he scouted, decided that
route was too rugged—too many mountains—to meet
his time limit," Tucker explained patiently. Then he
shrugged into his coat. "I must see about unloading the
wagon and Sol. You and *Maman* can stay here where it's
warm until I—"

"But what if the train starts up again? What if—"

Two large hands grasped her arms and Christine lost
herself in the depths of Tucker's smile. Her mood improved immediately.

"I will see to everything, *ma belle*," he murmured. "I
only ask that you wait for me—even if other men, they
make you better offers."

Several passengers were standing up, glancing her
way, as though curious about the young girl who'd been
plotting to meet her mother. Christine smiled sweetly—
because their attention confirmed her allure, and because she wanted to tease Tucker Trudeau a little.

"What better offers could they possibly make?" she
asked, allowing a hint of drawl to sweeten her speech.

"Don't ask! *Maman*, she will help them think of
something."

He kissed her quickly and then made his way down
the aisle to the door at the back of the car. How could
she not adore him? He stood head and shoulders above
the others, and she still felt the tingle of his lips on hers.

When Tucker grinned at her, Christine blew him a
kiss. But once she was sitting alone again, waiting as
other passengers filed past, she reminded herself that
they were detouring from his job for her; that her mission in Denver was much more than a parlor game
played around a dimly lit table. He'd been raising difficult questions earlier to remind her of what she was get-

ting into. If Mama were a practicing medium—and still lived here—they had to be very careful.

She couldn't allow her impatience—or the need to see her mother again—to overrule sensibility. Billy would never forgive her if she met up with Mama and bungled it. Agatha Vanderbilt and Mercy—and Michael, too—would be disappointed if she'd gotten this close to her goal only to fail because her quicksilver emotions won out over strategy.

Never forget that you are much like Mama. Not just in looks, but in smarts. You can fight fire with fire.

The thought made her grin wickedly. And when the gentleman from the seat in front of her stood up and turned around, she was still awash with a heady sense of adventure.

"Excuse me, miss, but I couldn't help overhearing some of your conversation, and—"

Christine's eyes widened. His top hat and stylish overcoat gave him an aura of enterprise, and he carried a cane with a carved knob of gold. When he smiled at her, his waxed handlebar mustache—

Oh my God, it's Richard Wyndham! He's blocking the way out of my seat because he heard us talking about Mama, and he knows Tucker is gone and—

"—I was wondering if you might possibly be talking about Madame Bristeaux, the medium who . . . oh, my word, you could be her—her younger sister!" he said in an awestruck voice. "I didn't mean to eavesdrop, or to upset you, miss—"

Upset me?

Christine began swallowing convulsively, unable to think—much less answer this man. The blood rushed from her head. The seats and people began to spin at a frightening tilt.

Stop this! You can't let him win without even putting up a fight! He hasn't even touched you—yet! What if he—

"—but I'm a close friend of Madame, and I—" He blinked. "Are you all right, miss? May I help you—?"

Without a sound, Tucker's mother had come up the aisle and slipped an arm around her shoulders. Veronique Trudeau only stood as high as this gentleman's chest, yet there was no denying the power that surrounded her like a host of invisible, invincible angels.

"I believe you are disembarking, sir?" she demanded coolly.

He blinked, as though startled or disarmed by those spirits he couldn't see. "Yes—yes, of course," he mumbled.

As he touched his cane to his hat, however, he dropped a small vellum card into Christine's lap.

Mrs. Trudeau watched him with those probing black eyes, releasing Christine after he had left the car. She returned to her seat and gathered her shawl and rosary, as though nothing out of the ordinary had just happened.

What *had* happened?

When Christine could draw breath again, she realized Tucker's mother had not only driven away that stranger with the incredible force of her presence but had spoken perfect English. Had used the word *disembark* as confidently as Miss Vanderbilt would have said it.

She gaped back at Veronique, her pulse still racing. If that had been Richard Wyndham, he might be waiting for them when they stepped off the train, or—

The calling card in her hand bore an angular, mannish script: MADAME V. BRISTEAUX, TRANCE MEDIUM, he'd written, along with a house number on Thirteenth Street. And when she turned it over, the front of the card announced him as Carlton Harte, of the Harte Detective Agency.

If this man were really an investigator—and had called Mama a close friend—what should she anticipate? Her heart was still pounding too fast. At any moment Mr. Harte might return and not be so cordial. After all, he'd heard how she and Tucker were planning to beat Mama at her own game. He might even go straight to her at this address in Denver and—

This is Mama's address. We're nearly there.

The air rushed from her lungs. And as she dared to look up, to see if Mr. Harte was coming back to abduct her, she noticed that three of the men standing up to stretch wore handlebar mustaches. Waxed and curved into perfect circles at the ends. Devilish when they smiled at her, yes, but a sign of impeccable grooming.

It was a popular way to wear a mustache, after all.

Christine deflated in her seat. She closed her eyes, chiding herself for falling prey to her imagination—to the wicked associations she'd had since she first saw that photograph of Mama and Richard Wyndham. If one look—one mustache among dozens—sent her into conniptions, she was in serious trouble. How could she face her wily mother and get the answers she needed if she behaved like such a witless ninny?

"*Chérie?* You are ready to go?"

Now *there* was a question. She opened her eyes, so relieved to see Tucker that she threw her arms open, begging shamelessly for his embrace. His beard rippled with his grin as he leaned down.

"I cannot refuse you, you know," he murmured, his breath tickling her ear. "Your wish is my command, *ma princesse.*"

And *here* was her answer—wrapped in this man's strong, loving arms. When had she ever felt so safe and cherished? Well . . . not since Mama held her, as a child.

Christine kissed his cheek with unabashed enthusiasm, causing those around them to chuckle indul-

gently. Then she handed Tucker the calling card Fate itself had dropped into her lap.

"We must go to Mama—*now*," she murmured urgently. "I can't do this alone, Tucker. I'll love you forever
if you see me through this."

Chapter Twenty

"Why are we in this empty church instead of looking for Mama's house?" Christine whispered impatiently. "We've already lost so much time. And it's cold in here!"

She swatted at the dark lace scarf his mother had insisted she cover her head with, a better sign of reverence than her own stylish hat, supposedly. How it had galled her, that this mismatched witch presumed to tell her what apparel was acceptable. As though enduring endless days with that woman on the rugged, snowy road—being passed by stagecoaches that swept along behind sleek, sure-footed teams—weren't enough of a challenge

"*Maman*, she wants to pray. To renew herself," Tucker replied. He glanced through the dimness of the drafty chapel to where his mother was lighting candles in front of the Blessed Virgin. "More than two months it's been since we left home—left behind the priest she knows, and the comforts of the confessional and the mass."

Christine sighed, more intrigued by the wisps of va-

por that escaped his lips than by his mother's religious
life. But still—they were in Denver at last! Didn't he realize she had to find Mama soon, before that detective
messed everything up?

Her first glimpse of this city, a grid of wintry streets
that bustled with business, had made her heart skip
into triple-time. How would they ever find Mama's
house among all these impressive brick buildings? Odd
enough that her superstitious mother lived on Thirteenth Street; it seemed a worse omen that Tucker was
letting his mother have her way again, when finding
Mama was *her* mission.

Slipping her frigid fingers beneath her arms to warm
them, Christine glanced at the little woman standing
before the statue of the Virgin Mary—apparently in a
trance of adoration. "Why did she ask for something of
Mama's? I wasn't about to let her read the diary, so I
gave her a lace handkerchief instead."

Tucker indulged her with a smile. "She will consecrate it, *chérie. Maman*, she is sorry for the way those
widows in North Platte persecuted you," he said softly.
"She wants to help you. She is searching for your
mother's spirit, which resides in her personal items. She
also needs the blessing of God and the angels she calls
upon."

Maman was kneeling before Mary now, praying with
the handkerchief between her hands.

"Some think her a witch, you know," he went on. "But
Maman, she does nothing without calling upon Our Father and His son, Jesus. This is why we trust she is working divine magic rather than sorcery."

Divine magic.

Christine shivered. All around her, on the walls and
vaulted ceilings, Christ in his crown of thorns reminded
her of the supreme sacrifice He made so long ago. In
stained glass and dark, polished statuary He bore His

cross to Calvary and then died on it, His eyes filled with compassion and sadness.

Their church back home hadn't been filled with such artwork. So many reminders of the way Jesus suffered and died.

Beside her, Tucker went to his knees. She felt like an intruder. She didn't want to eavesdrop on his prayers but didn't know what else to do with herself.

"Would—would it be improper to walk around and look at things?" she whispered.

He smiled kindly. "Of course not. It is a beautiful place, *non?* A fitting place to worship and rest in the Lord."

Christine smiled nervously and stood. If she didn't get moving soon, she'd freeze to the pew—or say something she'd regret—and Tucker would know how out of place she felt among the symbols of his faith.

Silently she sidestepped a larger-than-life statue of Saint Matthew in the corner and ambled along the outer aisle. Above her, ornately carved pictures with Roman numerals at the bottom depicted scenes of Christ on His way to be crucified. STATIONS OF THE CROSS, GIVEN IN LOVING MEMORY OF MURIEL BANCROFT, she read on a plaque at the back of the sanctuary.

An arched doorway opened to a hall where she guessed the priest might have his office. Another statue—Saint Luke—ruled over this corner.

Christine continued along the back wall, tempted to slip out through the door they'd come in a while ago. She could be asking someone how to get to Thirteenth Street. She could use this time to do some sleuthing— and be back before the Trudeaus even missed her.

Here, the light from a magnificent round window of stained glass bathed the back aisle in a pastel rainbow, even though the sun wasn't shining. The air around her seemed to glow, warming her like an invisible cloak.

THE ROSE WINDOW, A GIFT OF THE GILMORE FAMILY TO HONOR MARY, OUR HOLY MOTHER, the brass plaque near the door read.

It caught her eye then, a painting she hadn't seen when they came inside. Mary and Jesus were arrayed in shimmering shades of blue and cream so soft she wanted to reach out and touch them. Their hearts, afire with love for all to see, were portrayed on the outside of their flowing clothes. Their faces were alight with kindness and tender mercy.

Jesus was looking right at her.

Christine knew it was only a painting, but the eyes looked so real. When she'd caught her breath and gotten her imagination under control, something compelled her to look again.

Don't be afraid.

Sucking in her breath, she glanced back at Tucker. But he was still kneeling, with his hands and face resting on the pew in front of him. He hadn't spoken . . . which meant she must be hearing things.

I am with you always. Believe this with all your heart and miracles can happen.

Her throat tightened and a tear rolled down her cheek. Had someone spoken, or was that voice inside her head? It spooked her, standing here in this huge sanctuary lit only by candles, empty except for the three of them. This was absolutely crazy, because she wasn't a Catholic—

You can hear me because you're ready for a higher understanding.

Squeezing her eyes shut, Christine fought the urge to bolt for the door. If it weren't snowing—if she knew how to get back to the hotel—if it weren't horribly impolite to run out of a church—

Be still and know that I am God. Look at me again, my child.

Very slowly, half afraid of what she might see, Christine turned her head. When she opened her eyes, the painting had not changed. Jesus and Mary still smiled invitingly, their faces aglow from their haloes and the fires in their hearts. Their open, extended hands beckoned her.

And yes, Christ was looking at *her*! As though it were the most natural, normal thing in the world for Him to whisper inside her head—because He knew only a very blatant sign of His presence would make her stop and listen.

He smiled as though He knew her by name. Knew her every thought, and loved her anyway.

Of course I know your name! You are my lamb, Christine—named for me.

Her skin prickled with gooseflesh. She swallowed hard and her hand fluttered to her throat. This was divine magic, and it was happening to *her*.

Christine suddenly realized the meaning of *holy*; suddenly understood the phrase *hallowed be Thy name*, which she'd prayed since she was a child. She'd been mimicking Mama as she learned the Lord's Prayer, and after that she'd said the words because everyone around her was. Divine magic now made these ideas real. As real and alive as the heart pounding faster in her chest.

But if divine magic hadn't saved the perfect Son of God from those thorns and the nails of the crucifixion, why did she think *she* had the slightest chance?

It was a daunting question. One that hadn't occurred to her as she'd sat in the pew beside Mama, whispering about what the other women wore—or on the benches in Mercy's yard, wishing she were someplace else as the circuit rider droned on. She'd never thought about the meaning of her faith, or her salvation, because church had been mostly a social gathering. Something families did on Sundays.

She turned to see if Veronique was casting a spell on her.

But Tucker's mother was still on her knees, draped in a black lace veil before the rows of flickering candles at Mary's feet.

Something odd was going on here. Voices. Paintings come to life. Profound thoughts about what Christ and His cross had to do with *her*. Yet it was something that moved her to silent tears she didn't wipe away. And as she gazed fixedly at the tiny flames dancing in the sanctuary's draft, the Virgin Mary seemed to gather the glow of all those candles and magnify them into a single, focused beam.

Christine suddenly saw the light: She had always gone to church, but she'd never really gone to God.

He'd remained a distant patriarch, veiled in mystery, the One she prayed to when she needed something or wanted things to go her way. Even when attending services with the girls at Miss Vanderbilt's academy, she'd remained removed from the realities of religious faith. Church was a place she went with her friends, like the library or the orphanage, and then went away from.

Here in this dusky, silent sanctuary, mystical with incense and decorated with sacred paintings, Christine stood in awe of all she'd never noticed.

It's all right. You're not alone. And I love you anyway.

She pivoted, thinking she'd catch the trick of the picture—an optical illusion that talked in a calming male voice in her mind. But those serene, smiling faces hadn't changed.

"All right, then," she whispered, afraid to respond—but afraid not to. "Help me catch Mama! Help me bring her home. How am I supposed to do that?"

Silence. The light from the rose window dimmed, so the colors paled around her.

"I asked you a question," she murmured more insistently. "Don't start talking to me and then just stop. It's terribly rude. Not to mention . . . confusing."

Christine shuddered, trying not to cry. Here she was, finally realizing why Judd Monroe and Mercy and Michael Malloy so staunchly believed in the Scriptures, teachings she'd given mere lip service to. Yet when she called upon the Lord for help with the most important mission of her life, He didn't answer!

I always answer prayers. Maybe not the way you expect me to.

"What sort of a—"

"Christine? You are ready to go, *chérie?*"

Flushing furiously, she turned to see Tucker and his mother standing in the aisle between the last two pews, waiting for her. Had they heard her conversation with Christ? Did they think she was crazy—or disrespectful—to carry on this way with the Savior?

More importantly, had they heard His voice? Did she dare ask?

Christine blinked, aware that her face felt wet. Wearing clothes creased from being crammed in her valise, with her hair in a knot at her nape because it needed washing, she'd never felt more unpresentable for being seen in church—

Being seen. It seemed a pretty shallow reason for showing up on Sundays—

Showing up or showing off?

That was her own voice, but it was as maddening to argue with her conscience as to be caught talking to a painting. Tucker was smiling kindly, like the Christ who had said He'd always be with her. But Veronique must be watching her with those beady, bright eyes, ready to write her off.

Christine fidgeted. Tucker's mother was just a few feet away, but with that lace veil draped around her head and face, it was impossible to know what Veronique was looking at. Or what her facial expressions said. As Tucker helped his mother with her bulky old coat, Christine also realized that his *maman* looked like a different woman in a plain gray skirt and ivory blouse.

Why, she looks like a normal, everyday—

It struck her then, like a bolt from the blue—*or an answered prayer*—how they could approach Mama at her séance table without being detected. Yes, it would take practice and mental preparation for her to pull it off—but hadn't Billy always yammered about what an actress she was?

And it would require this arrogant Cajun healer to speak the same perfect, unaccented English she'd used to get rid of Carlton Harte. No guarantees on that front if Veronique decided this idea wasn't to her liking.

But it was a plan. It would at least get them into the address on the detective's card, to see Madame Bristeaux, the trance medium.

Because if Mama was pretending to be someone she wasn't, why couldn't they?

Chapter Twenty-one

"Again! What is your name, and why do you want this sitting?"

Christine bit back a retort, her gaze flitting around the hotel room where she, Tucker, and Veronique were preparing to confront Mama. Finally this witchy woman was speaking to her in English, but she felt like a prisoner at an inquisition.

"I am Emma Clark, and you are my mother, Rachel," she recited. "We want Madame Bristeaux to contact my recently deceased—"

"Say it like you mean it! I don't believe you are Emma Clark."

"Well, that's too damn bad! I'm sick and tired of making up this story—"

"Which is why she'll see right through your flimsy disguise," Veronique snapped. "I can't help you if you don't follow through on *your* plan."

Christine returned her glare. "Then why help me at all? I can go there by myself—"

"Christine, *chérie*—and *Maman*," Tucker crooned. He

came to stand beside the table where they were facing off, and placed placating hands on their shoulders.

"We must be calm and show patience," he reminded them. "Now that we have found your mother, *ma princesse*, it would be a shame to spoil your big moment with a mistake. *Maman* is helping you because she knows how you have missed your—"

"I am helping so this whole ridiculous mother hunt will end," Veronique said. "The sooner you are with her again, the sooner you are out of my life."

"*Maman,* You don't mean—"

"Oh, yes, she does!" Christine blurted out. "She's never liked me—has never seen my side of this story. And she never will."

"Because you don't believe in *me*," the little Gypsy shot back. "If you had trusted me with your mother's diary, I would know so much more. But no! You show no faith in my God-given gifts as a seer. You think of me as an old witch, when your mother is the deceiver here. So why should I cooperate?"

Christine's mouth fell open. Once again Veronique Trudeau had been poking around in her private thoughts, and she was tired of it.

"If you can see so much, why wasn't her handkerchief enough?" Christine demanded. "Do you think I like it that my mother has behaved so badly? Why would I want anyone else reading her diary?"

"I've told you, young lady, that merely holding her book will bring me the visions I need to—"

"Why does that sound even phonier than those Bibles Mama sold to the ladies in North Platte?"

Even as she said it, Christine knew she'd gone too far. Tucker's mother, exasperating when she spoke Cajun French and stared at her with those penetrating eyes, now looked livid enough to slap her out of her chair.

"I—I'm sorry," she said, turning away. "I didn't sleep at

all last night. Do you know how hard this is—preparing to see Mama after three years, knowing the awful things she's done? Anyone would be distracted. And agitated. And very, very angry."

"So your talk with Jesus yesterday changed nothing?" Veronique demanded with a haughty rise of her eyebrows. "If He assured you of His help, and you have already forgotten the relief His promises brought you, why should I try? Oh, ye of little faith."

"Enough!" Tucker cried. "You are two cats scratching out each other's eyes. You cannot show up at her house this way."

His expression darkened like an oncoming storm. If Tucker had reached the end of his patience, saint that he was, Christine felt she should heed his warning.

She would've preferred to meet Mama alone—to suffer the humiliation and get answers she wanted no one else to hear—but Mama would probably recognize her and run. Far better to beat Madame Bristeaux at her own deception when she had help from this man who loved her. If only he would silence his hateful old mother. Or just make her stay behind.

But that wasn't going to happen. And neither would tonight's séance, if they didn't settle themselves.

Christine drew a deep breath and sat taller, as Miss Vanderbilt had taught her. A true lady rose above the sticks and stones others threw; a true Christian turned the other cheek, suffering for the higher good of all. They had one chance to make her dream a reality. It could not be *her* fault if the evening fell to pieces.

"Does it strike you as odd that Mr. Harte—supposedly a close friend of Madame Bristeaux—arranged this sitting for us?" she ventured.

That was another of Miss Vanderbilt's rules for navigating rough conversational waters: When the going gets rough, change the subject.

"After all, he overheard parts of our conversation on the train, about why we wanted to see her," she added. "And how we intend to trap her."

Tucker considered this, tapping his chin with his fingertips.

"Your meeting him, it felt too—providential to pass up," he replied in a low voice. "Mediums, they do not invite just anyone to their séances. Mr. Harte was the connection we needed—and he didn't have to drop that card in your lap."

"His motivations are as dubious as our own," Veronique confirmed, "but he has his reasons—as I do—for helping you, Miss Bristol. All the more incentive to have your story in order if we have to outwit two opponents."

Christine kept her sigh to herself. Why did so many things seem ready to go wrong tonight? If the seer seated across from her knew so much, why didn't she act upon it?

Why did it have to be so difficult to see her own mother?

"All right, let's try this again," she murmured. "My name is Emma Clark, and you're my mother, Rachel. We're here to contact my beloved father—your husband—Owen Clark, who died last month of . . ."

Veronique rapped sharply with the brass door knocker. Then she crossed herself, whispering, "Saint Michael, protect us from all evil . . . Saint Gabriel, give us the right words . . . Mary, Blessed Mother, wrap your grace around us like a cloak. . . ."

The coppery tang of fear filled Christine's mouth. Beneath the drabbest black dress, borrowed from Tucker's mother, her knees knocked. The mourning veil of black lace she'd sewn to an old hat made it very difficult to see. She'd tripped coming up the stairs to this imposing house, situated in a neighborhood noted for its mine owners and millionaires. Would her disguise be her undoing, rather than a way to enter Mama's home unrecognized?

But here they were—on the doorstep at last! Besides being the answer to her prayers and the fulfillment of her mission, this was her chance to outfox Mama. Her chance for answers after three years of dealing with a betrayal of the basest sort.

Yes, this little scheme was underhanded, but they all agreed Virgilia Bristol wouldn't see Christine any other way. Mama's activities suggested she wanted no reminders of the family she'd abandoned.

Light footsteps on the vestibule floor made her stiffen. The cold night air stung her lungs. As though to keep her from running off, Veronique slipped an arm around her shoulders. Even through their two heavy veils, Christine could read those dark, shining eyes: *It will be your fault if she suspects our ruse and sends us away.*

Christine glanced across the street, where Tucker awaited them in a parked carriage. As the door opened, she braced herself, pressing her lips into a tight line to keep from crying out.

Oh God, it was Mama.

She wore a simple dress of deep green silk that set off her elegant figure and complemented her auburn hair. Her smile looked so warm as she welcomed them inside.

"You must be the Clarks," she said, with just a hint of a French accent. "I'm so happy you could come this evening. We've been waiting for you."

Christine stifled a sob—which Veronique covered by pulling her closer.

"We thank you so much for allowing us a place at your table," Tucker's mother replied just as graciously. "Emma has been inconsolable since her daddy died."

How much of this could she stand? Why had she thought it would be so easy to foil her mother—or to pass herself off as someone this woman had never met? Mama looked downright radiant with her success as a trance medium. Much more self-assured than she'd been back home.

Don't think about home, her whirling thoughts warned. *Watch Mama for cues, so you won't make stupid mistakes!*

"I understand your husband passed just recently, Mrs.—"

"Yes, my dear Owen was out tending our horses—he raised the finest registered Arabians in Colorado—" Veronique cut in with a quiver in her voice. "That is, until rustlers rode in one night and shot him down, along with Emma's twin brother. Poor dear saw the whole thing. She's hardly said three words or eaten a meal since."

As Tucker's mother had predicted, Mama would make pleasant conversation to gain information, which would render her messages from the Beyond more accurate and believable. They had concocted a story that closely resembled the circumstances of Mrs. Bristol's husband's murder, so they could watch her reaction. They hoped to keep her off-balance.

The face Christine knew so well—the face that looked even lovelier and livelier than she remembered—tightened with the details of Daddy's own death.

"I—I'm so sorry for your loss," she murmured, blinking rapidly.

Was she faking? Or had Veronique's first arrow struck its mark?

Not that it mattered, because when Mama squeezed her hand, Christine nearly fainted. The blood left her head and she drew a desperate breath, thankful the lace veil hid her stricken expression.

Straighten that spine! Hold your head up and forge forward! Miss Vanderbilt encouraged in her mind.

This is what you've lived for, Christine, came Mercy Malloy's softer voice. *I'm so proud of you for not giving up on your mother—for having the gumption to follow through on your dreams.*

What she wouldn't give to have those two women with her now. Somehow Christine found the strength to nod. She then withdrew her hand and knew to keep her mouth shut. They had agreed to let Mama do most of the talking—to let "grief" be their cover, if Christine lost her nerve.

Who could've guessed it would be this difficult?

"Well! Shall we join the others in the parlor?" Mama asked lightly.

She gestured toward a room off the vestibule, where the only light was a single candle. "As you may—or may not—know, the spirits of our dearly departed prefer a setting where everyone at the table believes in them, and feels comfortable inviting them to manifest themselves."

She looked at them pointedly, as though penetrating their veils with her gaze. "If either of you ladies has doubts about contacting those on the Other Side—or if you don't believe I, through my spirit guide, am truly able to summon them—we won't waste your time. And we won't interfere with the wishes of others who've come here tonight."

There it was: Veronique had told her that for most sitters, believing was seeing. Mediums removed any naysayers before the séance started.

"Oh, it was Emma's idea to come," Mrs. Trudeau assured Mama. "She was the apple of her daddy's eye, and she *so* hopes he's happy now. Living beyond the pain of his sudden, agonizing death—so she can live again, too."

Christine nodded, making her veil flutter with her eager consent.

"Very well, then," Mama said. "Let's meet the others
and begin."

In the parlor sat a round table draped in a dark cloth,
with a prismed candle lamp flickering in its center. Five
faces turned their way with expectant smiles as
Madame Bristeaux gestured toward the two empty seats
nearest the door.

"This is Mrs. Clark and her daughter, Emma, who
wish to contact their husband and father, Owen," she
said as she took the empty chair across from them.
"Mr. and Mrs. Grantham wish to contact their little
boy, Lewis. Justine and Anna Merritt are regulars at
my table, as they ask advice of their dear departed
mother—and I believe you already know Carlton
Harte, my associate. Shall we begin by joining hands in
a moment of silence, to invoke the presence of those
we love?"

What was Carlton Harte doing here? And if he was
Mama's associate, what had happened to Richard Wyndham?

Christine grasped Veronique's bony hand on her left
and the very damp, fleshy one of Anna Merritt on her
right. Her pulse pounded. They hadn't anticipated the
detective's presence. In the unnerving silence that felt
like forever, she wondered whether the man she'd met
on the train had led them into a trap. He had to know
they were trying to catch Mama—had to realize the
medium was her mother.

Had he told Mama why they were coming? And why,
after arriving in Denver ahead of them on the stagecoach, had he gone to the trouble of locating them at
the hotel?

Swallowing hard, she tried to concentrate. In this
darkened room, her black lace veil made it difficult to

discern the finer points of facial expressions. She wished she'd devised a different disguise.

"I will now contact Lewis through my spirit guide, William Henry," Mama's low voice broke the silence. "I will remind you to keep your hands clasped on the table at all times, so the circle of welcoming love remains unbroken for the Granthams."

William Henry? That's Billy's name!

Christine quickly bowed her head again, disguising her dismay. As she peered through her veil at the others, however, they seemed familiar with Madame Bristeaux's ritual and her spirit guide—the unseen guest who served as a medium's liaison with those on the Other Side.

Across the table, Mama closed her eyes and lifted her face toward Heaven. She looked so lovely by the light of the lamp, Christine almost cried. Moments later her head dropped gracefully forward until her chin rested on her chest—the classic pose of entering a trance.

Veronique had discussed what to expect—and she herself had read and heard enough to assume there might be disembodied voices and floating objects. Perhaps even table tipping and tapping in response to yes-or-no questions.

Maybe this was where Richard came in. Phony mediums had an accomplice pulling strings and doing things in the darkness to cause such otherworldly effects. Sometimes sitters came to detect such fakery—or marvel at the lack of it—as much as to receive word from their departed loved ones.

"William Henry, are you here?" Mama asked in a faraway voice.

The heavy table rapped twice in response, rising amazingly high before landing on the floor each time. Everyone leaned forward in anticipation, clasping hands more urgently.

Christine swallowed hard, hoping she could handle whatever happened next.

"William Henry," Mama went on in a detached tone, "we would have you contact the spirit of our dear Lewis Grantham now. The poor boy drowned last month, and his parents wish to hear how he's doing."

Quiet crying, probably Mrs. Grantham's, caused a ripple of grip-tightening. And then Christine swore she smelled . . . fresh, warm cinnamon rolls. Indeed, the room became cozier, as though someone had just opened the oven to take them out!

"Maaaamaaaa? Paaaapaaaaa?" came a high, young voice.

"Lewis, thank God—"

"Oh, darling, it's you!" the Granthams cried in a heartrending duet.

Christine wanted to scream. That was Billy's voice! Just as she remembered it, from when he was a frightened little child crying in the nursery.

Why hadn't she accepted her brother's offer to bring her west? Her nerves were stretched to the snapping point and she was afraid to breathe—but her *brother!* Billy would've called this mockery to a halt by unmasking himself. To call Mama's bluff.

Sheer force of will made her open her eyes to watch as the eerie conversation continued between the Granthams and the supposed ghost of their son. Young Lewis was saying, yes, he was being a good boy, and in Heaven there were cinnamon rolls for breakfast every day. Mama's head remained bowed. Her mouth hung slightly ajar, but her lips didn't move.

Beside her, Carlton Harte penetrated the darkness with his gaze. And he was watching *her*. Very closely.

Veronique tapped three times with her thumb against Christine's wrist—the signal for her to settle down and concentrate.

Now Lewis Grantham's voice sounded like Billy when he was whining about Wesley making fun of him. With difficulty, Christine squared her shoulders and took a deep breath.

She had to remain calm; had to remember the details of their story for when their turn came—in case Owen Clark spoke directly to his dear daughter Emma. They'd chosen the names of Mercy Malloy's neighbors so Christine would remember them more easily—and because Mama wouldn't recognize anyone's name except Daddy's. And they'd agreed that Veronique would do the talking, as she herself was supposed to be mute with grief.

Still, she wished Billy were here. Their made-up story and veils would be unnecessary if he'd come along, because Madame Bristeaux wouldn't have bolted at the sight of her best boy. Mama would've gone soft like a cream pie and surrendered to them without a fuss.

Christine blinked. While she'd been lost in thought, Madame Bristeaux had contacted the Merritt sisters' mother, and the woman beside her was nearly squeezing her hand off.

"Mother! Mother, thank you so much for coming to us tonight!" Justine was gushing.

"It's such a comfort, knowing you're all right," Anna added with a hitch in her voice. She had a death grip on Christine's hand, and her ample bosom was quivering. "We're doing our best to disburse your bequests as you wished, Mother, but we're wondering about your gift to the church. Reverend Wilkes has suggested several uses for it, but we can't decide—"

From somewhere behind Mama came sonorous chords, which modulated into the melody for "Amazing Grace." Everyone at the table gasped with delight at this manifestation, and Justine seemed beside herself.

"The organ fund! Of course, Mother!" she cried.

As the two sisters rhapsodized over the hymn and this

answer from Above, Christine rolled her eyes. She knew an accordion when she heard one! Her guess was that someone was playing it in the large cabinet against the far wall. Richard Wyndham, perhaps?

Carlton's cough brought her back to the present. Unless Mama was going to contact someone for Mr. Harte, their turn was next.

She reminded herself of the plan they'd gone over a dozen times. She was to let Veronique do the talking; she was to refrain from challenging anything Mama said, or from baiting her with mannerisms and reminders of their life in Missouri. When the séance ended, they would linger after the others left to express their gratitude—so she could grasp Mama by one hand while Veronique grabbed the other. Then she could reveal herself! Mama would be her captive audience!

But how much could the detective see through her veil? His presence put a cramp in their plan. They'd have to be ready for anything—for she still didn't know why Madame Bristeaux's "associate" was here. If things went wrong—if it seemed they would be the captives—Christine was to gag as though she needed to vomit, and they would leave immediately.

As agitated as she felt, while everyone else sang along with that damned accordion music, vomiting might be the most authentic thing she did this evening. When the hymn ended she inhaled deeply, preparing herself.

The room went silent. Mama, her eyes closed and her porcelain complexion aglow in the lamp's light, raised her face again.

Christine noticed the sparkle of earrings—diamonds, perhaps?—beneath her stylishly arranged auburn hair. While genuine mediums didn't charge their sitters money, Mama had received some very generous gifts from either her grateful guests or whichever man was looking after her these days. This palatial home was a testament to her success.

I could wear my hair that way. Her thoughts strayed. *And maybe someday those earrings will be mine . . . Mama's reward for the way I've come after her, and never forgotten her. . . .*

"William Henry, are you still with us?" Mama asked in that wraithlike voice. "Mrs. Clark and young Emma would like to speak with Owen, please."

The candle went out.

Everyone gasped, grabbing hands in the darkness with fearful faces—everyone except Harte, who gazed sharply around the table and then up toward the ceiling. Not a breath of air stirred, so how had the flame inside the glass globe been extinguished?

"Madame Bristeaux?" he asked in a controlled voice. "Do you wish me to light the candle again?"

Mama's eyes flew open. A ripple of her surprise went through the circle of hands around the table.

"No," she finally whispered, sounding dazed and disoriented. "I sense the presence of an uninvited spirit."

All present looked from one neighbor to the other. The room grew tense.

Christine held fast to the hands on either side of her. Was it growing colder, or was her imagination playing tricks? The parlor had stayed quite cozy after the Lewis boy and his cinnamon rolls departed, yet now the velvet draperies at the two tall windows were rippling—as though the windows behind them had been opened.

But that was nonsense. No one in the room had moved, and it was snowy outside.

On her left, Veronique began to sway slightly and murmur in Latin. Christine jabbed her hand three times with her thumb—this was no time to summon saints or angels! At least not until they saw whether Mama could summon the ghost of Owen Clark. This was not a part of their plan.

But the veiled woman beside her moaned loudly enough that everyone heard her. The temperature had dropped with the cold hiss of the wind coming in behind the curtains. The table began to vibrate, until the prisms dangling on the lamp whispered ominously—just as the guests were doing.

Suddenly Mama stood up.

"For your own safety, I must ask you all to leave," she announced, dropping the hands she held. "William Henry has departed, and somehow a powerful spirit beyond my control has taken his place."

The Granthams shoved their chairs back, as did the Merritt sisters, who looked frightened for their lives. Carlton Harte stood up beside Mama, his arm slipping protectively around her waist as he glanced around the shadowy room.

"Can you tell it to go away?" he asked her quietly.

Christine was having none of it. For three years she'd endured the disgrace of being abandoned—of living as Mercy Malloy's charity case—of learning firsthand of her mother's connivery. Christine refused to leave until she got the answers she'd come for. She sprang from her chair so fast it tipped over backward, landing with a loud *whack* against the floor.

"I didn't get my turn!" she protested, all her pretenses fleeing in the emotion of the moment. "We came here to talk with Daddy—to be sure he was out of pain! To ask if he recognized the man who shot him! To ask him what to do, now that Leland Massena has foreclosed on the horse farm! Dammit, Mama, you *will* talk to me!"

The room felt suddenly airless, even with the wind still whistling at the windows. She'd made a grave mistake, but there was no going back. She yanked off the hat with its annoying lace veil and faced her mother squarely from across the table.

Veronique Trudeau sat like a statue in her chair. The other guests froze in place near the doorway, staring first at her and then across the table at the medium who so closely resembled her.

By the light drifting in from the vestibule, Christine noted a flicker of Mr. Harte's waxed mustache—like the whiskers of a cat following a mouse. His eyes narrowed. He stood fast beside Mama.

And Mama . . . Mama's pale, perfect face had lost its glow. She gripped the edge of the table, her eyes wide with amazement—or was it fear? Twice she opened her mouth to speak, but nothing came out.

"It's been three years since you abandoned us at the stage station, Mama," Christine whispered. Every syllable tore at her throat; every vowel and consonant cost her. "I've come a long way to find out why. If you won't answer to me, can't I at least take an explanation back to Billy?"

A little moan escaped Mrs. Grantham. The Merritt sisters clasped each other's hands, staring raptly.

"I'm sorry for your . . . inconvenience," the medium replied in that same detached voice of moments before. "But you've mistaken me for someone else."

"No!" Christine slapped the table, leaning on it for support. "Even in the darkness, you know it's me, Mama. Everyone in this room can see—"

"Carlton, will you please escort our guests to the door? The séance is over."

For a moment, everyone seemed suspended in time and space. Mr. Harte looked ready to comment, while Anna, Justine, and the Granthams kept staring in shocked silence, not wanting to miss this unexpected drama. Christine was shaking so hard she couldn't breathe, but by God she would not be dismissed like some inconsequential—

Footsteps crossed the room behind the parlor and went quickly down some stairs. The back door slammed.

Mama blinked and pivoted, walking quickly toward where this distraction had come from. Carlton followed close behind her.

"Madame Bristeaux, in the interest of your reputation, I believe you should—"

"I don't care what you believe!"

Christine let out the breath that burned her lungs. It came out as a sob when Mama disappeared into the next room with a swish of her fine skirts.

Then Veronique was beside her, steering her out of the dark parlor.

"We must leave," she announced with quiet urgency. "There are indeed some powerful spirits afoot in this place, and a nasty storm is blowing in. You'd all best go home and forget what took place here tonight."

Chapter Twenty-two

"You had to jump in with both feet—and that mouth!—and ruin it! We nearly had her—"

"*Me?*" Christine retorted, glaring at Mrs. Trudeau, who paced her hotel room. "If you hadn't made the light go out—"

"I had nothing to do with that."

Her mouth fell open. "Are you saying Mama *did*?"

"*Maman*, Christine, *s'il vous plaît*," Tucker said soothingly, although his patience was unraveling. "It's late, and the other hotel guests, if they complain, we could be put out in this snowstorm, *non?*"

It *was* late, and she wanted to fall into her bed and sleep like the dead. But no, Veronique kept picking at her like a scab. As though she'd *wanted* the séance to go wrong. As though she'd gone there to be turned away by her own mother.

Her challenge was giving Tucker's mother something to think about, however. Clad in her mismatched clothing, Veronique was once again the witchy woman who wasn't happy unless she made everyone else miserable.

She plucked Mama's embroidered handkerchief from her pocket to study it.

"Your mother conducts one of the most convincing séances I've ever attended," she mused aloud. "She's a mistress of misdirection, which is why her accomplice—Mr. Wyndham, I suspect—could slip out from under the table he'd been tipping for the Granthams to play that hymn for the sisters. No doubt he keeps a number of things besides an accordion in that cabinet, to create such dazzling effects."

Christine crossed her arms tightly. It irritated her that Veronique had such rational answers, for Mama's performance fascinated her. "But how could anyone have gotten in? We were looking right at that cabinet the whole time."

"It could have an open back, and there's probably a trap door in the wall behind it," the seer explained. "While we were focused on your mother's face and smelling those cinnamon rolls, her helper could have crawled to that other room in the darkness. Then he ran out the back door when he heard you challenging her."

Christine bristled, determined not to let mere logic diminish what had happened in that mysterious room.

But Veronique turned, her expression pensive now. "I haven't figured out Mr. Harte's motives for being there. Very odd, wouldn't you say?"

How could this woman look like a shiftless Gypsy and speak with the eloquence of an orator? What was her secret—*her* motive—for analyzing all they'd seen this evening? Why was Veronique finally asking for her opinions after so many weeks of acting as if she wasn't even there?

Christine slumped with exhaustion. Too many things had gone on tonight, and she was too confused to deal with them. Humiliated . . . and so very disappointed.

But that would have to wait for later, too, for she refused to break down while this Gypsy was watching.

"Maybe you should go to your room now, Tucker," she murmured, hoping his mother would leave with him. "It's been a very long day, and I have a lot to think about."

His expression softened. Ignoring his mother's raised eyebrow—for she despised having her questions ignored—he sat on the edge of the bed beside Christine. The dark dress she'd borrowed from *Maman* made her look older and unusually pale, although her dejection came from what he had *not* heard about the séance.

A dozen times he'd almost entered that house, to be sure things were proceeding safely for this brave young lady. But his intrusion would've ended the evening even sooner.

He brushed a strand of auburn hair away from her face. "What happened tonight, *chérie?*" he whispered. "After waiting so long to see your mama, what did you find out?"

Pain stabbed her heart like jagged glass. But Veronique's hard gaze made her sit ramrod straight when she wanted to melt into Tucker's embrace.

"Everything—and nothing," she replied. "My mother refused to see me. She sent us all away, even though everyone knew damn well who I was."

He held her close, shutting his eyes against such agony. Mon Dieu, *how could that woman refuse to— how can this poor girl bear such rejection?*

"*Si désolé* . . . so sorry, my love," he murmured. Words couldn't repair the damage her heartless mother had done.

Christine sank against his warm, solid body. "Why wouldn't Mama talk to me?" she asked in a childlike voice. "She acted like she didn't have a daughter—like she wished I'd never been born!"

Tucker's empathy had cracked the wall of pride and self-preservation she'd built around herself. A hic turned into a cough, which could no longer camouflage her agony.

"Why doesn't Mama love me anymore, Tucker?" she whispered as the tears streamed down her cheeks. "What did I do to deserve this?"

Pulling her into his lap, Tucker hugged her against his shoulder while he searched for answers. This wasn't the right time to profess his deepest feelings for her. That was supposed to happen when there was moonlight and a joyful anticipation in the air—when he could kiss her without *Maman* watching.

"But *I* love you, Christine," he whispered anyway.

Cradling her in his lap, he adored the childlike way her arms slipped around his neck. "My love for you is not the same as your mother's—and I know how badly you need that, *chérie*. But it's enough love to see you through this, *ma belle*. Enough love to last for all your life."

She raised her head, sniffling. "H-how do I know you're not just saying—"

"As *Maman* is my witness," he said, eyeing the woman who watched them with her arms crossed tight, "I fell for you, *ma petite*, when you first came into my shop, and I have never recovered. Love at first sight, it was. And it has only grown stronger over time—no matter how badly my mother would like to change that."

There, he'd stated his case before both women, despite how they would probably fight about it.

Christine's eyes widened, green and lovely even when filled with tears—even more beautiful than usual, for she was usually too proud to show her face in such vulnerable moments. Her watery smile reminded him of the sun peaking from behind a dark cloud, with the inverted curve of a rainbow.

"You loved me even though you knew I was . . . fibbing about my age?"

"You were the bravest, dearest, strongest girl I'd ever met," Tucker said, "and you still are, *ma princesse.* Few daughters would follow their mothers this far, knowing what you know."

"We can't tell Billy what Mama's done," she cautioned. "He'll be crushed."

Tucker smiled. Even now, in her hour of greatest heartbreak, she was watching out for her younger brother. Would things be different had Billy come along? Mothers had stronger feelings for sons, no matter how much their daughters pleased them.

"Maybe matters of faith don't seem to fit right now," Tucker offered in a thoughtful voice, "but Jesus, He had the same problem—a family who didn't believe in Him as the Messiah, or believe He had any special power. His own brothers did not stand up for Him, even when He was falsely accused. Condemned by Pilate to die."

"Ah, but his mother Mary was at His side on His most difficult days," Veronique pointed out. "Mothers love that way."

She was still across the room, still aloof, yet *Maman* hadn't retaliated when he'd professed his love for Christine. Considering how the séance had ricocheted like a bad bullet, she was behaving with great restraint.

"She stood with Him at Calvary, despite the mockery of the crowd and the agony of seeing her perfect son— God's gift to the world—hanging on the cross, with nails hammered through His hands," she went on. "I—I cannot imagine her pain."

The sorrow in Veronique's voice made Christine peer over Tucker's shoulder. His mother wiped a spot in the frosted window, to check the snowstorm. When she turned, compassion had softened those piercing eyes.

"Your mother is running scared, Christine," she said. "When you revealed yourself tonight, I saw delight and pride on her face. For a moment, she wanted to rush over and hug you—but then she hid behind her lies."

"But why—"

"Because something else is going on. Something your presence has threatened."

Veronique sighed tiredly. A sad smile overtook her face. "I must give you credit, Christine, for handling the evening with more fortitude than I expected. Myself, I would have leapt across the table and grabbed that woman around the neck—or given myself away much faster than you did."

Christine blinked. It was a major victory to hear Veronique Trudeau's admission, but why now?

"If you're a seer, why didn't you predict all this?" she blurted out. "If you're a healer, why can't you fix the wounds Mama inflicted?"

The room grew silent, except for the wind that howled like a pack of phantom wolves outside.

Impatience flickered in those all-seeing eyes. Yet—even though her presence threatened Veronique, as well—Tucker's mother didn't turn away.

"We must believe God was showing us other forces at work, and that He's in control of them," she said in a low voice.

Gone was the Cajun cadence and the arrogance that had excluded her from the seer's mystical world before now. "You are disappointed, yes. But when that candle went out, it might've been an answered prayer—God's way of telling us, perhaps through His angels, that the situation was moving beyond our control."

"Divine magic," Christine whispered. It was the same

goose-bumpy sort of revelation she'd had with that painting of Jesus and Mary. It sounded right.

Had they really reached an agreement? A truce? Christine was too tired to put all the pieces of this puzzle together, but a milestone had been reached. Better to let things settle on this positive note and get some rest.

"Thank you for going with me, Veronique," she whispered. "I couldn't have done it without you."

"What does the Lord require of you, Christine?"

She shifted, realizing this was a dream yet feeling fully awake. That voice was unmistakably Judd Monroe's, and as Mercy's first husband spoke to her, she saw the dark log walls of the house he'd built—the home she'd despised, even though she'd yearned for the approval of the man who had taken in her and Billy. He looked vital and alive, his raven hair framing a face bronzed by hard work in the sun, and—excited as she was to see him again—he wouldn't let her wiggle out of a tough spot *now,* either.

Judd pointed to Mercy's embroidered sampler on the parlor wall. *"I'm not asking you to recite a Bible verse, Miss Bristol. I'm telling you to live it,"* he insisted.

It wasn't real, yet it was. Judd Monroe was saying hello from Heaven in a way she didn't dare ignore. Her body tensed, but she knew better than to wake herself before he'd shared his entire message. In life—and in his afterlife—this man resonated with purpose. He always made her reach farther and aim higher.

"To do justly, to love mercy, to walk humbly with your God," she replied with the impatience of the girl she'd been then. *"I have always wanted justice, or I wouldn't have chased after Mama—"*

"Whose justice? Yours? Do you consider that walking humbly?"

She swallowed her retort. Judd had the damnedest way of nailing her to her own pathetic, self-serving cross.

"*Consider carefully what your mother lost when those Border Ruffians shot your father and made off with your brother. Not just a husband and a son, but her whole way of life. 'Ripe and ready to fall'—remember that phrase?*"

She nodded, but she didn't like his sermon much.

Judd's face softened, achingly handsome in the light from the little window in that log parlor. "*Maybe she fell farther than she figured on, honey. Maybe she needs justice, and your mercy, more than you will ever know. And maybe she's too afraid—too ashamed—to ask you for it.*"

What could she say to that? She'd never looked beyond the flirtatious delight in Mama's diary entries. Or how happy she'd looked with her arms around Richard Wyndham in that picture Tucker had taken. Judd's suggestion echoed with what Veronique had hinted at. . . .

"*The Lord has been with you on this mission since your mother left you, Christine. He's had His reasons for bringing you this far. If you turn away from Him—from her—now, will you be able to live with your doubts and fears?*"

Tears sprang to her eyes. She turned quickly so he wouldn't see them.

"*I didn't think so.*"

When she turned again to quiz him, she was alone. "*Wait—Judd! Don't go! I—I need you to tell me—*"

"*Ask your mother.*"

Shaken by seeing and hearing him so clearly, Christine awoke with a gasp—to find herself looking into a face framed with raven waves so much like Judd's, she thought this might be the next phase of her dream. But this man had a beard along the line of his jaw, and the hands squeezing her shoulders were so strong and warm, their heat penetrated the sleeves of her nightgown.

She glanced around her room. "You're here without your—?"

A finger to his lips silenced her. "*Maman*, she has taken our clothes to be washed and is getting a bath. I have been to Carlton Harte's office—"

"What time is it?" She struggled to sit up, squinting at the bright sunlight that peeked in around the curtains.

Tucker chuckled, savoring the sight of her auburn hair splayed over her pillow and the sleepy look in her eyes. "You needed your rest after such an eventful evening, *chérie*. *Et moi*, I could not sleep anyway. The note on Harte's door says he is away on a case indefinitely."

Christine frowned. "Does that mean he's chasing Richard Wyndham—or whoever ran out Mama's back door?"

"Possibly." He kissed her brow—to indulge his senses in her warm sweetness, and to soften his other information. "I also went there—to your mama's house again. To catch her off-guard, when she couldn't refuse to talk to me. But she was gone."

"What do you mean . . . gone?"

"The back door, was hanging open, blowing in the breeze. So I took the liberty of—"

"You just went inside? What if she—or Richard—"

Tucker shrugged, grinning. "That door, it would wake the dead—or bring the neighbors in, soon enough. So I shut it behind me."

He watched her lovely face for signs that he was saying more than she could bear. "The furnishings were all there, but her clothes were gone, *ma chère*. The agent at the depot, he said a stagecoach got out last night, ahead of the storm—but they are delayed now, until the mountain roads can be cleared."

"And Mama was on that coach?

"*Oui.*" He sighed. "Or at least a couple who signed as Mr. and Mrs. Wynn Richards."'

Christine struggled enough this time that he finally let her sit up.

"That's not fair!" she protested, punching her feather pillow. "I wanted to take Mama by surprise today, and then check that cabinet—"

"It has no back, as *Maman* suggested. The hole through the wall is covered by another cabinet that has nothing in it. I knew you'd want to know, *ma princesse*. But I am no thief," he added with a teasing grin. "I left the accordion, and the tambourine, and the other noisemakers."

Her green eyes sparkled with fascinated fury.

"This leaves us with a decision, *chérie*, and I want you to consider it carefully," he continued. "I know how badly you want to be with your mama again, and we will follow until we find her, if that's what you decide. But I also know how badly your mama hurt you last night."

Christine blinked to keep from crying again. Hadn't she run out of tears yet? Why was it upsetting when Tucker was so kind to her?

"So if you want to go back—back to Abilene, or back to school, or whatever else you were doing—" he continued softly, "then we will go."

I want to go back to before all this happened. Before Mama ran off in the first place.

Yet she would never have met Tucker Trudeau had she stayed in Missouri; would never have attended Miss Vanderbilt's Academy for Young Ladies and developed her talent for dress design had Mercy and Judd Monroe not taken her in.

She reached for Tucker's hand, her pulse pounding

harder. "But you have your commission with the Union Pacific to—"

Tucker shrugged again. "That is my job, *oui,* but this is a mission. Your happiness—your wishes—are more important than any pictures I might take of all this white snow, *non?*"

The firm squeeze of his hand made her heart skip. She'd received gifts from earnest young men in St. Louis, but all of them lumped together didn't hold a candle to what Tucker had just said, and the affection with which he'd expressed it.

Christine wove her fingers between his, her thoughts driven like the snow in last night's wind. This was the chance—the choice—of her lifetime. Her answer tickled the tip of her tongue, but she wanted to be sure. She'd never forgive herself if Tucker gave up valuable time and considerable pay to chase after the loving mother who might only exist in her childhood memories.

"Where do you think they went? How will we ever find them?" she asked. "If they don't want to be found— if they realize Carlton Harte is tailing them—"

Christine blinked as another possibility occurred to her. "Or what if Mr. Harte is with them? Their partner in crime?"

"We can't know everything, *oui?* But I can tell you, the stagecoach last night was headed west rather than back to Nebraska." He smiled, admiring her quick wit and courage. "Just my guess, *ma joie,* but I'm thinking they will board the train again to escape us."

She considered this, nodding. "How far might they go? Where would the train take them?"

Tucker held her brave, green-eyed gaze, watching for a breaking point. "The Union Pacific, it heads west across Wyoming to Utah, veering south through Nevada to California—Sacramento, California," he explained. "That is the main route. But just as Kansas has its Kansas Pacific line, other small railways could take them to dozens of towns with train stations. Or they could disappear on a stagecoach to almost anywhere, as well, *chérie.*"

"California?" Christine let out a long sigh, boggled by all the possibilities. "Good Lord, we could search . . . we could be looking forever, Tucker. Like for a needle in a haystack. Like Michael tried to tell me."

"Three needles," he corrected. "This improves our odds, *non?*"

His attempt at humor made her smile. But as he was leaning in for another soft, delicious kiss, *Maman* bustled through the door.

"And what have you learned, *mon fils?*" she demanded of her son. A single arched eyebrow expressed her opinion of him sitting on Christine's bed.

"They got out before the storm last night. I'm guessing they'll board the train in Cheyenne—which, on the hotel express, could take them to California in just a few days."

"Or they could disappear in any no-name town between here and there." She gripped her carpetbag, gazing toward the windows as though she could see the couple who had eluded them. Then she focused on Christine.

"And what do you think? No doubt Tucker is letting you decide our fate."

Christine pushed her sleep-mussed hair back from her face, noting that Veronique had arranged her own dark tresses in a neat upsweep and was wearing a simple red dress. Amazing how much younger—how fetching—she could be when she didn't dress like the fortune teller at a carnival.

When she looked into Veronique's dark, penetrating eyes she saw a flash of—what? Challenge? Anticipation? Encouragement?

Not the arrogance she had expected. Not a lecture on the impropriety of Tucker being in her room—or about how she was more trouble than she was worth, or less of a woman than her son deserved.

The room seemed a-flutter with a sense of fresh beginnings, as though angels had arrived to take charge— as though last night's confrontation with Mama had cleared the air. And didn't *that* sound like something the magical, mystical Veronique would say!

Christine reached under the bed for her valise, the one she'd carried whether they camped in the wagon or rode the train, the one she'd stashed beneath her bed at school and when she'd visited the Malloys. The bag she'd packed both times she rode away on a horse that wasn't her own to find Mama.

With trembling hands she reached in and gripped the little diary. Its velvet was worn smooth now from damp hands holding it. She knew certain passages by heart; knew the pages where the ink had smeared from teardrops, Mama's and her own.

She handed it to Veronique.

"Help me," she whispered. "We must find Mama before it's too late. I'll go with you to the church, to consecrate—"

The moment Tucker's mother touched the diary, the transformation began. Her eyes widened and glazed, as though she stared inward, at scenes no one else should see. The air left her lungs in a rush. She began to shake, and then vibrated to a high, manic pitch played on a wild violin.

Christine fell back, awed by the powerful force that now possessed Veronique Trudeau. "Tucker, should we—"

"Shhh," he whispered, his gaze fixed on his mother. "This happens when *Maman* feels the spirit of an item's owner. It's part of being a seer. It brings her the visions."

Mama's words must've sucked Tucker's mother into an invisible tempest. The slender face that had looked so sophisticated moments ago was now contorted in agony, as though the diary were scorching her hands, her eyes. Her soul. Veronique's hair was coming loose and drops of sweat—or were they tears?—ran down cheeks that now looked drawn with age.

Gasping, the seer released the diary. It landed on the bed, but Christine didn't dare pick it up. Instead, she watched *Maman*'s recovery, greatly relieved that she was breathing again and blinking to regain her normal sight.

Veronique shuddered one final time and looked at her. "*Tu as raison*—you are right," she rasped in her Cajun accent. "I have seen your mother with Richard Wyndham. They sit together on the train, but they plan separately. Secretly."

She touched her mussed hair, as though she didn't recall how it got that way. Then she looked at Christine again.

"They're going all the way to the coast—to San Francisco. There's going to be trouble, Christine. Your mother's in grave danger."

Chapter Twenty-three

"Why look—it's a present!"

Tucker grinned as Christine tore into the box that had awaited them at the Cheyenne station. Before boarding the train for Sacramento, he'd sent General Dodge a message saying his photographs would be delayed—and then one to Michael Malloy, telling him they'd seen Virgilia Bristol and were now following her west again. He'd let Christine share whatever she cared to with Billy and the Malloys after they'd completed their quest.

In the seat beside him, she was opening the enclosed letter. "It's from Mercy," she said, smoothing its folds. " 'Dear Christine,' she writes, 'we didn't know when you might reach Wyoming, but we wanted to remember your birthday—' "

Her mouth fell open. "Well, isn't that the nicest thing?" she said, stunned.

Tucker took her hand, hoping whatever she'd received wouldn't upset her. She'd had enough of that these past few days. "And your birthday, when is it?" he asked with a sly smile. "I have an idea for a present myself."

That made her smile!

"December eighteenth, but—excuse me!" she hailed the conductor collecting tickets in the aisle. "What's today's date, please?"

"It's the second of December, miss."

Christine nodded, yanking the ribbon from one small package. "Everyone knows I can't wait that long to open my—oh, it's a lace collar! I bet Miss Vanderbilt tatted it for me! And here's—"

She quickly unwrapped the other little item, holding it up with delight. "A cutwork handkerchief, monogrammed with a *C*. How . . . well, I never expected this!"

To hide the hitch in her voice, Christine read the rest of Mercy's letter to herself.

> *—and to wish you all the best as you look for your mother. Aunt Agatha tucked in a lace remembrance so you'll know how much she and the girls at school miss you, dear. Lily picked out the handkerchief at the Great Western Store in town. My satin stitching isn't nearly as perfect as yours, but it was done with loving thoughts of you as you turn seventeen. We are all so proud of the young woman you've become.*

A tear was trickling down each cheek now, and two little wet spots appeared on the pressed ivory linen. After all the selfish, hateful things she'd done to Mercy Malloy, she hardly deserved—

"What a pretty piece!" Veronique leaned forward from the seat facing them. "And how nice that Mrs. Malloy sent you a gift. You must miss receiving such things from your mother. I know I did."

Nodding mutely, Christine passed the collar and handkerchief across to her. She loved presents; had gotten plenty of them back home before the war. But why did her birthday—and every holiday—have to be so difficult now?

"My parents put me in a convent school, you see," Tucker's mother continued. "When Mama realized I'd inherited the second sight, and the ability to heal that *her* mother had struggled with, well—"

Veronique glanced out the train's window as though these memories haunted her. For a moment, there was only the chugging of the train as it accelerated, and the other passengers' quiet conversations.

"She claimed it was to protect me from the rumors that plagued *Grandmaman* throughout her lifetime. But I knew my visions and spirit summonings made her . . . very nervous."

"You grew up in a convent?" Christine focused on the woman who was gazing raptly at her satin-stitched hanky. "That makes the Academy for Young Ladies sound very free and lenient. How did you ever meet Tucker's father?"

Veronique's pointed stare made her wish she'd kept her mouth shut. Beside her, Tucker shifted on the seat.

Fine dang can of worms you opened now, came Billy's voice in her head.

Tucker's mother composed herself; those small, dark eyes shone with purpose rather than regret. "It is a natural question for you to ask," she said quietly, "and it is an answer my son has long deserved. Growing up with only a mother's love has been difficult for him at times."

"*Maman*, if you don't want to—"

"No, it is time," she insisted. "When parents hide the truth from their children, the real stories often get revealed at the wrong times. Raising you alone wasn't easy, *mon fils,* but you have been the light of my life."

She sighed, and then began in a pensive voice. "The Sisters at the convent believed I brought on my 'seizures'—that I was trying for their attention in a dramatic way, when I spoke to spirits they couldn't see."

"Even though they believe in angels?" Christine asked. "And miracles? And the immaculate conception of Jesus?"

Veronique shrugged prettily. "I *did* win favor with my healing skills, since no one else birthed babies or knew about herbal remedies. So, although they wouldn't allow me to take my vows, I developed my medical skills and received an education far beyond most women's. I was the only student ever allowed to use the abbot's extensive library."

"Which explains why you're talking as you do now, instead of like a Cajun," Christine surmised.

"My bayou neighbors wouldn't have trusted a *traiteur* who sounded citified," she replied with a wry smile. "My accent and habits helped me fit in. And they coincided with my other quirks, as outsiders saw it."

Christine considered this, suspecting Tucker's mother knew a lot more than she was telling. But then, wasn't she learning firsthand how mothers sometimes did things their children didn't want to hear about?

"So you met my father outside the convent? While you were healing people?"

Christine felt the thrum of Tucker's apprehension in the hand that held hers so tightly. Had his mother made up stories when he was a boy? Or had intuition told him not to ask about his other parent?

Veronique drew a deep breath and let it out. Then she smiled at him, coming to terms with her memories. Her past.

"Your father was overjoyed that he was about to have his first child," she replied, "and I see his excitement every time you smile, *ma joie*. You can understand his despair when that baby was stillborn, and his wife succumbed to birthing fever just a few days later.

"I, too, was devastated," she continued, shaking her head. "I was only seventeen—Christine's age—dabbling in the mysteries of life and death and medicine. I'd done my very best to save her, but it was a hard lesson, learning that some things are beyond our control no matter how skilled we are."

Christine's jaw dropped. Beside her, Tucker tensed, as though he'd guessed the rest of the story.

"To comfort him, I summoned the spirit of his wife. Zach Tucker and his Adelaide had been so much in love, I felt honored to give them a few more moments together."

She sat as in a trance, recalling these events in a far-away voice. "Zach found it a comfort to know she and the baby were beyond their pain. It was my chance to bring a happier ending to the most difficult situation I'd ever faced. We embraced afterward and . . ."

Veronique paused, flushing. "It was my first time with a man. You were conceived in joyful innocence and exuberance, my son."

"But he would not marry you?"

Was it her imagination, or did everyone around them become very, very quiet? Christine wondered if her hand would survive his grip, but she dared not pull away. Tucker looked incensed. Yet his glower disguised a vulnerability she'd never seen on his strong, handsome face.

"The Sisters knew what had happened the moment I returned. It was written all over my face," she said with a rueful laugh. "They could allow no such goings-on with a *traiteur* in their charge, so they sent me home. I prayed night and day that Zach would find me . . . that we would become a family. But I realize now that the Sisters would've refused him any information."

Veronique sighed with her recollections. "Mama and Papa wanted no further scandal with a daughter whose arcane abilities already threatened their standing in the upper circles of New Orleans. So a colored servant whisked me away to her family's little hut back in the bayou to have my baby.

"I knew better than to return home with my boy," she said. "So I made do. Learned more about herbal healing from the woman I stayed with—who delivered Tucker. Made my own way, with the gifts God gave me."

Her smile became fragile, imploring Christine to understand without begging forgiveness. "So do you see how Tucker is all I have? Why he's my reason for being, after twenty-four years? Maybe this explains why I'm not so good at sharing him."

Veronique smiled, reaching out her hands. Tucker grabbed them, and then pulled his *maman* into an embrace that had them laughing and hugging and crying all at once.

Christine could only watch in envy as the love between this protective mother and her devoted son deepened with a joy she'd never seen her own reserved family share, even in the best of times.

It was an awesome thing to witness, this love. And although she'd once despised the woman in Gypsy attire whose eyes knew her every secret, Christine now felt a profound admiration for Veronique Trudeau. Tucker's mother wasn't laying blame, or cursing her fate, or sniffling pitifully into her hanky. She'd made a worthwhile life for herself. She'd depended upon God's gifts to her, rather than falling back on prostitution or charity or . . . con artistry. She'd raised her son the best way she knew how.

And she was preparing to set him free.

A torrent of affectionate Cajun French surged between them as they reaffirmed the bond that had seen them through Tucker's entire life. And now as they chattered, Christine could appreciate the comfort of their Cajun ways. This time, she didn't feel she was being left out.

Then Tucker slung an arm around her shoulder. And

when she felt Veronique's embrace from within his, Christine knew, for the first time in years, how it felt to belong.

The next day, the train took them through a garden of earthly delight such as Christine had never seen. The flatlands of Nebraska and snow-capped mountains of Colorado had given way to spectacular rock formations and vast stretches of desert, which became fertile, rolling hills as they approached Sacramento. How odd to be seeing green grass and trees when it was the dead of winter back in Kansas.

Another short train ride took them into San Francisco—and civilization. The bustling city of businesses and established neighborhoods easily rivaled St. Louis. She'd studied about the gold rush that brought the Forty-Niners here—recalled reading about Spanish land grants and the immigration of the Chinese, and the way shipping had established this port city as a major trade center. But seeing all these things from her train window made them real.

And it made something very clear, as well: Mama and Richard Wyndham could operate from a dozen different pockets of commerce here, and it might take months to find them. As she stood on the platform with Veronique, while Tucker got Sol and the wagon off the train, Christine felt totally overwhelmed.

All these people! Many wore the stylish suits and bowlers of successful businessmen, while others appeared to be penniless immigrants, huddling in conversations that rang with exotic vowel sounds and rhythms. Mama and her consort wouldn't even have to leave the train station to run a devious scheme that would make them a living.

And wasn't that a scary thought?

Christine sighed. There was no backing out now. No

honorable way to say she'd seen enough of her mother's shenanigans and wanted to leave the whole thing alone. If Veronique Trudeau's instincts were correct—and she'd been right a number of times—they had arrived at their final destination.

This was where she'd find Mama and get her answers, once and for all. Or not, if that "trouble" Tucker's mother predicted found Virgilia Bristol before *she* could.

Christine glanced at the woman beside her. Veronique stood with her eyes closed and her face lifted slightly, as though listening for messages from her angels. She appeared removed from the cacophony of accented chatter and the heavy scents of locomotive smoke and unwashed bodies, a single serene soul operating on a different plane from those hurrying around her.

Christine envied that serenity.

She stood quietly, watching the sea of faces—the ebb and flow of passengers boarding or leaving trains from other platforms. A fellow in a stovepipe hat gazed at her, but then went on his way; just one man of many who wore such a hat and a wicked little waxed mustache. Why did he look vaguely familiar?

Because in this crowd, you might see anyone. Or think you did.

One face, however, separated itself from the others, and her toes wiggled inside her shoes. Who wouldn't adore that distinctive black beard—cropped more closely than the mutton chops and bushy thickets most men sported—and the aquamarine eyes that shone so when they looked at her?

Tucker swooped her up into a kiss and the world went still. For those blissful moments, she knew only the warm softness of his lips and the strength of his arms holding her off the ground, and the little moan that escaped him as he released her.

"I have parked the wagon and paid a boy to stand with Sol," he said. "In this crowd, who knows what might happen to such a fine horse?"

Then he glanced at his mother, hesitant to interrupt her state of mental suspension. "Have you sensed anything, *Maman?* In a city this size—"

"I hear . . . male voices. Odd, squawking music and languages . . . black hats and braids," she murmured in a rush. "Back rooms, behind . . . steam. A strong odor of incense and . . . soap."

"Do you feel Christine's mother?"

Veronique swayed, squeezing her eyes tighter. "She . . . she is here, in this city, yes."

Christine's pulse pounded. "Is Mama all right? Is she with—"

"Anger! Harsh words! I see—I see secret keys and—"

Veronique shuddered, her eyes flying open. She sucked in a few desperate breaths, reaching for their hands as she regained her composure. "We must find her soon. He has left her in an . . . alley. Left her for dead."

Chapter Twenty-four

How much more impossible could this be? Christine fretted. *How many men in black hats? How many odd languages? How many alleys?*

They sat crammed together on the seat of the red wagon, peering down one narrow street after another, moving very slowly because the mass of jabbering Oriental humanity kept Sol to a walk. It was nearly dusk, and in their urgency they hadn't gotten a room—didn't want to stay someplace that might be city blocks away from whatever had happened to her mother.

Hands clasped tightly in her lap, Christine forced herself to remain calm. If what Veronique had envisioned was true, Mama might already be dead. Her body could be crammed into a doorway where these Chinese people would never see her. Not that they'd help a white woman in this part of town.

"Have you seen anything like what went on in your vision?" she asked Veronique quietly. "Or had any new impressions?"

"Are we close? Going the right way?" Tucker joined in.

The woman between them shook her head. She, too, was gazing in all directions, trying desperately to match their surroundings with those fleeting images in her head. Lamps were being lit behind curtains, and exotic aromas wafted from upstairs windows where people lived above their shops.

"We must get a place to stay, *Maman*. Or I must park where Sol will be safe while we sleep in the wagon."

His eyes followed the sidewalks—or what he could see of them, with so many people milling about. They were eyeing his red wagon and huge horse with suspicion, not offering help to foreigners so obviously lost.

"Are we going in the right direction? Or have we passed what you saw?"

Veronique sighed, looking drained. "The images went so fast. But yes, these men are wearing black hats and braids, speaking a strange language. Who could have known Chinatown was so huge?"

"Why would Richard take Mama *here?*" Christine blinked back tears, wondering if this whole miserable trip would come down to finding her mother lifeless on—

Don't think about that! Just keep looking. Ask questions.

"Was that incense you mentioned like what they burned in the church?" she quizzed. "Or was it—"

"Opium?" Tucker finished.

Christine hugged herself, more from fear than the breeze blowing in from the bay.

Veronique frowned. "I didn't think so at the time. The Chinese use incense as part of their daily rituals— offerings to their gods. It's the impression of hidden places that remains so strong."

She stiffened, and then pointed to the corner ahead of them. "Is that steam coming from that window? A laundry, perhaps?"

Christine sat straighter. Steam—scent of soap—they fit together!

But the trio of short men in black Mandarin-style jackets, with long queues and odd little shoes, hardly seemed to be leaving a place where washing was done. A burst of twangy music followed them onto the street as they gesticulated in their excited conversation.

"That's what I heard! Music like that!"

Veronique would have sprung down from the wagon if Tucker hadn't stopped her. "*Maman*," he said tiredly, "If you can call that awful noise music, it sounds like the same song we've heard for the past hour. We need to—"

"Let me ask the angels. We're very close."

Christine pressed her knuckles to her lips to keep from screaming. Night was falling in an area where she didn't feel one bit safe, even with Tucker here. And his mother wanted a consultation!

Fools rush in where angels fear to tread, she fretted. But when Veronique, already entering her trance state, asked for Mama's diary, Christine reached into her valise. What else could she do?

When the seer's hands closed around the velvet-bound book, she sucked in air. Her body went rigid. She underwent the same facial contortions as before, only this time they seemed more intense. The wagon seat vibrated with her pent-up energy. Then she slumped between them with her eyes squeezed shut, murmuring incoherent phrases and sounds.

Veronique suddenly sat bolt upright. Her eyes flew open and she pointed ahead of them.

"One more block. Turn and enter the alley from the other side," she directed. "Wyndham knocked her against the building to scare her. We must find her before he returns."

Tucker clucked to Sol and they lurched ahead. The streets were clearing. Apparently the Chinese men who'd clogged the streets earlier had gone home for their evening meal. The huge horse's hoofbeats ricocheted off the tall buildings. They rounded the corner, found the narrow passageway that doubled back to the laundry, then proceeded more slowly.

Silently, they scanned the dark, fetid passageway. The stench of rotten vegetables and human waste stung Christine's nose; Mama would be mortified if her daughter knew Richard Wyndham had dumped her here like a pailful of garbage. They simply had to find—

"There! Is that someone—?"

Tucker scrambled down from the seat, holding up his arms to assist his mother, then Christine. The only light came from a window where steam still emerged, so they stepped carefully toward what he saw.

When she spotted a pale face at an odd angle to its body, Christine's stomach lurched. *I will not vomit,* she vowed as she knelt beside the eerie figure. *I will not collapse or make this any harder than—*

"Oh, Mama," she breathed. "Oh, my God, Mama . . ."

"Are you sure?" Tucker squatted on the woman's other side. "Something tells me that in this part of town victims get left this way a lot."

"It *is* Mrs. Bristol," *Maman* affirmed. Her hands began an assessment, checking for blood and broken bones. "She wasn't shot or stabbed, at least. Pick her up carefully, Tucker, while I open the wagon door."

Stunned, Christine tucked Mama's limp arms and long skirts close to her body while Tucker gently gathered her into his arms. Dozens of possibilities whirled in her frightened mind, but she didn't dare think about them. Better to remain separated from reality and just do something. Better to keep moving from one little task to the next so she wouldn't be overwhelmed by a sense of defeat as dark as this alley.

As they stepped up into the wagon, Tucker balanced himself carefully, adjusting Mama's weight in his arms. His mother had lit a lamp with a reflector, and the candles on her angel altar; she was kneeling in the corner, out of the way. Her hurried, whispered prayers were in Latin, but Christine understood their urgent undertone perfectly: Veronique didn't think Mama was going to make it.

And indeed, Mama looked far removed from this world as Tucker laid her on the back bunk. He stepped away, slipping his arm around Christine as his mother again checked for breathing and a heartbeat. The *traiteur* then lifted one of Mama's eyelids to reveal a pupil that was barely visible.

"I suspect a large dose of opium," she said, brushing debris from Mama's shoulders.

She positioned the limp head on her pillow and smoothed Mama's loose auburn hair. "It fits with what flashed through my mind—that they were having a disagreement . . . something about keys. He could've slipped the drug into anything she ate or drank. That bruise on her face is from hitting against the building, or the ground."

"But—but will she . . . ?" Christine choked on her worst thoughts. Mama resembled a rumpled corpse laid out for burial, and she just couldn't talk about that right now.

"It depends on how much opium he gave her, and how resistant to it she is," Veronique replied. "And we don't *know* that she lost consciousness from hitting her head. I can't revive her with strong coffee because she can't swallow it. And we can't get her up and walking to move the drug through her system faster."

Veronique straightened, her dark eyes sorrowful. "If she survives the night and tomorrow, she stands a fair chance of recovery. Until then, all we can do is wait. And pray."

It was the longest night of her life.

While Tucker drove, Christine sat beside her mother.

She held the hand that had caressed her face and arranged her hair in ribbons and led her with disciplinary determination when she'd disrupted church as a child. How vividly she recalled Mama's touch from those moments!

She would've given five years of her life to be yanked down an aisle that way right now—*ten* years for one more time when Mama smoothed her hair, smiling with such love in those beautiful green eyes. Love Christine had taken for granted, thinking it would never end. Thinking it would always be her mother's special gift to her.

But Mama lay so still.

Christine felt she was already sitting vigil beside a coffin. It was awful enough to endure those long hours in the crepe-draped parlor where Daddy was laid out before his burial, but this—this was *Mama*. This was the woman she'd turned to for direction, approval, and true understanding—the woman she'd never stopped loving these last three years, even though she'd behaved in unmotherly ways.

"If it helps you," Veronique's voice broke the silence, "at least your mother is feeling no pain. She is beyond whatever that wicked man did or said to her because we found her. And she is breathing. For these things we can be very thankful."

Christine nodded. Her throat was so tight she didn't try to talk.

"I've asked the angels for assistance," the seer went on. "I've implored Saint Raphael to minister to her as we cannot. I've prayed to Saint Michael for his supreme protection while she's in this suspended state. I've asked the Archangel Gabriel to whisper words of encouragement in her ear—assurances that she is safe, and with people who love her. Who *need* her. Sometimes we mothers can get by on very little if we know we are needed."

Tears slithered down Christine's face again.

Oh, Mama, if you only knew how I've needed you! How I've missed you—even though my questions about why you abandoned us seemed more important than anything else, she mused miserably.

If I could turn back time to when I saw you last week, I'd shuck that veil and just hug you—no questions asked. It was my selfish questions that drove you away . . . my need to make you suffer for the way you treated me. It was my deception that made Wyndham desperate enough to leave town—and to poison you.

What an awful thought, but it was true, wasn't it? If she hadn't sent that Englishman fleeing into the night, he'd still be in Denver. Mama would still be conducting séances, instead of lying here as pale as a china plate.

Oh God, if You let her live, I promise I'll never again ask why she abandoned Billy and me. It—it really doesn't matter anymore.

"It's normal to blame yourself for this sad chain of events, Christine." *Maman's* soft voice came from behind her. "But we all make our choices. And sometimes it only takes one bad choice to require another, and another—to convince ourselves we've done the right thing. To believe we had no other choice that first time.

"Despite what you might think," she went on gently, "I'm guessing your mother's had more than her share of regrets since she left you. When she rode off with Richard Wyndham, she was trying to fill a desperate need inside herself. She would never have intentionally hurt you, dear."

Christine kept rubbing Mama's cool, limp hand, as though it might revive her—or hold her here, so she couldn't slip away to the Other Side.

There was nothing else she could do.

I love you, Mama. Please don't go.

Chapter Twenty-five

"Christine, *ma princesse*," Tucker murmured. "Come outside for some air. Come see the sunrise—and the ocean."

Her eyes were so red-rimmed, and the circles beneath them so dark, he wanted to enfold this poor girl in his arms and hold her forever. She'd been awake nearly twenty-four hours now, refusing to rest in case her mother came around. But Virgilia Bristol hadn't even shifted in her sleep—if indeed she was only asleep.

From the corner, *Maman* looked up from her prayers. "Yes, Christine, you should stretch your legs. Breathe the fresh morning air. I'll call you if I see the slightest change, dear."

Christine rose stiffly from the padded storage bin where she'd kept watch. How many times had she held the mirror over that pale face to catch the vapor of such shallow breathing? How many times had she probed the underside of Mama's wrist for a pulse?

How many prayers had she said to God—to those angels and saints and anyone else who might listen—asking for a sign? A way to know if Mama would live or if she was slipping away.

About the same number of times I've kicked myself for confronting her in Denver. Sighing, she let Tucker help her down from the wagon.

On the mist-shrouded horizon, the sun glowed like a fireball, shimmering above water that went on endlessly, bounded only by the shoreline on her left. Buildings constructed shoulder-to-shoulder clung to the hillsides above the piers, where magnificent sailing ships and little fishing boats bobbed peacefully in their slips. After feeling like a mouse caught in the maze of those terrifying Chinatown streets last night, she'd never expected this panoramic view of land and sea and sky.

"Oh, my," she breathed, unable to stop staring. "This is San Francisco?"

"And *this*," Tucker said with a sweep of his arm, "is the Bay, which is part of the Pacific Ocean, *chérie*. We're standing on the very edge of America."

Butterfly wings of excitement fluttered inside her. Not only could she see streets and buildings, but normal, everyday people were walking about, as though this enchanting world had been created especially for her enjoyment. Why had she been afraid of this city last night?

You thought your mother was dead. And not a soul offered to help.

"It—it's so different from St. Louis. Or Kansas," she murmured. She tugged her shawl tighter around her shoulders, marveling at the mist, which gave the city such mystique. "Why, back home it's probably snowing, or—"

Had she really said that? *Back home?*

Tucker caught it, too. He pulled her closer, his heart thundering with a sense of grand destiny. Yes, they'd come here in search of Christine's mother, but what he'd found was a city he loved at first sight—the same way he'd fallen for this slender girl in his arms. He knew what he wanted without thinking twice.

He kissed her warm hair as he gazed at the Bay, praying for the right words to woo her. Surely she knew his intentions were honorable? Surely she understood that when he'd stopped in Abilene, it wasn't because *Maman* felt compelled to help with that other girl's baby?

But Christine was young, and right now she was exhausted. She was thinking only of her mother and what was at stake—as she should be. She needed to hear exactly what he had in mind for their future . . . but perhaps this wasn't a good time. Would she feel he was taking advantage of her agitated state? If she said yes—or no—would she change her mind when she'd had a chance to think about it?

"Thank you for coaxing me out here, Tucker," she said, resting her head against his chest. "The morning air is exactly what I needed."

He closed his eyes against a wave of wanting, of *needing* to express his innermost thoughts. For a moment more he simply held her, keenly aware of her fragility and her strength; her youth and her maturity. Few girls of sixteen would've had the gumption to come after such a mother—and then return to the search after the rejection she'd received in Denver. But Christine Bristol had always known what she wanted, and pursued it.

Did she want *him?*

"Christine," he began, hoping the words would flow like magic. "Right now, maybe it's not the best time to—to ask about your feelings—"

She raised her head. Those green eyes gazed up at him, and despite her worries, she smiled.

He could only stare back, mesmerized. He was losing the moment—losing the nerve to—

"I said that if you helped me find Mama, I would love you forever," she said. "Well, you did your part. But what I said wasn't entirely true."

His heart clenched into a knot. "You—you've been known to fib about—"

Her fingertip silenced him. A good thing, since that was such a stupid path to go down right now. Then damned if she didn't trace the edge of his lips with that finger, driving him absolutely mindless with her touch.

"What I meant was," she continued, "by the time I was asking you that, I was too lost in love to find my way out. You're stuck with me, Tucker."

Was she going to—? Tucker cleared his throat, not daring to drop her gaze. "Does this mean you'd marry me if I asked?" he asked.

Her smile turned coy. "Why not find out?"

Tucker gasped as though she'd punched him. He was trying to be proper and eloquent—considerate of her worries—and she was toying with him. He stood taller, tightening his embrace. Around them, the gulls cried and the gentle lapping of the waves called up ancient rhythms: the ebb and flow of life's own tides.

"If I wanted to settle here, to open a photography shop, and you—if you wanted to—could design fine dresses for San Francisco's richest women," he said, his words tumbling out in somersaults, "would you still marry me? It's a long way from your brother Billy and—"

"Why not find out?"

Sacre bleu, but she was making this difficult! Why wasn't she an excited little thing who just threw her arms around his neck and squealed *yes?* Christine knew what he was asking and she was leading him around by the—

"Christine! She's shifting!" *Maman*'s voice rang inside the wagon.

He held her, with his arms and his gaze, and then realized she'd made no move to leave. Her face took on the glow of the dawn. With wisps of auburn hair blowing loose in the breeze and her eyes as deep green as an eternal forest, she was the loveliest thing he'd ever seen.

Tucker kissed her. Thank God she rose on her toes to press her lips into his, for if she'd pulled away at this fragile moment, he might've—

"Her eyes are open!" his mother cried.

Christine's heart raced, just as her legs wanted to. But it had occurred to her, after all these miles and days, that whatever happened with Mama, her life was her own to design—much like the gowns she'd fashioned these past three years. She'd developed that talent with Miss Vanderbilt's help, and at Mercy's encouragement, hadn't she? She loved her mother and had desperately wanted to find her, but she was her own woman, after all was said and done. Mama or not.

She kissed Tucker more insistently. She'd come so far, across the country and in personal wisdom, because Tucker Trudeau had believed in her—had overlooked her fibs to see the fear behind them, and found her worthy anyway. So he deserved her unswerving attention in this moment she'd been dreaming of forever. Mama had promised her that a wonderful man would sweep her off her feet someday. And here he was!

He was going to drown in this kiss if he didn't speak up *now.* "Christine, *ma princesse, ma chérie*—"

"Christine—she's asking for you! She's frightened and disoriented, waking up in a strange place."

Tucker sighed. She couldn't possibly be interested in what he had to say, even if her kiss suggested otherwise. "Perhaps you should go inside—"

"Ask me."

What man wouldn't melt in the warmth of her smile and delight in that dreamy-eyed look? Bless her, she wasn't rushing off, or giving any hint she might refuse

him. To have a beautiful young woman so focused on
him—as though she saw only the *best* in him, the very
things he tried to bring out in his photographs—well,
when would life ever smile at him this way again?

"Will you marry me, Christine?" he whispered. His
heart was pounding so hard, that was the loudest he
could speak. "I—I love you so—"

"Yes, I will, Tucker," she breathed back. Her cheeks
blossomed as she stretched up to kiss him again. "I've
waited all my life for you to ask."

The kiss ended in a mutual sigh—and *Maman*'s more
insistent summons. "All this way we've come, for *your
mother.* She's fading fast! If you don't—"

With a sad smile, Christine slipped from his embrace.
She stepped over the wagon's threshold, glanced back
at Tucker—where had his Cajun exuberance gone, now
that she'd said yes?—and then let her eyes adjust to the
dimness inside. Mama was lying on the bunk at the
back of the wagon, deathly pale in the altar's flickering
candlelight.

"She came around?" Christine clasped Veronique's
trembling hand. "And she asked for me? And now she's
fading away again?"

"I—I'm so sorry," the seer murmured. "I saw sure signs
of her recovery, and then—"

"Do you have camphor and a hanky?" she whispered.

Veronique blinked. "Yes. Yes, of course."

While Tucker's mother fetched these things, Christine
walked over to stand beside her mother. It could have
been her own face she gazed at, except for the network
of tiny lines around the eyes—and lips curved down-
ward into a scowl she hoped Tucker never saw as she
slept.

She grasped Mama's hand. "Mama? Can you hear me?"

Nothing.

The hand remained limp in hers, so she laid it on the

bed. Dousing Veronique's handkerchief with the pungent camphor made her eyes water and sting—or was it because, after all this time and trouble, her mother simply refused to recover?

Leaning closer, she stood with her face mere inches from Mama's. She recalled staring this blatantly at Billy in his bed when they were kids . . . looking for that undetectable quiver beneath his eyelids . . .

Heart pounding wildly, Christine held the saturated rag over Mama's nose. "Mama? Come on now—snap out of it!"

Seconds ticked by.

Still holding the reeking camphor rag in place, Christine smiled slyly. "Mama? Mama, wake up! I—I'm getting married—"

This realization finally washed over her, as though Tucker had tossed her into the icy waters of the Bay. Christine laughed out loud.

"Mama, I'm getting *married!*" she crowed. "I'm getting married—just like we've always planned. Now dammit, stop playing 'possum or you'll miss the wedding!"

Her mother's eyes flew open. She gasped for air, sputtering from sucking in such a snootful of the camphor. Arms and legs flailing, Mama swatted the hanky away.

"Right now?" she rasped. "But—I—have nothing to wear!"

Veronique Trudeau's mouth fell open. "Christine, you're shameless!"

Christine shrugged, chuckling. "I was raised that way."

Chapter Twenty-six

"You're sure Richard's not here? And he won't find us?"

"It's all right, Mama. That's why Tucker got us this hotel room and parked the wagon several blocks away."

Christine grasped her mother's hand. Now that the pranks were over, this woman had a morbid fear of the man who'd abandoned her. The greenish-purple bruise on the side of her head would take several days to go away, but otherwise Mama was recovering pretty well—for a woman who had only the filthy clothes on her back.

"Why did he try to poison you? And then knock you down in that alley, for God's sake?" Christine asked vehemently. "From what I saw in Denver, you were the goose laying his golden eggs."

Mama closed her eyes, scowling. "Goose? Really, Christine! Didn't I raise you to show more respect for your—"

Christine crossed her arms, raising her eyebrows in a silent challenge.

"Oh, all right," her mother said with an injured sniff. "Yes, I was conducting those séances for well-to-do—"

"*Fake* séances, Mama."

"—people who were generous with their . . ." Her mother slumped against the bed head. "What else do you know?"

Christine considered how much to reveal. While she hated being her mother's inquisitor, she also knew the value of knowledge kept to herself. Not just to use later, at a more advantageous moment, but because if she upset this wily woman, Mama might run off again. Calling her a liar wasn't a good strategy either, considering how successfully she'd created her own versions of the truth these past few years.

"I know a fourteen-year-old boy who was devastated when you left us but has carried on and made something of himself," she replied quietly. "And I know a family who sent you all the money they could scrape together only to discover that a certain homestead in Kansas was *not* theirs to claim. And I know some widows who'd like to bury you beneath those cheap Bibles you sold them."

She paused, looking Mama in the eye. "And we haven't even approached the way *my* heart was broken when you left us—and then again last week, when you wouldn't even speak to me."

Bitterness rose in her throat and she had to stand up to keep from shaking the woman on the bed. Christine gulped a deep, uneven breath. How she wished for Tucker's quiet strength and sense of perspective now— or for Veronique to enter with their lunch tray.

But wasn't this what she'd always wanted? A chance to hold Mama accountable?

Perhaps her need for vengeance wasn't serving her purpose. Finding Mama alive should've compensated for her heartache these past three years. But dammit, this woman was still up to her old tricks! Still sidestepping questions and the consequences of what she'd done to people.

"I'm so sorry, honey," Mama murmured. "I never meant to hurt you—"

Christine whirled around. "How can you say that?" she demanded. "How could you just ride away from your own children, dammit?"

There it was, without frills or trimming. She'd shouted it out in her frustration, so now the silence between them rang just as loudly.

Mama looked away. "I had no idea he was—Richard told me he'd found us a nice house in Atchison, knowing we'd lost our home—"

"Knowing you were ripe and ready for the picking."

She'd blurted out Judd Monroe's line without a second thought, startling Mama—and herself as well. But she was no longer a young girl unaware of Wyndham's devious ways. There was no sense in pretending.

Her mother's mouth moved, but no sound came out. She blinked rapidly, fishing for the handkerchief in her skirt pocket.

"All right then, let's go back to the other matter at hand," Christine said in a lower voice. "Why did Richard bring you here to San Francisco, then try to kill you?"

Mama sighed, the dark bruise in sharp contrast to the pallor of her face. "When . . . when he knew you'd found me again, he assumed you'd brought the law with you."

"Why? There's nothing illegal about conducting séances in your home. And the unknowing guests couldn't associate Mr. Wyndham with your sittings, since he remained . . . under the table. Or in the dark."

Mama's crushed look sent a shimmer of victory up her spine. Miss Vanderbilt was right: Knowledge was power. She had Mama exactly where she wanted her. Not that it was as satisfying as she'd imagined.

"When did you become so cynical? So wise to the ways of the world?" her mother asked. "You were only a sheltered, spoiled little girl when—"

"I did some fast growing up," Christine said. "And, thanks to the wise, generous woman who took us in, I've attended an academy in St. Louis. The headmistress teaches us to think for ourselves and look beyond the surface of any situation."

She turned to face her mother straight-on then. "But before that, I read the diary you left in your trunk, with all the other belongings you'd packed to take us west—supposedly to that new *opportunity* you kept talking about. That alone was quite an education, Mama."

Her mother's face went pale, and she began to cough like an old woman with consumption. But when Christine refused to fall for this ploy, Virgilia Bristol let out a long, resigned sigh. Gingerly she fingered her huge bruise.

"When Richard and I left Denver to beat the storm, we were all but clawing at each other," she began. She looked toward the window, as though these scenes were playing themselves out in the glass.

"He insisted we leave town—assuming the long arm of the law was ready to snatch him up—before we could pack properly. And then, when he discovered I hadn't brought along the jewelry case . . . but I outfoxed him on that one."

Christine relaxed. She was by no means satisfied with this explanation, but at least they were getting somewhere. Mama only smiled that way when she was keeping a tasty little secret.

"What was in the case? Not jewelry, I'm guessing."

"Oh, there was that," she said with a coy roll of her

eyes. "Richard could be quite generous when repaying my favors—"

Mama stopped, blushing. "That's where we kept the keys to . . . the post offices boxes. I suppose you know about those, too."

Recalling all those newspaper ads Tucker had sent her, she nodded.

"Well, when he thought I'd left those keys behind—which meant we couldn't collect on the—"

"Why didn't *he* have them?"

Mama shot her an incredulous look. "Because he's a man, dear. And packing is woman's work."

Christine was ready to strangle her—until her mother began to giggle. It started slowly, as though she was out of practice at laughing. Mama raised the hem of her stained, smelly dress up over her knees and began to tear at the stitching—except by then she was laughing so hard her fingers were shaking.

"Mama, what on earth are you—?"

"I did grab those keys, Christine," she said with a conspiratorial grin, "because when I heard him run out the back, after you revealed yourself, I knew we'd be on the run again. And I knew he'd blame me that you'd gotten so close this time—"

She looked away suddenly, her fingers still.

"Mama, I never meant to put you in danger," Christine murmured. "I—I just wanted to see you again."

"I know that, sweetheart. I'm your mother, after all."

Mama got control of herself and then groped along the hem of her skirt again. "And I also had a feeling that if I didn't see to my own . . . resources, I wouldn't have any. But now I have at least—"

Another tug pulled a long section of hem loose, and then she fished out six keys. "Atchison . . . Kansas City . . . Abilene . . . Omaha . . . Cheyenne—and Denver," she said as she held them up. "I slipped them into my hem when I used the washroom on the train. Richard was due to check the boxes for money, so I figured I'd have something to get by on if I could slip onto an eastbound train without him knowing—"

Mama had been in Abilene? And hadn't gone to see Billy while Christine had been away at school? Christine filed this away for later, preferring to pursue the subject at hand.

"But he drugged you and beat you. Because you didn't bring the keys."

"Because he guessed that I *did*. And he couldn't make me give them up."

Christine shivered, reliving the fear and stench and horror of that awful Chinatown alley. "Dear God, Mama, what kind of man—"

"Richard Wyndham was a prince of a fellow—a man any woman would fall for," she said wistfully. "He had that continental air about him. An irresistible wit. He dressed well, and was attentive and adventurous and—all the things I'd ever wanted in a man."

Mama sighed, her expression forlorn. "Your father was a wonderful provider, honey, but he never knew how to have *fun*."

Christine's jaw dropped. "Wyndham was writing worthless checks and cheating people out of their lives' savings. Sending children to Denver to fend for themselves! And you call that fun, Mama?"

At least she looked apologetic now.

"I—I didn't know he'd done all that. My grief over losing your father and Wesley and—our home—kept me from seeing his darker side," she said softly. "All I knew was that Richard wanted to be with me. He made me laugh and—and feel alive again. Christine, you have no idea—you were too young to understand—"

"Oh, Billy and I understood that we'd be inconvenient to a charming Englishman who dressed and talked—"

"How do you know that?"

It was just like old times, baiting her hook to see which fish she'd catch with it. Yet now that Mama was snapping at her lines, the sport was losing its appeal.

"I spied on you, Mama," she replied matter-of-factly. "From the stairs. I saw Richard when he came with Leland Massena, pretending to be interested in the ranch. After that, you invited him while we'd be doing our lessons."

When Mama's face clouded over, Christine widened her eyes pointedly. "You're not the only one who's used the necessary at opportune times. At least that's what I told our teacher."

She turned away again, haunted by the memories of that fateful day in Leavenworth. "I just wish I'd—*held* it—at the stage depot. Because believe you me, we would've chased down Wyndham's surrey if Billy hadn't refused to leave me in the privy by myself. At least *he* looked after me."

Her verbal arrows finally found their mark. Mama crumpled into a sniffling little ball on the bed.

Christine reminded herself that her mother had always softened her opponents this way—or at least this ploy had worked on Daddy and Billy. She and Billy's twin had seen right through it. She'd perfected the Miss Pitiful act herself—until Agatha Vanderbilt ignored her fits and taught her better methods for getting what she wanted.

Like leaving people to dangle in silence. Until they blurted out what she needed to know out of sheer nervousness.

So Christine stood in the center of the hotel room, contemplating the worn spots in the rose-patterned rug. Waiting Mama out. It might be her only chance to hear these stories, because her mother tended to embellish things when she wanted the approval of listeners who didn't know her tricks.

When did you become so cynical? So wise to the ways of the world?

A sad question. But they both knew the answer, didn't they?

Behind her, Mama sighed. "Christine, sweetheart, I can never make up for the heartache I've caused you," she said, "but please believe that I had no idea about the schemes Richard was involved in—until I was too involved myself to get out of them. Or to get away.

"It was so pleasant at first—such a relief from wondering where my next meal would come from," she went on. "He situated me in nice houses while he tended to his business. Told me he was sending messages along the stage line to locate you and Billy. As the weeks passed without any word of you, I convinced myself you'd found a home and were being cared for. It was the only way I stayed sane.

"And when Richard introduced me into some of his . . . *business*, I was so desperate for a purpose—something to do!—that I overlooked the consequences of our advertisements and devious schemes," she continued. "By the time I realized I'd probably never see you again, it—it didn't matter to me that I was cheating people."

Mama got off the bed to walk to the window, but Christine didn't turn around. Best not to interrupt the flow of this story.

"When your nice photographer mentioned that you'd come to Atchison looking for me—the day before we claimed our portrait—" Mama went on, "It sent Richard into such a rage, I knew he'd been deceiving me—just like all his other victims. But what was I to do?" she asked urgently. "I had no money, no chance to break away . . . no place to go. By then, the gilding had come off the lily—"

Just like it came off those Bibles, Christine mused.

"—and I was as much Richard Wyndham's prisoner as his accomplice," she said bitterly. "He never let me out of his sight, on the chance I'd reveal his activities to the Pinkertons and other lawmen who were beginning to figure him out. That's why we kept moving west, of course.

"I—I can't tell you how amazed I was—how overjoyed!—to see your face last week, Christine," she went on. Her voice was rising with excitement, and she came to stand right behind her.

Christine closed her eyes, bracing herself. Parts of the story didn't add up, but if she raised objections she'd never hear it all before someone interrupted them. Veronique should've returned with that tray long ago—

"But when I heard Richard's footsteps fleeing out the back way—when you asked such incriminating questions in front of clients who trusted me—where was I to turn?" she pleaded. "Even Mr. Harte—a man I encouraged to come often because I sensed he'd protect me—ran out on me when you showed your face, Christine. It all happened so suddenly, I didn't know what to do!"

Christine stood stock-still, wanting to believe her mother—*needing* to believe she wasn't making excuses. Most women were cast into roles they couldn't change or escape, but still . . . hadn't Mama missed her—or missed Billy, her best boy—enough to *try* to find them?

Or was she feeling sorry for herself? Licking the wounds Mama didn't seem to care she'd inflicted—

"Christine! For God's sake, look at me when I'm talking to you. I'm baring my soul to—"

Two hands grabbed her shoulders, and with an amazing display of strength, Mama spun her around. The face she saw, mere inches in front of her own, looked as haunted and fearful as she felt inside right now. Christine kept her cool reserve until huge tears tumbled over her mother's lower lashes, to dribble unchecked down her cheeks.

"I *love* you, honey!" Mama's breathless sentiment shook her to the core when those wet green eyes bored into hers. "I never stopped loving you—or Billy! I've made some mistakes, and done things I've come to regret, but being your mother was never one of them."

Something snapped inside Christine—or rather, it melted. She surged forward so hard they both gasped from the sheer force of it, the utter *love* of it. Together they cried and shook and held on tight, releasing the fear and heartache of three long, desperate years.

When she could quit crying enough to talk, Christine whispered, "Mama, I'm sorry I've been so mean and rude, but—"

"You had every reason to ask such questions—"

"—I just couldn't stand it, not knowing where you were and if you were all right—"

"Not a day went by that I didn't wonder the same about you, honey. I was just too weak and spineless to—"

"I missed you so much, Mama."

Her mother hugged her so hard that neither of them could breathe.

"You've always been the strong one, Christine," Mama whispered. "I hope, as time goes by, you'll find it in your heart to forgive the many ways I've sold you short. I am so, so sorry."

Christine nestled her head against Mama's shoulder as she'd done as a child, except now she didn't have to reach *up* to do that. She realized then that it was far more satisfying to *hold* her mother than to hold her accountable.

So she did.

A knock at the door announced Veronique Trudeau, bearing a napkin-draped tray. She smiled at them, her dark eyes shining when she noted their embrace.

"Carlton Harte is downstairs in the parlor to see you, Mrs. Bristol," she said. "I told him you needed solid food and freshening up before you could receive visitors, so Tucker is keeping him company."

She set the tray on the nightstand, smiling evasively. "Take your time. You'll want to have your wits about you and your story in place before you meet with him."

Chapter Twenty-seven

As they descended the stairs into the front parlor of the hotel, Christine paused behind Mama. Just as Veronique had said, Tucker was talking with a fellow dressed in a frock coat and trousers. Somehow the detective appeared different from the way she remembered him. Of course, she'd only seen him briefly on the train, and in the darkness surrounding Mama's séance table, so she could've forgotten what he really looked—

My God, "Mr. Harte" is Sheriff Carson! What's he doing out here? He and Tucker rose and turned toward the staircase as Mama reached the bottom step. Tucker's purposeful gaze warned Christine something was amiss—and that she was to keep any outbursts of recognition to herself.

She realized then why Tucker's mother had been grinning like the fabled Cheshire cat. She also noticed a WANTED poster on the table.

Mama hesitated, smoothing the simple dress of cotton sateen Christine had loaned her. Then she smiled with that prettily dazed expression Southern women passed on to their daughters, extending her arm.

"How good of you to see me, Virgilia," the detective said. He clasped her hand, scowling at the bruise on her face. "After the tale Tucker has told me, I'm thankful you're alive. What an ordeal you've endured!"

"Carlton?" Mama allowed him to kiss her hand, but she was clearly confused. "When did you shave off your mustache? Why is your hair a lighter shade of—?"

Christine clenched her teeth, for Tucker's raised eyebrows warned her to hold her curiosity in check. How ironic, after all the aliases Mama and Richard had taken, that she didn't recognize her *associate* from Denver. Probably because he looked like a man who went by a different name when they'd hopscotched across the country earlier.

Still holding Mama's hand in one of his, the phony Mr. Harte reached into his breast pocket and pulled out a fake handlebar mustache.

Mama gasped, trying to pull free of his grasp, but then the detective produced a leather wallet. When he unfolded it, Christine saw a small certificate with a sketch of a human eye and the words PINKERTON NATIONAL DETECTIVE AGENCY—WE NEVER SLEEP curved around it.

"We have some explaining to do to each other, and I'll begin," he said, still gripping her hand. "In my Denver office, I'm known as Carlton Harte—"

"You're a Pinkerton operative?" Mama stiffened, struggling harder when he wouldn't release her hand. "What kind of a—this is a trap! I've considered you my *friend,* and now—"

"And I still am, my dear Virgilia," he cut in earnestly, "because you were right to suspect Richard Wyndham might tip the tables—if you'll pardon the pun—when things didn't go his way. And now that he's—"

"Then why didn't you introduce yourself as the

Harley Carson named on this—" Mama's eyes widened further, and she wrenched her hand from his. "This is the most despicable—I trusted you! I believed you when you told me—"

Sensing trouble, Christine slipped her arm around her mother. No telling what might happen now that this lawman from North Platte had revealed himself, but things would only get trickier if Mama bolted.

"I apologize for my deception and disguise," Mr. Carson said. "But to catch Mr. Wyndham at his swindling—and protect you from any repercussions—I've had to—"

"Richard Wyndham, he's run another piece in the *San Francisco Chronicle*," Tucker cut in. He stepped around to Mama's other side as he unfolded a page of the newspaper. "A national lottery this time, designed to bring in donations from big contributors. And he's put your name on it."

Christine felt Mama's pulse and temperature rising with her agitation. It was a bigger, showier advertisement than before, to raise funds for a School of Spiritual Enlightenment—and Madame Bristeaux, the renowned medium, was not only named but pictured. The oval portrait—cut from the photograph Tucker had taken in Atchison—had an ornate frame sketched around it.

"But that's—you all *know* I had nothing to do with this! I was left for dead in that alley—"

"Which suggests Wyndham has used your name on other schemes as well, to divert attention from himself," Mr. Carson pointed out. "It gives me this opportunity to protect you, and to . . . assure you my intentions are honorable, Virgilia. Please believe my association with you has become so much more than an assignment from Mr. Pinkerton."

Now *this* was getting interesting! Christine giggled, while her mother glared indignantly at the detective, who looked as plain as a sparrow without his fancy mustache.

"In Mr. Carson's defense," Christine chimed in, "he was kind enough to rescue me from a pack of irate widows in North Platte. They thought you'd had the gall to come back after selling them those chintzy personalized Bibles when their husbands died."

Mama scowled, now even more confused. "But why would he need to rescue you—"

"The resemblance is striking, Mrs. Bristol. Your daughter was marched to jail, direct from Mrs. Padgett's bathtub, to atone for your trickery."

Carson's face softened, perhaps with the recollection of that day. "I'm hoping you'll be gracious enough to apologize to those ladies in person on your way back home—although that's entirely up to you," he added quickly.

"I would've helped Miss Christine anyway—would've reunited mother and daughter—even if I hadn't been fascinated by your . . . powers of persuasion, Virgilia. It was your vibrant mind—your sense of adventure!—that first caught my attention, you see."

He's asking her to make amends with Harrie Butt! Not just to prove his prowess as a detective, but to rub his mother's nose in—

Christine blinked. The look in Harley Carson's eyes was not one of professional detachment or sentiment for his own mother. He was in *awe* of Mama. Thought she had a vibrant mind, and a sense of—

He can't possibly have romantic notions about—this is my mother he's gawking at! Like a lovesick puppy.

Mama's sudden ramrod posture brought Christine out of her thoughts.

"Of all the nerve! To—to lure me downstairs by pretending—as you've been doing all along!—that you *care* for me, Carlton!"

Her voice was high and girlish; on the verge of breaking into a wail—a pattern Christine recognized from when Mama used to manipulate Daddy, or divert his correctional conversations. Her face paled and her breathing became shallow, as though she'd succumb to the vapors any moment now.

"No, my dear, I came to tell you that, with the help of the local police, I cornered Mr. Wyndham—at the postal box listed in this advertisement. We've brought this hoax to a halt!" Mr. Carson replied with a decisive nod. "I've revealed my true identity to you, hoping that we may become . . . better acquainted, now that you're no longer under his influence."

"*Hope* all you want to, Mr. Harte—or whoever you are," Mama said, her rage building. "But now that I see you for the snake you really are—"

"I think of myself as a chameleon," Mr. Carson interjected, "changing my appearance to bring criminals to justice."

"—not to mention a presumptuous little skunk, for thinking I wanted Richard to be caught. For crimes you can't prove he committed!"

Again the detective's smile was patient. "We've sent telegrams to banks he's written bogus checks on, and other businesses he's cheated—not that I believe you knew of his financial activities, my dear. So I am meanwhile clearing your name and the reputation he might've ruined by association—"

Mama's gaze wandered, for she'd never been able to look men in the eye while they were finding fault with her.

"And what is *this?*" she demanded, snatching up the WANTED poster. "If it's your way of cowing me into submission—making me believe the police or the Pinkertons have issued this—"

The detective's expression sharpened subtly; he exchanged glances with Tucker in a way Christine couldn't dismiss.

"No, Virgilia," he said more pointedly, "this portrait was instrumental in bringing Wyndham to justice. Because other Pinkerton operatives and the local police finally knew who they were looking for—and who might need their protection. Someday, when all this commotion's behind you, you might wish to thank Tucker Trudeau for . . . providing it."

What was Mr. Carson saying between the lines? And why had Tucker's jaw tightened enough to make his beard ripple?

He'd sent Christine that WANTED poster nearly three years ago to alert her to Mama's activities with Richard Wyndham. Yet now, she felt a shift in the conversation. The playful Cajun she'd come to love looked as nervous as when he'd proposed to her beside the Bay.

Mama, meanwhile, was glaring at both of them as though she despised the male gender in general. "Are you telling me Mr. Trudeau took that portrait of Richard and me to the authorities? If the Pinkertons have been circulating it, they've done a damn poor job, because this is the first I've seen of it."

Tucker's Adam's apple bobbed, he swallowed so hard. Then he glanced up, toward the stairway.

Christine turned to see his mother approaching with an expression that suggested some sort of cue—from her angels, perhaps. How different she looked in a gown of gold damask that set off her olive complexion. Civilized to the point of being sophisticated.

"When Christine first came to Atchison hunting for you," Tucker explained, "*Maman* and I, we wanted her to find you. To be with her mother—and be a family again!"

"It was my idea," Veronique continued. "My main reason for finding you, Virgilia, was so you Bristols would go back home—so my son would forget his instant affection for a young girl who'd be more trouble than she was worth. We asked the newspaper editor to print several of these posters so Atchison storekeepers wouldn't do business with the man who'd already scammed the banks.

"I've changed my mind about Christine, however," Tucker's mother went on, smiling fondly at her, "because she's proven herself a young woman of unswerving purpose who sincerely wished to see her mother again despite the . . . unfortunate scandals you've been associated with. I hope you'll be proud of your daughter, Virgilia—"

"So the posters were a hoax, too?" Christine could barely get the words out, her throat felt so tight. "You're saying I've chased halfway across the country believing the police might catch my mother before I could?"

Her stomach ached as though someone had kicked her, and a bitter sense of betrayal came up her throat like bile.

"I didn't mean to mislead you, *ma chérie*," Tucker pleaded, "but I went along with *Maman*'s plan—hoping you would find her sooner."

"You lied to me." Christine blinked rapidly, determined not to show how devastated she felt. How betrayed! "This whole mission has been based on—"

"An assumption anyone would make," Harley Carson pointed out. "But when I noticed there was no reward listed—no record of which bank or agency was looking for Wyndham—"

"You knew. That's why you were so interested in seeing the poster back in North Platte, wasn't it?" she demanded. "What you wouldn't tell me is that you're a—a glorified bounty hunter."

Now she didn't know who to be angrier with—Tucker, for going along with his mother's underhanded scheme, or Carson, for not telling her what he knew that day she was in his jail.

Or should she blame Veronique Trudeau for this whole charade? She was beginning to see all three of them in a haze of red that signaled a tantrum like she hadn't pitched for a long time.

"Excuse me," she muttered, "but I can't spend another minute with any of you!"

Spinning on the heel of her kid slipper, Christine stalked toward the staircase, crying quietly so none of them would know how they'd ripped her heart out. Behind her, Mama was adding fuel to the fire. Burning their bridges.

"Well! If you think you can treat my daughter this way," she huffed, "don't believe we'll ever speak to any of you again!"

Chapter Twenty-eight

I'm heading back. Mama is with me!

Intensely satisfied that she could finally write those words, Christine handed her note to the telegraph operator. "This goes to Billy Bristol, in care of Michael Malloy, who lives just outside of Abilene, Kansas."

"Yes, ma'am! I'll send it right now!"

It seemed a miracle that this man's rapid tapping on a lever would travel through lines that spanned the entire country now, to end up as a message delivered to her brother. Maybe by tomorrow.

Christine watched, her heart thumping as fast as the man's fingers. It was finally true! She'd found Mama and they were going *home*—even though she couldn't name its geographical location yet. Right now, it was enough to be boarding the eastbound train with her mother. Her mission, the journey of the past three years, was nearly complete.

It is finished.

She frowned slightly. What an unhappy omen that the

final words of Christ had come to her mind: words of
suffering and death, when she should be feeling elated.

"Wasn't that a fine how-do-you-do?" Mama remarked
as they settled on an upholstered seat. "I *thought* something smelled fishy, the way Carlton Harte insinuated
himself into my séances. I did feel safer with him
around, since Richard became more devious in
Denver—"

Mama widened her green eyes, grabbing Christine's
hand. "But now we'll just stop at the post office boxes
along the way and have money to burn! Who needs
men like that? We have each other again!"

Christine's heart pattered rapidly, for Mama's excitement was contagious. For so long she'd awaited this
victory—this togetherness—

But it's not like I'd planned, is it?

Christine looked out her window as the train's whistle
blasted its all-aboard warning. They had managed to
leave the hotel without encountering the Trudeaus. Despite her fury at their deception, she was still a bit disappointed that Tucker had not made more of an effort
to seek her out—she *was* his fiancée, after all.

And would Mr. Carson resume his pursuit of Mama
once Richard Wyndham was behind bars? An article in
yesterday's *Chronicle* had listed Richard's schemes in
several states, leaving her mother too mortified to be
faking innocence. Along with charges of fraud posted
by banks and businesses, three women had reported financial scandals of a more personal nature. To her
credit, Mama had accepted this information with a mar-
tyrlike lifting of her chin.

"So I wasn't the only poor fool sucked in by his charm,"
she'd mused aloud. "Well! Life rolls on—like a train on its
tracks—and I'm leaving him behind. Thank God!"

As the train lurched away from the platform, however,
Christine felt a pang of regret. She searched the crowd

one last time for Tucker's midnight hair and boyish grin—the man she'd promised herself to on the shoreline, because she'd loved him since the moment they'd met. Why, she'd practically bullied him into proposing—

Have we learned anything from our mistakes? Miss Vanderbilt asked in her mind's ear.

Maybe Tucker's hesitation then was a sign of his guilt. Even so, she wished he'd kept it to himself that he and his mother had been behind that WANTED poster. She'd learned enough things she wished she hadn't, these past weeks.

Mr. Carson led him into it. That's what they were talking about—with Veronique—while they waited for us to come downstairs.

"Don't you just *love* riding the train?" Mama trilled beside her.

She leaned across Christine's lap to gaze out the window, where the city's impressive buildings passed by more quickly with each minute. "I could live forever in a Pullman car—my own little world!—until I cared to come out for dinner, where polite darkie waiters in their white coats indulged my every whim!"

Christine bit back a retort. This woman was in for a rude awakening—quite a comeuppance!—when she sat down to old Asa's cooking in Abilene.

Yet she envied the privileges Richard Wyndham had obviously bestowed upon her mother. Just as she envied Mama's appetite for life, now that she'd left that shyster behind. She hadn't seen her mother this happy since—when?

Since she and her lady friends sipped too much of Beulah Mae's elderberry wine. When Daddy wasn't there to scold her for it.

A sobering thought. One that followed right behind Judd Monroe's line about Mama being ripe and ready to—

"Why such a glum look, sugar? I thought you'd be excited about the two of us going home."

Christine gazed at her mother's face. While the bruise still haunted the upper side of her cheek, Mama's skill with powder and rouge had camouflaged the ugly reminder of her last minutes with Richard Wyndham.

Mama's good at covering things, remember? The mistress of misdirection.

"I—I wasn't ready to hear about that WANTED poster being Veronique's idea," Christine replied. "She and I were just starting to understand each other—"

"You'd rather believe your mama had a price on her head? And that she'd helped such a huckster with his life of crime?"

Christine blinked. "Mama, I sat at your séance table and watched while you—"

"Brought peace to Lewis Grantham's lonely parents, and helped the Merritt sisters donate their mother's money to a worthwhile project."

Mama sat straighter, looking right into her daughter's eyes. "There is nothing illegal—or immoral—about contacting the Other Side, Christine. Especially since I never charged for my services. It's my God-given ability to bring hope from the Hereafter to those who need it."

"But they paid you—"

"Voluntarily." Mama looked away with that familiar lift of her chin. "Had I been smarter, I would've put the donations jar where Richard couldn't get to it first. But that's all behind me now—and beside the point, considering we were talking about that WANTED poster."

When the talking gets tough, change the subject. The technique she'd learned at this woman's knee didn't feel any better, now that she was once again Mama's conversational victim.

"And we must look at the silver lining, Christine," her mother said. "Tucker and his mother designed that poster so you could find me, sweetheart. And thank God you didn't give up on that, because I'd be—well, I can't imagine how utterly disgusting I'd smell by now, lying dead in that alley."

"Which is again beside the point," Christine said, and then wished she hadn't.

It meant she'd have to admit how empty she felt without Tucker . . . and how she'd reverted to her old habit of storming off before she'd heard his explanation. What was it about Mama's presence that made her behave like a spoiled child again?

Mama sighed wistfully. "I have to remind myself that you're all grown up now. Not the sheltered little girl I raised in Richmond. Did you love him, Christine?"

"Yes, I did," she whispered miserably. "I *do.*"

Another sigh, like the sweet, satisfied sound of reading THE END when the heroine of a romance made good. "He'll come around, sweetheart. If he's your destiny—if it's really love—he'll be back for you."

Why did that answer sound so trite? So patently false? All her life she'd thrived on the images of the handsome prince sweeping her off her feet to love her forever—and indeed, Tucker had promised her that.

But was that how love really happened?

She'd never witnessed such overblown emotion between her parents, after all. And as she recalled the girlish joy in Mama's diary entries about the debonair Englishman who'd hauled her up from the miry bog of her grief and listened to her sentiments about Wyndham *now*, well—where was Prince Charming? And if Harley Carson were so smitten by Mama's mind and adventurous spirit, why wasn't he in the seat across from them?

So much for fairy tales. Maybe that's why Miss Vanderbilt never married: too much the realist to get sucked in by romance.

And yet . . . when she recalled the sweetness Michael

and Mercy Malloy shared—even before she'd seen
them cavorting naked—Christine had believed the feelings she and Tucker Trudeau explored would evolve
into the same everlasting bond.

Was it really over between them? All because of a
poster—a photograph that had haunted her with the
joy he'd captured on her mother's face?

It was too long a trip to sit brooding—or wondering
how much to believe of what Mama told her—so Christine reached beneath her seat for the carpetbag. The
red velvet diary would remain at the bottom of it, out of
Mama's sight, but the prints Tucker gave her might
make her feel better. And they'd be something to talk
about with the mother who felt like a stranger in so
many ways.

"Photographs!" Mama cried. "And how do I know
your Mr. Trudeau was behind the lens?"

Christine smiled at the thought of Tucker beneath his
black camera cape, waiting for just the right moment to
squeeze the shutter bulb.

"That's how I came west," she explained as she lifted
the prints from their box. "Tucker has been appointed
the official photographer for the Union Pacific railroad.
But when Veronique had visions of you going to
California—being in danger—Tucker said my
mission—finding *you*—was more important than taking his pictures."

"Well, then, that tells me he's very devoted to—oh,
who's *this?* Why, she could be your little girl, Christine!"

Why did her heart leap up into her throat every time
she saw this picture? Christine couldn't gaze at that little
face, even on paper, without feeling those downy blond
curls brushing her cheek and seeing the pink of that
gingham dress, and hearing that reedy little voice saying, "Kwis-teen!"

She smiled proudly. "That's our Lily, the mystery girl.

She was left on Mercy's porch in a basket last spring, with a note pinned to her collar."

"Mercy?"

Christine blinked. So much had happened—so many lives had entwined with hers—since Mama ran off, it would be impossible to catch her up on all those stories in one sitting. She leafed through the box until she came to the portrait of Mercy and Michael standing against the porch pillar.

"Mercedes Malloy, and her new husband Michael," she explained, letting her fingertip trail over the carved *M*s between their faces. "Mercy and her husband Judd took us in when Michael—who was driving the stage-coach we were on—asked if they'd keep us until he could . . . find our mother. They're very kind, decent people. Billy took to them—"

"And what happened to Judd?"

She smiled wryly: Mama had switched the direction of their conversation, much like railroad men diverted a train's cars onto side spurs. "He was killed in an Indian raid last year. Mercy was carrying Solace—"

As she looked for the picture of the entire family, Mama scowled. "And where was Billy during the raid? You're not going to tell me—"

"He went down into the root cellar to hide with Mercy and Asa and the two dogs," she replied, knowing Mama would never remember all the names. "It's a good thing, too, because that winter, during a snow-storm, he and Asa and Michael delivered the baby! See—there she is! Looks just like her daddy."

Mama snatched the picture where all of them sat on the front steps. "My God, he's—he's so grown up! My little Billy is—"

"He's fourteen now, Mama," she said, more tersely than she intended. "Hardly anyone's baby boy anymore."

"He'll always be my baby. You'll never know how I suffered, watching as those godless Border Ruffians snatched Wesley—"

She drew a ragged breath, gazing at the picture to compose herself. "And this is the baby he—you can't mean Billy assisted with the birthing? What sort of woman would allow—"

"Yes, Mama, this is Solace," Christine answered with clenched teeth. "Since there were no ladies nearby, because a blizzard kept everyone—"

"What an odd name, Solace. She won't like that when she gets older."

Christine stifled a remark about how Judd's daughter had been the solace that kept Mercy alive, for Mama had challenged every single thing she'd said about this patchwork family . . . a family who now seemed far dearer than she'd once believed.

"And this must be Michael's son? Mr. Malloy hardly looks old enough to have been married before."

"That's Joel, yes, Mama. He's three now, and quite a handful."

Two could play at Mama's conversational cat-and-mouse. Christine kept smiling, gazing at those faces so she wouldn't say things she'd regret. Lord, but she missed these Malloys more than she realized.

"And these are Billy's Border collies, Snowy and Spot," she went on, trying to remain patient. "Smartest dogs you ever saw, the way they keep the children corralled and—"

"Who's *that* old biddy? She must've played with God when He was a boy!"

Christine clenched her fist until her nails stung her palm—so she wouldn't slap the woman beside her. When had Mama forgotten those high-and-mighty manners she'd drilled into her children? Did she have no regard for anyone—other than Billy and herself?

"That," she replied, elevating her voice with pride, "is

Miss Agatha Vanderbilt, headmistress of the Academy for Young Ladies. I've nearly completed my studies there, and have earned an apprenticeship with the most exclusive couturiere in St. Louis. You should see the gowns I've designed, Mama!"

Surely the topic of fashion would make for more pleasant conversation. Mama had fled Denver on short notice, but her trunk—which they'd fetched from the hotel room she and Richard checked into—was filled with gowns in the latest styles.

"You? A seamstress? Well, *there's* something I'd never have imagined."

"Not just a seamstress, Mama—although the gowns I made over to go to school were what caught Miss Vanderbilt's eye," she explained proudly. "I even convinced her I should design a new school uniform—"

"My daughter went away to school in made-over clothes?"

Mama flipped back through the pictures, studying what she and Mercy and Aunt Agatha were wearing. "What sort of woman is Mrs. Malloy that she'd subject a pretty young girl—from a highly respected family—to the humiliation of cast-off clothing?"

Something inside her snapped. Christine snatched the photographs from Mama's hand and put them back in the box. "If you have to ask me such a question—you, the mother who abandoned her children—you wouldn't understand the answer!"

She stared out her window then, seething. It was still a long, long way to Abilene.

Chapter Twenty-nine

Christine awoke from a fitful nap to find Mama gone. What a relief, since talking had made them hostile—or revealed more things she didn't want to know. While she believed her mother was mostly unaware of—and uninvolved in—the major swindles Richard Wyndham had masterminded, Mama's attitude appalled her.

Nothing measured up to her standards. Nothing pleased her. Unless the conversation centered on Mama and her own whims, she got bored and asked for those photographs again—so she could gaze at Billy and chatter about *him*.

A flirtatious laugh floated from a few rows behind her. Christine sighed, watching Mama's animated expression and hand gestures as she carried on with a well-dressed gentleman twice her age . . . a man who acted anything but grandfatherly as he leered at her—and then kissed her cheek!

Mama, realizing she was being watched, gave him a playful peck in return. She returned to the seat with a triumphant giggle.

"We're dining in style tonight, my dear," she whispered breathlessly. "Compliments of Mr. Acree, who *so* looks forward to our company in the diner—and who is requesting that a Pullman car be made ready for us at Cheyenne."

Christine wiped the sleep from her eyes, dumbfounded. "And what did you tell him, to wrangle such an invitation from—"

"Young lady, we left San Francisco in a hurry—with not five dollars between us after paying our fares," Mama whispered viciously. "If Miss Vanderbilt is such a wonderful headmistress, has she not taught you the fine art of enticing gifts from men who appreciate pretty women?"

"I thought once we got to those post office boxes, we'd be rich beyond our wildest—"

"We must seize opportunities when they present themselves, Christine. She who hesitates is lost."

Mama turned to smile fetchingly at Mr. Acree again. When she wiggled her fingers at him, he did the same.

"Now—take a lesson from your mother," Mama instructed in a low voice. "You will behave graciously—and say nothing—when we join him for dinner tonight, understand me? Mr. Acree believes we've been to San Francisco seeking treatment for a mysterious ailment which has left you unable to utter a sound.

"He felt so sorry for your misfortune—and the fact that your doctor bills have bankrupted your poor widowed mother," she purred, "that he's going to ticket our Pullman hotel express car all the way to Abilene, even though he himself is getting off in Cheyenne."

Christine's eyes widened. "Why on God's earth did you tell him I'm—"

"So you wouldn't spoil it, of course." Mama looked downright gleeful. "And because an old goat like Mr. Acree is so damned grateful when a woman pays attention to him, he'll go along with anything I say. We'll get off in Cheyenne with him, secure the ticket for our Pullman car—and then dismiss him. For being such a desperate old toad!"

Christine's cheeks grew hot and she looked away. Not only was Mr. Acree being played for a fool, but Mama had made *her* a pawn in this despicable game—a bargaining chip for his sympathy.

"We're not getting off in North Platte, as Mr. Carson suggested?"

"Whatever for?" Mama scoffed.

"Because you cheated those ladies! In their darkest hour, you stripped them of their dignity—even though you knew how lost—"

"You feel sorry for them? After they believed you were *me?*" Her mother's face displayed extreme disbelief. "Christine, dear heart, when P.T. Barnum said 'There's a sucker born every minute,' he must've just left North Platte, Nebraska. Let us hope you will never become the sucker of the minute."

Christine's mouth fell open. Her mother, a woman of beauty and breeding, gazed at her with coldly calculating green eyes that made her soul freeze over. Mama was already plotting some excuse—some way to get rid of her tonight—before she could foil any of these devious plans.

Not only does Mama disregard the pain of others, she won't admit she inflicted it. Nor does she care.

Her mother had no conscience.

What a frightening thought.

As Christine caught her own reflection in the window glass, she was reminded of how much she resembled her mother—and how she'd taken it as a compliment to be compared to her. Other images came back to her, too: times when she'd flounced out of Tucker's red wagon and ridden off on his horse like a thief in the night, and stalked off before he could further explain that WANTED poster, back at the hotel.

The apple hadn't fallen too far from the tree, had it?

Lord, don't let me be like her! Not anymore! Christine pleaded. *I've treated Tucker and his mother badly, behaving like a pampered brat.*

What can I do to fix this?

Dinner with Mr. Acree was yet another ordeal. The old fellow's face bore several scars, probably from smallpox, so it was an effort not to stare at them as he talked with Mama. He looked so obviously flattered, so happy to be in their company, that Christine pitied him. Just as well that she was only to smile forlornly and keep silent.

Mama was in rare form. She'd pinned a fabric poinsettia at the crown of her upswept hair, with a black veil that swooped coquettishly over one eye—

Like a spider's web, Christine mused.

—to offset her black velvet gown. It was acceptable attire for a widow at her evening meal, except, perhaps, that its daring décolletage left little to anyone's imagination. The waiters fawned over her, expounding upon menu items as though she were a queen.

And Mama was behaving regally indeed. Living out the fantasy of splendor and refinement she felt she deserved as she daintily sipped her wine and played upon Mr. Acree's unsuspecting nature.

"Oh, would you look at this!" she twittered, batting her lashes beneath that veil. "Years it's been since I tasted Blue Point oysters! Or oxtail soup! But I really can't expect you to—"

"Of course you shall have them, my dear Mrs. Bristol," the old fellow said, nodding at their waiter. "And when we arrive in Cheyenne, I'll escort you to places—"

"Oh, no, no, kind sir!" she replied, patting his mottled hand. "I've already told you Christine and I must return to Abilene. In time to place flowers on her daddy's grave for Christmas, you know."

Mama turned to her then, widening her green eyes.

What could she do but play along? Never mind that Mama had never decorated Daddy's grave back home; she and Billy had placed wildflowers on the river rock that marked his spot, as the only memorial they could afford. If she spoiled Mama's charade by speaking now, there'd be hell to pay for the rest of the trip.

So Christine pointed to her menu choices with a very real sense of despair. Not only did Mr. Acree's fawning make her ill, but she felt downright mousy compared to Mama. She'd left her better dresses at the Malloys', so the only adornment she wore on her green tweed gown was the lace collar Miss Vanderbilt had tatted for her birthday.

Bad enough that the red candles and holly sprigs on the tables proclaimed a Christmas spirit she didn't feel; the festive printed menu had made her aware of the date, after days of being too caught up in Mama's drama to notice it.

December eighteenth. Mama hadn't even wished her a happy birthday.

The waiter flashed them a grin and went to place their order. Christine distanced herself from her mother's flirtation with Mr. Acree by staring out at the moonlit plains, which passed at an amazing clip. Memories of sixteen candles last year, with her academy friends and Miss Vanderbilt, gave way to recollections of Beulah Mae's high, light angel cakes with pink sugar roses like only that old Negro cook knew how to make.

Mama had insisted those cakes be placed on the crystal cake pedestal and served on the white china with the roses that matched the cake—"because my Christine Louise is a *lady*," she proudly proclaimed each year.

But the War Between the States and those Border Ruffians had changed everything, hadn't they? Christine hadn't known how deep the wounds went that first night at the Monroe house, when she'd insisted to Billy that it was their *duty* to save Mama because they were all she had.

" *'If she can't be the same Mama we had before we lost Daddy, then there's nothin' left worth savin'!'* " he'd blurted through his tears.

He was only ten when he said that, but maybe Billy was the smart one.

Maybe her mission to find Mama had been a major mistake.

"Now, not *one word* about how all the envelopes came to be in this box, young lady."

Mama glanced around the Denver post office, as though wondering if Mr. Acree had tailed them here from Cheyenne. Had he seen her paying the railyard workers to leave that Pullman car on a side spur until they returned to take a later train? Was he lovesick enough to follow the wily woman who'd detoured to Denver to fetch more of her clothing and jewelry—and the windfall that awaited her from Wyndham's advertisements?

Or would Mr. Acree retaliate? Have the car canceled in their absence?

Christine sighed, tired of being treated like a child—and disgusted by her mother's devious ways. What a show Mama had put on, kissing that poor old fool and promising she'd write to him. Was this how she'd won Richard Wyndham's attentions, too? And Carlton Harte's?

Mama fished the key from her reticule. "Thank God Richard rented one of these larger boxes. I could never remember the combination on the smaller ones."

Why did that line ring so false?

Because Mama could've sweet-talked the postmaster into opening any box she wanted. Because she made a beeline back here to this one, as though she knew exactly where it was—because she's been here many times before.

So many stories, so little truth.

Christine held her tongue, squelching a retort that would ruin Mama's fine mood. All the way here, she'd grinned like a little girl ready to make her wildest dreams come true. Her hand shook as she slid the brass key into the lock and twisted it, anticipating a pile of mail from the various schemes she'd supposedly never known about.

Mama threw open the shiny hinged door—and then her smile curdled. "What in the name of God—?"

She pulled out a single sheet of paper with a short note scrawled on it.

"Who do they think they're dealing with? Don't just stand there gawking, Christine," she snapped as she stalked off. The echo of her steps announced her wrath as surely as her scowl. "It seems we must claim our mail at the front counter—as though we were ordinary customers!"

Every fiber in Christine's body told her it was a trap. Perhaps they'd better march out the door rather than follow the note's instructions. Heads turned as her irate mother stormed past, with the sides of her stylish coat flapping behind her. Christine remained in Mama's wake, too mortified to meet anyone's eyes, already shaking her head at the high drama about to unfold.

"And what is the meaning of *this?*" her mother demanded of the clerk. She slapped the note down in front of him, her fist returning to her hip.

The man smiled. "Ma'am, if you'll be so kind as to wait until I've finished with this man's transaction—"

"According to this, I'm to see a Mr. Klinestettler—

whoever the hell he is!" She glowered at the customer in question, daring him to defy her.

"Ah. Yes, of course." The postman rapped sharply on a door behind his counter. "Mr. Klinestettler will be with you shortly."

"Damn right he will."

Christine's stomach lurched. Why wasn't Mama suspecting a problem—which might get worse if she acted so hostile? The post office was bustling with people who carried packages wrapped in brown paper and string and handfuls of Christmas cards, but they were setting aside their holiday cheer to watch the little lady with the big mouth.

And when that office door opened and a stocky man with thinning brown hair stepped out, Christine's worst fears were confirmed.

"Carlton—Carson—whoever the hell you are!" Mama sputtered. "What is the meaning of this?"

"Step inside please, Mrs. Bristol," he replied. "We've been waiting for you."

Chapter Thirty

"I'll just wait here in the—"

"You'd best come with her, Christine," the detective said with an apologetic smile. "We'll be discussing matters you should . . . be aware of."

Shutting out the curious stares—the humiliation of being associated with a striking redhead who swore like a stevedore—Christine stepped into the postmaster's sanctum behind her mother.

Her thoughts were spinning. How had Harley Carson arrived in Denver before they did? How had he known to be lying in wait to pounce on Mama when she retrieved that note from Wyndham's box?

Is Tucker here, too?

She had to save her own concerns for later, however. A tall, intimidating man was standing behind his desk when they entered. He was studying Mama—and her!—very closely, as though comparing their appearances to what the detective had already told him.

"Mrs. Virgilia Bristol and Miss Christine," Mr. Carson

said, gesturing at each of them, "may I introduce the postmaster, Theodore Klinestettler."

"Good day, ladies. Please have a seat."

While he gestured eloquently and spoke in a low, controlled voice, Christine already knew she didn't like this man. Or was it the nature of his inquisition she detested?

"I have what you were looking for, Mrs. Bristol," he continued, stuffing his hands in his trouser pockets. "And I've confiscated it because—"

"You can't do that!" Mama popped up from her chair with a finger pointed like a pistol. "You've taken personal property from a post office box belonging to—"

"Richard Wyndham," Carson cut in, although he didn't look happy about it. "And because the box was rented in his name—and because he instructed me to empty it after we caught him in San Francisco—I can't let you have whatever you were looking for just now."

"And what might that be, Mrs. Bristol?"

The postmaster leaned forward to gaze down at Mama, but his expression held none of the gratitude or adoration Mr. Acree's had shown. Klinestettler was the cat who'd grabbed the canary and wanted to play with it before he ate.

"And why is that *your* business?" Mama countered. She stood ramrod straight; only the clenching of her jaw gave away her rage. She would've torn Wyndham limb from limb had he been here.

Christine let out the breath she'd been holding. This could take all day if Mama kept waltzing around the men's questions.

Harley Carson stepped closer, looking as if he'd rather not be there. "When Wyndham told us you'd be checking the various mailboxes for money, I asked Mr. Klinestettler to be lenient," he said quietly. "Because you left San Francisco in a rush—"

"My comings and goings are not your concern, Mr. Carson," Mama snapped. "Why should I trust a man who disguised himself and changed his name to deceive me?"

Christine grimaced at the irony of this.

"Part of my job, I'm afraid." The detective shifted, imploring her with his eyes. "I want to help you, dear. I led your daughter in your direction because I believe families should be together and—"

"Horse hockey! You knew I was Richard Wyndham's partner and lured me away from him. Because you wanted me!"

"Because I knew he'd cause you trouble!" Mr. Carson came to stand in front of her. Hesitantly, he took hold of her hands. "Virgilia, he left you to rot in that Chinatown alley. Like garbage thrown out the window."

Mama pulled away, smirking. "Your concern is touching, Carlton—or whatever your real name is. But I'm not buying it. It was all a part of your scheme to latch on to me—or to catch Richard at something illegal— because I was so successful as a medium. Men just can't stand it when a woman does well for herself!"

"That's not true. I've always admired your agile mind—"

"Shall we get to the point?" the postmaster demanded.

Mr. Klinestettler stood at his full height then, looking down his nose at Mama. "Richard Wyndham has confessed to more than fifteen fraudulent schemes involving the United States mail these past five years. He named you as his partner, Mrs. Bristol. Which means you'll be called into court when—"

"Court? You can't touch me!" Mama tilted her head defiantly, crossing her arms beneath her breasts. "You yourself said I didn't know about Richard's financial affairs, Mr. Carson. So why am I being treated like a criminal?"

The Pinkerton agent's face hardened subtly. "If you

hadn't been so cavalier about selling those Bibles to the widows in North Platte, maybe I'd defend your honor more strenuously. But you tricked Harriet Butterfield—my *mother*—and her best friends. And I've been paying ever since."

"Oh, spare me, Mr. Carson!" Mama said with a roll of her eyes. "If you can't handle your mama by now, you deserve to rot like this crock of—*kraut*—you're stirring up here."

"Mama, really!" Christine slapped the arms of her chair, glaring. "You told me yourself we'd be raking in the windfall from Richard's big schemes. High time you were held accountable for deceiving so many innocent people!"

Mama spun on her heel. "And what did you plan to get by on, Miss Idealist? We spent what little money we had on train fares. I'm your mother. It's my duty to take care of you."

Christine stood then, shaken but not dropping Mama's gaze. "If I spent even a dollar of your misbegotten money, I couldn't face Billy or the Malloys—or Miss Vanderbilt!—ever again. I—"

"Well, then, you've never gone hungry. Or been widowed. Or lost your home—and nearly lost your mind—after your son was snatched away from you."

Mama's eyes widened into deep green pools, transforming her face into a fragile mask of tragedy. She assessed the effect she was having on the men.

"Until you've suffered as I have, dear daughter," she went on with a catch in her voice, "you have no right to judge a woman left utterly destitute after the war. You were a child. You had no idea of the grief and heartache I endured after your daddy was shot dead."

Christine took a deep breath. *Here it comes: She's going to whimper and raise that pretty chin and stick out that lower lip like the spoiled brat she is. Lord, deliver me!*

This brief plea settled her. She stood erect, her head high as she recalled the lessons Miss Vanderbilt had taught about dealing with adversity—and impossibly difficult people. It was time to make her stand.

"You dumped us like unwanted puppies, Mama," Christine replied in a tight whisper. "You broke Billy's heart, and betrayed all that was sacred to your family. You lied to us all the way to the stage station because you *knew* Richard Wyndham was going to send us west—out of sight, out of mind. And you never really married him, did you?"

Christine's fisted hands quivered at her sides, but she couldn't stop now. She had to state her case in front of these witnesses, who might help her, or forever endure her mother's unspeakable behavior.

"I can't be part of this anymore!" she cried, wishing the tears weren't dribbling down her cheeks. "From the start, I insisted on coming after you—I've spent the past three years with that as my mission. And from the start, Billy saw the situation for what it was. "If she can't be the same Mama we had before we lost Daddy,' he said, 'then there's nothin' left worth savin." I'm going home now, to tell him he was right. And I'm going without you, Mama. I can't let him see what you've become."

Swiping at her eyes, Christine left the postmaster's office and crossed the lobby, a tight smile concealing the wild throbbing of her heart. Once outside, she walked slowly, gazing at the ornate building facades. No sense in considering the hotel where she and the Trudeaus had stayed, for she hardly had money enough for a meal. Although the intersecting street looked familiar, she wouldn't walk that way. Mama planned to return to that splendid house for the finery she'd left behind.

But that wasn't her concern right now.

An invisible hand seemed to lead her. Christine passed more shops until she spotted the brick building with its arched windows of stained glass. She looked up at the rose window above the massive double doors and stepped inside. Divine magic.

The sanctuary was deserted, as she'd hoped. The Virgin Mary stood in the front corner, her porcelain face aglow from the flickering candles at her feet. The dark, carved statuary waited in the dim silence with the patience of saints.

Christine grinned. If her little speech had worked, she'd have company soon. And if not, well—she was exactly where she needed to be, wasn't she?

Chapter Thirty-one

"Christine! What in God's name are you—this is a Catholic church!"

She remained silent, gazing at the radiant faces of Christ and his mother—the painting at the back of the sanctuary, where the rose window blessed her with its breathtaking pastel tenderness. As before, Jesus and Mary returned her affection, their hearts aflame with heavenly purpose. They had welcomed her back, warming her with their holy presence and unconditional love, so she was in no hurry to break the peaceful spell they'd cast.

It was Divine magic, just like last time. And despite the trials of these past several days, Christine believed this grace and love was still hers for the asking.

"Answer me!" Mama's insistent whisper came again. "I had to promise those men—"

"I'm talking to Jesus, Mama. It's rude of you to interrupt."

She kept gazing at that beautiful bearded face.

Please, Jesus, help me do the right thing. Even if it means walking away for real this time.

"All right, then, Miss Holier-Than-Thou. Now I suppose you'll tell me He's answering you back."

Breathing deeply, drawing upon the ageless serenity reflected in the faces above her, Christine faced her mother.

"Matter of fact, He is," she replied quietly. "Don't tell me a medium can't believe we hear messages from the Spirit if we ask our questions and then *listen.*"

Mama blinked. Then she arched her eyebrow. "You may be sixteen, but you are still my—"

"Seventeen, Mama. The day we ate with Mr. Acree. Remember?"

Somehow she found the nerve to keep looking at her mother, resigned to the conversational shenanigans that would follow. And somehow she remained dry-eyed as Mama's face registered disbelief, and then realization, and then . . . remorse?

"It doesn't seem possible I have a daughter that old. Why, when I was your age, I had *you,* dear," she mumbled. Then she gazed at the walls around them, searching for an easier topic. "This is all very strange to me, Christine. I—I don't know what to do in a church where Jesus and Mary have flaming hearts and—"

Christine heard her mother's rising agitation and refused to knuckle under. "What you do now isn't my concern, Mama," she stated. "For you, I turned my back on a wonderful man and the life we were planning together. I hope it's not too late to correct that mistake."

How odd it seemed—how disheartening—to explain proper church behavior to the very woman who'd taught *her* such things! Christine walked slowly up the aisle, with Mama following like a petulant child.

"If you don't want to pray, you can sit in a pew until

I've finished," she suggested, gesturing toward the front row. "I have a lot of things to discuss."

Mama gasped. "Then why are you walking up to Mary? We Protestants don't believe in praying to—"

Christine pivoted, to silence her mother with the same pointed glare she'd received as a child.

Mama slipped into the front pew, looking nervous.

What was going on here? It didn't seem right, bullying her mother in a church, so Christine took a deep breath. She lit a candle at Mary's feet, and then another—not knowing why, except that it felt like the right thing to do. A way to shed light on an unfamiliar path.

"Mary knows a lot about a mother's love," she began, looking up to the Blessed Virgin for assistance.

And Mary's love shone down on her, while the candles flickered their encouragement as well.

With a grateful smile, she went on.

"Mary knew that no matter how much she loved her son, He had to suffer and die—for fools like you and me, Mama," Christine explained with sudden enlightenment. "We try to arrange things *our* way. We believe we can handle everything by ourselves. And then we whine and cry when it doesn't turn out right."

Glancing back, she took Mama's wary expression as a sign she'd better make her point. "Jesus must be very disappointed about how long it takes us to live His way. I need all the help I can get, Mama, if I'm to win Tucker back. So if you'll excuse me—"

Christine walked slowly back to the painting, focusing on it despite her jumbled thoughts. What sort of theological corner had she painted herself into? Why was she preaching to a mother who'd gone to church to see what the other women wore, when she herself had paid so little attention to Scripture and its lessons?

And yet, as she stood again before that sacred painting, Christine felt peaceful for the first time in weeks.

What can I say to make this work out? she mused as she gazed into Jesus's loving face. *I'm in over my head, you know. If Judd were here—or Michael—they'd be turning to precisely the right Bible passage to—*

What does the Lord require of you, Christine?

Her jaw dropped. In her mind she was thirteen again, reading Mercy's stitched samplers in that log-walled parlor with Judd Monroe. The voice of that handsome, righteous man rang in her ears now, just as it had in her dream:

To do justice, to love mercy, and to walk humbly with your God.

It was that simple—and that difficult—wasn't it?

Humility—and its close cousin, humiliation—were easier to come by these days, so maybe the Lord was pleased that she was trying to walk with Him, and trying to bring Mama along. Mercy was a little harder to manage, considering the stunts her mother had pulled. But *justice*—now there was something that seemed a feasible, tangible goal.

Christine turned to find Mama standing at the end of a pew, watching her closely. She smiled. This was her mother, after all. She was alive and well, even if she was proving herself a real handful.

"So what did you promise the postmaster and Mr. Carson, Mama?"

Mama blinked. Had she already forgotten that conversation? Or was she revising it?

"I told Carlton—for he will always be Carlton Harte to me," she added, "that, if it would make him happy, we'd stop in North Platte to make amends."

Christine nodded. Why did she suspect Mama had blurted out whatever pretty promises the two men required to get out of going to court—and then get out of that office to follow *her?*

"That's a start," she said, watching Mama's eyes for

signs of insincerity. "And how did you convince the postmaster? Mr. Klinestettler impresses me as a man who likes to make ladies stew in their own juices."

Mama let out a disgusted snort. "I wasn't happy about it, but I signed a statement saying the money in those envelopes will be returned to the fools who sent it. Nasty man—wouldn't let me open even a few for traveling cash! And he assured me the other mailboxes were empty, too. Life was a lot easier before the telegraph, dear."

Christine wanted so badly to laugh, but she kept her mirth to herself. "They've let you off, then. What else did they say?"

Virgilia Bristol smoothed her hair with the air of a very satisfied woman. "I pointed out what a fine, upstanding young lady you've become, and assured them that if they released me into your custody, I would return home a changed woman. No more land schemes. No more lotteries. Just a mother happy to be back in the bosom of her family."

Christine caught the sparkle in Mama's eyes. *"And?"*

Her mother feigned innocence, but then chuckled. "Detective Harte intends to check on me from time to time. I insisted he darken his hair and grow a mustache, however. He looks as bland as a baby's backside without one, don't you think?"

"Mama, you're incorrigible!"

Her mother shrugged, unhooking the gloves from her reticule. "There are women in this world who thrive without a man, my dear, but I've never been one of them."

She paused, as though that statement had cost her something. "Take your time here, Christine. I'll be waiting for you at the house. We'll head back to Cheyenne, and catch that Pullman car to Kansas, whenever you're ready."

She sensed Mama had emerged the winner of this conversation—of this entire situation in Denver. But they were still speaking to each other, and the proceeds from the schemes she and Richard had concocted would be returned. If a Pinkerton operative said he'd remain involved, well—things would stay legal, anyway.

Christine looked at the painting of Mary and Jesus again, smiling. "Thank you," she murmured. "I should've known You were in charge all along."

When they were once again rolling along the tracks full-speed, Christine had to admit this Pullman hotel car had its advantages. While the reclining seats in the first-class cars were quite comfortable, it was much nicer to sleep in a real bed, and to watch the passing scenery from a wing chair beside their plate-glass window.

As she glanced at the listing of towns along their way, she estimated they'd arrive at North Platte in about an hour. Mama must've composed her apology during the night, for she poured her morning tea and buttered a slice of warm, nut-studded Christmas bread as though she were ready to meet Harriet Butterfield again. Making amends, so her budding romance with Harley Carson wouldn't have that black cloud of deceit hanging over it.

And yet, as Christine watched the signs and depots whizzing past, she realized they weren't stopping in all the smaller towns. Usually it was farmers taking things to market in larger cities who got on in these places, or travelers visiting family members. Now that stage-coaches had all but disappeared along the Union Pacific route, it was more convenient to ride the train.

Had that last sign said North Platte? Wasn't that the depot they'd just rolled past?

Christine scowled through the window at the tracks behind them. "Mama, we missed our stop! I'd better go tell the conductor—"

Mama's smiled, wide-eyed but hardly innocent.

"Sit down and finish your breakfast, dear," she said smoothly, spooning up some strawberry preserves. "This is the express train, which only stops where ticketed passengers get on and off. And our tickets are for Abilene, aren't they?"

Chapter Thirty-two

A blast of snowy wind whipped at her mantle as Christine stepped from the Pullman car's warmth onto the platform.

The porter gripping her hand flashed a wide grin that looked especially white against his dark skin. "Merry Christmas to you, Miss Bristol! You and your mama have a wonderful holiday!"

Christmas? While it had to be at least the twenty-second of December, her mind had been so occupied with Mama—with the journey of her lifetime—that she'd shoved holiday thoughts aside.

You've done it! she realized. *You've brought Mama back, just like you vowed to three years ago.*

Now what?

Her mother stepped down beside her, gazing around as she smoothed the red fox trim on her bonnet. "Well, now! Abilene's a much bigger town than when I last saw it. No doubt we'll find plenty of opportunities to—"

"Mama, we have no gifts for the Malloys. No—"

"Christine! Christine, over here!"

She turned to see a wiry redhead dashing toward her, and her heart pounded into a gallop. "Billy! How did you know—"

"You did it, Sis! Just like you always said! And now here's—here's Mama!"

The gangly young man, now a few inches taller than she was and speaking in a voice that cracked with adolescence and emotion, stood gazing at their mother as though he couldn't believe what he was seeing.

"My stars, Billy," Mama murmured, her gloved fingers fidgeting as she gazed at him. "Last time I saw you— why, you've become a man!"

He lunged at her with a cry that rang around the platform. As his arms encircled her, Mama's laughter and tears mingled with his—ascending into a delirious whoop of joy when he whirled her around. His hat blew off, but he didn't notice. Passengers around them chuckled and stepped out of their way.

Now why didn't I think of that?

Christine watched them with an envious sigh. Hadn't Billy always cut through the emotional underbrush to the love that really mattered instead of questioning every detail? Three years of Mama's connivery hadn't changed the fact that he would always be her baby— her best boy—while Christine remained the responsible daughter.

"Billy! Oh, Billy!" she cried as she embraced him. When he set her down again, Mama stepped back to smooth his windblown hair and study the changes in his face.

"Your sister has taken it upon herself to become my conscience," she said with a wry chuckle, "so thank God you can just be my son!"

With a wave of some invisible wand, their mother had erased—or at least pardoned herself for—the torment she'd caused Billy when she took off in Richard Wyndham's surrey. Christine watched them sadly, managing a smile for Michael Malloy as he slipped his arm around her.

"Welcome home, honey. It's so good to see you!"

His mustache tickled when he kissed her cheek, and then she threw her arms around him. She blotted her hot tears against the rough wool of his coat, determined not to get sappy—or to appear bitter about how Mama was still making over her younger brother.

"Guess things got scary out in San Francisco," Michael murmured, rocking her as he held her close. "And maybe . . . maybe finding your mama hasn't been the rose-colored reunion you dreamed it would be."

Christine clung to him, soaking up the warmth of words intended just for her. More than once she could've strangled this man for bossing her around, but right now he knew exactly how to soothe her battered soul.

"Maybe she doesn't love you the way you want to be loved," he went on softly, "but I've met a lot of mothers in my day, and most of them love us as best they can. My sisters were all jealous of the way Ma coddled me, too—as her baby and the apple of her eye. But it wasn't because she loved me more, honey. She just overlooked more."

Christine sniffled, listening closely. Michael made her feel like she was entering a warm, sunny parlor after getting caught in a blizzard.

"We're so proud of you, Christine," he went on. "Going all the way across the country—not letting the unfortunate facts change your mind or your mission. I understand you saved her life . . . in ways she might not thank you for. I hope what you've just given Billy for Christmas will turn into a gift for you, too, honey."

Blinking, she raised her head to give him a tremulous

smile. "He and I have a lot to talk about—but I won't bother him with the details just yet," she added. "One of us might as well be happy."

She looked directly into Michael's soulful eyes. Was it her imagination, or did they match the ones she'd seen when she talked to Jesus?

"How do you know so much about my trip?" she quizzed. "And how 'd you and Billy know which train we'd be on?"

Michael's mustache twitched. "What did we do before we had the transcontinental railroad—and the telegraph?" he teased. "All right, I'll confess: I asked Tucker to keep us informed of your progress, and any important information, as you made your way west—although his telegrams left more out than they revealed. And we got your mother's message, saying you were ready to leave Cheyenne."

He steered her aside then, as the porters stacked their trunks and valises on the platform.

"Let's go home, Christine," he added before she could protest his methods. "I know some folks who just can't wait to see you."

She quivered with excitement as Michael's carriage pulled into the familiar driveway. A white wrought-iron archway proudly proclaimed the Triple M Ranch, displaying its cattle brand between ornamental horse heads. The picket fence was capped in snow, and wreathes with huge red bows decorated the twin pillars of the front porch. This was not her home, yet—

Why not? Home is where the heart is, right?

Christine let Billy point things out to Mama as they rolled past the white two-story house, where wisps of smoke rose cozily from the chimneys. She was determined not to neglect a single detail of this place she didn't realize she'd missed so much.

"There's Snowy and Spot," he said, waving at the two Border collies that ran from the porch to greet them. "They were born in the barn at Mercy's place, and my friends Emma and Gabe raised the other two."

But it wasn't the dogs Christine was gazing at. There in the corral—could that be Sol? Or did the Malloys now breed Percherons in addition to the Morgans they'd always raised?

She pondered this mystery as Billy opened the carriage door for them.

"Ever'body comes in through the kitchen, Mama," he said as he helped her down. "Just like back home—'cept we don't have no Beulah Mae chasin' us out with her broom!"

Mama sniffed indignantly, stepping onto the shoveled path so her pumps wouldn't be ruined. "Any darkie who comes after *me* better hope there's another stove to cook on in the Hereafter!"

Christine caught the cautious look Billy tossed her.

"The war's over, Mama. The help here gets paid," she remarked. "And in this house, Asa and the others are treated pretty much like family. It'll feel different, eating with them in the dining room—but *you'll get used to it.*"

Her mother's startled expression was the response she'd hoped for; she was all too happy to let Mama's best boy escort her inside. *He* could make those introductions, now that she'd completed her part of this mission.

For a few peaceful moments, Christine remained on the back porch, drinking things in. She'd forgotten the energy of those dogs as they chased the carriage into the barn. She'd missed the sight of these plowed fields, blanketed in white, that rolled on beyond the river, where the trees reached up with bared limbs toward a pale gray sky.

That tall black horse nickered at her. Like he knew her. He was standing at the corral fence, looking right at her, until—ignoring the snow that was ankle-deep—Christine stepped off the porch to see, once and for all—

"Christine! Come inside before you freeze. It's *so* good to have you home, sweetheart!"

She turned and gazed at that gentle face, framed in chestnut hair that accented shining brown eyes. Mercy's calico sleeves were pushed up past her elbows, and her flour-sack apron bore bright red smudges that could only be cherry pie filling. She opened her arms as she rushed forward, and for the first time Christine did that, too.

The phrase *goodness and mercy,* from one of the few psalms she'd ever memorized, popped into her mind—and as those strong arms closed around her, Christine knew why those two words belonged together. Mercy Malloy *was* goodness. And here in this kitchen, filled with aromas of yeast rolls and roasting meat, she could feel the love that had always been here. Just waiting for her to accept it.

Maybe all wasn't lost if meeting up with Mama had made her realize how lucky she and Billy were that day Mike Malloy sat them down at this woman's table. Maybe—

"Merry Christmas, Miss Christine!" an ancient voice cut into her thoughts. "We sure happy to have you home, child! And don't you look *just* like your mama—'cept prettier!" he added slyly.

"Asa! You must've started cooking before dawn!" She glanced around the cluttered kitchen, at a sink piled with dirty dishes and a cookstove where bubbling pots gave off wonderful aromas—and, of course, there was a line of pies along the table's edge.

Christine frowned. "You'll have to excuse me for losing track of the days, but . . . *is* today Christmas?"

"It might as well be. Look who's here—at last."

"Miss Vanderbilt!"

Once more Christine rushed into open arms, and once more she knew the unrestrained hug of a woman who loved her in ways no one else ever had.

"I wasn't expecting you to be here—"

"I got Mercy's telegram that you were on your way back and I couldn't stay away," her headmistress replied. "Partly because the train makes the trip so easy these days, and partly—"

She looked toward the doorway to be sure her words weren't overheard. "Partly because I just had to know how things have gone, Christine. From what we've heard, the trip was more . . . *enlightening* than you anticipated."

How like this pillar of the Academy for Young Ladies to transform a conversational sow's ear into a pretty silk purse. Christine laughed, relieved to be among women who would appreciate what she'd endured and wouldn't think less of her for feeling, well—disappointed.

"To paraphrase the Bard," she said in an elevated tone, "it's been 'Much Ado About Mama' these past weeks. I—I'll save my stories for a more appropriate time."

Agatha Vanderbilt and her niece exchanged a conspiratorial grin.

"When you can't think of anything nice to say—" Mercy began.

"—come sit by me!" her aunt chimed in.

The laughter that filled the kitchen gave her the best kind of comfort: balm to a soul that needed healing. Christine shrugged out of her coat, eager to see everyone . . . wondering just who might be here.

"You remember Temple," Mercy said, as they entered the dining room. "Reuben and Sedalia are settled in my old home, caring for the horses and ready to help plant come spring. But Temple's become my right hand. I don't know how I would've managed this household without her."

The young woman looked up from placing silverware around plates at the long table, and Christine stood amazed: Temple Gates wore a radiant smile—and one of the dresses Christine had left behind.

"Well, don't you look pretty!" she blurted. "It's good to see you filling out that amber gown—looking *almost* as fine in it as I did!"

Temple laughed aloud, curtsying playfully. "This one's my favorite, Miss Christine. Now, don't tell me you didn't make it just for me! And thank you," she added with a warm smile. "I've found my purpose here with Miss Mercy and Mr. Mike. I'm truly blessed to call this my home."

There it was again: *home.* Spoken with conviction; much more solid than her wistful notions of belonging when she felt she had no place to go.

Christine walked over to the colorful quilt of Mercy's homestead and this patchwork family, hanging proudly on the wall—and then she grinned at the framed photographs on the sideboard below it. Beloved faces greeted her, the smiles and dogs and love Tucker Trudeau had captured with his camera.

And there *she* was, standing between a proud Agatha Vanderbilt and Mercy Malloy . . . leaning against the porch pillar . . . nose-to-nose with Lily, and—

Right smack in the middle of this happy family. Surrounded by the children she loved, and by the adults who had loved her even when she didn't want them to—even when she'd defied and challenged their affection with her every unkind word and selfish deed.

It's divine magic, that little voice whispered. *And it's with you always, just as I am.*

Had anyone else heard that? Christine glanced around the cheerful dining room to see that Mercy and Miss Vanderbilt had returned to the kitchen, and Temple was taking glasses from the cabinet across the room. The young woman smiled, as though she *had* heard that still, small voice—and was quite comfortable with it, because she listened for it all the time.

"I'm glad you found your mama, Miss Christine," she said softly. "It sounds like quite a story, and I'd love to hear it sometime."

Christine could only nod, awed by the sense of blessing and light in Temple's presence. Recalling how this girl had come here under the worst circumstances, lost her baby, and then nearly died from an infection, Christine realized she herself had a long way to go—and a lot to be thankful for, even if Mama sorely tried her patience.

Strains of a Christmas carol drifted in from the front parlor. Her heart halted midbeat as an accented male voice began to sing.

" 'A-wayyyy in a manger, no crib for His bed—' "

Christine rushed toward the music. Little voices chimed in with a high, angelic sweetness that made her cry. There in that sunny room, where the window's beveled glass made a rainbow on the wall, sat Tucker Trudeau. He was beaming at the boy and girl who stood on each side of him, fascinated by the bellows and buttons of his accordion. His gentle voice encouraged them with the words they were just learning.

" 'The lihhttle Lord Jesus lay down His sweet head.' "

Christine held her breath in the doorway. Overhead, footsteps told her Billy was showing Mama her room, so she could powder her nose before dinner. From a wing chair near the window, Veronique grinned at her, and she wiggled her fingers in greeting. But she wanted nothing to interrupt this wonderful moment—this music sent from angels high above and long ago. Just for her.

" 'The stahhhhrs in the sky-y looked down where He lay . . . The lihhhtle Lord Jesus, asleep on the hayyyyyy.' "

Tucker embellished the final chord, and she sighed. Was it the sentiment of that carol—the first she'd learned as a child—or the sight of that big, sable-haired Cajun singing with those little children, that filled her with an inexplicable tenderness?

This, too, is divine magic, Christine. And it can be yours.

When she gasped with the power of this whispered message, they all looked up at her.

"*Kwis-teen!* Kwis-teen, it's weelly *you!*"

Lily launched herself across the braided rug, arms flung forward, while Joel whirled in excited circles. Christine caught the little blonde and held her high, until her shrill giggles filled the room. She wore a dress of candy pink velveteen with a white pinafore, and the bows in her hair were already loose from the morning's commotion. Joel landed against her thigh, nearly toppling them all. Luckily, there was a large upholstered chair to catch them.

She had a lapful of wiggling, giggling children, and she'd never been happier.

But it was Tucker's smile that made her heart stop. She hugged Joel and Lily close, so she could return his gaze above their bobbing heads.

"Tucker, I—wasn't expecting—how'd you *get* here?"

He slipped his arms from the accordion's straps and came over to crouch beside the chair.

"*Maman* and I, we thought you needed time alone with your mother, *chérie,*" he said, placing his hand on her arm. "We got on the same train you did in San Francisco. Mr. Carson, he followed you off at the Cheyenne station, but we came back here. To wait for you. Everything went all right there, with your mama?"

Christine dodged two little heads, smiling wryly. "Well, Mama was in for a shock when the money from Wyndham's mailboxes had been confiscated, but she still had the last word. Made a big show of coming clean, saying she'd apologize to those ladies in North Platte—already knowing our train wouldn't stop there to . . ."

His aquamarine eyes were fixed on her lips.

Christine swallowed hard. Should she break such a mesmerizing mood with an apology?

"I—I'm sorry I ran out on you, Tucker. It was rude and childish—like Mama's way of handling things."

"But I understood, *ma princesse*," he whispered.

He was still watching her talk, the same way she focused on *his* mouth—such firm, lush lips, accented by his dark, curling beard.

"You know, I hope," he went on softly, "that *Maman et moi*, we had good intentions—printing that poster to find your mother. But I didn't mention it earlier, so you learned of it at a bad time. I'm sorry you were hurt, Christine. Disappointed in me."

"I could never be disappointed in you, Tucker. I love you."

The words slipped out as she leaned toward him to make her point. He caught her up in a long, lovely kiss, to clarify things between them.

"Mama kisses Papa like that *allllll* the time," Lily chirped. And she clapped her hands on their cheeks to hold them that way.

"You will still marry me, *oui?*" Tucker asked. His eyes shone with a pale blue fire that sent a sunburst through her.

"Oh, *oui*, Tucker! Next spring? Right here?" The words tumbled out as she studied his rugged face, amazed at the love and longing she saw there. "The flowers will be blooming, and—"

"Of course, *ma princesse.* You are absolutely right."

Joel laughed, wiggling down from her lap. "Papa says that to Mama *alllll* the time! Don'tcha, Papa?"

Tucker chuckled, watching the boy rush across the room. "Your papa, he is a wise man, Joel. A wise and happy man, *non?*"

"A wise and happy man, yes," Christine echoed.

Michael Malloy smiled at them from the arched doorway, looking truly contented as he surveyed the parlor, the Christmas tree, and the three of them near the picture window. He scooped Joel up to his shoulder, kissing him noisily.

"I come, like the angel Gabriel, with tidings of great joy!" he announced. His sandy hair fell softly around his face and his grin held the promise of Christmas joy— and perhaps a secret—that made Christine hold her breath.

"It's time for dinner! So come to the table. And you—" he said to the boy who looked so much like him, "you may go upstairs to fetch Billy and Mrs. Bristol. Please and thank you."

Joel squirmed to the floor and then shot up the oak stairway, his footsteps thundering grandly. "Come 'n' eeeeeat!" he hollered as he reached the top. "Bihl-eeeee!"

"Kwis-teen! Sit by *me!*"

Christine blinked. Even though she'd just made up with Tucker and reaffirmed her love for him—even though she was so caught up in the familiar rhythms of this family, feeling as though she'd never left—the little girl in her lap had just taken her breath away. With the grip of those fingers, urging her out of her chair, Lily was showing her the joy of being chosen by a child. A child whose blue eyes sought her out; a child who loved her without limits or conditions.

Why—that little girl could be yours! her mother repeated in her mind.

Christine smiled; it was probably the most worthwhile thing Mama had said on the whole trip.

As they reached the dining room, Mama was coming downstairs ahead of Billy. Her mother stopped to watch her: Christine was being led by a blond toddler, and she was leading a tall, dark-haired Cajun. And they all wore happy smiles, as though Tucker had posed them in front of his camera.

It was an image that would remain imprinted on her heart, for it was the moment Christine realized she had a life of her own to look forward to. A life separate from her mother's. A life that revolved around her own abilities and purposes, because God had a plan for her.

Everyone took seats around the extended table while Asa placed the last of the steaming bowls in its center. Michael was thumbing through the large Bible he'd taken from the sideboard.

How many times did I watch Judd Monroe do this? And Billy? And this fine man, Michael, who has changed every life in this room with his simple, honest faith.

They settled into their places, waiting for the reading that would grace the meal. Christine's stomach rumbled as she gripped Tucker's hand under the table. Slices of gravied roast beef filled one platter and pieces of golden fried chicken another. A jellied cranberry salad shone like a huge ruby in its glass bowl. Steam rose from buttered, seasoned potatoes, along with three other bowls heaped with vegetables preserved from Mercy's large garden.

But it wasn't Christmas dinner. This feast was spread because she'd come home.

"We've all waited for this day," Michael began, smiling at her, "because there were plenty of times we wondered if Christine's dream would really come true. It's a pleasure and an honor to have you at our table, Mrs. Bristol."

Mama's cheeks flushed and she sat up straighter. In a dress of olive and bronze stripes, with her hair pulled into a braid that encircled her crown, she looked younger and more vibrant than Christine had seen her in years. Probably because she sat beside her beloved Billy—

And that's as it should be, she reminded herself. *Good things come to those who wait, and Billy did his share of that. It's his turn to watch over Mama now.*

"I'd like to grace this meal with a reading that befits the season, and tells of a special surprise, too," Michael went on.

Faces lit up with anticipation as he found his place. Miss Vanderbilt beamed fondly at Christine over Lily's tousled curls, while across the table, Asa and Temple winked at each other. Mercy sat beside her husband, looking sleek and queenly even in calico; she and Veronique exchanged a glance that put a feline smile on *Maman's* exotic face.

"This passage comes from the first chapter of Luke, about a very famous angel visitation. For we've each felt the presence of angels, and they're with us now, seated around this table."

Michael cleared his throat, smiling like he couldn't contain his excitement. "And the angel Gabriel was sent by God to a city of Galilee named Nazareth, to a virgin betrothed to a man named Joseph. And the virgin's name was Mary," he paraphrased. His voice was low and loving, caressing the familiar story as though it were one of his children.

"And the angel came inside, and said, 'Hail, you who are highly favored! The Lord is with you; blessed art thou among women.' When Mary saw him she was afraid, and wondered what sort of greeting this would be.

"So the angel said, 'Fear not, Mary! You've found favor with God, and behold, you shall conceive and bring forth a son, and you'll call his name Jesus. He shall be great, and shall be called the Son of the Highest. The Lord God shall give Him the throne of His father David, and He shall reign forever and ever, and His kingdom will never end.'"

Michael closed the Bible. He slipped an arm around Mercy's shoulders, grinning like a kid. "You'll never mistake me for the angel Gabriel, but I'm saying that Mercy's going to have my child! Just like Tucker's mother predicted."

Excited cries went up around the table, and hands clapped together with the joy of it. Mercy beamed at them.

"The baby will be here next summer," she said. "Probably in July. This will mean four children under the age of five in this house! So Temple will become even more of a guardian angel, and we'll be very, very busy."

"And very happy," Michael added. Then he smiled at Christine. "We're glad you made it home when you did, honey, because we couldn't keep this to ourselves much longer."

Christine laughed. As everyone congratulated Mercy and Michael, she once again felt honored by their attention. And after a moment's hesitation, she, too, stood up.

"While we're sharing good news," she said, her hand fluttering to Tucker's shoulder, "I would like to announce that Tucker and I are getting married—"

More cries of excitement circled the table. Christine kept talking before her courage ran out—and before

Mama's wounded expression made her feel she'd been too bold and independent.

"—and we'd like to have the ceremony here, next summer—"

"Of course you will!" Michael blurted, while beside him, Mercy looked extremely pleased.

"—and that in the meanwhile I'll return to St. Louis to finish my schooling."

The room was quiet. Christine focused on Miss Vanderbilt, and then looked at Mercy with a grateful smile.

"I've realized, in these weeks while I searched for Mama, that I'd be foolish not to get my diploma and spend a few months working with Madame Devereaux. If she'll still have me."

She leaned against Tucker, drawing strength from his broad shoulders and the way his gaze never wavered.

"It's smart, *oui*, to have that designer's blessing," he remarked. "Because—if you still will go to San Francisco with me—you will have the skills to bring those wealthy women flocking to your shop, *chérie*."

"Shop? San Francisco?" Mama said in a weak voice. "Why was I never asked about—? What if I need you for—?"

"Christine has always known her own mind, and has developed her talents well," her headmistress cut in firmly. "We all know she's perfectly suited to such a career, while being a natural with children. You should be very proud of your daughter, Mrs. Bristol."

Christine grinned. Mama still looked pathetically peeved, but she didn't dare argue with Agatha Vanderbilt.

"I would also be remiss—would be throwing away the hours you've spent with me at the academy," Christine stammered, "and the sacrifices Mercy made for me, so I could become more than a hot-headed little runaway. I owe you both more than I can say."

"I was pleased to help you," Mercy replied, her dark eyes shining. "I'm so tickled to hear about you and Tucker—and your plans, Christine. Now you're really going somewhere!"

"And this success is your own doing, dear," Miss Vanderbilt chimed in. "We provided the opportunities, but *you* made the most of them. Every one of us is so proud of you."

Were those tears in her teacher's eyes? Christine nipped her lip. She'd once considered this woman a battle-ax who had to be older than God and now realized she'd become a dear friend. Like a mother, when she needed one most.

"Thank you," she whispered. "Thank you all for never giving up on me. These last few weeks, things have fallen into place like—like—"

"Divine magic."

Everyone looked at Veronique Trudeau. She smiled serenely, so different from the Gypsy witchy woman who'd tried to keep Christine from going west with her son.

"The Virgin Mary, Mother of God, bestows her grace on all who aspire to her loving ways, Christine," she said quietly. "For who would know better about a mother's love than the mother of Christ Himself?"

It was the blessing she could never have asked for. Christine could only nod, speechless. Had this woman overheard her conversation with that painting? Read her thoughts once again?

It didn't matter, did it? Veronique Trudeau, who routinely invoked divine magic in her own right, had passed her a symbolic torch—much like those that burned in the two holy hearts Christine had reached out to in the church.

"I can only add my amen to divine magic," Michael

said happily. "May God bless us every one—and let's eat before it gets cold!"

"Magic!" Lily echoed in an awed whisper. Then she looked up at Christine with sparkling blue eyes. "Magic like *me*, Kwis-teen!"

Epilogue

July 1870

Resplendent in the beaded ivory gown she'd designed for Mercy's wedding, Christine grinned at Billy from behind her shimmering veil. They stood in the shade of the house, looking out over the backyard where benches and the dais had been arranged for the ceremony. It was just like when the circuit rider conducted Sunday services at Mercy and Judd's place, when they first came to Kansas. And that felt exactly right.

"Emma Clark's giving you that look, little brother," she teased.

Billy ran a finger inside his tight shirt collar. "*Her* I can handle. It's that man Mama's with I'm not so sure about."

She watched Reverend Larsen place his Bible on the podium. White ribbons and mock orange adorned it and the bridal arch, which glowed in the afternoon sunlight. Mama was sitting next to the inside aisle, arrayed in a gown of mint green silk that Christine had designed. Mr. Carson—or Carlton, as Mama called him—was sitting too close to be considered proper, looking devilishly dapper in his darkened hair and handlebar mustache.

Christine snickered. The detective was having a much better time today than Billy was. While she dearly loved her brother, it was a treat to watch him sweat for a change.

"At least he has a legitimate career," she remarked. "And, Pinkerton operative that he is, he's seen Mama at her worst. Yet he admires her *mind*."

Billy choked. "Yeah, I'm sure she gives him a piece of *that*, too. But how'm I s'posed to keep track of her now? She'll say she's on her way out to see you, and for all I know, she'll be operatin' a lottery outta those mailboxes again."

Christine shrugged. "She doesn't need our permission, does she? And she certainly won't *ask* you for it."

His exasperated sigh made her smile.

"But she's never home!" His whispered exclamation made some of the guests turn to look at him. "You'd think, since Mercy and Mike've let her live in the Barstow house, she'd *be* there when I rode over to visit."

Recalling the dark log houses most homesteaders had built, and the way the wind whistled through their chinking, Christine knew why Mama seldom stayed at that isolated place.

"A queen without a staff or subjects?" she asked with a raised eyebrow. "How long did you think Mama would last like that? Now, hush! The music's starting, and I don't want to miss a minute of my ceremony."

Mrs. Reid sat down at the pump organ with a flourish. As her prelude began, Christine assessed the friends and neighbors gathering in her honor. Emma Clark, once a dyed-in-the-wool tomboy, now sat primly beside her parents. She fingered the folds of her cornflower frock, stealing backward glances at Billy—who was ignoring her. Her cousin, Gabe Getty, looked very scholarly in his new suit and spectacles, despite being a few years younger than her brother.

Nell and Clyde Fergus had come, as had friends from the church in Abilene. Back a few rows, Sedalia and Reuben Gates sat beside Asa—who grinned proudly at her. She waved at the old cook, grateful for his kindness and patience over the years. Lord knows she hadn't always been nice to *him*.

. On a bench near the front, Temple Gates sat talking quietly to the children. How pretty she looked in that new gown of buttercup watered silk.

Beside her, Lily sat swinging her legs and shaking her head—to feel the bounce of her first ringlets. The soft, springy columns of gold nearly reached her shoulders and transformed her from a baby into a beauty who already knew how to rule. According to the note her father had pinned on her, she'd be two next month, but—as *Maman* had prophesied last autumn—they suspected she was either older or an extremely bright little girl.

Solace, at sixteen months, toddled around the end of the bench, beating her hands in time to the music. With a mop of dark brown curls, distinctive eyebrows, and that dimple beneath her lips, she looked so much like Judd, Christine could believe he'd come back in childlike form.

Joel was growing restless, and Miss Temple was scolding him.

"He's gonna bolt," Billy warned. "Probably while the preacher's sayin' your vows."

"He's Joel. He's four. He gets agitated when people expect something of him."

Christine smiled sadly. She'd miss these children when she and Tucker headed for California tomorrow.

Her groom had been busy these past six months, selling his shop in Atchison and setting up a new one with a view of the San Francisco Bay. Union Pacific had paid him well for his photography work along the railroad, so he'd found her a little shop, too—a quaint place with flower boxes and a porch swing, and an apartment above it for their first home.

And *home* it would be, because the handsome man walking up to the bridal arch would share it with her.

Michael joined him there, brushing his sandy hair back and looking understandably nervous. Today of all days, Mercy's water had broken. *Maman* was inside tending her. An occasional moan came from the bedroom window behind her, but so far, the music and the guests' chatter camouflaged them.

Then, with a loud fanfare, the organist modulated into a wedding march. Christine's pulse played its own solo. It was time!

Here came Miss Vanderbilt with her bouquet, an assortment of day lilies, roses, and mock orange blossoms she'd picked this morning. Her headmistress laid them in the crook of her elbow with a wistful smile.

"Don't tell Mercy," she murmured, "but you're an even lovelier bride than she was. I wish you all the happiness this world—and that man—has to offer, young lady."

Christine nodded, misty-eyed. "How's it going in there?"

"Moving right along—just as we should be, if you're to remain the star of this ceremony." She watched Temple directing Lily and Joel toward them, and then turned with a wry smile. "Of course, since you made such a racket, leaving while Mercy and Michael exchanged vows, maybe it would be poetic justice for this baby to make some ruckus of its own!"

As they'd rehearsed, Miss Vanderbilt positioned the children for their walk down the aisle. Like a fairy princess in her dress of pale pink tulle, Lily led the procession, strewing rose petals from her basket on the grassy path. When she reached the white archway, she curtsied flirtatiously to Tucker and Michael and then turned to watch Joel.

Miss Vanderbilt handed the boy a white satin pillow with the rings carefully laced in place. She whispered something in his ear.

He'd balked at having his hair cut. He'd squirmed and fussed when they dressed him in a little blue suit, buttoned his collar, and made him wear shoes. And now, with all the guests watching him, and Lily anxiously crooking her finger, Joel stood stock-still, gripping the pillow.

He looked like a cornered rabbit. Too frightened to move.

And then he was off like a shot! He tossed the pillow and out toward the barn he ran, with Snowy and Spot barking raucously behind him.

Billy was ready to call them back, but Christine squeezed his arm.

"No harm done," she whispered. "Leave them be."

Rusty eyebrows shot up above startling blue eyes. "You weren't that nice about it when we practiced with 'im," Billy whispered. "How many times did you tell him to make us all proud? And promise extra ice cream if he behaved on your big day?"

Christine gazed at her brother—dear, protective, *dependable* Billy. And realized she would miss him most of all.

"Maybe no one's going to behave as perfectly as we'd

like," she replied quietly. "Maybe we should forgive them as best we can and go on."

Her brother sighed as if he wanted to say something. His Adam's apple bobbed as he swallowed. Then he tucked her hand around his arm again.

The guests were still chuckling as Miss Vanderbilt brushed off the pillow. Then the headmistress straightened her shoulders to walk up the aisle so gracefully she could've balanced half a dozen schoolbooks on her head.

Christine watched fondly as this white-haired angel in lavender taffeta passed through the archway and took Lily's hand. When she turned with a proud smile, the chords of the organ brought the guests to their feet. Suddenly they were all gazing at *her*.

Dear Lord, don't let me trip over my hem.

For one glorious moment, with all the dignity instilled during hours of practice at the Academy for Young Ladies, Christine stood at the end of the aisle while her guests paid her tribute with their admiring eyes. Some of these people had watched her run away, to defy Judd and Mercy and Michael, behaving like the ungrateful little girl she'd been when she came here.

And where would she be if she hadn't landed here? What might've happened had Mercy thrown up her hands and thrown her out? Or if Michael Malloy hadn't brought her back after she ran away?

She didn't want to think about that. Better to let these people celebrate the woman she'd become—because that's what *she* intended to do. What a difference it made, to consider herself a part of this patchwork family. To count her time here as a blessing rather than a cruel twist of fate.

She caught Mama's eye—saw tears sparkling in the afternoon sun—and then tugged on her brother's elbow.

She walked slowly, keeping the music's majestic beat

as she approached the man who made her so happy. Closer to the ground, a blur caught her eye—and here came Solace! She was laughing with the sheer joy of propelling herself away from those who would've grabbed her. She bounced down the aisle with steps that made her curls and pinafore flutter, her bright eyes fixed on her best buddy.

Billy swooped, caught her up against his shoulder, and kissed her cheek with a resounding smack. Solace crowed again and kissed him back, as she'd done since she was an infant in her crib.

"Emma's getting jealous," Christine teased.

"Let her," Billy said. "Can I help it if I drive all the girls wild?"

They chuckled, resuming their promenade. At the bridal arch, an apologetic Temple took Solace again, and Billy handed Christine off to Tucker, just as they'd rehearsed—

But then her brother grabbed her back and quickly kissed her. "I love you, Sis. Be happy," he murmured before taking his seat beside Mama.

Christine's jaw dropped. They hadn't practiced that!

And then she felt a warm hand wrapping around hers, and she basked in the tender urgency of eyes that sparkled like aquamarines.

"Dearly beloved, we are gathered here . . ."

For a few moments, all else blurred except the love shining on Tucker's face. His black hair fluttered in the breeze, and in his dark frock coat and striped cravat, he'd never looked more dashing. Yet Christine loved him even better in the earthy flannel shirts that strained across his shoulders when he adjusted his cameras. And she dared to dream of frolicking in the mist with him, wearing no clothes at all.

"Miss Bristol has asked Michael Malloy to share to-day's Scripture—"

"And it is indeed an honor," Michael replied as he stepped up to the podium. His glance flickered to the house, where his wife was giving birth. But when he gazed at her with those steadfast hazel eyes, Christine felt the blessing he was about to bestow upon her.

"After all," he continued with a grin, "when I was reading this passage at our wedding in October, Christine was running off, determined to catch the man she thought had forgotten her. What a joy, that she's marrying Tucker Trudeau today—and that she was actually *listening* enough to request this same Scripture from First Corinthians!"

When the laughter drifted away, he glanced at the page before him. Then, in a voice magnificent with commitment, he looked out over the crowd.

"If I speak in the tongues of men and of angels, but have not love, I am a noisy gong or a clanging cymbal," he began.

A lot like me. I hope I've changed, Christine mused. Michael's eyes were closed with the sheer beauty of the verses, and she had to swallow hard to keep from crying.

"Love is patient and kind. Love is not jealous, or boastful—it is not arrogant or rude." He looked at both of them, as though he were teaching the most important lesson of their life to come. "Love does not insist on its own way. It is not irritable or resentful. It does not rejoice at wrong, but rejoices in the right. Love bears all things, believes all things . . . hopes all things and endures all things. Love never ends."

Behind her, Mama let out a dramatic whimper and blew loudly into her handkerchief. But then it was a different cry—a loud, lusty bawling from the house—they heard.

Christine giggled. Mama had just been upstaged by a baby. Mercy's baby!

"Praise be!" Temple Gates exclaimed, while Michael's face lit up brighter than the Fourth of July.

"If you folks'll excuse me," he said, "I hear the voice of an angel. A man should never ignore that!"

Everyone chattered excitedly as they watched him race toward the house. Christine hugged Tucker's arm— and then noticed that Reverend Larsen seemed at a loss for restoring order. Poor man. Had he ever performed a service for this family that hadn't been disrupted?

She gave him her brightest smile. "I think we should exchange our vows, and enjoy Asa's splendid cake while we wait to see that baby. That's the real highlight of this day! *Oui,* Tucker?"

"Ah, *oui,* Christine! You are absolutely right."

For nearly half an hour, the guests milled about the table where Asa's three-tiered marvel of a wedding cake held court. They complimented the old cook and sipped lemonade punch while Christine savored her last day with Lily, Joel, and Solace. In an attempt to dodge Emma Clark's advances, her brother and Gabe had carried their cake to the corrals.

Tucker had set up his camera for a wedding photo, so Christine stood patiently inside the bridal arch as he prepared some glass negatives. When he had the shot framed to his satisfaction, he took his place beside her and asked Harley Carson to squeeze the shutter bulb.

Lily watched with wide eyes. "Oh, Kwis-teen, you look like a pwincess—an angel pwincess!" she exclaimed. She was holding Solace by the hand, doing an admirable job in her big sister role. Looking like a princess herself in those ringlets. Christine couldn't resist.

"Tucker, may we take a photograph of just us girls?" she asked. "How often will we three be together, all dressed up—"

"There's the baby!" Temple called out.

Michael stood in the doorway, his coat and cravat removed, cradling a bundle in one elbow. He wore the most lovestruck smile Christine had ever seen.

"On second thought," she murmured, "*there's* the picture to commemorate this wonderful day! Look at him! He's just beaming."

"Here she is," Michael announced as he approached the waiting crowd. "Just like Tucker's mother predicted, it's a girl. We've named her Grace. Grace Christine Malloy."

Christine sucked in her breath. She grabbed Tucker's hand and squeezed between people to see the baby— a baby they'd named for *her*.

"Would you look at that sweet little face!" she cooed.

True, Grace's cheeks were still red and puckery, and she looked ready to bawl. But who wouldn't love that tiny turned-up nose and those wisps of light brown hair?

"You would like a photograph with your new daughter, *oui?*" Tucker suggested.

Michael's eyes lit up. "A fine idea! And I want one with *all* my daughters, too. Come on, girls!"

As they watched this proud papa gazing at his baby for the camera, and then gathered around him, Christine knew a blissful completeness. And as she stood beside Michael, holding Solace, while Miss Lily posed proudly in front of them, she knew again what it meant to be part of a family.

Mama saw this, for she stood off to one side with Harley Carson, watching. Seeing how the Malloys had taken her daughter and Billy not just into their home but into their hearts. Her chin lifted; her aloofness kept her at a safe distance from such intense emotion.

For the first time ever, Christine felt sorry for her. Mama looked brittle—not like the wayward, freewheeling mistress of misdirection she'd been with Richard Wyndham—even though she and Mr. Carson clearly enjoyed each other. While Tucker took more pictures, she went over to spend some final moments with her mother. By this time tomorrow, Christine would be on the train to San Francisco.

"It's been quite a day, Mama," she said. "I'm glad you were here to share it with me."

Mama shrugged with a wounded sniff. "You certainly didn't need me here. Made all your plans without even asking me to—"

"Mama."

Christine squeezed her mother's hands. "I wanted you here or I wouldn't have followed you all the way to California," she said. "We see things differently than we did before the war, but you'll always be my mama. I'll always love you."

For just a moment, Mama was stunned enough to bat her eyes. "Fine way you have of showing it, going to California to live. Leaving me to—"

"Make your own decisions," Christine finished pointedly. "Just like your leaving *me* has taught me to design a life of my own."

Christine gazed into green eyes that didn't want to see reason, but Harley Carson's expression encouraged her. He was sipping punch in the shade, allowing them these moments alone.

"A lot of girls never learn how to do that, Mama. So thank you for teaching me how *not* to be a helpless, clingy little thing," she continued. Then she grinned, thinking of what awaited her. "I'll be running a shop soon—designing fine gowns. I'll be a wife and a mother, and I'll spoil my children and show them off, just like you did.

"And Mama," she added, "You should know that every

time I look in the mirror, I'll be seeing *you*. If we think of it that way, we can spend time together every day, even if we're miles apart."

She managed a smile, squeezing her mother's hand again. "And I bet, if you sweet-talk him just right, Harley'll bring you out to see us. You'll only be a stranger if you choose to be, Mama."

Behind her, the baby cut loose with a series of ear-splitting cries that had everyone looking her way sympathetically.

As though drawn by an inexplicable magnet, Christine turned. With open arms, she walked toward Michael Malloy and his tiny, bawling daughter. Yes, she felt wondrously happy as her beautiful dress whispered around her and drew admiring smiles from the crowd. And yes, she counted herself lucky to have Tucker Trudeau gazing at her with such love on his handsome face.

But when Michael placed baby Grace in her arms, Christine felt an awe that could only come straight down from Heaven, as though God Himself held them both in His warm, comforting hand.

Grace hicced and then gazed quietly up at her. She kept rocking side-to-side, in that innate rhythm, her eyes locked on the baby's until she could see into the depths of that little soul.

Christine sighed. She'd just fallen in love all over again.

"Tucker," she murmured, her gaze still on little Grace, "I can't wait to have babies. *Your* babies."

As the man beside her stroked Grace's cheek, his chuckle had a devilish edge to it. "Whatever you want, *ma femme*," he whispered. "Today you've been the darling of everyone here—their bright and shining star. But tonight you become the moon of my desires and you will shine only for me. *Oui?*"

A delicious little thrill tickled all the way up her spine. It was a moment for embracing all the ways of love she'd learned: its patience and kindness, its endurance and faith. But also its passion and joy.

"*Oui, mon amour,*" she whispered. "I will shine, always and only, for you."

A Patchwork Family

CHARLOTTE HUBBARD

Meet Mercy Malloy. No matter what she does, God's love fills her life. So when two orphaned children appear on her doorstep, she hesitates only a moment before opening her heart and her home to them. Perhaps this is the Lord's way of sending her and Judd the babies they've prayed for.

Out on the Kansas plains the years bring hardship and heartache—Indian attacks, a runaway daughter, an abandoned baby in a basket—but also precious new life and the unlooked for joy of a surprise love. Through it all, Mercy's faith holds her family together, creating a patchwork of strength and beauty.

BOBBI SMITH

Writing as
Julie Marshall

MIRACLES

For the devout members of Lydia Chandler's prayer group, faith provides a shining light through even the darkest times. To George Taylor is given the grace to face his cancer and leave a lasting memorial. To Jim Hunt is granted the wisdom to turn away from the temptations of alcohol and peer pressure. And for lovely Lydia, who refuses to despair in the ugly side of life that her reporting often uncovers, there is an earthly love to bring laughter and joy to all of her days.